THE HOUSE OF
SPECIAL PURPOSE

THE HOUSE OF SPECIAL PURPOSE

John Boyne

WINDSOR
PARAGON

First published 2009
by Doubleday
This Large Print edition published 2009
by BBC Audiobooks Ltd by arrangement with
Transworld Publishers Ltd

Hardcover ISBN: 978 1 408 43089 7
Softcover   ISBN: 978 1 408 43090 3

British Library Cataloguing in Publication Data available

Printed and bound in Great Britain by
CPI Antony Rowe, Chippenham and Eastbourne

For Mark Herman,
David Heyman
&
Rosie Alison,
with thanks

1981

My mother and father did not have a happy marriage.

Years have passed since I last endured their company, decades, but they pass through my thoughts almost every day for a few moments, no longer than that. A whisper of memory, as light as Zoya's breath upon my neck as she sleeps by my side at night. As gentle as her lips against my cheek when she kisses me in the first light of morning. I cannot say when they died exactly. I know nothing of their passing other than the natural certainty that they are no longer of this world. But I think of them. I think of them still.

I have always imagined my father, Daniil Vladyavich, dying first. He was already in his early thirties by the time I was born and from what I can recall of him, he was never blessed with good health. I have memories of waking as an infant in our small timber-framed *izba* in Kashin, in the Grand Duchy of Muscovy, pressing my hands to my tiny ears to repel the sound of his mortality as he choked and coughed and spat his phlegm into the fire burning in our small stove. I think now that he may have had a problem with his lungs. Emphysema, perhaps. It's difficult to know. There were no doctors to administer to him. No medicines. Nor did he bear his many illnesses with fortitude or grace. When he suffered, we suffered too.

His forehead extended in a grotesque fashion from his head, I remember that also. A great mass

1

of misshapen membrane protruding with smaller distensions on either side of it, the skin stretched taut from hairline to the bridge of his nose, pulling his eyebrows north to give him an expression of permanent disquiet. My older sister, Liska, told me once that it was an accident of birth, an incompetent doctor taking hold of the cranium rather than the shoulders as he emerged into the world, pressing too hard on the soft, not yet solidified bone beneath. Or a lazy midwife, perhaps, careless with another woman's child. His mother did not live to see the creature she had produced, the deformed baby with his misshapen skull. The experience of giving my father life cost my grandmother her own. This was not unusual then and rarely a cause for grief; it was seen as a balance of nature. Today, it would be unexpected and worthy of litigation. My grandfather took another woman soon after, of course, to rear his young.

When I was a boy, the other children in our village took fright when they saw my father walking along the road towards them, his eyes darting back and forth as he returned home from his farm labours, perhaps, or shaking his fist as he stepped out of a neighbour's hut after another argument over roubles owed or insults perceived. They had names for him and it excited them to shout these in his direction—they called him Cerberus, after the three-headed hound of Hades, and mocked him by pulling off their *kolpak*s and pressing their wrists to their foreheads, flapping them maniacally while chanting their war cries. They feared no retribution for behaving like this in front of me, his only son. I was small then and weak. They were not

2

afraid of me. They pulled faces behind his back and spat on the ground in imitation of his habits, and when he turned to cry out like a wounded animal they would scatter, like grain seeds tossed across a field, disappearing into the landscape just as easily. They laughed at him; they thought him terrifying, monstrous and abhorrent all at once.

Unlike them, I was afraid of my father, for he was liberal with his fists and unrepentant of his violence.

I have no reason to imagine it so, but I picture him returning home some evening shortly after I made my escape from the railway carriage in Pskov on that cold March morning and being set upon by Bolsheviks in retaliation for what I had done. I see myself rushing across the tracks and disappearing into the forest beyond in fear of my life, while he shuffles along the road for home, coughing, hacking and spitting, unaware that his own is in mortal danger. In my arrogance, I imagine that my disappearance brought great shame upon my family and our small hamlet, a dishonour that demanded retribution. I picture a crowd of young men from the village—in my dreams there are four of them; they are big and ugly and brutal—bearing down upon him with cudgels, dragging him from the street towards the darkness of a high-walled lane in order to murder him without witness. I do not hear him crying out for mercy, that would not have been his way. I see blood on the stones where he lies. I glimpse a hand moving slowly, trembling, the fingers in spasm. And then lying still.

When I think of my mother, Yulia Vladimirovna, I imagine her being called home to God in her own bed a few years later, hungry, exhausted, with my sisters keening by her side. I cannot imagine what hardships she must have faced after my father's death and I do not like to think of it, for despite the fact that she was a cold woman and betrayed her disappointment in me at every juncture of my childhood, she was my mother nevertheless and such a person is holy. I picture my eldest sister, Asya, placing a small portrait of me in her hands as she clasps them together for the final time in prayer, preparing in solemn penitence to meet her maker. The shroud is gathered to her thin neck, her face is white, her lips a pale shade of periwinkle blue. Asya loved me but envied my escape, I remember that too. She came to find me once and I turned her away. It shames me now to think of this.

None of this may have happened, of course. The lives of my mother, my father and my sisters may have ended differently: happily, tragically, together, apart, in peace, in violence, there is no way for me to know. There was never a moment when I could have returned, never a chance that I could have written to Asya or Liska or even Talya, who might not have remembered her older brother, Georgy, her family's hero and shame. To return to them would have put them in danger, put me in danger, put Zoya in danger.

But no matter how many years have passed, I think of them still. There are great stretches of my life that are a mystery to me, decades of work and family, struggle, betrayal, loss and disappointment that have blended together and are almost impossible to separate, but moments from those years, those early years, linger and resonate in my memory. And if they remain as shadows along the

4

dark corridors of my ageing mind, then they are all the more vivid and remarkable for the fact that they can never be forgotten. Even if, soon, I shall be.

*   *   *

It has been more than sixty years since I last laid eyes on any member of my blood family. It's almost impossible to believe that I have lived to this age, eighty-two, and spent such a small proportion of my given time among them. I was remiss in my duties towards them, although I did not see it like that at the time. For I could no more have changed my destiny than altered the colour of my eyes. Circumstances led me from one moment to the next, and the next, and the next, as it does with any man, and I followed each step without question.

And then one day I stopped. And I was old. And they were gone.

Do their bodies remain in a state of decomposition, I wonder, or have they already dissolved and become one with the dust? Does the act of putrefaction take several generations to complete or can it advance at a faster rate, dependent on the age of the body or the conditions of burial? And the speed of corporeal decay, does that depend on the quality of the wood from which one's coffin is made? The appetite of the soil? The climate? In the past, these are the types of questions that I might have pondered over while distracted from my night-time reading. Typically, I would have made a note of my query and researched it until a satisfactory answer had been arrived at, but my routines have all fallen apart this year and such investigations seem trivial to me now. Indeed, I have not been to the library for many months, not since before Zoya became ill. I may never go there again.

Most of my life—most of my adult life, that is— has been spent within the tranquil walls of the library at the British Museum. I began my employment there in the early autumn of 1923, shortly after Zoya and I first arrived in London, cold, fearful, certain that we might yet be discovered. I was twenty-four years old at the time and had never known that employment could be so peaceful. It had been five years since I had shed the symbols of my previous life—uniforms, rifles, bombs, explosions—but I remained branded by their memory. Now it was soft cotton suits, filing cabinets and erudition, a welcome change.

And before London, of course, was Paris, where I developed that interest in books and literature that had first begun in the Blue Library, a curiosity that I hoped to pursue in England. To my eternal good fortune, I noticed an advertisement in *The Times* for a junior librarian in the British Museum and I applied in person later that day, hat in hand, and was immediately taken in to meet a Mr Arthur Trevors, my potential new employer.

I can remember the date exactly. August the twelfth. I had just come from the Cathedral of the Dormition and All Saints where I had lit a candle for an old friend, an annual gesture of respect to mark his birthday. *For as long as I live*, I had promised him all those years ago. It seemed appropriate, somehow, that my new life was to commence on the same day that his own short life

6

had begun.

'Do you know how long the British Library has existed, Mr Jachmenev?' he asked me, peering over the top of a pair of half-moon spectacles, which were perched uselessly towards the base of his nose. He didn't struggle even slightly with my name, which impressed me since so many English people seemed to make a virtue out of being unable to pronounce it. 'Since 1753,' he replied immediately, giving me no opportunity to hazard a guess. 'When Sir Hans Sloan bequeathed his collection of books and curiosities to the nation, and thus the entire museum was born. What do you think of that?'

I could scarcely think of any response other than to praise Sir Hans for his philanthropy and common sense, a reply which Mr Trevors wholeheartedly approved of.

'You're absolutely right, Mr Jachmenev,' he said, nodding his head furiously. 'He was a most excellent fellow. My great-grandfather played bridge with him regularly. The difficulty now, of course, is one of space. We're running out of it, you see. Too many books being produced, that's the problem. Most of them written by half-wits, atheists or sodomites, but God help us, we're obliged to carry them all. You don't have any truck with that faction, do you, Mr Jachmenev?'

I shook my head quickly. 'No, sir,' I said.

'Glad to hear it. Some day we hope to move the library to its own premises, of course, and that'll help matters no end. But it's all down to Parliament. They control all our money, you see. And you know what those fellows are like. Rotten to the core, every last one of them. This Baldwin

7

chap's frightfully good, but other than him . . .' He shook his head and looked as if he might be ill.

In the silence that followed, I could think of nothing to recommend myself other than to speak of my admiration for the museum, which I had spent a mere half-hour in before my interview, and the astonishing collection of treasures which were gathered inside its walls.

'You've worked in a museum before, Mr Jachmenev, haven't you?' he asked me and I shook my head. He appeared surprised by my answer and took off his glasses as he questioned me further. 'I thought perhaps you were an employee of the Hermitage? In St Petersburg?'

He did not need to qualify the name of the museum with its location; I knew it well enough. For a moment I regretted not having lied, for after all it was unlikely that he would seek proof of my employment there and any attempt to seek references would take years to achieve, if they arrived at all.

'I never worked there, sir,' I replied. 'But of course I am very familiar with it. I spent many hundreds of happy hours at the Hermitage. The Byzantine collection is particularly impressive. As are the Numismatics.'

He considered this for a moment, trilling his fingers along the side of his desk, before deciding that he was satisfied with my response. Leaning back in his chair, he narrowed his eyes and breathed heavily through his nose as he stared at me. 'Tell me, Mr Jachmenev,' he said, dragging each word out as if their elocution was painful to him. 'How long have you been in England?'

'Not long,' I told him truthfully. 'A few weeks.'

'You came directly from Russia?'

'No, sir. My wife and I spent several years in France before—'

'Your wife? You're a married man, then?' he asked, appearing pleased by my admission.

'Yes, sir.'

'Her name?'

'Zoya,' I told him. 'A Russian name, of course. It means *life*.'

'Does it indeed?' he muttered, staring at me as if my statement had been entirely presumptuous. 'How charming. And how did you make your living in France?'

'I worked in a Parisian bookshop,' I said. 'Of average size, but with a loyal client base. There were no quiet days.'

'And you enjoyed the work?'

'Very much.'

'Why was that?'

'It was peaceful,' I replied. 'Even though I was always busy, there was a serenity to the atmosphere that appealed greatly to me.'

'Well, that's how we run things here too,' he said cheerfully. 'Nice and quiet, but lots of hard work. And before France, you travelled extensively throughout Europe, I expect?'

'Not really, sir,' I admitted. 'Before France was Russia.'

'Escaping the revolution, were you?'

'We left in 1918,' I replied. 'A year after it took place.'

'Didn't care for the new regime, I suppose?'

'No, sir.'

'Quite right too,' he remarked, his lip curling a little in distaste at the thought of it. 'Bloody

9

Bolsheviks. The Tsar was a cousin of King George, did you know that?'

'I was aware of that, yes, sir,' I replied.

'And his wife, Mrs Tsar, a granddaughter of Queen Victoria.'

'The Tsaritsa,' I said, carefully correcting his irreverence.

'Yes, if you must. It's a damn cheek, if you ask me. Something should be done about them before they spread their filthy ways across Europe. You know that chap Lenin used to study here at the library, of course?'

'No, I didn't,' I said, raising an eyebrow in surprise.

'Oh it's quite true, I assure you,' he said, sensing my scepticism. 'Sometime around 1901 or 1902, I believe. Well before my time. My predecessor told me all about it. He said that Lenin used to arrive every morning around nine and stay until lunchtime when that wife of his would arrive to drag him off to edit their revolutionary rag. He tried to smuggle flasks of coffee in all the time but we were on to him. Nearly got himself barred over it. You can tell the kind of man he was from that alone. You're not a Bolshevik, are you, Mr Jachmenev?' he asked, leaning forward suddenly and glaring at me.

'No, sir,' I said, shaking my head and glancing down at the ground, unable to meet his piercing stare. I was surprised by the opulence of the marble floor beneath my feet. I thought that I had left such glories behind me. 'No, I am definitely not a Bolshevik.'

'What are you then? Leninist? Trotskyite? Tsarist?'

10

'Nothing, sir,' I replied, looking up again, a determined expression on my face now. 'I am nothing at all. Except a man recently arrived in your great country who seeks honest employment. I have no political allegiances and seek none. I desire nothing more than a quiet existence and the ability to provide a decent living for my family.'

He considered these remarks quietly for a few moments and I wondered whether I was debasing myself a little too much before him, but I had prepared these lines on my walk towards Bloomsbury in order to secure the position and thought them humble enough to satisfy a potential employer. I didn't care if they made me sound like a servant. I needed work.

'Very well, Mr Jachmenev,' he said finally, nodding his head. 'I think we'll take a chance on you. A trial period to begin with, let's say six weeks, and if we're happy enough with each other at the end of that time we'll have another little chat and see if we can't make the position permanent. How does that sound?'

'I'm very grateful, sir,' I said, smiling and extending my hand in a gesture of friendship and appreciation. He hesitated for a moment, as if I was taking a tremendous liberty, before directing me to a second office where my details were recorded and my new responsibilities outlined.

I remained in the employment of the library at the British Museum for the rest of my working life, and after my retirement I continued to visit almost every day, spending hours at the desksI used to clear, reading and researching, educating myself. I felt safe there. There is nowhere in the world I have ever felt so safe as within those walls. My

11

whole life I have waited for them to find me, to find us both, but it seems we have been spared. Only God will separate us now.

*　　　*　　　*

It is true that I have never been what you might term a modern type of man. My life with Zoya, our long marriage, was of the traditional variety. Although we both worked and returned home from our jobs at similar times in the evening, it was she who prepared our meals and took care of such domestic chores as laundry and cleaning. The idea that I might help was never even considered. As she cooked, I would sit by the fire and read. I liked long novels, historical epics, and had little time for contemporary fiction. I tried Lawrence when it seemed daring to do so, but I stumbled over the dialect, Walter Morel's *dost*s and *nimbler*s and *threp'ny bit*s, Mellors' *niver*s and *theer*s. Forster I found more attractive, those earnest, well-intentioned Schlegel sisters, the free-thinking Mr Emerson, the wild Lilia Herriton. Sometimes I might feel moved to recite a particularly affecting passage aloud and Zoya would turn away from the sweating of the roast or the broiling of the pork chops to rest the front of her hand against her forehead in exhaustion and say *What, Georgy? What is it you're telling me?* as if she had half forgotten that I was even in the room. It seems wrong that I did not play a greater part in the running of our home, but this was how family life was conducted in those days. Still, I regret it.

I had not always intended my life to be quite so conservative. There were even moments, fleeting

12

instances over more than sixty years together, when I resented the fact that we could not stand clear of our parents' shadows and create our own individualized lifestyle. But Zoya, perhaps in recognition of her own childhood and upbringing, desired nothing more than to create a home which would fit in exactly with those of our neighbours and friends.

She wanted peace, you see.

She wanted to blend in.

'Can't we just live quietly?' she asked me once. 'Quietly and happily, behaving like others behave? That way, no one will ever notice us.'

We made our home in Holborn, not far from Doughty Street, where the writer Charles Dickens lived for a time. I passed his house twice every day as I walked to and from the British Museum and, as I became more familiar with his novels through my work at the library, I tried to imagine him seated in the upstairs study, crafting the peculiar sentences of *Oliver Twist*. An elderly neighbour once told me that her mother had cleaned for Mr Dickens every day for two years and that he had presented her with an edition of that novel with his signature upon the frontispiece, which she kept on a shelf in her parlour.

'A very clean man,' she told me, pursing her lips and nodding in approval. 'That's what Mother always said about him. Fastidious in his ways.'

My morning routine never changed. I would wake at half past six, wash and dress, and step into the kitchen by seven o'clock, where Zoya would have tea and toast and two perfectly poached eggs waiting for me on the table. She had a miraculous technique for preparing the eggs so that they

13

retained their oval shape outside of the shell, a talent she put down to creating a whirlwind effect in the boiling water with a whisk before plunging the albumen and the yolk inside. We said little to each other as I ate but she would sit at the table next to me, refilling my mug of tea when it ran low, taking my plate away the moment I had finished and rinsing it beneath the tap.

I preferred to walk to the museum, regardless of the weather, in order to take some exercise. As a young man, I was proud of my physique and I worked hard to maintain it, even as middle-age approached and I became less enamoured by my reflection in the glass. I carried a briefcase and Zoya placed two sandwiches and a piece of fruit inside it every morning, alongside whatever novel I was reading at the time. She took such good care of me and, through the nature of daily repetition, I rarely thought to comment on her kindness or offer her my thanks.

Perhaps this makes me sound like an old-fashioned creature, a tyrant making unreasonable demands of his wife.

Nothing could be further from the truth.

In fact, when we were first married, in Paris in the autumn of 1919, I could not bear the idea of Zoya placing herself in a servile position towards me.

'But I am not waiting upon you,' she insisted. 'It gives me pleasure to take care of you, Georgy, can't you see that? I never imagined I would have such freedoms as this, to wash, to cook, to maintain my own home as other women do. Please don't deny me something that others take for granted.'

'That others complain about,' I replied with a smile.

'Please, Georgy,' she repeated, and what could I do but accede to her demands? Still, I remained uneasy with this for some years, but as time went by and we were blessed with a child, our routines took over and I forgot about my initial discomfort. The arrangement suited us, that is all I can say of it.

My shame, however, is that she has looked after me so well throughout our life together that I find myself unable to cope with basic responsibilities now that I am alone in our home. I know nothing of cooking and so eat cereal for my breakfast every day, flakes of dry oats and bran, fossilized currants made soggy by the addition of milk. I take lunch at the hospital at one o'clock when I arrive on my daily visit. I eat by myself at a small plastic table overlooking the infirmary's unkempt garden, where the doctors and nurses smoke side by side in their pale-blue, almost indecent scrubs. The food is dull and bland but it fills my stomach and that is all I ask of it. It is basic English food. Meat and potatoes. Chicken and potatoes. Fish and potatoes. I imagine that some day the menu will offer potatoes and potatoes. It can excite no one.

Naturally, I have grown to recognize some of my fellow visitors, the widows and widowers in waiting who wander the corridors in terrified loneliness, deprived for the first time in decades of their favourite person. We have a nodding acquaintance, some of us, and there are those who like to share their stories of hope and disappointment with each other, but I avoid conversation. I am not here to form friendships. I am here only for my wife, for

15

my darling Zoya, to sit by her bedside, to hold her hand in mine, to whisper in her ear, to make sure she knows that she is not alone.

I remain in the hospital until six o'clock and then I kiss her cheek, rest my hand on her shoulder for a moment, and say a silent prayer that she will still be alive when I return the next day.

* * *

Twice weekly, our grandson Michael arrives to spend a little time with me. His mother, our daughter Arina, died in her thirty-sixth year when she was hit by a car as she returned home from work. The scar that was left by her absence has never healed. We had been convinced for so long that we were unable to bear children that when Zoya finally became pregnant we thought it a miracle, a gift from God. A reward, perhaps, for the families we had lost.

And then she was taken from us.

Michael was only a boy when his mother died, and his father, our son-in-law, a thoughtful and honourable man, ensured that he maintained a relationship with his maternal grandparents. Of course, like all boys, his appearance changed constantly throughout his childhood, to the point where we could never decide whose side of the family he favoured the most, but now that he has reached manhood, I find that he reminds me very much of Zoya's father. I think she must have noticed the similarity too, but has never spoken of it. There is something in the way that he turns his head and smiles at us, in how his forehead furrows unexpectedly when he frowns, the depth of those brown eyes that combine a mixture of confidence and uncertainty. Once, when the three of us were walking in Hyde Park together on a sunny afternoon, a small dog came scampering towards us and he fell to his knees to embrace the puppy, allowing it to lick his face a she gurgled delighted inanities in the dog's direction, and as he looked up to grin at his doting grandparents, I am sure that we were both taken by the sudden and unanticipated resemblance. It was so unsettling, it caused our minds to fill with so many memories, that the conversation immediately grew stilted between us and an otherwise pleasant afternoon became spoiled.

Michael is in his second year of studies at the Royal Academy of Dramatic Arts, where he is in training to become an actor, a vocation which surprises me for as a child he was quiet and withdrawn, as a teenager sullen and introverted, and now, at the age of twenty, he displays an extrovert's talent for performance which none of us had ever expected. Last year, before she became too ill to enjoy such things, Zoya and I attended a student production of Mr Shaw's *Major Barbara*, in which Michael played the part of the young, smitten Adolphus Cusins. He was quite impressive, I thought. Convincing in the role. He seemed to know a little about love too, which pleased me.

'He's very good at pretending to be someone he's not,' I remarked to Zoya in the lobby afterwards as we waited to offer our congratulations, unsure as I said the words whether I meant them as a compliment or not. 'I don't know how he does it.'

'I do,' she replied, surprising me, but before I could respond he introduced us to a young lady,

Sarah, Major Barbara herself, his on-stage fiancée and, as it transpired, his off-stage girlfriend. She was a pretty thing but seemed a little confused as to why she was being forced to make small talk with two elderly relatives of her lover, and perhaps a little irritated by it too. Throughout our conversation I felt as if she was talking down to Zoya and me as if she believed that a correlation somehow existed between age and stupidity. At nineteen years old she was full of pronouncements about how terrible the world was, and how both Mr Reagan and Mr Brezhnev were entirely to blame. She declared in a harsh, condescending voice, which put me in mind of that awful Thatcher woman quoting St Francis of Assisi on the steps of Downing Street, that the President and the General Secretary would destroy the planet with their imperialist policies, and spoke with deluded authority of the arms race, the cold war, matters that she had only read about in her student magazines and about which she presumed to lecture us. She wore a white T-shirt which made no attempt to conceal her breasts; a dripping, blood-red word—Solidarność—was scrawled across it and when she caught me staring—at the word, I swear it, not her breasts—she proceeded to deliver a sermon about the heroic nature of the Polish ship-worker, Mr Wałeşa. I felt utterly patronized by her, insulted even, but Zoya linked arms with me to ensure that I remained composed and finally Major Barbara informed us how absolutely marvellous it had been to meet us, that we were perfectly adorable, and vanished off into a sea of grotesquely painted and no doubt similarly opinionated young people.

I didn't criticize her to Michael, of course. I know what it is to be a young man in love. And, for that matter, to be an old man in love. Sometimes I find it absurd to consider the fact that this magnificent boy is now experiencing sensual delights; it seems like such a short time ago that he wanted nothing more than to sit on my lap and have me read fairy-tales to him.

Michael makes sure to visit his grandmother in the hospital every few days; he is diligent in his attendance. He sits with her for an hour and then comes to lie to me, to say how much better she looks, that she woke for a few moments and sat up to speak with him and appeared alert and more like her old self, that he's sure it's only a matter of time before Zoya will be well enough to come home. I wonder sometimes whether he really believes this or if he thinks that I am foolish enough to believe it myself and he is doing me a great service by putting such wonderful, impossible notions in my stupid old head. Young people have such disrespect for the elderly, not by design perhaps, but simply by the fact that they refuse to believe that our brains still function. Either way, we perform the farce together two or three times a week. He says it, I agree with him, we make plans for things that we three—four—might do together when Zoya is well again, and then he checks his watch, seems surprised by how late it is, kisses me on the head, says 'See you in a couple of days, Pops, call me if you need anything' and is out the door, bounding up the steps on his long, lean, muscular legs, and jumping almost instantaneously on board the lower deck of a passing bus, all in the space of a minute.

There are times when I envy him his youth but I try not to dwell on that. An old man should not resent those who are sent to take his place, and to recall when I was young and healthy and virile is an act of masochism that serves no purpose. It occurs to me that even though Zoya and I are both still alive, my life is already over. She will be taken from me soon and there will be no reason for me to continue without her. We are one person, you see. We are GeorgyandZoya.

*   *   *

Zoya's doctor's name is Joan Crawford. This is not a joke. The first time I met her, I couldn't help but wonder why her parents inflicted such a burden on her. Or was it the result of her marriage, perhaps? Did she fall in love with the right man but the wrong name? I didn't remark on its familiarity, of course. I imagine she has spent a lifetime enduring idiotic comments. By coincidence, she bears a certain physical similarity to the famous actress, sporting the same rich, dark hair and slightly arched eyebrows, and I suspect that she encourages the comparison by the manner in which she presents herself; whether or not she beats her children with wire clothes-hangers is of course open to conjecture. She usually wears a wedding ring but occasionally it's missing from her hand. Whenever that is the case her manner is distracted, and I find myself wondering whether her private life is a source of disappointment to her.

I have not spoken to Dr Crawford for almost two weeks and so, before visiting Zoya, I wander through the white, antiseptic-scented corridors in search of her office. I've been there before, of course, several times, but I find the oncology department difficult to negotiate. The hospital itself is labyrinthine and none of the young men and women who rush by, consulting clipboards and charts as they scurry along, biting into apples and half-sandwiches, seem inclined to offer any assistance. Finally, however, I find myself standing outside her door and knock gently. An eternity seems to pass before she answers—an irritable *Yes?*—and when she does I open it only a fraction, smiling apologetically, hoping to disarm her with my elderly civility.

'Dr Crawford,' I say. 'I must apologize for disturbing you.'

'Mr Jachmenev,' she replies, impressing me by the fact that she remembers my name so quickly; over the years, there have been some who have had great difficulty in either recalling or pronouncing it. And there have been others who have felt it beneath their dignity to try. 'You're not disturbing me at all. Please come in.'

I'm glad that she is so welcoming today and step inside, sitting down with my hat in my hands, hoping that she might have some positive news for me. I can't help but look towards her ring finger and wonder whether her good humour is a result of the shining gold band winking at me as it catches the sunlight. She's smiling noticeably as she takes me in and I stare at her, a little surprised. This is a cancer department, after all. The woman treats cancer patients from morning till night, tells them terrible things, performs horrible surgeries, watches as they struggle their way out of this world

21

and on to the next. I can't imagine what she has to look so happy about.

'I'm sorry, Mr Jachmenev,' she says, shaking her head quickly. 'You'll have to forgive me. I'm just always impressed by how beautifully you're dressed. Men of your generation, they seem to wear suits all the time, don't they? And I don't often see men with hats any more. I *miss* hats.'

I look down at my clothing, unsure how to take the remark. This is how I dress, how I have always dressed. It does not seem worthy of comment. I'm not sure that I care for the distinction between our generations either, although it is true that I must be nearly forty years older than her. Indeed, Dr Crawford would be around the same age that Arina, our daughter, would have been. Had she lived.

'I wanted to ask you about my wife,' I say, dispensing with these pleasantries. 'I wanted to ask you about Zoya.'

'Of course,' she replies quickly, all business now. 'What would you like to know?'

I feel at a loss now, despite the fact that I have been preparing questions in my mind ever since I left the hospital the previous afternoon. I search my brain for the correct words, for something approaching language. 'How is she doing?' I ask finally, four words which do not seem sufficient to carry the great weight of the questions they support.

'She's comfortable, Mr Jachmenev,' she replies, her tone softening a little. 'But, as you know, the tumour is at an advanced level. You remember I spoke to you before about the development of ovarian cancer?'

I nod, but cannot look her in the eye. How we cling to hope, even when we know that there is none! She has spoken at some length over the course of several meetings with Zoya and me about the four individual stages of the disease and their inevitable ends. She's talked about ovaries and tumours, the uterus, the fallopian tube, the pelvis; she has used phrases such as *peritoneal washings*, *metastases* and *para-aortic lymph nodes* which have been beyond my level of comprehension, but I have listened and asked appropriate questions and done my best to understand.

'Well, at this point the most that we can do is try to manage Zoya's pain for as long as possible. She responds extremely well to the medication, actually, for a lady of her years.'

'She has always been strong,' I say.

'I can see that,' she replies. 'She has certainly been one of the most determined patients I've encountered in my career.'

I don't like this use of the phrase 'has been'. It implies something, or someone, which is already past. Which once was, and is no more.

'She can't come home to . . . ?' I begin, unwilling to finish the sentence, looking up at Dr Crawford hopefully, but she shakes her head.

'To move her would accelerate the progression of the cancer,' she tells me. 'I don't think her body could survive the trauma. I know this is difficult, Mr Jachmenev, but—'

I don't listen to any more. She is a nice lady, a competent doctor, but I do not need to hear or report platitudes. I leave her office shortly after this and return to the ward, where Zoya is awake now and breathing heavily. Machines surround her. Wires slip beneath the arms of her nightdress; tubes worm their way beneath the rough covers of the bedspread and find purchase I know not where.

'*Dusha*,' I say, leaning over and kissing her forehead, allowing my lips to linger for a moment against her soft, thin flesh. *My darling*. I inhale her familiar scent; all my memories are wrapped up in it. I could close my eyes and be anywhere. 1970. 1953. 1915.

'Georgy,' she whispers, and it is an effort for her even to speak my name. I motion to her to reserve her energy as I sit by her side and take her hand in mine. As I do so, her fingers close around my own and I am surprised for a moment by how much strength she can still summon from within. But I reproach myself for this, for what human being have I ever known whose strength can compete with that of Zoya? Who, dead or alive, has endured as much and yet survived? I squeeze her fingers in return, hoping that whatever feeble strength remains in my own weakened body can be passed along to her, and we say nothing, simply sit in each other's company as we have throughout our whole lives, happy to be together, content when we are one.

Of course, I was not always this old and weak. My strength was what led me away from Kashin. It is what brought me to Zoya in the first place.

The Prince of Kashin

It was my eldest sister, Asya, who first told me of the world that existed outside of Kashin.

I was only nine years old when she breached that naive insularity of mine. Asya was eleven and I was a little in love with her, I think, in the way that a younger brother may become entranced by the beauty and mystery of the female who is closest to him, before the urge for a sexual component appears and the attentions are diverted elsewhere.

We had always been close, Asya and I. She fought constantly with Liska, who was born a year after her and a year before me, and barely tolerated our youngest sister, Talya, but I was her pet. She dressed me and groomed me and saw to it that I was kept away from the worst excesses of our father's temper. To her good fortune, she inherited our mother Yulia's pretty features, but not her disposition, and she made the most of her looks, braiding her hair one day, tying it behind her neck the next, loosening the *kosnik* and allowing it to hang loosely around her shoulders when she was so inclined. She rubbed the juice of ripe plums into her cheeks to improve her countenance and wore her dress pinned up above her ankles, which made my father stare at her in the late evenings, a mixture of desire and contempt deepening the darkness of his eyes. The other girls in our village despised her for her vanity, of course, but what they really envied was her confidence. As she grew older they said she was a whore, that she spread her legs for any man or boy who desired her, but she didn't care about any of that. She just laughed at their taunts, allowing them to slip away like water off a rock.

She should have lived in a different time and place, I think. She might have made a great success of her life.

'But where is this other world?' I asked her as we sat together by the stove in the corner of our small hut, an area which acted as bedroom, kitchen and living area for the six of us. At that time of the day, our mother and father would have been returning home from their labours, expecting us to have some food prepared for them, content to beat us if we did not, and Asya was busy stirring a pot of vegetables, potatoes and water into a thick broth which would act as our supper. Liska was outside somewhere, causing mischief, as was her particular talent. Talya, always the quietest of children, was lying in a nest of straw, playing with her fingers and toes, observing us patiently.

'Far away from here, Georgy,' she said, placing a finger carefully into the foam of the bubbling mixture and tasting it. 'But people don't live there like they live here.'

'They don't?' I asked, unable even to imagine a different manner of existence. 'Then how do they live?'

'Well, some are poor, of course, like we are,' she conceded in an almost apologetic tone, as if our circumstances were something of which we should all have been ashamed. 'But many more live in great splendour. These are the people who make our country great, Georgy. Their houses are built from stone, not wood like this place. They eat whenever they want to eat, from plates encrusted with jewels. Food which is specially prepared by cooks who have spent all their lives mastering their art. And the ladies, they travel only by carriage.'

'Carriage?' I asked, crinkling my nose as I turned to look at her, unsure what the word could possibly mean. 'What is this carriage?'

'The horses carry them along,' she explained with a sigh, as if my ignorance had been designed for no other reason than to frustrate her. 'They are like . . . oh, how can I put this? Imagine a hut with wheels that people can sit inside and be transported in comfort. Can you picture that, Georgy?'

'No,' I said firmly, for the idea seemed both preposterous and frightening. I looked away from her and felt my stomach start to ache with hunger, and wondered whether she would allow me a spoon or two of this broth before our parents returned.

'One day I shall travel in such a carriage,' she added quietly, staring into the fire beneath the pot and poking at it with a stick, hoping perhaps to find some small coal or twig that had not yet caught flame and which could be cajoled into providing us with just a few more minutes of heat. 'I don't intend to stay in Kashin for ever.'

I shook my head in admiration for her. She was the most intelligent person I knew, for her awareness of these other worlds and lives was astonishing to me. I think that it was Asya's thirst for knowledge which fuelled my own growing imagination and desire to learn more of the world. How she had come to know of such things I did not know, but it saddened me to think that Asya might be taken from me one day. I felt wounded that she should even want to seek a life outside of the one that we shared together. Kashin was a dark, miserable, fetid, unhealthy, squalid, depressing wreck of a village; of course it was. But until now I had never imagined that there might be anywhere better to live. I had never stepped more than a few miles from its boundaries, after all.

'You can't tell anyone about this, Georgy,' she said after a moment, leaning forward in excitement as if she was about to reveal her most intimate secret. 'But when I am older, I am going to St Petersburg. I've decided to make my life there.' Her voice became more animated and breathless as she said this, her fantasies making their way from the solitude of her private thoughts towards the reality of the spoken word.

'But you can't,' I said, shaking my head. 'You would be alone there. You know no one in St Petersburg.'

'At first, perhaps,' she admitted, laughing and putting a hand over her mouth to contain her mirth. 'But I shall meet a wealthy man soon enough. A prince, perhaps. And he will fall in love with me and we will live together in a palace and I will have all the servants that I require and wardrobes filled with beautiful dresses. I'll wear different jewellery every day—opals, sapphires, rubies, diamonds—and during the season we will dance together in the throne room of the Winter Palace, and everyone will look at me from morning till night and admire me and wish that they could stand in my place.'

I stared at her, this unrecognizable girl with her fantastical plans. Was this the sister who lay on the moss-and-pine floor beside me every night and

28

woke up with the imprint of the grainy branches upon her cheeks? I could scarcely comprehend a single word of which she spoke. Princes, servants, jewellery. Such concepts were entirely alien to my young mind. And as for love. What was that, after all? How did that concern any of us? She caught my look of incomprehension, of course, and burst out laughing as she tousled my hair.

'Oh, Georgy,' she said, kissing me now on either cheek and then once on the lips for luck. 'You don't understand a thing I'm saying, do you?'

'Yes,' I insisted quickly, for I hated her to think of me as ignorant. 'Of course I do.'

'You've heard of the Winter Palace, haven't you?'

I hesitated. I wanted to say yes, but if I did, then she might not explain it in further detail and the words were already holding a certain allure. 'I *think* I have,' I said finally. 'I can't remember exactly. Remind me, Asya.'

'The Winter Palace is where the Tsar lives,' she explained. 'With the Tsaritsa, of course, and the Imperial Family. You know who they are, don't you?'

'Yes, yes,' I said quickly, for His Majesty's name, and that of his family, was invoked before every meal as we offered a prayer for his continued health, generosity and wisdom. The prayers themselves often lasted longer than the eating. 'I'm not stupid, you know.'

'Well then you should know where the Tsar makes his home. Or one of his homes, anyway. He has many. Tsarskoe Selo. Livadia. The *Standart*.'

I raised an eyebrow and now it was my turn to laugh. The notion of more than one home seemed ridiculous to me. Why would anyone need such a

29

thing? Of course, I knew that Tsar Nicholas had been appointed to his glorious position by God himself, that his powers and autocracy were infinite and absolute, but was he possessed of magical qualities also? Could he be in more than one place simultaneously? The idea was absurd and yet somehow possible. He was the Tsar, after all. He could be anything. He could do anything. He was as much a god as God himself.

'Will you take me to St Petersburg with you?' I asked a few moments later, my voice sinking almost to a whisper, as if I was afraid that she might deny me this ultimate honour. 'When you go, Asya. You won't leave me behind, will you?'

'I could try,' she said magnanimously, considering it. 'Or perhaps you could come and visit the prince and me when we are established in our new home. You can have a wing of our palace entirely for yourself and a team of butlers to assist you. And we will have children, of course, too. Beautiful children, many of them, boys and girls. You will be an uncle to them, Georgy. Would you like that?'

'Certainly,' I agreed, although I found myself growing jealous at the idea of sharing my beautiful sister with anyone else, even a prince of the royal blood.

'One day . . .' she said with a sigh, staring into the fire as if she could see depictions of her glorious future flickering and bursting into life within the flames. Of course, she was only a child herself at the time. I wonder whether it was Kashin that she hated or just a better life that she longed for.

It saddens me to recall that conversation from such a distance of time. My heart aches to think

30

that she never achieved her ambitions. For it was not Asya who found her way to St Petersburg and the Winter Palace. It was not she who ever knew how it felt to be surrounded by the seductive power of wealth and luxury.

It was me. It was little Georgy.

*   *   *

The closest friend of my youth was a boy named Kolek Boryavich Tanksy, whose family had lived in Kashin for as many generations as my own. We had many things in common, Kolek and I. We were born only a few weeks apart, during the late spring of 1899. We spent our childhood playing in the mud together, exploring every corner of our small village, blaming each other when our escapades went wrong. We both came from a family of sisters. I, of course, was blessed with only three, while Kolek was cursed with twice that number.

And we were both frightened of our fathers.

My father, Daniil Vladyavich, and Kolek's father, Borys Alexandrovich, had known each other all their lives, probably spending as much of their boyhood in each other's company as their sons would thirty years later. They were passionate men, both of them, filled with degrees of admiration and loathing, but their political opinions diverged considerably.

Daniil treasured the country of his birth. He was patriotic to the point of blindness, believing that man was given life for no other purpose than to obey the dictates of God's messenger on earth, the Russian Tsar. However, his hatred and resentment of me, his only son, was as incomprehensible as it

31

was upsetting. From the moment of my birth, he treated me with disdain. One day I was too short, the next I was too weak, on another I might be too timid or too stupid. Of course, it was the nature of farm labourers that they wanted to breed, so why my father saw me as such a disappointment after already siring two girls is a mystery. But nevertheless, it was how things were. Having never known anything different, I might have grown up believing that this was how all relationships between fathers and sons were cultivated, were it not for the other example that played out before me.

Borys Alexandrovich loved his son very much and considered him to be the prince of our village, which, I suppose, means that he thought himself to be its king. He praised Kolek constantly, brought him everywhere with him and never excluded him from adult conversation in the way that other fathers did. But unlike Daniil, he nurtured an obsession with criticizing Russia and its rulers, believing that his own poverty and perceived failure in life was entirely the result of the autocrats whose whims dictated our lives.

'One day, things will change in this country,' he told my father on any number of occasions. 'Can't you smell it in the air, Daniil Vladyavich? Russians will not stand to be ruled over by such a family for much longer. We must take control of our own destinies.'

'Always the revolutionary, Borys Alexandrovich,' my father replied, shaking his head and laughing, a rare treat, and one which was only ever inspired by his friend's radical pronouncements. 'All your life spent here in Kashin, tilling fields, eating *kasha* and drinking *kvas*, and still your head is full of these ideas. You will never change, will you?'

'And all *your* life, you have been content to be a *moujik*,' said Borys angrily. 'Yes, we work the land, we make an honest living from the soil, but are we not men like the Tsar? Tell me, why should he have everything, be entitled to everything, own everything, when we live out our days in such poverty and squalor? You still say prayers for him every night, don't you?'

'Of course I do,' said my father, starting to grow irritated now, for he hated even engaging in any conversation which criticized the Tsar. He had been bred with an innate sense of servitude and it flowed through his veins as freely as his blood. 'Russia's destiny is inextricably linked to that of the Tsar. Think, only for a moment, of how far back this generation of rulers goes. To Tsar Michael! That's more than three hundred years, Borys.'

'Three hundred years of Romanovs is three hundred years too many,' roared his friend, coughing up a mouthful of phlegm and spitting it on the ground between his feet without shame. 'And tell me, what have they given us during that time? Anything of value? I think not. Some day . . . some day, Daniil . . .' He hesitated there. Borys Alexandrovich could be as radical and revolutionary as he wanted, but it would have been a heresy, and perhaps a death sentence, to have continued.

Still, there was not a man in our village who did not know the words that he intended to come next. And there were many who agreed with him.

Kolek Boryavich and I, of course, never spoke of politics. Such matters meant nothing to either of us

33

as children. Instead, as we grew up, we played the games that boys played, found ourselves in the trouble that boys find themselves in, and laughed and fought, but were around each other so much that strangers passing through our village might have taken us for brothers, were it not for the difference in our physical appearance.

As a child, I was small in stature, and cursed with a mop of blond ringlets, a fact which might lie at the root of my father's contempt for me. He had wanted a son to carry on his name and I did not look like the kind of boy who might accomplish such a task. At the age of six I was a foot shorter than all my friends, earning myself the nickname Pasha, which means 'the small one'. Because of my golden curls, my older sisters called me the prettiest member of our family, garnishing me with whatever ribbons and fancies they could find, which caused our father to scream at them in fury and rip the garlands from my head, handfuls of hair often being extracted in the process. And despite the frugality of our diet, I had a tendency towards weight gain as a child too, which my father Daniil considered a mark of dishonour against him.

Kolek, on the other hand, was always tall for his age, lean, strong, and handsome in a very masculine way. By the age of ten, the girls in our village were looking at him with admiring eyes, wondering how he might develop in a few years' time when he had grown to manhood. Their mothers vied with each other for the attention of his own mother, a timid creature named Anje Petrovna, for there was always a sense about him that he would be a great man one day, that he would bring glory to our village, and it was their fervent desire that one of their daughters would eventually be taken to his bed as his bride.

He enjoyed the attention, of course. He was more than aware of the glances that came his way and the admiration everyone had for him, but he too had fallen in love and with none other than my own sister Asya. She was the only person who could make him blush and lose confidence in his remarks. But to his dismay, she was also the only girl in the village who seemed utterly immune to his charms, a fact which I believe only fuelled his desire for her. He hovered around our *izba* daily, seeking opportunities to impress her, determined to break through her steely exterior and make her love him as everyone else did.

'Young Kolek Boryavich is enamoured of you,' our mother remarked one evening to her eldest daughter as she prepared another miserable pot of *shchi*, a sort of cabbage soup that was almost indigestible. 'He cannot bear to look in your direction, have you noticed?'

'He cannot look at me, so that means he likes me,' remarked Asya casually, brushing his interest aside like something unpleasant which had found its way on to her clothing. 'That's a curious logic, don't you agree?'

'He is shy around you, that's all,' explained Yulia. 'And such a handsome boy too. He will make some lucky girl a worthy husband one day.'

'Perhaps,' she said. 'But not me.'

When I quizzed her about this afterwards, she seemed almost insulted that anyone would think that Kolek was good enough for her. 'He's two years younger than me, for one thing,' she

35

explained in an exasperated tone. 'I'm not interested in taking a boy for my husband. And I don't like him anyway. He has a sense of entitlement about him that I cannot bear. As if the world exists only for his benefit. He's had it all his life and everyone in this miserable village is responsible for giving it to him. And he's a coward, too. His father is a monster—you can see that, Georgy, can't you? A horrible man. And yet everything your little Kolek does is designed for no other purpose than to impress him. I've never seen a boy so in thrall to his father. It's loathsome to watch.'

I didn't know how to respond to such a litany of disdain. Like everyone else, I considered Kolek Boryavich to be the finest boy in the village and it had always been my secret delight that he had chosen me to be his closest friend. Perhaps it was the difference in our appearance which allowed our relationship to thrive. The fact that I was the short, fat, golden-curled subordinate standing next to the tall, slim, dark-haired hero, my pathetic proximity making him appear even more glorious than he really was. And this, in turn, made his father even more proud of him. On that, I knew Asya was correct. There was nothing that Kolek would not have done to impress his father. And what was wrong with that, I wondered. At least Borys Alexandrovich took pride in his boy.

But finally, I grew tired of being Pasha and wanted to be Georgy again, and around the time of my fourteenth birthday, the changes in my own appearance, from boy to man, finally took a sudden and unexpected hold, and I encouraged them through exercise and activity. Within a few months, I had grown a considerable amount and suddenly stood just over six feet in height. The heaviness which had cursed me throughout my childhood fell away from my bones as I began to run miles around our village every day, waking early in the morning to swim for an hour in the freezing waters of the Kashinka river that flowed near by. My body grew toned, the muscles at my stomach became more defined. My curls began to straighten out and my hair darkened a little from the shade of bright sunlight to the colour of washed sand. By 1915, when I was sixteen years old, I could stand beside Kolek and not be embarrassed by the comparison. I was still the lesser of the two, of course, but the gap between us had diminished.

There were girls who liked me, too, I knew that. Not as many as fell for my friend, that is true, but nevertheless, I was not unpopular.

And through it all, Asya shook her head and said that I should not aspire to be like Kolek, that he would never be the great man that people expected, and that sooner or later the young prince would not bring honour on Kashin, but shame.

*　　*　　*

It was Borys Alexandrovich who first imparted the news that would change my life.

Kolek and I were standing at the corner of a field near my family's hut, stripped to the waist on a frosty spring morning, laughing together as we chopped a pile of logs into firewood, while doing all that we could to impress the village girls who walked past us. We were sixteen years old, strong and handsome, and while some ignored us completely, others glanced in our direction and offered teasing smiles, biting their lips as they laughed and watched us swing our axes high in the air before bringing them down into the heart of the timber, cleaving it in half, the splinters spitting out from the wreckage like fireworks. One or two were flirtatious enough to make the kind of indecent comment that encouraged Kolek, but I was not yet confident enough to engage in such banter and found myself feeling self-conscious and turning away.

My father, Daniil, emerged from our *izba* and stared at us for a moment, curling his lip a little in distaste as he shook his head. 'You bloody fools,' he said, irritated by our youth and physicality. 'You'll catch pneumonia like that, or do you think that young men can't die?'

'I'm made of strong stuff, Daniil Vladyavich,' replied Kolek, winking at him as he lifted his muscular arms once again so his biceps might pulse and flex for all to see. The axe glistened in the air, its clean steel catching the light for a moment and sending a series of black and golden polka-dots dancing before my eyes, so that when I blinked away the obstruction, it seemed as if a magnificent halo had suddenly materialized around my friend. 'Can't you see that?'

'You might be, Kolek Boryavich,' he said, glaring at me as if he wished that it was Kolek who had been born his son and not I. 'But Georgy follows your example too much and lacks your strength. Will you take care of him when he's shivering in his bed, sweating like a horse and crying out for his mother?'

Kolek looked at me and grinned, delighted by the insult, but I said nothing and continued with my work. A group of young children ran past and giggled as they saw us there, delighted by our near indecency, but then looked towards my father, with his deformed head and terrible reputation for anger, and their smiles quickly faded as they hurried on their way.

'Are you going to stand there and watch us all afternoon or do you have any work of your own to do?' I asked finally, when Daniil showed no sign of leaving us to our labours and conversation. It was unusual for me to speak to him in this way. Typically I addressed him with some degree of respect, not out of fear, but because I did not wish to involve myself in any arguments. On this occasion, however, my defiant words were designed more to impress Kolek with my fortitude than insult Daniil with my insolence.

'I'll take that axe from your hands and slice you in two with it, Pasha, if you don't keep quiet,' he answered, stepping towards me and employing the diminutive which he knew could keep me in my place. I held my position for only a moment before retreating a little and hanging my head. He maintained a power over me, one that I did not fully understand, but he could intimidate me back to my childhood obedience with a simple word.

'My son is a coward, Kolek Boryavich,' he announced then, delighted by his triumph. 'This is what happens when you are reared in a family of women. You become one of them.'

'But *I* was reared in such a family,' said Kolek, burying the blade of the axe in the timber before him, the handle stretching upwards into the crease of his folded arms. 'Do you think me a coward too, Daniil Vladyavich?'

My father opened his mouth to respond, but before he could, Kolek's own father came stomping around a corner towards us, red-faced and angry, his breath transforming into steam in the chill of the morning. He stopped for a moment when he saw the three of us gathered together, shook his head and then threw his arms in the air in disgust in such a dramatic fashion that I found myself having to bite my lip to stop myself from laughing and insulting him.

'It's a disgrace,' he roared, so loudly and aggressively that none of us said anything for a moment, but continued to stare at him, waiting to learn the source of his displeasure. 'An absolute disgrace,' he continued. 'That I have lived to see such a moment! You have heard this news, I take it, Daniil Vladyavich?'

'What news?' asked my father. 'What has happened?'

'If I was a younger man,' he replied, wagging a finger in the air in the manner of a teacher chastising a group of errant schoolboys. 'I tell you now, if I was a younger man and had all my faculties about me—'

'Borys,' said Daniil, interrupting him and looking almost amused by his friend's fury. 'You are ready to kill this morning, I think.'

'Do not joke about it, my friend!'

'Joke? What joke? I don't even know what has caused you to feel such anger.'

'Father,' said Kolek, walking towards him, his face so filled with concern that I thought he was near to embracing him. It was a continual source of fascination to me, this obvious affection between father and son. Having never experienced such warmth myself, I was always curious to observe it in others.

'A merchant I know,' explained Borys finally, stumbling over his words in his anxiety and anger. 'A virtuous man, a man who never lies or cheats, has passed through our village this morning and—'

'I saw him!' I announced cheerfully, for it was unusual enough to see a stranger passing through Kashin, but an unfamiliar man had walked past our hut wearing a coat of fine goats' hair only an hour before and I had taken note of him as he had passed and offered him a good morning, which he had ignored. 'He came by here not an hour since and—'

'Hold your tongue, boy,' snapped my father, irritated that I should have some part in this at all. 'Let your elders speak.'

'I have known this man for many years,' continued Borys, ignoring us both, 'and a more sincere person it would be difficult to find. He was making his way through Kalyazin last night and it seems that one of the monsters intends to journey this way as he travels on to St Petersburg. He is passing through Kashin! Our own village!' he added, spitting out the words, so deep was the level of insult he felt. 'And of course he will demand that we all step out of our huts and bow down before him in adoration, as the Jews did when Jesus entered Jerusalem on a colt. A week before they crucified him, of course.'

'Which monsters?' asked Daniil, shaking his head in confusion. 'Who are you referring to?'

'A Romanov,' he announced, searching our faces

for a reaction. 'None other than the Grand Duke
Nicholas Nicolaievich,' he added, and for a man
who held the Imperial family in such low regard,
he rolled the royal name off his tongue as if every
syllable was a precious jewel that must be handled
with care and consideration, lest its glory be
shattered and lost for ever.

'Nicholas the Tall,' said Kolek quietly.

'The very same.'

'Why *the Tall*?' I asked, frowning.

'To distinguish him from his cousin, of course,'
snapped Borys Alexandrovich. 'Nicholas the Short.
Tsar Nicholas II. The tormentor of the Russian
people.'

My eyes opened wide in surprise. 'The cousin of
the Tsar is to pass through Kashin?' I asked. I
could not have been more astonished if Daniil had
thrown his arms around my shoulders, embraced
me and praised me as his son and heir.

'Don't look so impressed, Pasha,' said Borys
Alexandrovich, insulting me for not joining him in
his anger. 'Don't you know who these people are?
What have they done for us anyway other than—?'

'Borys, please,' said my father with a deep sigh.
'Not today. Your politics can wait until another
time, surely. This is a great honour for our village.'

'An honour?' he asked, laughing. 'An honour, you
say! These Romanovs are the ones who keep us in
our poverty and you think it a privilege that one of
their number chooses to use our streets to stop for
a moment to allow his horse to drink our water and
take a shit? An honour! You dishonour yourself,
Daniil Vladyavich, with such a word. Look! Look
around you now!'

We turned our heads in the direction in which he

42

was pointing; most of the villagers were rushing towards their huts. They had no doubt heard the news about our illustrious visitor and were seeking to prepare themselves in whatever way they could. Washing their faces and hands, of course, for they could not present themselves to a prince of the royal blood with streaks of mud stained across their faces. Stringing together a few small flowers to create a garland to throw beneath the feet of the Grand Duke's horse.

'This man's grandfather was one of the worst of all the tsars,' continued Borys, ranting now, his face growing redder and redder in his rage. 'Had it not been for Nicholas I, Russians would never even have heard of the concept of autocracy. It was he who insisted that every man, woman and child in the country believed in his unlimited authority on every subject. He saw himself as our Saviour, but do you feel saved, Daniil Vladyavich? Do you, Georgy Daniilovich? Or do you feel cold and hungry and desirous of your freedom?'

'Go inside and prepare yourself,' said my father, ignoring his friend and pointing a finger in my direction. 'You will not disgrace me by appearing before such a great man in your nakedness.'

'Yes, Father,' I said, bowing quickly to his own autocracy and rushing inside in search of a clean tunic. As I rustled through the small pile of clothes that constituted my entire wardrobe, I heard more raised voices outside the hut, followed by the sound of my friend, Kolek, telling his father that they should go home and prepare themselves too. That shouting on the street was of no use to anyone, loyalist or radical.

'If I was a younger man,' I heard Borys

Alexandrovich say as he was led away. 'I tell you, my son, if I was only—'

'*I* am a younger man,' came the reply, and I thought nothing of Kolek's words at the time, nothing at all. It was only later that I remembered them and cursed myself for my stupidity.

It was no more than an hour later when the first advance guards appeared on the horizon and began to make their way towards Kashin. Although common *moujik*s such as we knew only the names of the immediate Imperial family, the Grand Duke Nicholas Nicolaievich, the Tsar's first cousin, was famous throughout Russia for his military exploits. He was not loved, of course. Men such as he never are. But he was revered and blessed with a fearful reputation. During the revolution of 1905, it was rumoured that he had brandished a revolver in front of the Tsar and threatened to blow his own brains out if his cousin did not permit the creation of a Russian constitution, and for that he was admired by many. Although those who were more inclined towards radical thought, like Borys Alexandrovich, cared nothing for such bravery; they saw only a title and an oppressor and a person to be despised.

However, the idea that the Grand Duke was close at hand was enough to send a frisson of excitement and fear through my heart. I could not recall when we had last experienced such anticipation in Kashin. As the riders grew ever closer, almost everyone in the village swept the street clean before their *izba*, creating a clear route for the horses of this most illustrious of visitors.

'Who will he have to accompany him, do you

44

think?' my sister Asya asked me as we stood by our doorway, a family gathered together, waiting to wave and cheer. Her cheeks were even more rouged than usual and her dress was pulled up towards her knees, displaying her legs beneath. 'Some of the young princes from St Petersburg, perhaps?'

'The Grand Duke has no sons for you,' I replied, smiling at her. 'You will have to cast your net wider still.'

'*He* might notice me though,' she said with a shrug.

'Asya!' I cried, appalled but amused by her. 'He's an old man. He must be nearly sixty if he is a day. And he is married, too. You can't believe that—'

'I'm just teasing you, Georgy,' she replied, laughing as she slapped my shoulder playfully, although I wasn't entirely sure that she was. 'But nevertheless, there are sure to be some available young soldiers among his retinue. If one of them was to take an interest in me . . . oh, don't look so scandalized! I've told you before that I don't intend to spend my life in this miserable place. I'm eighteen years old, after all. It's time I found a husband before I grow too ancient and ugly to marry.'

'And what of Ilya Goryavich?' I asked, referring to the young man with whom she spent much of her time. Like my friend Kolek, poor Ilya was madly in love with Asya and she offered him a little affection in return, no doubt encouraging him to believe that she might give herself to him entirely in time. I pitied him for his stupidity. I knew that he was little more than a plaything for my sister, a marionette whose strings she controlled to stave

45

off her boredom. One day she would cast her doll aside, that much was obvious. A better toy would come along—a toy from St Petersburg, perhaps.

'Ilya Goryavich is a sweet boy,' she said with a disinterested shrug. 'But I think, at twenty-one, he is already everything that he will ever be. And I'm not sure that's enough.'

I could tell that she was about to make some unnecessarily disparaging comment about that good-hearted oaf, but the soldiers were starting to approach now and we could make out the lead officers, sitting tall on their horses as they paraded slowly along the street, resplendent in their black double-breasted tunics, grey trousers and heavy, dark greatcoats. I stared at the fur *shapka*s on their heads, intrigued by the sharp V cut through the front of them, just above the eyes, and fantasized about how wonderful it would be to be part of their number. They ignored the noisy cheers of the peasants who surrounded them on either side, calling out blessings to the Tsar and throwing garlands before the hooves of the horses. They expected nothing less from us, after all.

Little news of the war ever came to Kashin, but from time to time a trader might pass through our village with information about the military's successes or failures. Sometimes a pamphlet might arrive at the home of one of our neighbours, sent by a well-intentioned relative, and we would each be allowed to read it in turn, following the advance of the armies in our imaginations. Some of the young men of the village had already left for the army: some had been killed, some were missing, while others still remained in service. It was expected that boys like Kolek and I, when we

46

reached seventeen, would be called upon to bring glory to our village and join one of the military units.

The great responsibilities of Nicholas Nicolaievich were well known to all, however.

The Grand Duke had been appointed Supreme Commander of the Russian forces by the Tsar, fighting a war on three fronts, against the Austro-Hungarian Empire, against the German Kaiser, and against the Turks. By all accounts he had not been tremendously successful in any of these campaigns so far, but still he commanded the admiration and absolute loyalty of the soldiers under his command, and this in turn was filtered down through the peasant villages of Russia. We considered him to be among the very finest of men, appointed to his position by a benevolent God who sent such leaders to watch over us in our simplicity and ignorance.

The cheers grew even louder as the soldiers passed us by, and then, approaching like a glorious deity, I could make out a great white charging horse at the centre of the throng and seated atop the steed, a giant of a man in military uniform, his mustachios waxed, groomed and teased to a fine point on either side of his upper lip. He was staring rigidly ahead, but lifting his left hand from time to time to offer a regal wave to the gathered crowd.

As the horses passed before me I caught sight of our revolutionary neighbour, Borys Alexandrovich, standing among the crowd on the opposite side of the street and was surprised to see him there, for if there was one man who I thought would refuse to come out and pay tribute to the great general, it would have been him.

'Look,' I said to Asya, nudging her shoulder and pointing in his direction. 'Over there. Borys Alexandrovich. Where are his fine principles now? He is as enamoured of the Grand Duke as any of us.'

'But aren't the soldiers handsome!' she replied, ignoring me and playing with the curls of her hair instead as she studied each man that passed us. 'How can they fight in battle and yet keep their uniforms so pristine, do you think?'

'And there's Kolek,' I added, noticing my friend pushing his way to the fore of the crowd now, his face a mixture of excitement and anxiety. 'Kolek!' I cried, waving across at him, but he could neither see me nor hear me through the noise made by the marching horses and the cheering of the villagers. At any other time, I would not have thought anything of this unremarkable fact and would have turned to look back at the parade instead, but there was an expression on his face which confused me, a look of utter disquiet that I had never observed on the countenance of this thoughtful boy before. He stepped forward a little and looked around until he had reassured himself that his father, the man whose approval meant more to him than anything else in the world, was among the watching crowd, and when he was certain of Borys Alexandrovich's presence he turned back to stare at the Grand Duke as the white charger marched towards him.

Nicholas Nicolaievich was perhaps twenty feet away, no more, when I saw Kolek's left hand reach inside his tunic and remain there for a moment, trembling slightly.

Fifteen feet away, when I saw the wooden handle

48

of the gun emerge slowly from its hiding place, my friend's fist wrapped tightly around the grip, his finger hovering over the trigger.

Ten feet away, when he drew the gun, unobserved by any but I, and released the safety catch.

The Grand Duke was only five feet away when I shouted my friend's name—'Kolek! *No!*'—and tore through a gap in the passing riders, running across the street as the heads of the soldiers, aware of something untoward taking place, turned in my direction to see what was happening. My friend saw me now too and swallowed nervously before lifting the gun in the air and aiming it in the direction of Nicholas Nicolaievich, who was before him now and had finally deigned to turn his head to look at the young man to his left. He must have seen the flash of steel in the air but there was no time for him to draw his own gun, nor to turn his horse and make a quick escape, because the pistol went off almost immediately with a loud thunderclap, sending its murderous gunpowder in the direction of the Tsar's cousin and closest confidant at the very moment when I, failing to consider the consequences of such an action, leapt in front of it.

There was a sudden flash of fire, a piercing pain, a scream from the crowd, and I fell to the ground, expecting to feel the shod-hooves of the horses crush my skull beneath their enormous weight at any moment, even as a pain unlike any that I had ever felt before seared through my shoulder, a feeling that someone had taken an iron rod, smelted it in a furnace for an hour and driven it through my innocent flesh. I landed hard on the ground, experiencing a sudden sensation of peace and tranquillity in my mind before the afternoon went dark before my eyes, the noises became hushed, the crowds appeared to vanish into a misty haze, and there was only a small voice left whispering to me in my head, telling me to sleep— *sleep, Pasha!*—and I obeyed it.

I closed my eyes and was left alone inside an empty, soporific darkness.

*   *   *

The first face I saw when I awoke was that of my mother, Yulia Vladimirovna, who was pressing a wet rag across my forehead and staring down at me with a mixture of irritation and alarm. Her hand was trembling slightly and she seemed as nervous to be offering maternal consolation as I was to receive it. Asya and Liska were whispering in a corner while the child, Talya, was watching me with a cold and disinterested expression. I did not feel a part of this unusual tableau at all and simply stared back at them, confused as to what had taken place to inspire such a display of emotion, until a sudden explosion of pain in my left shoulder caused me to grimace and I let out an anguished cry as my hand reached across to ease the pressure on the injured area.

'Be careful there,' said a loud, deep voice from behind my mother, and the moment it spoke, she jumped noticeably and her expression transformed into one of frightened anxiety. I had never seen her so intimidated by anyone before and thought at first that it was my father, Daniil, who was ordering her to make way, but the voice did not belong to him. My vision was slightly blurred and I blinked several times in quick succession until the haze began to dissipate and I could see clearly again.

I realized then that it was not my father who was standing over me; he was positioned towards the back of the hut, observing me with a half-smile on his face, a look that betrayed his confused emotions of pride and hostility. No, the voice which had addressed me was that of the supreme commander of the Russian military forces, the Grand Duke Nicholas Nicolaievich.

'Don't try to move,' he said, leaning over me and examining my shoulder, his eyes narrowing as he scrutinized the wound. 'You've been injured, but you were lucky. The bullet went straight through the soft tissue of your shoulder but missed the arteries and the vein. It just shot directly out the other side, which was fortunate. A little more to the right and your arm might have been paralysed or you might have bled to death. The pain will continue for a few days, I imagine, but there won't be any lasting damage. A small scar, perhaps.'

I swallowed—my mouth was so dry that my tongue stuck uncomfortably to my palate—and I asked my mother for something to drink. She didn't move, just stood there with her mouth open as if the scene playing out before her was one in which she was too terrified to take a part, and it was left to the Grand Duke to take the hip flask from around his waist and fill it from a barrel that stood near by before handing it across to me. I was almost too intimidated by the finery of the leather to drink from it, particularly when I noticed the Imperial seal of the Romanovs that was stitched in golden thread across its casing, but my thirst was so

51

extraordinary that my hesitation did not last long and I gulped it down quickly. The sensation of the ice-cold water entering my body and making its way along my gut helped to alleviate the pain of my shoulder for a few moments.

'You know who I am?' asked the Grand Duke, raising himself to his full height now, filling the room with his imposing figure. At least six feet and the same number of inches in height. A large, muscular body. Handsome and imposing. And that extraordinary moustache which served to make him look even more dignified and majestic. I swallowed and nodded my head quickly.

'Yes,' I replied weakly.

'You know who I am?' he repeated, louder now, so I thought that I was in trouble of some sort.

'Yes,' I said again, finding my full voice now. 'You are the Grand Duke Nicholas Nicolaievich, commander of the army and cousin to His Imperial Majesty, Tsar Nicholas II.'

He smiled a little and his body jolted slightly as he offered me a small laugh. 'Yes, yes,' he said, dismissing the grandeur of my response. 'There's nothing wrong with your memory then, boy, is there? If you remember so well, can you recall what happened to you?'

I sat up a little, ignoring the shooting pains that were exploding along my left side from the top of my shoulder to the crook of my elbow, and looked down at my body. I was lying on the small hammock that functioned as my bed, wearing trousers but no shoes, and I was embarrassed to see the layer of filth from the floor of our hut that clung to my bare feet. My clean tunic, the one that I had worn especially for the Grand Duke's parade, was lying in a bundle on the floor beside me, and it was no longer white, but a malevolent mixture of black and dark red. I wore no shirt and my chest was streaked with blood from the wound on my arm, which was wrapped tightly in bandages. The first thought I had was to wonder where these dressings had been found, but then I remembered the soldiers who had been trooping through our village and assumed that one of them had attended to my wound with their own army supplies.

Which in turn led to a sudden recollection of the events of the afternoon.

The parade. The white charger. The Grand Duke seated astride it.

And our neighbour, Borys Alexandrovich. His son, my best friend, Kolek Boryavich.

The pistol.

'A gun,' I cried suddenly, leaping up, as if the events were taking place once again, directly before my eyes. 'He has a gun!'

'It's all right, boy,' said the Grand Duke, patting me on my uninjured shoulder. 'There is no gun now. You committed a great act, if you can recall it.'

'I ... I'm not sure,' I replied, struggling to remember what I might have done to earn such a compliment.

'My son has always been very brave, sir,' said Daniil, stepping forward now from the rear of the hut. 'He would have given his life for yours without question.'

'There was an assassination attempt,' continued Nicholas Nicolaievich, looking directly at me and ignoring my father. 'A young radical. He aimed his pistol at my head. I swear that I saw the bullet preparing to quit its chamber and plant itself in my skull, but you rushed before me, brave lad that you are, and took the bullet in your shoulder.' He hesitated before continuing. 'You saved my life, young Georgy Daniilovich.'

'I did?' I asked, for I could not imagine what might have inspired me to do such a thing. But the fog in my mind was beginning to lift and I could remember rushing towards Kolek in order to press him back into the body of the gathered crowd, so that he would not commit an act that would cost him his life.

'Yes, you did,' replied the Grand Duke. 'And I am grateful to you. The Tsar himself will be grateful to you. All of Russia will be.'

I didn't know what to say to such a remark—he certainly had a high regard for his importance in the world—and lay back, feeling a little dizzy and desperate for more water.

'He doesn't really have to go, does he, Father?' asked Asya suddenly, stemming her tears for a moment as she asked the question. I looked in her direction and was touched that she was so upset by what had happened to me.

'Quiet, girl,' replied my father, pushing her back against the wall. 'He will do as he is told. We all will.'

'Go?' I whispered, wondering what she could have meant by that. 'Go where?'

'You're a brave lad,' said the Grand Duke, putting his gloves back on now and taking a small purse from his pocket, which he handed to my father; it immediately disappeared inside the mysterious caverns of his tunic, out of sight of any of us. *I have been sold*, I thought immediately. *I have been traded to the army for a few hundred roubles.* 'A boy like you is wasted in a place like this. You were planning on joining the army this year, of course?'

'Yes, sir,' I replied hesitantly, for I knew that day was approaching quickly but I had hoped to delay it for a few months yet. 'It was my intention, only—'

'Well, I can't send you into battle, where you will only face more bullets. Not after what you have done today. No, you may stay here and recover for a few days and then follow me. I will leave two men to escort you to your new home.'

'My new home?' I asked, thoroughly confused now and attempting to sit up again as he stepped towards the door of our hut. 'But where is that, sir?'

'Why, St Petersburg, of course,' he said, turning around to smile at me. 'You have already proved that you would be willing to step in front of a bullet for a man such as I. Just imagine how much loyalty you would show to one even greater than a mere duke.'

I shook my head and swallowed nervously. 'Even greater than you?' I asked.

He hesitated for a moment, as if he was unsure whether to let me know what he had in mind, in case the shock of the revelation caused me to faint away entirely. But when he finally spoke again, he behaved as if this most extraordinary idea was the most obvious thing in the world. 'The Tsarevich Alexei,' he said. 'You will be one of those assigned to protect him. My cousin, the Tsar, mentioned in his most recent communication how he was looking for just such a young man and asked whether I knew anyone who might make an appropriate companion. Someone closer to his own age, that is. The Tsarevich has many guards, of course. But he needs more than that. He needs a companion who can also tend to his safety. I believe that I have found what he is looking for. I intend to make a gift of you to him, Georgy Daniilovich. Assuming that he approves of you, that is. But stay here for now. Recover. Get well. And I will see you in St Petersburg at the end of the week.'

And with that he stepped outside our hut, leaving my sisters staring at him in awe, my mother looking as scared as she had ever been, and my father counting his money.

I forced myself to sit up even further and as I did so, I could see through the door on to the street beyond, where a yew tree stood, in full flower, strong and thick and hearty. But something was not quite the same. A great weight appeared to be swinging from its branches. I narrowed my eyes to identify it and when I finally focussed, I could do nothing but gasp.

It was Kolek.

They had hanged him in the street.

1979

It was Zoya's idea to make one final journey together.

We had never been great travellers, either of us, preferring the warmth and security of our peaceful flat in Holborn to the exhaustion of holiday-making. After we left Russia, we moved immediately to France; once there, we spent a few years living and working in Paris, where we married, before settling ultimately in London. When Arina was a child, of course, we made our best efforts to take a week away from the city every summer, but it was usually to Brighton, or perhaps as far as Cornwall, to show her the sea, to allow her to play in the sand. To be a child among other children. But we never left the island shores once we arrived. And I thought we never would.

She announced her idea late one evening as we sat by the fire in our living room, watching as the flames diminished and the black coals hissed and spat for the final time. I was reading *Jake's Thing* and set the book aside in surprise when she spoke.

Our grandson, Michael, had left half an hour earlier after a difficult conversation. He had come for dinner and to tell us of how his new life as an acting student was progressing, but all the joy of the evening had been swept away when Zoya broke the news to him about her illness and the spread of the cancer. She didn't want to keep anything from him, she said, although she didn't want his sympathy either. This was life, after all, she suggested. Nothing more than life.

'I'm already as old as the hills,' she told him, smiling. 'And I've been very lucky, you know. I've been closer to death than this.'

Of course, being young he had immediately looked for solutions and hope. He insisted that his father would pay for any treatments that were necessary, that he himself would leave RADA and find proper employment to pay for anything she needed, but she shook her head and held his hands

57

in hers while she told him that there was nothing that anyone could do, and there was certainly nothing that money could do either. This thing was incurable, she told him. She might not have many months left and she didn't want to waste them searching for impossible cures. He had taken the news badly. Having spent so many years without a mother, it was natural that he hated the idea of losing his grandmother as well.

Before leaving, Michael had taken me aside and asked me whether there was anything he could do for his grandmother to ease her comfort. 'She has the best doctors, right?' he asked me.

'Of course,' I told him, moved by the tears that were pooling in his eyes. 'But you know, this is not an easy disease to battle.'

'She's a tough old bird, though,' he said, which made me smile and I nodded.

'Yes,' I said. 'Yes, she is that.'

'I've heard of people that find a way to beat it.'

'As have I,' I told him, not wishing to offer him any false hope. Zoya and I had already spent weeks arguing over her decision not to seek any treatment but to allow the disease to work its way through her body and take her when it was finally bored of her. I had tried everything I could to dissuade her from this path, but it was useless. She had simply decided that her time had come.

'Call me if you need me, all right?' Michael had insisted. 'Me or Dad. We're here whenever you need anything at all. And I'll stop by more often, OK? Twice a week if I can manage it. And tell her not to cook for me, I'll eat before I get here.'

'And insult her?' I asked, chiding him. 'You'll eat what she puts before you, Michael.'

'Well . . . whatever,' he said, shrugging it off, running a hand through his shoulder-length hair and presenting that lean smile of his to me. 'I'm here, that's all I'm saying. I'm not going anywhere.'

He has always been a good grandson. He's always made us proud of him. After he left, Zoya and I both confessed that we had been moved by his thoughtfulness.

'A trip?' I asked, surprised by her suggestion. 'Are you sure that you would be able to manage it?'

'I think so,' she said. 'Now, I could, anyway. A few months from now, who knows?'

'You wouldn't prefer to stay here and rest?'

'And die, you mean?' she asked, perhaps regretting the words as soon as she said them, for she caught the expression of dismay on my face and leaned across to kiss me. 'I'm sorry,' she said. 'I shouldn't have said that. But think of it, Georgy. I can sit here and wait for the end to come, or I can do something with whatever time is left to me.'

'Well, I suppose we could take a train somewhere for a week or two,' I said, considering it. 'We had some happy times on the south coast when we were younger.'

'I wasn't thinking of Cornwall,' she said quickly, shaking her head, and it was my turn now to feel regret, for the name inspired memories of our daughter, and in that direction lay grief and madness.

'Scotland, perhaps,' I suggested. 'We've never been there. I've always thought that it might be nice to see Edinburgh. Or is that too far? Are we being too ambitious?'

'You can never be too ambitious, Georgy,' she said with a smile.

'Not Scotland, then,' I said, imagining a map of Britain in my mind and looking around it in my imagination. 'It's too cold there this time of year anyway. And not Wales, I think. The Lake District, perhaps? Wordsworth country? Or Ireland? We could take a ferry over to Dublin, if you think you could manage it. Or travel south, towards West Cork. It's supposed to be very beautiful there.'

'I was thinking further north,' she said, and I knew by her tone that this was no idle conversation, but something that she had been considering for some time already. She knew exactly where she wanted to go and would settle for nowhere else. 'I was thinking of Finland,' she said.

'Finland?'

'Yes.'

'But why Finland, of all places?' I asked, surprised by her choice. 'It's so . . . well, I mean, it's Finland, isn't it? Is there anything to see there?'

'Of course there is, Georgy,' she said with a sigh. 'It's an entire country, like anywhere else.'

'But you've never expressed any interest in seeing Finland before.'

'I was there as a child,' she told me. 'I don't remember it very much, of course, but I thought . . . well, it's as close to home as we could get, isn't it? As close to Russia, I mean.'

'Ah,' I said, nodding slowly and considering it. 'Of course.' I pictured the map of northern Europe in my head, the long border of over seven hundred miles that stretched the length of the country, from Grense-Jacobsely in the north to Hamina in the south.

'I'd like to feel that I was close to St Petersburg

once again,' she continued. 'Just one more time in my life, that's all. While I still can. I'd like to look into the distance and imagine it, still standing. Invincible.'

I breathed heavily through my nose and bit my lip as I stared into the fire, where the last of the coals were turning to embers, and considered what she had asked. Finland. Russia. It was, in the most literal sense of the phrase, her dying wish. And I confess that the idea excited me too. But still, I was unsure of the wisdom of such a journey. And not just because of the cancer.

'Please, Georgy,' she said, after several silent minutes had passed. 'Please, just this.'

'You're sure that you're strong enough?'

'I am now,' she said. 'In a few months' time, who knows? But now, yes.'

I nodded. 'Then we will go,' I told her.

*   *   *

There was a range of signs to predict Zoya's illness which, taken together, should have been warning enough to me that she was not well, but separated by several months as they were, and appearing alongside the typical aches and pains of old age, it was difficult to recognize the connections between the symptoms. Added to this was the fact that my wife kept the details of her suffering private for as long as possible. Whether she did this because she didn't want me to know of the agony she was enduring or because of a reluctance on her part to seek treatment to alleviate it is a question I have never asked her, for fear of being wounded by the answer.

61

I did notice, however, that she was more tired than usual and would sit by the fire in the evenings with a look of sheer exhaustion on her face, her breathing a little more laboured, her countenance a little more pale. When I asked her about this fatigue, she shrugged it off and said it was nothing, that she simply needed to get a better night's sleep, that was all, and that I shouldn't worry about her so much. But then her back began to trouble her too and I could see her wincing in pain as she put a hand to an area at the base of her spine, holding it there for a moment until the agony passed, her expression contorted with distress.

'You need to see a doctor,' I told her when the pain seemed to be lasting for longer than she could possibly cope with. 'Maybe you've pulled a disc and it needs to be rested. He could give you an anti-inflammatory or—'

'Or maybe I'm just getting old,' she said, making a determined effort not to raise her voice. 'I'll be fine, Georgy. Don't fuss.'

Within a few weeks, the pain had begun to spread towards her abdomen and I noticed a distinct lack of appetite as she sat at the table, pushing her food around the plate with her fork, taking only small morsels into her mouth and chewing on them carelessly before pushing the dish away and claiming that she wasn't hungry.

'I had a big lunch,' she said to me, and fool that I was I allowed myself to believe her. 'I shouldn't eat so much in the middle of the day.'

However, when these symptoms continued for several months, and she had started not only to lose weight but to be unable to sleep with the agony of her condition, I finally persuaded her to visit our local GP. She returned to say that he was running some tests on her, and two weeks later my worst fears were confirmed when she was referred to a specialist, Dr Joan Crawford, who has been a part of our lives ever since.

It seems a curious thing to me that I took the news of Zoya's illness worse than she did. God forgive me, but she seemed relieved, almost happy, when the results came through, imparting them to me with consideration for my feelings but without any fear or devastation for her own condition. She didn't cry, although I did. She didn't seem angry or frightened, both of which emotions poured over me throughout the days that followed. It was as if she had received . . . not good news exactly, but a piece of interesting information with which she was not entirely dissatisfied.

A week later, we sat waiting for Dr Crawford in her office. Zoya appeared perfectly at ease but I was restless in my chair, fidgeting nervously as I stared at the framed certificates that hung on the walls, convincing myself that someone who had been trained in this disease and had received so many qualifications from famous universities would surely be able to find a way to combat it.

'Mr and Mrs Jachmenev,' said Dr Crawford when she arrived, late but brisk, her manner entirely businesslike. Although she was not unsympathetic towards us, I felt immediately that she lacked a degree of compassion, which Zoya put down to the fact that she was dealing with patients suffering the same illness every day and it was difficult to view every case as tragically as the relatives of its victims would. 'I'm sorry to have kept you waiting. As you can imagine, it gets busier and busier here every day.'

I wasn't entirely reassured to hear that, but said nothing as she studied the dossier which lay on the desk before her, holding an X-ray up to the light at one point, but betraying nothing in her expression as she examined it. Finally, she closed the folder, placed her hands on top of it and looked at the two of us, her lips pursed in what was an approximation, I thought, of a smile.

'Jachmenev,' she said. 'That's an unusual name.'

'It's Russian,' I said quickly, not wishing to entertain any small talk. 'Doctor, you've examined my wife's file?'

'Yes, and I had a conversation with your GP, Dr Cross, earlier this morning. He's spoken with you, Mrs Jachmenev, about your condition?'

'Yes,' she said, nodding her head. 'Cancer, I was told.'

'More specifically, ovarian cancer,' replied Dr Crawford, using both hands to smooth out the papers before her, a habit which for some reason put me in mind of bad actors who never know what to do with their hands on stage; perhaps this was my way of not entering the conversation entirely. 'You've been suffering for some time, I expect?'

'There were symptoms, yes,' replied Zoya cautiously, her tone suggesting that she did not want to be chastised for her tardiness in reporting them. 'Some back pain, fatigue, a little nausea, but I didn't think anything of it. I'm seventy-eight, Dr Crawford. For ten years now I've woken every day with a different complaint.'

The doctor smiled and nodded, hesitating for a moment before speaking in a more gentle tone. 'This is not uncommon, of course, in women of

64

your age. Older women are more at risk of ovarian cancer, although typically they will develop it between their mid-fifties and mid-seventies. Yours is a rare, late-in-life case.'

'I've always tried to be exceptional,' said Zoya with a smile. Dr Crawford smiled in return and the two women stared at each other for a few moments, as if they each understood something about the other one of which I was necessarily ignorant. There were only three of us in the room, but I felt terribly excluded from their company.

'Can I ask, do you have any history of cancer in your family?' asked Dr Crawford after a few moments.

'No,' said Zoya. 'I mean yes, you can ask. But no, there is none.'

'And your mother? She died of natural causes?'

Zoya hesitated for only a moment before answering. 'My mother did not have cancer,' she said.

'Your grandmothers? Any sisters or aunts?'

'No,' she said.

'And your own medical history—have you suffered from any major traumas during your life?'

There was a moment of vacillation on her part and then Zoya suddenly burst out laughing at the doctor's question and I turned to look at her in surprise. Seeing the look of hilarity on her face, the fact that she was doing all that she could to stop herself from shaking with a mixture of amusement and grief, I didn't know whether to join her in her laughter or bury my face in my hands. I wanted to be elsewhere, suddenly. I wanted none of this to be happening. It had been the most unfortunate choice of words, that was for sure, but Dr

Crawford simply stared at her as she laughed without any comment; I suspected that she witnessed any number of bizarre reactions during conversations such as this one.

'I have suffered no medical traumas,' said Zoya finally, composing herself and stressing the penultimate word in her sentence. 'I have not had an easy life, Dr Crawford, but I have been in good health throughout it.'

'Well, indeed,' she replied, sighing as if she understood only too well. 'Women of your generation have suffered a lot. There was the war, for one thing.'

'Yes, the war,' said Zoya, nodding thoughtfully. 'There have been many wars, in fact.'

'Doctor,' I said, interrupting her to speak now for the first time. 'Ovarian cancer, this is curable? You have some way to help my wife?'

She looked at me with a certain degree of pity, understanding of course that the husband might be the most terrified one in the room. 'I'm afraid the cancer has already begun to spread, Mr Jachmenev,' she said quietly. 'And as I'm sure you know, at the moment medical science is unable to offer a cure. All we can do is try to alleviate some of the suffering and offer our patients as much hope for a continued life as we can.'

I stared at the floor, feeling a little dizzy at these words, although in truth I knew that this was what she would say. I had already spent weeks at my usual desk in the British Library researching the disease that Dr Cross had spoken to us about and knew only too well that there was no known cure. There was always hope, however, and I clung on to that.

'There are some additional tests that I would like to run, Mrs Jachmenev,' she said, turning to my wife again. 'We'll need to do a second pelvic exam, of course. And some blood tests, an ultrasound. A barium enema will help us to identify the extent of the cancer. We'll take some CAT scans, of course. We need to determine how far the cancer has spread beyond the ovaries and into the pelvic area, and whether it has travelled towards the abdominal cavity.'

'But the treatments, doctor, ' I insisted, leaning forward. 'What can you do to make my wife better?'

She stared at me, a little irritated, I felt, as if she was accustomed to dealing with devastated husbands but they were outside of her concern; she was interested only in her patient.

'As I said, Mr Jachmenev,' she replied, 'the treatments can only slow down the progress of the cancer. Chemotherapy will be important, of course. There will be surgery, almost immediately, to remove the ovaries, and it will be necessary to perform a hysterectomy. We can take biopsies at the same time of your wife's lymph nodes, her diaphragm, her pelvic tissue, in order to determine—'

'And if I don't have treatment?' Zoya asked, her voice low but determined, cutting through the cold granite of these medical phrases which Dr Crawford had no doubt uttered a thousand times in the past.

'If you don't have treatment, Mrs Jachmenev,' she replied, clearly accustomed to this question too, which shocked me; how simple it was for this lady to discuss such terrible notions, 'then the

67

cancer will almost certainly continue to spread. You will be in the same amount of pain that you are in now, although we would be able to give you some medication for that, but one day it will take you quite unawares and your health will deteriorate rapidly. That will be when the cancer has advanced to the later stages, when it has passed out of the abdomen to attack your organs— the liver, the kidneys and so on.'

'We must begin the treatment immediately, of course,' I insisted and Dr Crawford smiled at me with the tolerance of a doting grandparent towards a half-wit grandchild, before looking at my wife again.

'Mrs Jachmenev,' she said, 'your husband is right. It's important that we begin as soon as possible. You do understand that, don't you?'

'How long would it take?' she asked.

'The treatment would continue indefinitely,' she replied. 'Until we could control the disease. That might be a short time, it might be for ever.'

'No,' said Zoya, shaking her head. 'I mean, how long would I have left if I don't seek treatment?'

'For pity's sake, Zoya,' I cried, staring at her as if she had lost her reason entirely. 'What type of question is that? Didn't you understand what—'

She held a hand in the air to silence me, but did not look in my direction. 'How long, doctor?'

Dr Crawford exhaled loudly and shrugged her shoulders, which did not fill me with confidence. 'It's difficult to say,' she replied. 'We would of course need to run these tests anyway to determine exactly what stage the cancer is at. But I would say no more than a year. Perhaps a little longer if you were lucky. Although there is no saying how the

68

quality of your life would be affected during that time. You could be healthy until near the end, and then the cancer could attack quite quickly, or you could begin to deteriorate very soon. It really is for the best that you take action immediately.' She opened a heavy diary that lay in the centre of her desk and ran a finger along one of the pages. 'I can schedule you for the initial pelvic exam for—'

She never got to finish that sentence, interrupted by the fact that Zoya had already stood up, taken her coat from the stand beside the door, and left.

*   *   *

Originally, we planned to go no further east than Helsinki, but then, on a whim, we travelled on towards the harbour town of Hamina, on the Finnish coast. The Matkahuolto bus drove us slowly through Porvoo and just north of Kotka, names which sixty years before had been as familiar to me as my own, but which had slowly dissolved from my memory over the intervening decades, replaced by the experiences and recollections of a shared adulthood. Reading those words again on the bus timetable, however, pronouncing their lost syllables under my breath, jolted me back to my youth, the sounds echoing with the regret and familiarity of a childhood nursery rhyme.

Zoya and I were offered seats at the front of the bus owing to our advanced years—I had celebrated my eightieth birthday four days before leaving London and my wife was only a couple of years younger than I—and we sat together quietly, watching the towns and villages pass us by, in a country which was not home, which had never been home, but which made us feel closer to the place of our birth than we had been in decades. The landscape along the Gulf of Finland reminded me of long-forgotten sailing trips along the Baltics, my days and nights filled with games and laughter and the sound of girls' voices, each demanding more attention than the last. If I closed my eyes and listened to the cries of the seagulls overhead, I could imagine that we were dropping anchor once again at Tallinn on the Northern Estonian coast, or sailing northwards from Kaliningrad towards St Petersburg with a light wind behind us and the sun burning down on the deck of the *Standart*.

Even the voices of the people who surrounded us offered a sensation of familiarity; their language was different, of course, but we could recognize some of the words, and the harsh guttural sounds of the lowlands blending with the soft sibilant language of the fjords made me question whether we should have come here many years before.

'How do you feel?' I asked Zoya, turning towards her as the sign for Hamina indicated that we would arrive there in no more than ten or fifteen minutes. Her face was a little pale and I could see that she was moved by the heartbreaking experience of travelling east, but she gave nothing away in her expression. Had we been alone, perhaps she might have wept out of a mixture of sorrow and joy, but there were strangers sharing the bus with us and she would not confirm their prejudices by allowing them to observe the weakness of an old woman.

'I feel as if I don't want this journey to end,' she replied quietly.

We had been in Finland for almost a week and

Zoya was enjoying particularly good health, a fact which made me wonder whether it might not be a good idea to relocate to the climate of the north indefinitely if it meant that her condition would improve. I was reminded of the biographies of the great writers whose lives I had studied during my retirement at the British Library, of how they had left their homes for the frosted air of the European mountain ranges in order to rally against the illnesses of the day. Stephen Crane, allowing tuberculosis to extinguish his genius in Badenweiler; Keats staring out at the Spanish Steps as his lungs filled with bacteria, listening to the voices of Severn and Clark bickering with each other as they consulted over his treatment. They went there to look for revitalization, of course. To live longer. But all they found was their graves. Would it be different for Zoya, I wondered? Would a return to the north offer hope and the possibility of extended years, or a crushing realization that nothing could defeat the invader which was threatening to take my wife from me?

A small café in the town offered us a traditional *lounas* and we took a chance and sat outside, swaddled in overcoats and scarves as the waitress brought us warm plates of salted fish and seed potatoes, replenishing our hot drinks whenever they ran low. As we watched, a group of children ran past us and one of the boys pushed a smaller girl over, sending her toppling backwards into a mound of snow with a terrified scream. Zoya sat forward, prepared to remonstrate with him for his cruelty, but his victim quickly recovered herself and took her own revenge, which brought a satisfied smile to her face. Families passed by, on

71

their way to and from a nearby school, and we settled back with our thoughts and our memories, peaceful in the knowledge that a long and happy relationship negates the need for constant chatter. Zoya and I had long perfected the art of sitting silently in each other's company for hours on end, while never running out of things to say.

'Do you notice the scent in the air?' Zoya asked me eventually as we finished the last of our tea.

'The scent?'

'Yes, there's a . . . it's hard to describe it, but when I close my eyes and breathe in slowly, I can't help but be reminded of childhood. London always smelled to me of work. Paris smelled of fear. But Finland, it reminds me of a much simpler time in my life.'

'And Russia?' I asked. 'What did Russia smell of?'

'For a time it smelled of happiness and prosperity,' she said immediately, without needing to pause to consider it. 'And then of madness and illness. And religion, of course. And then . . .' She smiled and shook her head, embarrassed to finish her sentence.

'What?' I asked, smiling at her. 'Tell me.'

'You'll think me foolish,' she replied with an apologetic shrug, 'but I've always thought of Russia as a sort of decaying pomegranate. It hides its putrid nature, red and luscious on the outside, but split it in two and the seeds and arils spill out before you, black and repugnant. Russia reminds me of the pomegranate. Before it went rotten.'

I nodded but remained silent. I had no particular feelings about the scent of our lost country, but the people, the houses and the churches that

72

surrounded me in Finland reminded me of the past. These were simpler notions, perhaps—Zoya had always had a greater tendency towards metaphor than I, perhaps because she was better educated—but I liked the idea that I was near home again. Close to St Petersburg. To the Winter Palace. Even to Kashin.

But how I had changed since I had last set foot in any of those places! Glancing in the mirror as I washed my hands after our lunch, I caught sight of an old man staring at his reflection, a man who had been handsome once, perhaps, and young and strong, but was none of those things any more. My hair was thin and wispy, pure white strands clumped together at the side of my head, revealing a liver-spotted forehead that bore no resemblance to the clear, tanned skin of my youth. My face was thin, my cheeks sunken, my ears appeared to be unnaturally large, as if they were the only part of my physiognomy not in retreat. My fingers had become bony, a lean layer of skin covering the skeleton beneath. I was fortunate in that my mobility was not suffering as I had often feared it would, although when I awoke in the mornings it took much longer now before I could muster all my strength and resources to drag myself from our bed, perform my ablutions and dress. A shirt, a tie, a pullover every day, for my life from the age of sixteen had been constructed on formality. I felt the cold more and more as every month passed.

At times I thought it strange that a man as old and ravaged as I could still command the love and respect of a woman as beautiful and youthful as my wife. For she, it seemed to me, had barely changed at all.

'I've had an idea, Georgy,' she said as I returned to our table, wondering whether I should risk sitting down again or wait for her to rise.

'A good idea?' I asked with a smile, deciding on the former, since Zoya herself showed no sign of standing.

'I think so,' she replied hesitantly. 'Although I'm not sure what you will think.'

'You think we should move to Helsinki,' I said, predicting what she was about to say and laughing a little at the absurdity of the idea. 'Live out our final days in the shadow of the *Suurkirkko*. You've fallen in love with Finnish ways.'

'No,' she said, shaking her head and smiling. 'No, not that. I don't think we should stay here at all. In fact, I think we should keep going.'

I looked at her and frowned. 'Keep going?' I asked. 'Keep going where? Further into Finland? It's possible, of course, but I would worry that the travelling might—'

'No, not that,' she said, interrupting me, keeping her voice clear and steady as if she did not want to risk my refusal by appearing overly enthusiastic. 'I mean we should go home.'

I sighed. It had been a concern of mine when we set off from London that this trip would prove too much for her and she would regret her decision to leave, and long for the warmth and comfort of our familiar Holborn flat. We were not children any more, after all. It was not easy for us to spend so much time in transit.

'Are you feeling ill?' I asked, leaning forward and taking her hand, searching her face for any signs of distress.

'No worse than I was.'

'The pain, has it become too much for you?'

'No, Georgy,' she replied, offering a small laugh. 'I feel perfectly fine. Why do you say that?'

'Because you want to go home,' I said. 'And we can, of course we can, if it's what you really want. But we have only four days remaining of our trip anyway. It might be easier to return to Helsinki and rest there until it's time for our flight.'

'I don't mean go back to London,' she said quickly, shaking her head as she looked towards the children again, playing noisily in the mounds of snow. 'I don't mean *that* home.'

'Then where?'

'St Petersburg, of course,' she replied. 'We've come this far, after all. It wouldn't take too many hours more, would it? We could spend a day there, just a day. We never imagined that we would stand in Palace Square again, after all. We never thought we would breathe Russian air. And if we don't go now, when we are so close, we never will. What do you think, Georgy?'

I looked at her and didn't know what to say. When we had decided to undertake this journey, there had undoubtedly been a part of both of us that had wondered if this conversation would arise and if so, which of us would suggest it first. The idea had been to come to Finland, to go as far east as the weather and our health would allow, and to look into the distance and perhaps to make out the shadows of the islands in the Vyborgskiy Zaliv once again, even the tip of Primorsk, and remember, and imagine, and wonder.

But neither of us had spoken aloud of travelling the last few hundred miles to the city where we had met. Until now.

'I think . . .' I began, rolling the words slowly over my tongue uncertainly before shaking my head and starting again. 'I wonder . . .'

'What?' she asked me.

'Is it safe?'

The Winter Palace

I was struggling to stop myself from trembling too visibly.

The long, third-floor corridor of the Winter Palace, where the Tsar and his family made their home when they were in St Petersburg, stretched out coldly on either side of me, its golden walls fading into an intimidating darkness as the candles dimmed and flickered in the distance. And at its centre was a young boy from Kashin, who could hardly breathe for thinking of all those who had passed along these hallways in the past.

Of course, I had never witnessed such majesty before—I had scarcely believed that such places existed outside of my imagination—but glancing down, I could see the knuckles on both my hands turning white as they clutched the arms of my chair in a tight embrace. My stomach was alive with tension and every time I halted my right foot from tapping upon the marble floor in anxiety, it lay still for only a moment before beginning its nervous dance once again.

The chair itself was an object of the most extraordinary beauty. Its four legs were carved from red oak, with intricate detailing flowering along the ridges. Set into the wings were two thick layers of gold and they, in turn, were encrusted with three different types of jewel, only one of which I recognized, a dotted trail of blue sapphires that sparkled and changed colour as I examined them from different angles. The fabric was wrought tight against a cushion heavily stuffed with the softest feathers. Despite my anxiety, it was difficult not to emit a pleasurable sigh as I rested upon it, for the previous five days had offered no consolation, save the unforgiving leather of the saddle.

The journey from Kashin to the capital of the Russian empire had commenced less than a week after the Grand Duke Nicholas Nicolaievich had journeyed through our village and suffered the attempt on his life. In the days that followed, my sister Asya had changed the dressing on my shoulder twice daily, and when the discarded bindings were no longer spotted with blood, the soldiers who had been left behind to escort me to my new home announced that I was fit for travel. Had the bullet entered my body a little more to the right, my arm might have been paralysed, but I had been fortunate and it took only a day or two for harmony between the shoulder, elbow and wrist to be restored. From time to time, a stinging pain just above the healing wound offered a sharp rebuke as a reminder of my actions and I grimaced at such moments, not out of tenderness but in consideration for how my impetuous actions had cost the life of my oldest friend.

The body of Kolek Boryavich had remained where the soldiers had hanged him, swinging from the yew tree near our hut, for three days before the soldiers gave permission to his father, Boris

Alexandrovich, to cut him down and allow him a decent burial. He did so with dignity, the ceremony taking place a mile or so from our village on the afternoon before I left.

'Do you think we could attend the interment?' I asked my mother the night before, the first mention I had made to her of my friend's death, so guilty did I feel at what I had done. 'I'd like to say goodbye to Kolek.'

'Have you lost your reason, Georgy?' she asked, her brow furrowing as she turned to look at me. She had been attentive towards me over the last few days, showing more consideration than she had over the previous sixteen years, and I wondered whether my brush with death had caused her to regret our virtual estrangement. 'We would not be welcome there.'

'But he was my closest friend,' I insisted. 'And you have known him since the day that he was born.'

'From that day until the day he died,' she agreed, biting her lip. 'But Borys Alexandrovich . . . he has made his feelings clear.'

'Perhaps if I spoke to him,' I suggested. 'I could visit him. My shoulder is healing. I could try to explain—'

'Georgy,' she said, sitting down on the floor beside me and placing her hand flat against the muscle of my uninjured arm, her tone softening to a point where I thought she might even be moved towards humanity. 'He doesn't want to talk to you, can't you understand that? He isn't even thinking about you. He has lost his son. That is all that matters to him now. He walks the streets with a haunted expression on his face, crying out for

78

Kolek and cursing Nicholas Nicolaievich, denouncing the Tsar, blaming everyone for what has happened except himself. The two soldiers, they've warned him about his treasonous words but he doesn't listen. He'll go too far one of these days, Georgy, and end up with his head inside a noose too. Trust me, it's best that you stay away from him.'

I was tortured with remorse and could hardly sleep for guilt. The truth was that I didn't really believe it had been my intention to save the life of the Grand Duke at all, but rather I had hoped to prevent Kolek from committing an action which could only result in his own death. The irony that in doing so I had cost him his life was not lost on me.

To my shame, however, I was almost relieved by his father's decision to refuse me an audience, for had I been allowed to speak I doubtless would have apologized for my actions, which might have resulted in the guards realizing that I was not quite the hero that everyone believed me to be and my proposed new life in St Petersburg might have come to an early end. I couldn't allow this, for I wanted to leave. The possibility of a life outside of Kashin had been placed before me and as the week drew to a close and the moment of my departure loomed, I began to wonder whether it had even been my intention to save Kolek at all, or whether I had been hoping to save myself.

On the morning that I emerged from our hut to begin the long journey towards St Petersburg, I could see my fellow *moujik*s staring at me with a mixture of admiration and contempt. It was true that I had brought great honour on our village by saving the life of the Tsar's cousin, but every man and woman who watched me gather my few belongings together and place them in the saddlebags of the horse which had been left behind for my journey had watched Kolek grow up on these very streets. The fact of his untimely death, not to mention my part in it, lingered in the air like a stale odour. They were loyal subjects of the Romanovs, this was true. They believed in the Imperial family and the right of autocracy. They credited God with putting the Tsar on the throne and believed his relatives to exist in a state of glory. But Kolek was from Kashin. He was one of us. In such a situation, it was impossible to decide where loyalties should lie.

'You will come back for me one day soon?' Asya asked as I prepared to leave. She had been negotiating with the soldiers for several days to allow her to accompany me to St Petersburg, where she, of course, hoped to begin her own new life, but they would hear nothing of it and she was facing up to a lonely future in Kashin without her closest confidant at hand.

'I will try,' I promised her, although I didn't know whether I meant this or not. I had no idea, after all, what lay in store for me. I could not commit to making plans for others.

'Every day I will await a letter,' she insisted, clutching my hands in hers and staring at me with imploring eyes that were ready to spring forth with tears. 'And with one word, I will set off to find you. Don't leave me here to rot, Georgy. Promise me that. Tell whoever you meet about me. Tell them what a worthy addition I would be to their society.'

I nodded and kissed her cheek, and those of my

other sisters and mother, before walking over to shake my father's hand. Daniil stared at me as if he did not know how to respond to such a gesture. He had made his money off me finally, but with his profit came my departure. To my surprise, he looked stricken by this fact, but it was too late for reparation now. I wished him well but said little more before mounting the fine grey stallion, offering a last goodbye and riding out of Kashin and away from my family for ever.

The journey itself passed with little incident; it was simply five days of riding, resting, with little or no conversation to relieve the tedium. Only on the second-to-last night did one of the soldiers, Ruskin, show me a little sympathy as I sat around our campfire, staring into the flames.

'You look unhappy,' he said, taking his place beside me and poking at the burning sticks with the toe of his boot. 'You aren't looking forward to seeing St Petersburg?'

'Of course,' I said with a shrug, although in truth I had given it little thought.

'Then what? Your face tells me a different story. You're scared, perhaps?'

'I'm afraid of nothing,' I snapped immediately, turning to stare at him, and the smile that crept across his face was enough to dilute my anger. He was a big man, strong and virile, and there was no question of dispute between us.

'All right, Georgy Daniilovich,' he said, raising the palms of his hands before him. 'No need to be so angry. I thought you wanted to talk, that was all.'

'Well I don't,' I said.

A silence lingered between us for some time and

I wished that he would return to his friend and leave me alone, but finally he spoke again, quietly, as I knew he would.

'You blame yourself for his death,' he began, not looking at me now but staring into the flames. 'No, don't be so quick to deny it. I know you do. I've been watching you. And I was there on that day, remember, I saw what happened.'

'He was my oldest friend,' I said, feeling a great wave of remorse building up inside my body. 'If I hadn't ran across to him like that—'

'Then he might have killed Nicholas Nicolaievich and he would have been executed for his crime just the same. Perhaps worse. If the Tsar's cousin had been murdered, perhaps all of your friend's family would have been killed too. He had sisters, did he not?'

'Six of them,' I said.

'And they live because the General lives. You tried to stop Kolek Boryavich from committing a heinous act, that is all. A moment earlier and none of this might have happened. You cannot blame yourself. You acted for the best.'

I nodded my head, able to hear the sense in what he said, but little good it did. It was my fault, I was convinced of it. I had caused the death of my dearest friend and no one could tell me otherwise.

My first view of St Petersburg came the following night as we finally entered the capital. What I would soon recognize to be the glory of Peter the Great's triumphant design was diminished somewhat by the darkness of the evening, although that did not prevent me from staring in amazement at the breadth of the streets and the number of people, horses and carriages that travelled past me

82

in all directions. I had never seen such activity before. Along the side of the roads, men stood by caged wood fires, roasting chestnuts and selling them to the gentlemen and ladies who passed, each of whom was wrapped in hats and furs of the most exquisite quality. My guards appeared to be oblivious to these sights—I suppose they were so accustomed to them that they had lost their power to impress—but for a sixteen-year-old boy who had never before travelled more than a few miles outside the village of his birth, it was dazzling.

A crowd was gathered in front of one such fire and we stopped next to an elaborate carriage, pulling up our horses as the people parted to allow the guards through. I hadn't eaten in almost a day and longed for a bag of chestnuts, my stomach rumbling in anticipation of a warm supper. Around us the people were laughing and joking; at their head was a middle-aged lady who bore a severe expression, and next to her stood four identically dressed girls—sisters, obviously—each one a little younger than the next. They were quite beautiful and despite the hunger that pressed upon my stomach, my eyes were drawn to their faces. They were entirely unaware of me until one, the last in line—a girl of about fifteen, I imagined—turned her head and caught my eye. Typically, I might have blushed at such a moment, or looked away, but I did neither of these things. Instead I held her gaze and we simply stared at each other, as if we were old friends, until she became suddenly aware of the warmth of the bag she was holding and she let out a cry as it fell from her grip, half a dozen chestnuts rolling along the ground towards me. I stooped to gather them up and she ran over to collect them, but a stern rebuke from her governess halted her in her tracks and she hesitated for only a moment before turning back to join her sisters.

'Madam,' I cried, beginning to walk towards her with my prize, but I managed to cover only a few feet before one of my escorts grabbed me roughly by my injured arm, causing me to cry out in pain and drop the chestnuts once again. 'What are you doing?' I asked, turning furiously towards him, for, without knowing why exactly, I hated for her to see me weakened by something so simple as another man's grip. 'They belong to her.'

'She can buy some more,' he said, dragging me back to our horses, as hungry as I had been when we had stopped. 'Know your station, boy, or you will be taught it quickly enough.'

I frowned and looked over to my left, where the woman and her charges were entering the carriage once again and driving away, the eyes of all the crowd upon them, as well they might have been, for each girl was more beautiful than the last, except the youngest one, who outshone them all.

A few moments later and we were riding along the banks of the Neva River, my eyes fixed upon the granite embankments and the cheerful young couples who were strolling along the paths engaged in conversation. The people seemed happy here, a fact which surprised me, for I had expected a city torn apart by the war. It appeared, however, as if none of that unpleasantness had come to St Petersburg, and instead the streets and squares were filled with laughter, joy and prosperity. It was all that I could do to control my mounting excitement.

Finally, we turned into a magnificent square, where stretched out before me stood the Winter Palace. Despite the darkness of the evening, the full moon overhead allowed me to observe the green-and-white-fronted citadel with widened eyes. How anyone had constructed such an extraordinary edifice was beyond my comprehension, and still I seemed to be the only one of our number to be taken aback by its splendour.

'This is it?' I asked one of the guards. 'This is where the Tsar lives?'

'Of course,' he said gruffly, shrugging his shoulders and displaying the same lack of interest in talking to me that he and his partner had shown throughout our journey. I suspected that they had taken it as a great indignity to be left with such a mundane task as escorting a boy to the capital, while their fellows continued on in the retinue of the Grand Duke.

'And am I to live here too?' I asked, trying not to laugh at such an outrageous idea.

'Who knows?' he replied. 'Our orders are to deliver you to Count Charnetsky and after that, you can make your own way.'

We passed by the red granite of the Alexander Column, which stood almost twice as tall as the palace itself, and I stared up at the angel who presided at its summit, clutching a cross. Her head was bowed, as if in defeat, but her pose was one of triumph, a cry to her enemies to make themselves known, for the power of her faith would ensure her safety. Following the guards, I stepped below an archway which led directly into the body of the palace itself, whereupon my horse was taken from me. I was met by a portly gentleman who looked me up and down as I straightened myself from the long journey and seemed entirely unimpressed by what he saw.

'You are Georgy Daniilovich Jachmenev?' he asked as I approached him.

'I am, sir,' I replied politely.

'My name is Count Vladimir Vladyavich Charnetsky,' he announced, clearly enjoying the sound of the words as they tripped off his tongue. 'I have the honour of being in charge of His Imperial Majesty's *Leib Guard*. I am told that you performed a heroic gesture in your home village and have been rewarded with a place in the Tsar's household, is that correct?'

'It is what they say,' I admitted. 'In truth, the events of that afternoon all went by so quickly that I—'

'It doesn't matter,' he interrupted, turning around and indicating that I should follow him through another door into the warmth of the interior palace. 'You should know that such heroics are part of the everyday responsibilities for those who guard the Tsar and his family. You will be working alongside men who have put their lives at risk on any number of occasions, so do not think that you are anything special. You are simply a pebble on a beach, nothing more.'

'Of course, sir,' I said, surprised by his hostility. 'I never thought that I was anything more than that. And I do assure you that—'

'As a rule, I don't like having new guards imposed on me,' he announced, huffing and puffing as he led me up a series of wide, purple-carpeted staircases, maintaining such a pace that I was

86

forced to run a little to keep up with him, an unexpected fact considering the great difference in both our ages and weights. 'I grow particularly concerned when I am forced to oversee young men who have no training whatsoever and know nothing of our ways here.'

'Of course, sir,' I repeated, running along after him and doing my best to appear suitably deferential and subordinate.

Climbing the staircases in the palace, I stared in awe at the thick, gold frames that surrounded the mirrors and window-panes. White alabaster statues emerged from the walls and stood triumphantly on plinths, their faces turned away from the enormous grey colonnades which stretched from floor to ceiling. Magnificent tapestries and paintings could be glimpsed through open doors leading to a series of ante-rooms, most of which depicted great men on horseback leading their men into battle, and the marble floor beneath our feet sounded out as we marched along. It surprised me that a man of Count Charnetsky's girth—and his was quite an extraordinary girth—could move through the hallways with such dexterity. Years of practice, I decided.

'But the Grand Duke takes these fancies into his head from time to time,' he continued, 'and when he does, we must all fall in line with him. Regardless of the consequences.'

'Sir,' I said, stopping for a moment now, determined to avow my manhood, an aspiration which was rather spoiled by the length of time it took me to gather my breath, for I was doubled over with my hands on my hips, gasping for air. 'I must let you know that while I never expected to find myself in this most exalted of positions, I shall do everything in my power to act with fortitude and propriety, in the best traditions of your forces. And I am eager to learn whatever a guardsman is obliged to know. You will find me a quick study too, I promise you that.'

He stopped a few feet ahead of me and turned around, staring at me with such surprise for a moment that I did not know whether he intended to step forward and slap my face or simply throw me through one of the tall, stained windows that lined the walls. In the end, he did neither, merely shook his head and continued on, shouting after him that I should follow and be quick about it.

A few minutes later, I found myself in a long corridor and was told to sit down in that most exquisite of seats, and I was grateful for the rest. He nodded, satisfied with the completion of his task, and turned around to march away, but before he could vanish out of sight altogether I found the courage within myself to call after him.

'Sir,' I cried. 'Count Charnetsky!'

'What is it?' he asked, turning around and glaring at me as if he could not believe the audacity that I displayed to address him at all.

'Well . . .' I began, looking around and shrugging my shoulders. 'What am I to do now?'

'What are you to do, boy?' he asked, taking a few steps closer to me again and laughing a little, but out of bitterness, I thought, not amusement. 'What are you to do? You will wait. Until you are summoned. And then you will be instructed.'

'And after that?'

'After that,' he said, turning away from me again and disappearing into the darkness of the corridor, 'you will do what we are all here to do, Georgy Daniilovich. You will obey.'

*   *   *

The minutes that I sat there stretched out endlessly and I began to wonder whether I had been forgotten about. There was no movement on the corridor and, except for the sense that an entire community of dutiful servants was hovering on the other side of every door, little sign of life. Whoever was supposed to be instructing me on my duties showed no sign of appearing and I experienced a growing sense of unease, wondering what I should do or where I should go if no one arrived to take charge of me. I had hoped for a hot meal, a bed, somewhere to wash the dust of the journey off my body, but it seemed unlikely that such luxuries would be mine.

Count Charnetsky, unhappy with my presence at all, had vanished back into the heart of the labyrinth. I wondered whether the Grand Duke Nicholas Nicolaievich was waiting to interview me, but somehow I imagined that he would have returned to Stavka, the Army Headquarters, by now. My stomach began to grumble—it had been almost twenty-four hours since I had last had anything to eat—and I looked down at it, frowning, as if a stern rebuke would encourage it to remain silent. Its low growl, like the sound of an unoiled door being opened slowly, echoed along the corridor, bouncing off the walls and windows, growing louder and more embarrassing by the second. Coughing a little to mask the groan, I stood up to stretch my legs and felt a great ache pass from ankle to thigh, occasioned by the long ride from Kashin.

The passageway where I was standing did not look down over Palace Square, but was situated instead on the opposite side of the citadel with a view over the Neva River, which was lit up along its banks by a series of electric lights. Despite the lateness of the hour, there were still some pleasure boats sailing along, which surprised me, for it was a cold evening and I could only imagine how brisk the temperature would be upon the water. The people clearly belonged to the wealthier classes, however, for even from this distance I could see how swathed they were in expensive furs, hats and gloves. I imagined the decks of the boats to be lined with food and drink, a generation of princes and duchesses laughing and gossiping, as if they had not a care in the world.

No one watching such a scene could have imagined that our country had been engaged in a war for more than eighteen months and that thousands of young Russian men were dying by the hour on the battlefields of Europe. It was not quite Versailles before the arrival of the tumbrils, but there was evasion in the atmosphere, as if the landed classes of St Petersburg could not quite believe that unhappiness and discontent were breeding in the towns and villages outside the city limits.

I watched as one such vessel docked directly in front of the palace, perhaps the most lavish of all the boats, and two Imperial guards leaped the short distance from the deck to the promenade as the craft slipped gently into its mooring, then took a wide drawbridge from its resting place to provide safe transport across for its occupants. A heavy-set woman stepped off first and stood to the side as four young girls, all dressed identically in long grey dresses, overcoats and hats, followed her, talking among themselves. I craned my neck for a better look and was astonished to see that it was the same party from the roasted-chestnut stand. Their carriage must have taken them to the boat for a short journey to end a pleasurable evening, but standing where I was, on the third floor of the palace, I was too high to observe them for more than a few short moments. I wondered whether they had the sense that they were being watched, however, for just before they disappeared out of sight, one of them—the youngest one, the girl whose chestnuts had fallen on the ground and whose gaze had entranced me—hesitated, then turned her head upwards and caught my eye, a look of recognition on her face, as if she had expected me to be there all along. I saw her smile for only a moment before she vanished and I swallowed nervously and frowned, confused by the unfamiliar emotion that swept over me.

I had laid eyes on this girl for only the briefest of moments, and we had barely spoken at the chestnut stand, but there was a warmth, a kindness in those eyes that made me wish I could run down to find her again, to talk to her and discover who she was. I almost laughed at the absurdity of my emotions. *You are being ridiculous, Georgy!* I told myself, shaking my head quickly to rid myself of the images, and with still no sign of anyone to tell me any better, I started to walk along the corridor, away from those dangerous windows and the solitude of my exquisite chair.

And it was at that moment that I began to hear voices in the distance.

Every closed door was as ornate as the last and stood perhaps fifteen feet in height, with a semi-circular frieze placed above the intricate gold mouldings that ornamented each surface. I wondered how many hours of craftsmanship had gone into their elaborate detailing. How many doors like these were there in this palace? A thousand? Two thousand? The idea was too much for my brain to consider and I became dizzy at the thought of how many people must have struggled to complete work on such finery, which existed to serve the pleasures of only one family. Did they even notice how beautiful it was, I wondered, or did the delicate splendour just pass them by entirely?

Hesitating for only a moment, I turned a corner to where a much shorter corridor awaited me. There were no lights running to my left and its increasing darkness reminded me of some of the more terrifying stories that Asya had told me as an infant to induce nightmares, and I shuddered slightly and turned away. To my right, however, a number of candles were lit along the windowsills and I started to walk along in a spirit of exploration, carefully, quietly, so that my boots would not sound too loudly on the floor beneath my feet.

Again, each door was closed, but it wasn't long before I tracked the voices to a room a little further ahead. Intrigued, I continued along, pressing an ear to each door, but there was only silence behind them. What happened in each one, I wondered? Who lived there, worked there, issued orders from there? The sounds grew louder and at the end of the corridor there was one door slightly ajar, but I hesitated before approaching it. The voices were more distinct now, although the people from whom they emanated were speaking quietly, and as I looked around I observed a simple room before me, with a prie-dieu placed directly at its centre.

Kneeling upon it, her head buried in its cushion, was a woman. And she was crying.

I watched her for a moment, intrigued by her sorrow, before my eyes drifted to the room's other occupant, a man whose back was turned to me as he faced the wall, where a large icon was positioned upon a luminescent tapestry. He had the most extraordinary long dark hair and it hung down his back, thick and ragged, as if it was quite unclean, and he was dressed in simple peasant clothes, the type of tunic and trousers that would not have been out of place in Kashin. I wondered what on earth he could possibly be doing here in such simple apparel. Had he broken in? Was he a thief of some sort? But no, that was impossible, for the lady kneeling before him was dressed in the finest gown I had ever laid eyes on and clearly had reason to be here in the palace; had he been an intruder he would not have been commanding her attention quite so intently.

'You must pray, Matushka,' the man said suddenly, his voice deep and low, as if it came from the very depths of hell. He stretched his arms wide in a pose that recalled the crucified Christ upon on the cross at Calvary. 'You must put your faith in a greater power than princes and palaces. You are nothing, Matushka. And I am nothing but a

93

channel through which the voice of God may be heard. Before His grace you must supplicate yourself. You must give yourself to God in whatever disguise he presents himself. You must do whatever he asks of you. For the boy's sake.'

The woman said nothing, but buried her head deeper into the cushion at the front of the prie-dieu. I felt a chill enter my body and grew nervous as I watched the scene play out before me. However, I was hypnotized by the moment and found that I could not turn away. I held my breath, expecting the man to speak again, but in an instant he spun around, aware of my presence, and our eyes met.

Those eyes. To recall them even now . . . They were like circles of coal, mined from the centre of a diseased pit.

My own eyes grew wide as we stared at each other and my body became numb with fear. *Run*, I cried out in my mind. *Run away!* But my legs would not obey and we continued to stare at each other until finally the man cocked his head a little to the side, as if curious about me, and smiled widely, a horrible smile, a set of yellow teeth displayed in a cavernous darkness, and the dreadfulness of his expression was enough to break my spell and I turned and ran back the way I had come, finding myself at the junction once again and hesitating, already confused as to which direction would lead me back to where Count Charnetsky had instructed me to wait.

Running, convinced that he was giving chase to murder me, I twisted and turned, running along the wrong corridors and in opposite directions, lost in the palace now, scared, my breath gasping, my heart racing, unsure how on earth I could ever explain my disappearance, whether I should just descend as many staircases as possible until I found myself outside the palace again, at which time I could run away, home to Kashin, pretending that this entire experience had never taken place.

And then, as if by some curious magic, I found myself back on the corridor where I had started. I stopped and doubled over, catching my breath, and when I looked up I realized that I was not alone there any more.

A man was standing at the end of the hallway, just outside an open door, from where a great light shone, illuminating him almost as a god. I stared at him, wondering what other terrors this evening was to bring. Who was this man, bathed in white glory? Why had he been sent for me?

'Are you Jachmenev?' he asked quietly, his voice low and peaceful but making its way down to me without difficulty.

'Yes, sir,' I replied.

'Please,' he said, turning around and indicating the room behind him. 'I thought perhaps you had disappeared on me.'

I hesitated for only a moment before following him. I had never met this man before, of course, had never laid eyes on him. But I knew immediately who he was.

His Imperial Majesty, Tsar Nicholas II, Emperor and Autocrat of All the Russias, Grand Duke of Finland, King of Poland.

My employer.

*   *   *

'I apologize if I kept you waiting,' he said as I stepped into the room, closing the door behind me. 'As you can imagine, there are many matters of state to be taken care of. And this has been a very, very long day. I had hoped—' He stopped short as he turned around and stared at me in amazement. 'What on earth are you doing, boy?'

He was standing to the left of his desk, no doubt surprised to see me kneeling about ten feet away from him, supplicating myself on the floor with my hands outstretched on the rich carpet before me and my forehead touching the ground.

'Your most Imperial of Majesties,' I began, my words getting muffled in the purple and red weave in which my nose was buried. 'May I offer my sincere appreciation for the honour of—'

'All the saints in heaven, would you stand up, boy, so that I can see and hear you!'

I looked up and there was the hint of a smile flickering across his lips; I must have been an extraordinary sight.

'I apologize, Your Majesty,' I said. 'I was saying that—'

'And *stand up*,' he insisted. 'You look like some sort of whipped cur stretched out on my carpet like that.'

I stood and adjusted my clothing, attempting to discover some sort of dignity in my pose. I could feel the blood which had run to my head when I was on the ground causing my face to grow red and was aware that I must have seemed embarrassed to be in his presence. 'I apologize,' I said once again.

'You can stop apologizing, for a start,' he said, stepping behind his desk now and sitting down. 'All we've both done over the last two minutes is apologize to each other. There must be an end to it.'

'Yes, Your Majesty,' I said, nodding my head. I dared to look directly at him as he examined me and found myself a little surprised by his appearance. He was not a tall man, no more than five feet and seven or eight inches in height, which meant that I would have stood a good head above him had we been standing side by side. He was quite handsome, though, compact in his frame, trim and apparently athletic, with piercing blue eyes and a finely trimmed beard and moustache, the ends of which were waxed but drooping slightly, perhaps because of the lateness of the evening. I imagined that he tended to it once a day, in the mornings, or if there was a reception at night, then once again in preparation for his guests. It was not so important when receiving a lowly visitor such as I.

Contrary to my expectations, the Tsar was not attired in some outlandish Imperial costume, but in the simple garb of a fellow *moujik*: a plain, vanilla-coloured shirt, a pair of loose fitting trousers and dark leather boots. Of course, there was no question that these simple items of clothing were produced from the very finest fabrics, but they seemed comfortable and simple and I began to feel a little more at ease in his presence.

'So you are Jachmenev,' he said finally, his clear voice betraying neither boredom nor interest; it was as if I was simply another task in his day.

'Yes, sir.'

'Your full name?'

'Georgy Daniilovich Jachmenev,' I replied. 'Of the village of Kashin.'

'And your father?' he asked. 'Who is he?'

'Daniil Vladyavich Jachmenev,' I said. 'Also of Kashin.'

'I see. And he is still with us?'

I looked at him in surprise. 'He didn't accompany me, sir,' I said. 'No one said that he should.'

'He is still alive, Jachmenev,' he explained with a sigh.

'Oh. Yes. Yes, he is.'

'And what is his position in society?'

'He is a farmer, sir.'

'He has his own land?'

'No, sir. He is a labourer.'

'You said a farmer.'

'I misspoke, sir. I mean that he farms land. But it is not his land.'

'Whose is it then?'

'Yours, Your Majesty.'

He smiled at this and raised an eyebrow for a moment as he considered my reply. 'It is indeed,' he said. 'Although there are those who think that all the land in Russia should be distributed equally between the peasants. My former prime minister, Stolypin, he introduced that particular reform,' he added, his tone implying that it was not something he had been in favour of. 'You are familiar with Mr Stolypin?'

'No, sir,' I replied, honestly.

'You have never heard of him?' he asked in surprise.

'I'm afraid not, sir.'

'Well that doesn't matter, I suppose,' he said, rubbing carefully at a spot of dirt on his tunic. 'He's dead now. He was shot at the Kiev Opera House, while I sat in the Imperial box looking down at him. That's how close these murderers can get. He was a good man, Stolypin. I treated him unkindly.' He became silent for a few moments, his tongue pressing into his cheek as he lost himself in memories of the past; I had only been with the Tsar for a few minutes but I already suspected that the past weighed heavily on him. And that the present was hardly any more comforting.

'Your father,' he said eventually, looking up at me again. 'Do you think he should be granted his own land?'

I thought about it, but the concept, my very words, became confused and I shrugged my shoulders to indicate my ignorance. 'I'm afraid I don't know anything about such matters, sir,' I replied. 'I'm sure that whatever you decide will be for the right, though.'

'You have confidence in me, then?'

'Yes, sir.'

'But why? You have never met me before.'

'Because you are the Tsar, sir.'

'And what does that matter?'

'What does it matter?'

'Yes, Georgy Daniilovich,' he said calmly. 'What does it matter that I am the Tsar? Simply *being* the Tsar inspires confidence in you?'

'Well . . . yes,' I said, shrugging again, and he sighed and shook his head.

'One does not shrug one's shoulders in the presence of God's anointed,' he said firmly. 'It is impolite.'

'I apologize, sir,' I said, feeling my face grow red once again. 'I meant no disrespect.'

'You're apologizing again.'

'That's because I'm nervous, sir.'

'Nervous?'

'Yes.'

'But why?'

'Because you are the Tsar.'

He burst out laughing at this, a long, lingering laugh that went on for almost a minute, leaving me in a state of utter bewilderment. Truthfully, I had not expected to encounter the Emperor that night—if at all—and our meeting had come about with such little preparation or formality that I was still confused by the fact of it. It appeared that he wanted to question me thoroughly for a position I did not yet understand, but he was being deliberate and cautious in his queries, listening to my every answer and following up on it, trying to trap me in a mistake. And now he was laughing as if I had said something amusing, only for the life of me I could not think what that might have been.

'You look confused, Georgy Daniilovich,' he said finally, offering me a pleasant smile as his laughter came to an end.

'I am, a little,' I said. 'Was I rude in what I just said?'

'No, no,' he replied, shaking his head. 'It's just the consistency of your answers that amuses me, that's all. *Because I am the Tsar.* I am the Tsar, am I not?'

'Why, yes, sir.'

'And a curious position it is too,' he said, picking up a steel diamond-encrusted letter-opener from his desk and balancing it on its tip before him. 'Perhaps one day I shall explain it to you. For now, I believe I owe you my gratitude.'

'Your gratitude, sir?' I asked, surprised that he could possibly owe me anything.

'My cousin, the Grand Duke Nicholas Nicolaievich. He recommended you to me. He told me how you came to save him after an assassination attempt.'

'I'm not sure it was as serious as all that, sir,' I said, for the very words seemed astonishingly treasonous, even coming from the mouth of the Tsar.

'Oh no? What would you call it then?'

I considered the matter. 'The boy in question. Kolek Boryavich. I knew him since we were children. He was . . . it was a stupid mistake on his part, you see. His father was a man of strong opinions and Kolek liked to impress him.'

'My father was a man of strong opinions too, Georgy Daniilovich. I don't try to murder people because of it.'

'No, sir, but you have an army at your disposal.'

His head snapped up and he stared at me in surprise, his eyes opening wide at my impertinence, and even I felt utterly shocked that I had said such words.

'I beg your pardon?' he said after what seemed like an eternity had passed.

'Sir,' I said, scrambling to correct myself, 'I misspoke. I only meant that Kolek was in thrall to his father, that's all. He was trying to please him.'

'So it was his father who wanted my cousin murdered? I should send soldiers to arrest *him*, should I?'

'Only if a man can be arrested for the thoughts that are in his head and not the actions that he commits,' I said, for if I was responsible for the death of my oldest friend, I was damned if I was going to have his father's blood on my hands too.

'Indeed,' he said, considering this. 'And no, my young friend, we do not arrest men for such things. Unless their thoughts lead to plans, that is. Assassination is a terrible thing. It is a most cowardly form of protest.'

I said nothing to this; I could think of nothing to say.

'I was only thirteen years old when my own grandfather was assassinated, you know. Alexander II. The Tsar-Liberator, he was called at one time. The man who freed the serfs, and then they murdered him for his generosity. A coward threw a bomb at his carriage while he travelled through streets not far from here and he escaped unhurt. When he stepped outside, another ran at him and exploded a second. He was brought here, to this very palace. Our family gathered while the Tsar died. I watched as the life seeped out of him. I recall it as if it was yesterday. One of his legs had been blown off. The other was mostly missing. His stomach was exposed and he was gasping for breath. It was obvious that he had only a few minutes left to live. And yet he made sure to speak to each of us in turn, to offer us his final benediction, such was his strength even at a time like that. He consecrated my father. He held my hand. And then he died. Such agony he must have felt. So you see, I know the consequences of this kind of violence and am determined that no member of my family will ever suffer assassination again.'

I nodded and felt moved by his story. My eyes drifted to the rows of books which lined the wall to my right and I glanced at them, narrowing my eyes to make out the titles.

'You do not turn your head away from me,' said the Tsar, although his voice contained more curiosity than anger. 'It is I who turn away from you.'

'I'm sorry, sir,' I said, looking at him again. 'I didn't know.'

'More apologies,' he replied with a sigh. 'I can see that it will take some time for you to learn our ways here. They may seem ... curious to you, I imagine. You are interested in books?' he asked then, nodding towards the shelves.

'No, sir,' I said, shaking my head. 'I mean yes, Your Majesty.' I groaned inwardly, trying to make myself sound less ignorant. 'I mean ... I'm interested in what they say.'

The Tsar smiled for a moment, seemed almost about to laugh, but then his face clouded over and he leaned forward.

'My cousin is very important to me, Georgy Daniilovich,' he announced. 'But more than that, he is of extreme importance to the war effort. The measure of his loss would have been incalculable. You have the gratitude of the Tsar and all the Russian people for your actions.'

I felt it would be unworthy of me to protest any further and simply bowed my head in appreciation, holding it there for a moment before looking back up.

'You must be tired, boy,' he said then. 'Take a seat, why don't you?'

I looked around and a chair similar to the one in the outside corridor, but not quite as ornate as the one in which he sat himself, was standing behind me, so I sat down and immediately felt a little more relaxed. As I did so, I stole a quick glance around the room, not looking at the books now but observing the paintings on the walls, the tapestries, the objets d'art which sat on every available surface. I had never seen such opulence before. It was quite breathtaking. Behind the Tsar, just over his left shoulder, I saw the most extraordinary piece of ornamental sculpture and, despite my rudeness in staring, my eyes could not help but focus on it. The Tsar, taking note of my interest, turned around to see what had captured my attention.

'Ah,' he said, turning back and smiling at me. 'And now you have noticed one of my treasures.'

'I'm sorry, sir,' I said, trying my best not to shrug. 'It's just ... I've never seen anything quite so beautiful.'

'Yes, it is rather fine, isn't it?' he said, reaching across with both hands for the egg-shaped statue and placing it on the desk between us. 'Come a little closer, Georgy. You may examine it in more detail if you wish.'

I pulled my seat forward and leaned in. The piece was no more than seven or eight inches in height, and perhaps half that distance in breadth, a gold and white enamelled egg, patterned with tiny portraits, supported by a three-sided eagle standing upon a red, bejewelled base.

'It is what is known as a Fabergé egg,' the Tsar told me. 'The artist has traditionally presented one every Easter to my family, a new design every year with a surprise at its heart. It's striking, don't you think?'

'I've never seen anything like it,' I said, desperate to reach out and touch the exterior but terrified to do so in case I damaged it in some way.

'This one was given to the Tsaritsa and me two years ago, to celebrate the tercentenary of the Romanov reign. You see, the portraits are of the previous Tsars.' He spun the egg around a little and began to point out some of his ancestors. 'Mikhail Fyodorovich, the first of the Romanovs,' he said, indicating a small, unimposing, wizened man with a peaked hat. 'And here is Peter the Great, from a century later. And Catherine the Great, another fifty years hence. My grandfather, who I spoke of, Alexander II. And my father,' he added, indicating a man almost exactly like the one who sat opposite me. 'Alexander III.'

'And you, sir,' I remarked, pointing to the central portrait. 'Tsar Nicholas II.'

'Indeed,' he said, apparently pleased that I had noticed him. 'My only regret is that he did not add a final portrait to the egg.'

'Of who, sir?'

'My son, of course. The Tsarevich Alexei. I think it would have been quite fitting to see his face there. A testament to our hopes for the future.' He considered this for a moment before speaking again. 'And if I do this . . .' He placed his hand on the top of the egg and carefully lifted the hinged lid, 'you see the surprise which is contained within.'

I leaned forward again so that I was practically stretched across his desk and gasped when I saw the globe contained inside, the continents encased in gold, the oceans described by molten blue steel.

'The globe is composed of two northern hemispheres,' he told me and I could tell by his tone that he was delighted to have an interested audience. 'Here we have the territories of the Russias in 1613, when my ancestor Mikhail

Fyodorovich acceded to the throne. And here,' he continued, turning the globe over, 'are our territories three hundred years later, under my own rule. Somewhat different, as you can see.'

I shook my head, lost for words. The egg was composed of such fine detailing, such exquisite design, that I could have sat before it all day and night and not have grown tired of its beauty. That was not to be, however, for after staring at the lands over which he reigned for a few moments longer, he replaced the lid on the egg and returned it to where it had stood on the table behind him.

'So there we are,' he said, bringing his hands together and glancing across at the clock on the wall. 'It's getting late. Perhaps I should tell you the other reason why I wanted to talk to you.'

'Of course, sir,' I said.

He looked at me for a moment as if he was determining on the correct form of words. His stare pierced me so deeply that I was forced to look away and my eye caught a framed photograph on his desk. He followed my glance there.

'Ah,' he said, nodding. 'I suppose that is as good a place to start as any.' He lifted the photograph and handed it to me. 'You are familiar, I would assume, with the Imperial Family?'

'I am aware of them, of course, sir,' I said. 'I have not had the honour—'

'The four young ladies in that picture,' he continued, ignoring me, 'they are my daughters, the Grand Duchesses Olga, Tatiana, Marie and Anastasia. They are growing into very fine young women, I might add. I am supremely proud of them. The eldest, Olga, is twenty years of age now. Perhaps we shall marry her soon, that is a possibility. There are many eligible young men among the royal families of Europe. It's not possible at the moment, of course. Not with this blasted war. But soon, I think. When it is over. The youngest you see here is my own sweetheart, the Grand Duchess Anastasia, who is shortly to turn fifteen.'

I stared at her face in the portrait. She was young, of course, but then I was less than two years her senior. I recognized her immediately. She was the girl I had met at the chestnut stand earlier in the evening; the young lady who had looked up at me and smiled when she stepped from her boat an hour before. The one who had made me turn around in such a state of confusion, bewildered by my sudden rush of passion.

'There were moments—I think I can confide this in you, Georgy—when I thought I was never to be blessed with a son,' he continued, taking the frame off me and handing me a different one, in which a single portrait of a striking young boy had been placed. 'When I thought Russia was never to be blessed with an heir. But happily, my Alexei was born to the Tsaritsa and me some eleven years ago. He's a fine boy. He will be a great Tsar one day.'

I noted the cheerful countenance of the boy in the picture but was a little surprised by how thin he looked, how dark around the eyes. 'I have no doubt of that, sir,' I replied.

'Naturally, there are many members of the Leib Guard who protect him on a daily basis,' he said then, and to my mind he seemed to be struggling with his words a little, as if he was unsure how much he wanted to say. 'And they take good care of him, of course. But I thought . . . perhaps someone a little closer to his age as a companion. Someone old enough and brave enough to protect him too, should the need arise. How old are you, Georgy?'

'Sixteen, sir.'

'Sixteen, that's good. A boy of eleven will always look up to a lad your age. I think perhaps you might be a good role model for him.'

I exhaled nervously. The Grand Duke had mentioned something of this to me when he had visited my sick bed in Kashin, but I had doubted that such a task could possibly be entrusted to a *moujik*. It seemed so far beyond my expectations of the world that I was sure that at any moment I might wake up and discoverthat this had all been a dream, and that the Tsar, the Winter Palace and all the glories contained therein, down to the beautiful Fabergé egg, would dissolve before my eyes and I would find myself on the floor in our Kashin hut once again, being kicked into consciousness by Daniil, demanding his breakfast.

'I would be honoured, sir,' I said finally. 'If you think me worthy of the position.'

'The Grand Duke certainly thinks you are,' he said, standing up now, and of course I followed his example and stood too. 'And I think you seem like a very respectable young man. I think you might perform well in the role.' We walked towards the door and as we did so, he placed the Imperial hand upon my shoulder, sending a jolt of electricity through my body. The Tsar, the Lord's own appointed, was touching me. It was the greatest blessing that I had ever received. He gripped the bone tightly and I felt so overawed and honoured that I did not mind the searing pain he was sending through my arm from the bullet wound which he was so casually pressing upon.

'Now, can I trust you, Georgy Daniilovich?' he asked, looking me deep in the eyes.

'Of course, Your Majesty,' I replied.

'I hope so,' he said, and there was a hint of utter desperation and misery in his voice. 'If you are to undertake this responsibility, there is something . . . Georgy, what I say to you now must never leave this room.'

'Sir, whatever it is I will take it to the grave.'

He swallowed and hesitated. The silence between us lasted for more than a minute but I did not feel embarrassed now; I felt instead that I was at the centre of a great secret, something which the Lord of our land was about to entrust unto me. But to my disappointment, he seemed to change his mind for instead of confiding in me, he simply shook his head and looked away, releasing my shoulder and opening the door to the corridor.

'Perhaps this is not the time,' he said. 'Let us see how you develop at your task first. All I ask is that you take the utmost care of our son. He is our great hope, you see. He is the hope of all loyal Russians.'

'I will do everything in my power to keep him safe,' I assured him. 'My life is his in a moment.'

'Then that is all I need to know,' he replied, smiling again for a moment before closing the door in my face and leaving me alone once again in the cold and empty corridor, wondering whether anyone was going to collect me and where on earth I should go next.

1970

For the first year after my retirement, I deliberately chose not to go anywhere near the library at the British Museum. It wasn't because I didn't want to be there; on the contrary, after spending my entire adult life closeted within the erudite comfort of that peaceful chamber, there was almost nowhere that I felt quite so content. No, the reason I chose to avoid it was because I did not wish to become one of those men who cannot accept that his working life has come to an end and that the daily routine of employment, which provides order and discipline in our lives, has been replaced by the utter confusion—or what Lamb chose to call 'the deliverance'—of the superannuated man.

I could recall only too well the Friday evening in 1959 when a small party was thrown in honour of Mr Trevors, who had reached the age of sixty-five and was completing his last week of work at the library. Drinks and food were served, speeches were made, dozens of people showed up to wish him well with whatever was to follow. We offered the usual clichés that the world was now his oyster and felt no shame at our duplicity. The atmosphere was intended to be light and cheerful, but my former employer grew increasingly morose as the night wore on and wondered aloud, to the embarrassment of his guests, how he would fill his days after this.

'I'm alone in the world,' he told us with a wretched smile, pools of tears forming in his eyes as we all looked away, hoping that someone else would offer him comfort. 'What do I have if I don't have my work? An empty house. No Dorothy, no Mary,' he added quietly, referring to the family who should have been a consolation to him in his dotage but who had been taken from him. 'This job was my only reason for getting up in the mornings.'

The following Monday morning, he arrived at the library as usual, precisely on time, shirt and tie in perfect order, and insisted on helping us with the more menial tasks that he had never concerned himself with in the past. None of us knew quite what to do—he still maintained an air of authority in our minds, after all, having been our employer for so long—and so did nothing to impede him. But then, to our discomfort, he came in the day after that too, and the following day. On the Thursday morning, one of the directors of the museum took him aside for a quiet word and told him that he had to remember that the rest of us were there to work, that we were *paid* to work, and couldn't engage in conversation all day long. Go home and enjoy your retirement, he was told cheerfully. Put your feet up and do all those things that you could never do when you were stuck in here every day! The poor man did exactly that. He went home and hanged himself that very evening.

Of course, as I considered my own retirement I had no intention of allowing anything like that to happen to me. For one thing, Zoya and I were lucky enough to be in good health. We had each other, as well as our nine-year-old grandson Michael to keep us young. There was certainly no question of me succumbing to depression or a feeling of uselessness. But nevertheless, a year after my retirement began, I started to feel a longing, not to go back to my old employment but to revisit the atmosphere of scholarship which I so missed. To read more. To learn about those subjects of which I remained ignorant. After all, throughout my working life I had been surrounded by books but had rarely had the opportunity to study any of them. And so I decided to return to the tranquillity of the library for a few hours every afternoon, making sure not to cause any trouble for my former colleagues, usually hiding away from their view, in fact, so that they would feel no obligation to talk to me. And I felt content with this arrangement, happy to spend whatever years I had left engaged upon the act of self-education.

In the late autumn of 1970, however, shortly after my seventy-first birthday, I was seated at my usual desk one afternoon when I saw a woman—some thirty years my junior—I guessed, standing by one of the bookshelves, pretending to examine the titles when it was perfectly clear that she had no interest in them at all, but was intent on watching me. I didn't think too much of it at the time; she was probably lost in her own thoughts, I decided, and unaware that she was staring in my direction. I went back to my book and thought no more about it.

I noticed her again the following afternoon, however, when she sat at a desk three seats along from my own and I caught her glancing at me when she thought that I wasn't paying attention, and I confess, I began to find the experience both unsettling and annoying. Had I been a younger man, perhaps I would have thought that the woman was in some way attracted to me, but there was no possibility of that in this instance. I had entered my eighth decade, after all. What little hair remained on my head exposed a bumpy, speckled skull beneath. My teeth were my own, and remained passably white, but they added nothing to my smile, as they might have done when I was a younger man. And while my mobility had not been too badly impaired by ageing, I nevertheless had begun to employ the services of a fine Malacca cane, the better to ensure a steady balance as I walked to and from the library every day. In short, I was no matinée idol and certainly not a figure of desire for a woman half my age.

I considered moving seats, but decided against it. I had been sitting in that same place every afternoon for the previous five years, after all. The light was good, which assisted my reading, as my eyesight was not quite as perceptive as it had once been. Also, it was peaceful there, for I was surrounded by bookshelves that contained such unpopular subjects that few people ever disturbed me. Why should I move? Let her move, I decided. This is my place.

She left shortly after that, but not before hesitating as she passed me, as if there was something she wanted to say, but then thought better of it and moved on.

'You seem distracted,' Zoya said to me that night as we were preparing for bed. 'Is there anything wrong?'

'I'm fine,' I said, smiling at her, unwilling to go into the problem in any detail with her lest she thought I was imagining things and losing my mind. 'It's nothing. I'm just a little tired, that's all.'

Still, I lay awake that night, fretting about what

113

this woman wanted with me. Thirty years before, even twenty, such a visitation would have filled me with paranoid fantasies about who had sent her to spy on me, what they wanted, whether they were looking for Zoya too, but this was 1970. Those days had long since passed. I could think of no sensible reason for her interest in me and began to worry that she was not in fact the same woman I had seen before, or that I had imagined her entirely and senility was setting in.

That worry was put to rest the following day when I arrived at the library shortly after lunchtime, only to see the lady standing outside next to the great stone lions, wrapped up tightly in a dark, heavy overcoat, and she tensed noticeably when she saw me walking along the street towards her.

In return, I frowned and felt immediately nervous. I knew that she was going to speak to me, but thought that if I simply walked past her without an acknowledgement, then she might leave me in peace. For by now, I knew exactly who she was. It was perfectly obvious. I had never laid eyes on her before she started coming to the library—I hadn't wanted to—but now here she was, confronting me, which was a presumption in itself.

Walk on, I told myself. *Ignore her, Georgy. Say nothing.*

'Mr Jachmenev,' she said as I approached her and I lifted my gloved hand a little in the air and gave her a half-smile and nod as I passed by, realizing as I did so that I truly had become old. This was the action of an elderly man, a royal personage passing by in a gilded carriage. It put me in mind of the Grand Duke Nicholas Nicolaievich

114

offering a benediction to the gathered crowd as he paraded his horse through the streets of Kashin, ignorant of the dangers that lay ahead. 'Mr Jachmenev, I'm sorry, could I have a word—'

'I have to go inside,' I said, muttering the words quickly as I hurried on, determined not to allow any contemporary Kolek to take aim at me. 'I have a lot of work to do today, I'm afraid.'

'It won't take long,' she said, and I could see her eyes welling up with tears as she stepped in front of me, blocking my way. She was nervous too, that was obvious from her expression, and the way her hands trembled could not entirely be ascribed to the cold weather. 'I'm so sorry to disturb you, but I had to. I just had to.'

'No,' I muttered under my breath, shaking my head, unwilling to look at her. 'No, please . . .'

'Mr Jachmenev, if you tell me to go, then I'll do as you say and I promise I'll leave you in peace, but all I'm asking for is a few minutes of your time. Perhaps you'd let me buy you a cup of tea, that's all. I know I have no right to ask anything of you, I know that, but please. I beg of you. If you can find it in your heart . . .'

Her words trailed off as the tears came and I was forced to look at her now, feeling the great ache in my heart, that terrible pain that came upon me at the most unexpected moments of the day, times when I wasn't even thinking about what had happened. Moments when I hated her so much that I wanted to find her myself, to wrap my ancient hands around her throat and watch her expression as I squeezed the life out of her.

But now she had found me. And here she was, offering to buy me a cup of tea.

'Please, Mr Jachmenev,' she said and I opened my mouth to answer her, but heard nothing but a great cry of anger emerge from within, a mere fragment of the pain and suffering that she had caused me and that was twisted around my soul as tightly as any of my great secrets or torments.

* * *

We had waited so long to have a child. We had suffered so many disappointments. And then one day, there she was. Our healthy Arina, who it was impossible not to love.

When she was first born, Zoya and I would lay her down on the centre of our bed and sit on either side of her, smiling like people who had been touched by the moon. We'd place her feet in the palms of our hands, marvelling at how happy she was, astonished that we had finally been blessed in this way.

'It means *peace*,' we said when anyone asked us why we had chosen her name, and that was what she brought to us: peace, the satisfaction of parenthood. When she cried, we thought it shocking that someone so small could produce so musical a sound. For me, returning every day from the library, I could barely stop myself from breaking into a run as I walked along the street, so anxious was I to arrive home and see the look on her face when I stepped through the door, that expression that told me that she might have forgotten about me over the previous eight hours, but here I was, and she remembered me, and how good it was to see me again.

Growing up, she was no more or less difficult

116

than any other child; she did well at school, neither excelling at her studies nor giving cause for concern. She married young—too young, I had thought at the time—but the marriage was a happy one. Whether or not she faced similar difficulties to the ones her mother and I had faced I do not know, but it was seven years before she sat down before us, taking our hands in hers, to tell us that we were to become grandparents. Michael was born and his presence in a room was a constant joy. One evening over dinner, she mentioned that she would like to give him a younger brother or sister. Not immediately, but soon. And we were thrilled by the news, for we liked the idea of a house filled with visiting grandchildren.

And then she died.

Arina was thirty-six when she was taken from us. She worked as a teacher in a school near Battersea Park and late one afternoon, as she was walking home along the Albert Bridge Road, the wind took her hat and she ran out into the path of oncoming traffic without looking left or right and was hit by a car. As difficult as it is to admit, it was entirely her fault. There was no possibility that the car could have avoided her. Of course we had taught her to take care when running on to roads, it wasn't as if she didn't know that, but which of us does not get caught up in a moment and forget the things we have been taught? Arina's hat was blown off her head; she wanted it back. It was a simple thing that happened. And she died of it.

The first that Zoya or I knew of the accident was later that evening, when there was an unexpected knock on our front door. I opened it to see a pale young man standing outside, a man I half recognized but could not immediately place. He wore an anxious expression on his face, almost frightened, and was holding a brown cloth cap in his hands, which he passed between his fingers constantly. I didn't know why, but it was something I focussed on increasingly as he talked. His hands were quite bony, the skin almost transparent, not dissimilar to how my own hands had aged, although I was forty years older than him. I watched them as he talked, perhaps to keep myself steady, for there was something in his expression that suggested I would not like what he had come here to say.

'Mr Jachmenev?' he said.

'Yes.'

'I don't know if you remember me, sir. I'm David Frasier.'

I stared at him and hesitated, uncertain who he was, but Zoya appeared behind me before I had a chance to embarrass myself.

'David,' she said. 'What on earth brings you over here this evening? Georgy, you remember Ralph's friend, don't you? From the wedding?'

'Of course, of course,' I said, recalling him now. Drunk, he had attempted to perform the Hopak dance, arms folded, kicking his feet out while trying to keep his body upright. He thought it was a symbol of unity, a mark of respect to his hosts, and I didn't like to tell him that it was little more than an exercise to warm the body before battle.

'Mr Jachmenev,' he said, his face betraying his anxiety. 'Mrs Jachmenev. Ralph sent me round. He asked me to get you.'

'To get us?' I asked. 'What do you mean, *to get us*? What have we done to him?'

'Ralph did?' asked Zoya, ignoring me, the smile fading from her face a little. 'Why? What's happened? Is it Michael? Arina?'

'There's been an accident,' he said quickly. 'Now hopefully it's not too serious. I don't know the ins and outs of it, I'm afraid. It's Arina. She was on her way back from school. A car hit her.'

It occurred to me that he was talking in short, staccato-like sentences and I wondered whether it was his natural mode of speech. His diction was like gunfire. That's what I was thinking of as he spoke. Gunfire. Soldiers on the Front. Lines of boys, English, German, French, Russian, side by side, shooting at everything that stood before them, taking each other's lives without realizing their victims were young men just like them, whose return home was anxiously awaited by sleepless parents. The images floated through my mind. Violence. I focussed entirely on this. I didn't want to listen to what he was saying. I didn't want to hear the words that this man, this fellow who claimed he had been sent to get us, this boy who dared to suggest that he knew my daughter, was uttering. If I don't listen, I thought, then it won't have happened. If I don't listen. If I think of something else entirely.

'Where?' Zoya asked. 'When did it happen?'

'A couple of hours ago,' he said, and I couldn't help but hear him now. 'Somewhere near Battersea, I think. She's been taken to hospital. I think she's all right. I don't think it's too serious. But I've got Ralph's car outside. He asked me to collect you.'

Zoya pushed past him and out of the door, running up the steps towards the car, as if she

119

would have happily left for the hospital without either of us, ignoring the fact that we needed Mr Frasier to drive us there. I stayed where I was, feeling a certain numbness in my legs and a giddiness in my stomach, and the room began to sway a little.

'Mr Jachmenev,' said the young man, stepping towards me with one hand outstretched as if he might need to act as my balance. 'Mr Jachmenev, are you all right?'

'I'm fine, boy,' I snapped, turning and making for the door too. 'Come on. If you're to take us there, then for pity's sake let's go.'

The drive was a difficult one. The traffic was heavy and it took us almost forty minutes to make our way from our Holborn flat to the hospital. Throughout the journey, Zoya peppered the young man with questions, while I sat in the back of the car, silent as a mouse, listening, refusing to speak.

'You think she's all right?' Zoya asked. 'Why do you think that? Did Ralph say that?'

'I think so,' he said, sounding more and more as if he wished he was somewhere else entirely. 'He phoned me at work. I'm not far from the hospital, you see. He told me where he was, asked me to meet him at the reception desk immediately and to take my car and to come and find you both.'

'But what did he say?' asked Zoya, a note of aggression entering her tone. 'Tell me exactly. Did he say she was going to be all right?'

'He said she'd been in an accident. I asked whether she was all right and he sort of snapped at me. He said *Yes, yes, she'll be fine, but you've got to fetch her parents for me right away*.'

'He said she'd be fine?'

'I think so,' said Mr Frasier. I could hear the note of panic in his voice. He didn't want to say anything that he thought he shouldn't say. He didn't want to give false information. Offer hope where there was none. Suggest that we prepare ourselves when there was no need. But he had something that we had not and I could tell from his voice what it meant. He had seen Ralph. He had seen the look on Ralph's face when he'd collected the keys for the car.

Arriving at the hospital, we ran towards the reception desk and were immediately directed along a short corridor and up a flight of stairs. Looking left and right at the top we heard a voice calling our names—*Grandma! Grandpa!*—and then young feet, our Michael, only nine years old, running towards us, arms outstretched, his face bleached with tears.

'*Dusha*,' said Zoya, reaching down to pick him up, and as she did so I looked further along the passageway until I saw a man with a shock of red hair deep in discussion with a doctor and I recognized him as my son-in-law, Ralph. I watched. I didn't move. The doctor was talking. His face was serious. After a moment he extended an arm, placed his hand on Ralph's left shoulder and pursed his lips. There was nothing left to say.

Ralph turned then, sensing the commotion behind him, and our eyes met. He stared through me, his expression telling me everything that I needed to know as he focussed on my face for a long time before recognizing me.

'Ralph,' said Zoya, pushing Michael aside now and running towards him, dropping her handbag on the ground as she did so—when had she even

121

collected it, I wondered?—a hairbrush, clips, a notepad, a pen, some tissues, keys, a purse, a photograph, I remember it all, falling out and splashing across the white tiled floor as if her entire life had suddenly come apart at its centre. 'Ralph,' she shouted, grabbing him by the shoulders. 'Ralph, where is she? Is she all right? Answer me, Ralph! Where is she? Where is my daughter?'

He looked at her and shook his head and in the silence that followed, Michael turned to me, his chin wobbling slightly in terror at the unexpected nature of the emotions that surrounded him. He was wearing a football shirt, the colours of his favourite team, and it occurred to me that I might take him to see a home game soon, if the weather permitted it. He would need to know that he was loved, this boy. That our family was defined by those we had lost.

*   *   *

Please, Mr Jachmenev, she had said and finally I agreed to accompany the woman who had been watching me at the library to Russell Square, where we sat awkwardly on a bench, side by side. It felt strange to me to be sharing such an intimate setting with a woman who wasn't my wife. I wanted to run from the scene, to take no part in it, but I had agreed to hear her out and I would not break my word.

'I'm not trying to compare my suffering with yours,' she said, choosing her words carefully. 'I understand that they're completely different things. But please, Mr Jachmenev, you must believe me when I tell you how sorry I am. I don't think I have the words to express the remorse that I feel.'

I was pleased by the activity that surrounded us, for the noise and hum of conversation permitted me to pay a little less than my full attention to her. In fact, as she spoke I was half listening to a young couple seated only about ten feet away from us, engaged in a heated debate about the nature of their relationship, which was, I gathered, unstable.

'The police told me that I shouldn't contact you,' continued Mrs Elliott, for that was the name of the lady who had knocked down and killed my daughter on the Albert Bridge Road several months before. 'But I had to. It just didn't feel right to say nothing. I felt I had to find you and speak to you both and make some sort of apology. I hope I didn't do wrong. I certainly don't want to make things any worse for you than they already are.'

'Speak to us both?' I asked, picking up on that phrase as I turned to her and frowned. 'I don't understand.'

'To you and your wife, I mean.'

'But I'm the only one here,' I said. 'You came to see me.'

'Yes, I thought that was for the best,' she replied, looking down at her hands. I could see how nervous she was by the way she kept twisting and turning a pair of gloves between her fingers, an action that put me immediately in mind of David Frasier on the evening that he had stood outside our front door in a state of anxiety. The gloves were clearly an expensive pair. Her coat, too, was of a very fine quality. I wondered who this woman

123

was, how she had come into her money. Whether she had earned it, inherited it, married it. The police, of course, had been willing to tell me anything that I wanted to know and I think it surprised them that I wanted to know nothing. I needed to know nothing. What possible difference would knowledge have made, after all? Arina would still be dead. Nothing was going to change that.

'I thought if I saw you first, and talked to you, and explained to you how I felt,' she continued, 'then perhaps you could talk to your wife and I could meet her too. To apologize to her.'

'Ah,' I said, nodding my head and allowing a gentle sigh to escape my lips. 'I understand now. It's interesting to me, Mrs Elliott, the different way that people have approached my wife and me over these last few months.'

'Interesting?'

'There's a curious feeling among people that somehow it's worse for the mother than it is for the father. That the grief is somehow more intense. People ask me constantly how Zoya is holding up, as if I am my wife's doctor and not my daughter's father, but I don't believe they ever ask the same thing of her about me. I could be wrong, of course, but—'

'No, Mr Jachmenev,' she said quickly, shaking her head. 'No, you misunderstand me. I didn't mean to suggest that—'

'And even now, you come to talk to me first, to lay the groundwork for the much more difficult campaign ahead, as you see it. Of course, I don't think for a moment that it was easy for you to initiate this conversation. I admire you for it, if I'm

124

honest, but it's depressing that you think that I feel any differently about Arina's loss than my wife does. That her death is any less painful to me.'

She nodded and opened her mouth to speak, thought better of it and looked away. I said nothing for a moment, wanting her to think about what I had said. To my left, the young man was telling his companion that she needed to relax, that what did it matter, it had been a party, he had been drunk, she knew that he loved her really, and she was retaliating by calling him a series of vulgar names, each one more repugnant than the last. If her intention was to make him feel chastened, then she was failing, for he was laughing in mock-horror, an action which only exacerbated her wrath. I wondered why they felt the need for the world to overhear their quarrel. If, like film stars, their passion was only real when it had witnesses.

'I'm a mother too, Mr Jachmenev,' said Mrs Elliott after a few moments. 'I suppose it's only natural that I would immediately consider the feelings of another mother in this circumstance. But I certainly didn't mean to diminish your suffering.'

'You're a parent,' I said, countering her remark, but I softened a little nonetheless. It was easy to see how much pain this woman was in. I was in terrible pain too, but that could never be alleviated. It would be so easy for me to lessen her anguish, to assuage her conscience even by a small amount. It would be a gesture of infinite kindness and I wondered whether I was capable of it. 'How many children do you have?' I asked after a moment.

'Three,' she said, sounding pleased to be asked.

Of course she was; they all want to be asked about their children. *They*, now, not *we*. 'Two boys at university. A girl still at school.'

'Do you mind if I ask their names?'

'Not at all,' she said, surprised perhaps by the friendliness of the question. 'My eldest boy is John, that was my husband's name. Then Daniel. And the girl is Beth.'

'*Was* your husband's name?' I asked, turning to face her now, having picked up immediately on the tense.

'Yes, I was widowed four years ago.'

'He must have been quite young,' I said, for she herself was only in her mid-forties.

'Yes, he was. He died a week before his forty-ninth birthday. A heart attack. It was entirely unexpected.' She shrugged her shoulders and looked into the distance, lost now for a moment in her own grief and memories, and I glanced around the park, wondering how many of the people gathered there were suffering similar pain. The girl to my left was suggesting to the boy a variety of things he could do to himself, none of which sounded particularly pleasant, and he was trying to prevent her from standing up and leaving. I wished they would lower their tedious voices; they bored me intensely.

'Can I ask you about your daughter?' she asked me then and I felt my body grow a little more rigid at the audacity of her question. 'Of course, if you'd rather I didn't—'

'No,' I said quickly. 'No, I don't mind. What would you like to know?'

'She was a teacher, wasn't she?'

'Yes,' I said.

126

'What did she teach?'

'English and history,' I replied, smiling a little at how proud I had been that she had chosen such impractical subjects. 'She had other ideas though. She planned on being a writer.'

'Really?' asked Mrs Elliott. 'What did she write?'

'Poems when she was younger,' I said. 'They weren't very good, to be truthful. Then stories when she was older, which were much better. She published two, you know. One in a small anthology, the other in the *Express*.'

'I didn't know that,' she replied, shaking her head.

'Why would you? It's not the sort of thing that the police would tell you.'

'No,' she said, her jaw setting a little at my use of that terrible word.

'She was writing a novel when she died,' I continued. 'She had almost finished it.'

And now I must admit my own remorse at what I was doing to this woman, for not a word of this was true. Arina had never written any poems that I knew of. Nor had she published any stories or attempted to write a novel. That was not her calling at all. It was as if by inventing this creative side to her character I was suggesting that a great potential had been extinguished too soon, that she had killed more than just a person, but also all the gifts that she might have offered the world over the course of her lifetime. 'There was already some interest, I believe,' I continued, lost in the embellishment of my own lie. 'A publisher had read her stories and wanted to see more.'

'What was it about?' she asked me.

'How do you mean?

'The novel that she was writing. Did you read it?'

'Some of it,' I said quietly. 'It was a story of guilt. And of blame. Misplaced blame.'

'Did she have a title for the book?'

'Yes.'

'Can I ask what it was?'

'*The House of Special Purpose*,' I replied without any hesitation, frightened by how many truths my lie was placing before her, but Mrs Elliott said nothing, simply turned away from me now, uncomfortable with where our conversation had led us. I felt awkward too and knew that I could not continue with this charade for any longer.

'You must understand, Mrs Elliott,' I said, 'that I do not blame you entirely for what happened. And I certainly don't . . . I don't hate you, if that's what you're thinking. Arina ran out on the road, I am told. She should have looked. It doesn't matter, does it? None of it will bring her back. It was brave of you to come to see me, and I appreciate it. Truly, I do. But you cannot see my wife.'

'But Mr Jachmenev—'

'No,' I said firmly, bringing my hand down on my knee, like a judge descending his gavel upon the courtroom desk. 'That is how it must be, I'm afraid. I will tell Zoya that I have seen you, of course. I will let her know of your great remorse. But there can be no contact between the two of you. It would be too much for her.'

'But maybe if I—'

'Mrs Elliott, you're not listening to me,' I insisted, my temper growing a little more. 'What you are asking for is impossible and selfish. You wish to see us both, to have our forgiveness, so that in time you may move past this terrible event and, if not forget it, then at least learn to live with it, but we will not be able to do that, and it is no concern of ours how you manage to confront your own response to this accident. Yes, Mrs Elliott, I know it was an accident. And if it is of help to you, then yes, I forgive you for what you have done. But please. Do not seek me out again. And do not try to find my wife. She could not cope with meeting you, do you understand that?'

She nodded and started to cry a little but I thought no, this is not the moment where I become the protector. If she has tears, let her shed them. If she is in pain, then let her feel it. Let her children talk to her later and tell her the things that she needs to hear in order to find her way through these dark days. She still has hers, after all.

It was time for me to go home.

*   *   *

'You think it's your fault, don't you?'

Zoya turned to look at me, her expression a mixture of disbelief and antagonism. 'What do you mean?' she asked. 'I think *what*'s my fault?'

'You forget,' I said. 'I know you better than anyone. I can tell what you're thinking.'

More than six months after Arina's death and the normal routines of our lives had begun to reassert themselves, as if nothing untoward had ever happened. Our son-in-law, Ralph, had returned to work and was doing all that he could to keep his grief at bay for Michael's sake. The boy still cried every day and spoke about his mother as if he believed that we were somehow keeping her from him; her loss, the incomprehensibility of her death, was a matter with which he could not yet come to terms. There were sixty-two years between Michael and me, and yet we might have been twins for the similitude of our emotions.

We had just returned from our son-in-law's house, where Zoya and Ralph had argued about the boy. She wanted him to spend more nights with us, but Ralph didn't want him to sleep outside of his own bed just yet. In the past, he had been accustomed to staying over, to sleeping in the room that had been his mother's as she grew up, but that arrangement had come to an end immediately after her death. It wasn't that Ralph was trying to keep Michael from us, he simply didn't want to be without him. I understood this. I thought it entirely reasonable. For I knew what it was to want my child with me.

'Of course it's my fault,' said Zoya. 'And you blame me for it too, I know you do. If you don't, you're a fool.'

'I blame you for nothing,' I shouted, stepping towards her now and turning her around to face me. There was a hardness to her expression, a look that had hidden itself away for many years but had reappeared now, since Arina had been killed, that told me exactly what she was thinking. 'Do you think I hold you responsible for our daughter's death? The idea is madness. I hold you responsible for one thing only. Her life!'

'Why are you saying this to me?' she asked, her voice betraying how close she was to tears.

'Because you've always felt it and it has overshadowed our lives. And you are wrong, Zoya, can't you see that? You could not be more wrong to feel this way. Remember, I've seen how you've reacted every time. When Leo died—'

'Years ago, Georgy!'

'When we lost friends in the Blitz.'

'Everyone lost friends then, didn't they?' she shouted. 'You think I held myself responsible?'

'And every time you miscarried. I saw it then.'

'Georgy . . . please,' she said, her voice straining. I wasn't trying to hurt her, you understand, but it came from my heart. It needed to be said.

'And now Arina,' I continued. 'Now you think that her death is because of—'

'Stop it!' she shouted, rushing towards me, her hands twisted into fists that beat against my chest. 'Can't you stop it for even a moment? Why do you think I need to be reminded of these things? Leo, the babies, our friends, our daughter . . . yes, they're all gone, every one of them. What good does it do to talk of them?'

I sat down and ran my hand across my face in desperation. I loved my wife very much, but there had always been an unspoken thread of torment that had run through our lives. Her pain, her memories, were so much a part of her that she had very little room for anyone else's; even mine.

'There are things in life that it is impossible to ignore,' she said after a few silent minutes, huddled in an armchair beside me, her arms wrapped around her body defensively, her face as white as the snow at Livadia. 'There are coincidences . . . too many of them to justify our calling them that. I am a talisman for unhappiness, Georgy. That is what I am. I have brought nothing but misery throughout my life for the people who loved me. Nothing but pain. It's my fault that so many of them are dead, I know this is true.

Perhaps I should have died too when I was a child. Perhaps?' she added, laughing bitterly and shaking her head. 'What am I saying? Of course I should have. It was my destiny.'

'But that's madness,' I said, sitting up and trying to take her hand in mine, but she pulled away from me, as if my very touch would set her aflame. 'And what about me, Zoya? You've brought none of those things into my life.'

'Death, no. But suffering? Misery? Anguish? You don't think I've inflicted any of these things on you?'

'Of course I don't,' I said, desperate to reassure her. 'Look at us, Zoya. We've been married for more than fifty years. We've been happy. *I*'ve been happy.' I stared at her, pleading with her to allow my words to soften her distress. 'Haven't you?' I asked, almost afraid to hear her answer and watch our lives tumble apart around us.

She sighed, but finally nodded. 'Yes,' she said. 'You know I have. But this thing that has happened—to Arina, I mean—it's too much for me. It's one too many tragedies. I can't allow any more in my life. No more, Georgy.'

'What do you mean?' I asked.

'I'm sixty-nine years old,' she said with a half-smile. 'And I've had enough. I don't . . . Georgy, I don't enjoy my life any more. I never have, if I am honest. I don't want it. I don't want any more of it. Can you understand that?'

She stood up and looked at me with such determination on her face that it scared me.

'Zoya,' I said, 'what are you talking about? You can't speak like this, it's—'

'Oh, I don't mean what you think,' she said,

shaking her head. 'Not this time, I promise you. I just mean that when the end comes, and it will come soon, I won't be sorry about it. Enough is enough, Georgy, can't you see that? Don't you ever feel the same way? Just look at this life that I have lived, that we have lived together. Think about it. How have we even survived this long?' She shook her head and exhaled a long sigh, as if the answer was very simple and obvious. 'I want it to end, Georgy,' she told me. 'That's all. I just want it to end.'

The Prince of Mogilev

For weeks after I arrived in St Petersburg, I found my thoughts drifting back to Kashin, to the family I had left behind and the friend whose death weighed heavy on my conscience. At nights, lying on my thin bunk, Kolek's face appeared before me, his eyes bulging from his head, his throat bruised and scarred from the ropes. I imagined his terror as the guards led him towards the trees where the noose had been hung; for all his bravado, I could not imagine that he went to his death with anything other than fear in his heart and regret for the decades not lived. I prayed that he did not blame me too much; regardless, it could scarcely compare with how much I blamed myself.

And when I was not thinking of Kolek, it was my family who dominated my thoughts, particularly my sister Asya, who would have given anything to be living where I was now. Indeed, it was Asya who I was thinking of late one afternoon when I first encountered the great Reading Room of the Winter Palace. The doors were open and I turned, intending to leave, but an instinct made me change my mind and I stepped inside, where I found myself alone in the serenity of a library for the first time in my life.

Three walls were filled from floor to ceiling with books and a ladder was attached to each on a rail so that the browser could push himself across the floor. In the centre stood a heavy oak table, on which were placed two large volumes—open, to a series of maps. Great leather armchairs were situated at different points in the room and I imagined myself sitting there for an afternoon, lost in reading. I had never read a book in my entire life, of course, but they called to me, a whisper from the constant bindings, and I reached for one after the other, scanning the title pages, reading opening paragraphs as well as I could, placing my discarded volumes on the table behind me without a thought.

So lost was I in my examination that I failed to hear the door open behind me, and only as the heavy boots marched across the floor did I blink back into the moment and realize that I was not alone. I turned, throwing the book that I was holding in the air in surprise. It fell to the floor, crashing open at my feet, the noise echoing around the walls, while I dropped to my knees and bowed my head in the presence of the anointed one.

'Your Majesty,' I said, not daring to look up. 'Your Majesty, I must offer my sincere apologies. I was lost, you see, and—'

'Stand up, Georgy Daniilovich,' said the Tsar, and I stood slowly. Not long before, I had been grieving for my family; now I was in dread that I would be sent back to them. 'Look at me.'

I lifted my head slowly and our eyes met. I could feel my cheeks begin to redden but he looked neither angry nor displeased.

'What are you doing here anyway?' he asked me.

'I lost my way,' I said. 'I hadn't intended coming in here, but when I saw them—'

'The books?'

'Yes, sir. I was interested, that's all. I wanted to see what they contained.'

He breathed heavily for a moment, as if deciding how best to deal with this situation, before sighing and stepping away from me, walking behind the oak table and looking down at the volumes of maps, turning their pages and not looking at me as he spoke.

'I wouldn't have taken you for a reader,' he said quietly.

'I'm not, sir,' I explained. 'That is, I never have been.'

'But you *can* read?'

'Yes, sir.'

'Who taught you, your father?'

I shook my head. 'No, sir. My father would not have known how. It was my sister, Asya. She had some books she bought from a stall. She taught me my letters—most of them anyway.'

'I see,' he said. 'And who taught her?'

I thought about it, but was forced to admit that I did not know. Perhaps in her desire to escape our home village she had simply educated herself in order that she could, for the length of a story's few pages, escape to brighter worlds.

'But you liked it?' asked the Tsar. 'I mean to say,

135

something drew you in here.'

I looked around the room and thought for a moment, before offering an honest answer. 'There's something . . . interesting, yes, sir,' I said. 'My sister would tell me stories. I enjoyed hearing them. I thought I might find some here that would recall her to me.'

'I expect you're starting to miss your family,' said the Tsar, stepping back now towards the window, so that the soft light shining through illuminated him on all sides. 'I know that I miss my own when I am away from them for any length of time.'

'I haven't had any time to think of them, sir,' I replied. 'I've been trying to work as hard as I might. With Count Charnetsky, I mean. And the rest of my time I am honoured to spend with the Tsarevich.'

He smiled when I mentioned his son and nodded his head. 'Yes, indeed,' he said. 'And you are getting along well, the two of you?'

'Yes, sir,' I replied. 'Very well.'

'He seems to like you. I've asked him about you.'

'I'm gratified to hear it, sir.'

He nodded and looked away, his attention drawn back to the maps for a moment, and he marched towards them, stroking his beard as he looked down. 'These drawings,' he muttered. 'It's all in these drawings, do you realize that, Georgy? The land. The borders. The ports. How to win. If only I could see it. But I can't *see* it,' he hissed, more to himself than to me. I decided that I should leave him to his studies so I stepped back, never turning my back on him, as I made for the door.

'Perhaps we should get you some lessons,' he said loudly before I could take my leave.

136

'Lessons, sir?'

'Improve your reading. These books are to be read, I tell all the staff that they may read as they will, providing they take care of the volumes and return them in the condition that they found them. Would you like that, Georgy?'

I couldn't think for a moment whether I would or wouldn't, but didn't like to disappoint him so gave the answer that I believed he desired. 'Yes, Your Majesty,' I said. 'I'd like that very much.'

'Well, I'll see that the Count sends you to some of the classes attended by the boys in the Corps of Pages. If you are to spend so much time with Alexei, it's only right that you should be educated. You may leave now,' he said, dismissing me.

I turned and left the room, closing the door behind me, little knowing that a lifetime surrounded by books was initiated by that one conversation with the Tsar.

*   *   *

Before I exchanged a single word with the Grand Duchess Anastasia Nicolaevna, I kissed her.

I had seen her on three occasions previously, once at the chestnut stand by the banks of the Neva, and again later that night as I had waited to be received by the Tsar on my first evening at the Winter Palace, when I had looked out across the banks of the river and watched as the four Grand Duchesses emerged from their pleasure boat.

The third occasion came two days after that, when I was returning from an afternoon of training with the Leib Guard. Exhausted, worried that I would never be able to compete with their levels of energy or strength and would quickly be despatched back to Kashin, I was returning to my room in the late afternoon and lost my way in the labyrinth of the palace, opening a door which I believed would lead me to my corridor, but which led instead into a type of schoolroom that I entered and marched halfway across before lifting my tired eyes from the ground and realizing my mistake.

'Can I help you, young man?' said a voice from my left and I turned to see Monsieur Gilliard, the Swiss tutor to the Tsar's daughters, standing behind his desk and staring at me with a mixture of irritation and amusement.

'I apologize, sir,' I said quickly, blushing a little at my foolishness. 'I thought the door led towards my room.'

'Well, as you can see,' he replied, spreading his arms wide to indicate the maps and portraits which covered the walls, portraits of the famous novelists and great musicians who formed a part of the girls' studies, 'it does not.'

'No, sir,' I replied, offering him a polite bow before turning around again. As I did so I noticed the four sisters seated in two rows behind individual desks, staring at me with a mixture of curiosity and boredom. This was the first time that I had stood before them—they had barely noticed me at the chestnut stand—and I felt a little self-conscious, but also greatly privileged to be in their presence. It was quite a thing for a *moujik* like me to be in a room with the daughters of the Tsar; an indescribable honour. The eldest, Olga, looked up from her book with an expression of pity on her face.

'He looks worn out, Monsieur Gilliard,' she remarked. 'He's only been here a few days and he's already exhausted.'

'I am quite well, thank you, Your Highness,' I said, bowing deeply.

'He's the one who was shot in the shoulder, isn't he?' asked her younger sister, Tatiana, a tall, elegant girl with her mother's hair and grey eyes.

'No, that can't be him, I heard it was someone terribly handsome who saved Cousin Nicholas's life,' giggled the third sister, Marie, and I shot her a look of irritation, for I might have still been overawed by my new life at the royal palace, but I was far too tired from jousting and fencing and sparring with Count Charnetsky's men to allow myself to be bullied by a group of girls, regardless of their exalted status.

'It is him,' said a quieter voice and I turned to see the Grand Duchess Anastasia looking at me. She was almost fifteen years old then, a year or so younger than I, with bright-blue eyes and a smile that restored my vigour immediately.

'How do *you* know that, *Shvipsik*?' asked Marie, turning on her younger sister, who showed no sign of embarrassment or self-consciousness.

'Because you're right,' she said with a shrug. 'I heard the same thing. A handsome young man saved our cousin's life. His name was Georgy. It must be him.'

The other girls dissolved in giggles, hooting with laughter at the brazen nature of her remark, but she and I continued to stare at each other and in a moment I saw the corners of her mouth turn up a little and a smile appear on her face and, to my amazement, I found the impertinence to offer the same compliment in return.

'Our sister is in love,' cried Tatiana and at that, Monsieur Gilliard rapped the wooden edge of his chalkboard eraser on the desk in front of him, which made both Anastasia and me jump, breaking the connection which we had made with each other, and I turned to look at the teacher in embarrassment.

'I do apologize, sir,' I said quickly. 'I have disturbed your lesson.'

'You have indeed, young man. You have an opinion to share on the actions of Count Vronsky?'

I stared at him in surprise. 'I do not,' I said. 'I have never met the gentleman.'

'The infidelity of Stepan Arkadyvich, then? Levin's search for fulfilment? Perhaps you would like to comment on Alexei Alexandrovich's reaction in the face of his wife's betrayal?'

I had no idea what he was referring to, but seeing the novel that was open on each of the Grand Duchesses' desks, I suspected that these were not real people at all, but characters in a fiction. I glanced towards Anastasia, who was glaring at her teacher with a look of disappointment on her face.

'He doesn't understand, does he?' said Tatiana, perhaps noticing how I seemed unable to decide what I should do next. 'Is he a simpleton, do you think?'

'Be quiet, Tatiana,' snapped Anastasia, turning around to look at her sister with an expression of utter contempt. 'He's lost, that's all.'

'It's true,' I said, turning to Monsieur Gilliard, not daring to address the Grand Duchess directly. 'I am lost.'

'Well you will not find yourself in here,' he

replied, little knowing how untrue that statement was. 'Please leave.'

I nodded quickly and offered another quick bow before rushing to the door. Turning around as I closed it behind me, I caught Anastasia's eye once again. She was still watching me and I detected a flush of colour in her cheeks. In my vanity, I wondered whether she might not be able to concentrate any further on her lesson; I knew that my own evening was lost.

*   *   *

I spent the following afternoon in training with the soldiers once again. Count Charnetsky, who was entirely opposed to my appointment and lost no opportunity to make his displeasure known, had insisted that I spend a month learning the most basic skills which his men had spent years acquiring, and the need to be taught quickly was leaving me drained and weakened by the end of every day. I had spent just short of seven hours astride an efficient charger, learning how to control her with my left hand while brandishing a pistol in my right to fell a potential assassin, and as I passed through Palace Square, my tired legs and trembling arms were driving me towards nothing other than the comfort of my bed.

Pausing in the small covered atrium that acted as a passage between the square and the palace, I looked ahead at the garden that opened up before me. The trees that lined the short footpath towards the entry way were stripped of their leaves and, despite the frost in the air, I could see the Tsar's youngest daughter, her back turned to me, sitting by the edge of the central fountain, lost in thought, as still as one of the alabaster statues which lined the staircases and vestibules of the palace itself.

Sensing me, perhaps, her shoulders lowered as she sat a little more erect and then, cautiously, without moving her body, she turned her head to the left so that I could observe her in profile. Pink spheres blossomed in her cheeks, her lips parted, her hands lifted from the fountain's surround as if nervous for action and then settled where they lay. I could see the flutter of her perfect eyelashes in the cold air; I could feel every movement of her body.

And beneath my breath I whispered her name.

Anastasia.

She turned at that moment—impossible to have heard me, but she knew—her body remaining rigid but her face seeking my own. The dark-blue cloak she wore slipped a little around her shoulders and she gathered it around her, standing up then and walking towards me. Nervous, I found myself retreating behind one of the twelve six-pillared columns which surrounded the quadrangle and watched as she strode purposefully towards me, her eyes fixed on mine.

I knew not what to say or do while, standing before me, she stared at me with a mixture of desire and uncertainty; we had yet to exchange even a word in conversation. Her small pink tongue extended a little as she ran it along the surface of her lips, enduring the chilly frost of the air for a moment before returning to the warm cavern of her mouth. How enticing that soft tongue seemed to me. How it aroused my imagination into thoughts that filled me with a mixture of shame and excitement.

I remained rooted to where I stood, swallowing nervously, wanting her desperately. By rights, I should have offered her a deep bow and a greeting before continuing on my way, but I could not bring myself to behave as protocol demanded. Instead I stepped further back into the darkness of the colonnade, watching her, never letting my gaze slip away from her face as she approached me. My mouth was dry and lost for words. We faced each other silently until another member of the Leib Guard, patrolling the surround of Palace Square, raced past Anastasia on his charger so unexpectedly that she jumped and let out a small scream, afraid of being run down beneath the horse's hooves, and leapt forward into my arms.

And at that moment, like two lovers engaged upon the most graceful of dances, I spun her around so that her back was pressed against the tall oak door that loomed behind us. We stood together in the shadows, a place where we could be observed by no one, and stared into each other's eyes until I saw hers begin to close and I leaned forward and pressed my cold, chapped lips against the warmth of her soft, rose-coloured mouth. My arms wrapped themselves around her, one pressing firmly against her back, the other becoming lost in the fine softness of her auburn hair.

I could think of nothing at that moment other than how much I wanted her. That we had yet to exchange a word did not matter at all. Nor did the fact that she was a Grand Duchess, a daughter of the Imperial blood, while I was a mere servant, a *moujik* come to offer some small degree of security to her younger brother. I didn't care whether

143

anyone could see us; I knew that she wanted this as much as I did. We kissed for I know not how long and then, separating only a moment for breath, she placed a hand against my chest and looked at me, half frightened, half intoxicated, before turning away and looking at the ground, shaking her head as if she could not even begin to understand how she had been so bold.

'I'm sorry,' I said, my first words to her.

'For what?' she asked.

'You're right,' I replied, shrugging my shoulders. 'I'm not sorry at all.'

She hesitated for only a moment and then smiled at me. 'Neither am I,' she said.

We looked at each other and I felt ashamed that I didn't know what might be expected of me next.

'I have to go in,' she said. 'We dine soon.'

'Your Highness,' I said, reaching for her hand. I struggled with a sentence, having no clue what it was that I intended to say to her, only that I wanted to keep her here with me a little longer.

'Please,' she said, shaking her head. 'My name is Anastasia. And I can call you Georgy?'

'Yes.'

'I like that name.'

'It means *farmer*,' I replied with an embarrassed shrug and she smiled.

'Is that what you are?' she asked me. 'What you were?'

'It's what my father is.'

'And you,' she said quietly. 'What are you?'

I thought about it; I had never asked myself such a question before, but now, standing in the freezing cold beneath the colonnades with this girl before me, there seemed to be only one truthful

144

answer.

'I'm yours,' I said.

*   *   *

I was still a newcomer to the royal household when I boarded the Imperial train to travel towards Mogilev, the small Ukrainian town near the Black Sea where our Russian army headquarters were located. Seated opposite me, excited by the prospect of leaving behind the closeted world of the palace for the more rugged environment of a military base, was an eleven-year-old boy, Alexei Nicolaievich, the Heir, Tsarevich and Grand Duke of the House of Romanov.

At moments like this, it still seemed very strange for me to consider how dramatically my life had altered. Just over a month before, I had been a *moujik* like any other, chopping wood in Kashin, sleeping on a rough floor, starving and exhausted, dreading the freezing cold winter that would shortly arrive to stifle any chance of happiness. Now I was clothed in the tight-fitting uniform of the Leib Guard, preparing for a warm and comfortable journey, with the certainty of a lavish lunch and dinner to come and with God's anointed one sitting only a few feet away from me.

It was my first time to travel on the Imperial train and while I had started to grow more accustomed to extravagance and conspicuous consumption since arriving in St Petersburg, the opulence of my surroundings still had the power to astonish me. There were ten carriages in all, including a saloon, a kitchen, private studies for the Tsar and Tsaritsa, as well as apartments for each of the children, the servants and the luggage. A second, smaller train followed an hour behind and was populated by an extensive retinue of advisers and servants. Typically, the lead train held only the Imperial family, along with two doctors, three chefs, a small army of bodyguards and whichever of his counsellors the Tsar chose to honour with an invitation. As I had been by the Tsarevich's side for three weeks now as his protector and confidant, my place on the train was a matter of protocol.

Naturally, every floor, wall and ceiling was covered with the most lavish materials that the train's designers could lay their hands on. The walls were constructed from Indian teak, with stamped leather upholstery and a golden silk inlay. Beneath our feet, a rich, soft carpet ran the length of the carriages, while every item of furniture was built from the finest beech or satinwood and covered with a sparkling English cretonne, set with carvings or gilding. It was as if the entire Winter Palace had been transported on to a mobile platform so that no one travelling on board would ever have to consider that beyond our windows lay towns and villages where the people lived in abject poverty and were growing increasingly disillusioned by their Tsar.

'I'm almost afraid to move in case I damage something,' I remarked to the Tsarevich as we swept past the labourers' fields and the small hamlets, where the people came out to wave and cheer, although they looked miserable as they did so, their lips curled with distaste, their bodies gaunt from lack of food. There were almost no young men among their number, of course; most of them were either dead, in hiding, or fighting for the continuation of our curious way of life at the Front.

'How do you mean, Georgy?' he asked.

'Well, it's so magnificent,' I said, looking around at the bright-blue walls and the set of silks which hung on either side of the windows. 'Don't you realize it?'

'Aren't all trains like this?' he asked, looking across at me in surprise.

'No, Alexei,' I replied with a smile, for what was astonishing to me was quotidian life to the son of the Tsar. 'No, this one is special.'

'My grandfather built it,' he told me with the air of someone who assumes that everyone's grandfather was a great man. 'Alexander III. He had a great fascination with the railways, I am told.'

'There's only one thing I don't understand,' I said. 'The speed at which it travels.'

'Why, what's wrong with it?'

'It's just ... I don't know much about these things, of course, but surely a train such as this can travel much faster than it does?' I made the remark because ever since we had left St Petersburg, the train had been moving at no more than about twenty-five miles an hour. It was maintaining that speed almost perfectly, neither growing faster nor slower as the voyage continued, which made the journey extremely smooth but slightly frustrating too. 'I've known horses who could outstrip this train.'

'It always travels this slow,' he explained. 'When I'm on board, that is. Mother says that we can't risk any sudden jolts.'

'Anyone would think you were made of

porcelain,' I said, forgetting my place for a moment and regretting my words immediately, for he looked across at me, narrowing his eyes in disapproval and offering an expression that made my blood run cold, and I thought that yes, this boy could be Tsar one day. 'I'm sorry, sir,' I added after a moment, but he appeared to have already forgotten my transgression and had returned to his book, a volume on the history of the Russian army which his father had given him several nights before and which had been occupying his attentions ever since. He was a highly intelligent boy, I had already realized that, and cared as much for his reading as he did for the outdoor activities from which his protective parents were constantly trying to shield him.

My first introduction to the Tsarevich had taken place the morning after my arrival at the Winter Palace and I had liked him immediately. Although pale and dark-eyed, he had a confidence about him which I put down to the fact that he commanded the attention of everyone who passed through his life. He extended his hand to greet me and I shook it proudly, bowing my head out of respect as I introduced myself.

'And you are to be my new bodyguard,' he said quietly.

I immediately looked across at Count Charnetsky, who had delivered me into the royal presence, and who nodded quickly in assent. 'Yes, sir,' I said. 'But I hope I will also be your friend.'

His brow furrowed a little at the word, as if it meant nothing to him, and he considered this for a moment before speaking again.

'My last bodyguard ran away with one of the

cooks to get married, did you know that?'

I shook my head and gave a small laugh, amused by how seriously he took the offence. He might as well have said that he had tried to smother him in his sleep. 'No, sir,' I replied. 'No, I didn't.'

'I imagine that they must have been terribly in love to betray such a position, but it was an inappropriate match, for he was a cousin of Prince Hagurov and she was a reconstituted whore. Their families must feel great shame.'

'Yes, sir,' I agreed, hesitating for only a moment, wondering whether these were his own words or phrases he had overheard from his elders and which he was passing along now as his own. The frown on his face, however, suggested to me that he had been close to this bodyguard and regretted his loss.

'My father believes strongly in the propriety of an equitable marriage,' he continued. 'He won't countenance anyone who makes a match below their station. Before him, there was a fellow whom I did not like at all. His breath smelled, for one thing. And he could not control his bodily functions. I find such things vulgar, don't you?'

'I suppose so,' I said, anxious not to disagree with him.

'Although,' he continued, biting his lip a little as he considered the matter, 'sometimes I found it funny too. Like when Uncle Willy came to stay with Father and he made terrible noises when my sisters and I were brought in to say hello the following morning. That was comical, actually. But he was dismissed for it. The bodyguard, I mean. Not my uncle.'

'It does not sound like very appropriate

149

behaviour, Your Highness,' I remarked, shocked to think that anyone could refer to Kaiser Wilhelm, with whom our country was at war, as Uncle Willy.

'No, it wasn't. It cheapened him in my eyes, but my sisters and I were told to ignore his vulgarity. And then there was the bodyguard before him. I liked him very much.'

'And what happened to him?' I asked, expecting another curious story of illicit love affairs or unpleasant personal habits.

'He was killed,' replied Alexei without emotion. 'It was at Tsarskoe Selo. An assassin threw a bomb at the carriage I was riding in, but the driver saw it in time and drove on before it could land on my lap. This bodyguard was seated in the carriage directly behind us and it landed on him instead. It blew him up.'

'That's terrible,' I said, appalled by the violence of it and suddenly aware of how my own life might be in similar peril while I looked after such an illustrious charge.

'Yes,' he agreed. 'Although Father said that he would have been proud to have died like that. In the service of Russia, that is. After all, it would have been much worse if I had died.'

Coming from any other child, the remark might have seemed thoughtless and arrogant, but the Tsarevich delivered it with such compassion for the dead man and a thoughtful understanding of his own position that I did not despise him for it.

'Well, I don't plan on eloping, farting or getting blown up,' I said, smiling at him, imagining in my naivety that I could speak plainly, taking into account only his age and not his position. 'So hopefully I shall be here to guard you for some

150

time to come.'

'Jachmenev,' said Count Charnetsky immediately and I turned to look at him, ready to apologize before noticing how the Tsarevich was staring at me, his mouth wide open. I didn't know for a moment whether he was going to burst out laughing or call the other guards to have me hauled away in chains, but finally he simply shook his head, as if the common people were a source of endless interest and amusement to him, and in this manner we began our new roles.

In the weeks that followed, we developed a pleasant informality with each other. He instructed me to call him Alexei, which I was glad to do, as to spend my day referring to an eleven-year-old boy as 'Your Highness' or even 'sir' would have been almost too much for me. He called me Georgy, which he liked because he had once owned a pup by that name, until it had been run over by one of his father's carriages, a fact that I considered a grim portent.

He had his regular pastimes and wherever he went, I went too. In the mornings he attended Mass with his mother and father and then went directly to breakfast and on to private tuition with the Swiss tutor, Monsieur Gilliard. In the afternoons he went outside to the gardens, although I noticed that his parents, busy as they were, kept a close eye on him and he was not permitted to indulge in any activity which might be considered overly strenuous; I put this down to their worry about anything untoward happening to the heir to the throne. In the evenings, he ate dinner with his family, and afterwards he sat with a book, or perhaps we might play backgammon, a game he had taught me on our first evening together and at which I had yet to beat him.

And then there were his four sisters, Olga, Tatiana, Marie and Anastasia, whose rooms he invaded at every opportunity, and whose lives he tormented as much as they loved and fussed over him. As Alexei's bodyguard, I was in the company of the Grand Duchesses throughout the day, but they mostly ignored me, of course.

Except for one, that is, with whom I had fallen in love.

'Forget about the horses,' I remarked to Alexei as I sat there, staring out of the window. '*I* could run faster than this train.'

'Then why don't you, Georgy Daniilovich? I'm sure the driver would stop and let you try.'

I made a face at him and he giggled, a sure sign that he may have been many things—educated, well-spoken, intelligent, the heir to a throne, the future leader of millions—but at his heart he remained what every Russian man had been at some point in his life.

A little boy.

*   *   *

The Tsaritsa, Alexandra Fedorovna, had been opposed to this trip from the very beginning.

Of all the members of the Imperial family, she was the one with whom I had enjoyed the least contact since my arrival in St Petersburg. The Tsar himself was always friendly and personable, even remembering my name most of the time, which I took as a mark of great honour. He suffered greatly over the progress of the war, however, and

152

this was reflected on his face, which was lined and dark-eyed. His days were spent in his study in consultation with his generals, whose company he relished, or with the leaders of the Duma, whose very existence he seemed to loathe. But he never allowed his personal feelings on any given day to spill out into his dealings with those around him. Indeed, whenever I saw him, he always greeted me courteously and asked how I was enjoying my new position. Of course, my awe of him never lessened, but I also found that I was presumptuous enough to like him personally and I took great pride in being near his side.

Alexandra was different. A tall, attractive woman with a sharp nose and enquiring eyes, she considered a room to be empty if it was populated only by servants or guards, and conducted herself at such times, both in action and in conversation, as if she was alone.

'Never talk to her,' I was told late one night by Sergei Stasyovich Polyakov, a member of the Leib Guard with whom I had become friendly owing to the proximity of our quarters, which were adjacent to each other, our beds separated only by a thin wall through which I could hear him snoring in the night. At eighteen years of age, he was my senior by two years but was still one of the youngest members of Count Charnetsky's elite regiment, and I was flattered that he had adopted me as his friend, for he appeared much more worldly and comfortable about the palace than I. 'She would consider it a great mark of disrespect if you tried to engage her in conversation.'

'I never would,' I assured him. 'But sometimes we catch each other's eye in a room and I don't know whether I should greet her or bow.'

'She might catch your eye, Georgy,' he told me, laughing a little, 'but trust me, you don't catch hers. She sees right through people like us. We're ghosts, every one.'

'I am no ghost,' I insisted, surprised to find myself insulted by the charge. 'I'm a man.'

'Yes, yes,' he said, extinguishing half a cigarette on the heel of his boot as he stood up to leave me and placing the unsmoked portion in his jacket pocket for later. 'But you must remember how she was brought up. Her grandmother was the English queen, Victoria. Such an upbringing does not make you a sociable person. She never speaks to any of the servants if she can avoid it.'

Of course, I believed this to be perfectly reasonable. I had no kings or princes in my genealogy—I did not even know the names of some of my grandparents—so why should the Empress of Russia deign to hold discourse with me. Indeed, my trepidation for the Imperial family was such that I never expected any of them to notice me at all, but when I took into account how gracious her husband was, and her son, and her daughters, I wondered at times whether I had done anything to offend her.

I had seen her on my first night in the palace, of course, although I had not at the time realized who the lady kneeling at the prie-dieu with her back to me was. I could still recall how feverishly she prayed, how devoted to her God she seemed to be. And I had not forgotten that terrifying vision of darkness who stood before her, the priest who grinned his malevolent smile in my direction. Although our paths had yet to cross again, his

154

image had haunted me ever since.

The downside of her refusal to notice me was that she thought nothing of behaving in a less than regal fashion while I was in the room, something that embarrassed me on occasion, such as two days before I boarded the Imperial train, when the Tsar had proposed taking Alexei to Army Headquarters in the first place.

'Nicky,' she cried, marching into one of the parlours on the top floor of the palace where the Tsar was lost in thought, working on his papers. I was sitting in a darkened corner, for my charge, Alexei, was stretched out on the ground, playing with a group of toy trains and tracks which he had assembled across the floor. Naturally, the trains were plated with gold and the tracks were made of thin steel. Father and son were ignoring me entirely, of course, and engaged in intermittent conversation with each other. Although he was lost in his work, I had noticed that the Tsar was much more at ease when Alexei was near by and he looked up and grew anxious whenever he left the room for any reason. 'Nicky, tell me I have misunderstood.'

'Misunderstood, my darling?' he asked, looking up from his papers now with tired eyes, and for a moment I wondered whether he had in fact dozed off while he was seated there.

'Anna Vyrubova tells me that you are travelling to Mogilev on Thursday, to visit the army?'

'That's right, Sunny,' he replied, invoking the pet name by which he called her, a name which seemed in complete contrast to her often dark and fragile demeanour. I wondered whether their youth and courtship had been conducted in a very different manner to the one in which they lived now. 'I wrote to Cousin Nicholas last week and said that I would spend a few days there to encourage the troops.'

'Yes, yes,' she said dismissively. 'But you are not taking Alexei with you, surely? I've been told that—'

'I had intended on it, yes,' he said quietly, looking away from her as he said this, as if he was only too aware of the argument that would follow.

'But I can't allow it, Nicky,' she cried.

'Can't allow it?' he asked, a note of amusement entering his gentle tone. 'And why ever not?'

'You know why not. It's not safe there.'

'It's not safe anywhere any more, Sunny, or hadn't you noticed that? Can't you feel the storm clouds gathering around us?' He hesitated for a moment and the ends of his moustache rose a little as he attempted a smile. 'I can.'

She opened her mouth to protest, but that comment appeared to confuse her for a moment and she turned her head instead to look at her son, seated a few feet away on the floor, who was looking up from his trains now and watching the scene unfold before him. She smiled at him for a moment, an anxious smile, and wrung her hands together nervously, before turning back to her husband.

'No, Nicky,' she said. 'No, I insist that he stay here with me. The journey itself will be intolerable. And then who knows whatthe conditions will be like when you get there. And as for the dangers at Stavka, I need hardly tell you! What if a German bomber locates your position?'

'Sunny, we face these dangers every day of the

week,' he said in an exhausted tone. 'And we are nowhere more easy to locate than here in St Petersburg.'

'*You* face those dangers, yes. And *I* face them. But not Alexei. Not our son.'

The Tsar closed his eyes for a moment before standing up and walking to the window, where he looked out across the River Neva.

'He must go,' he said finally, turning around and staring directly into his wife's face. 'I have already told Cousin Nicholas that he will be accompanying me. He will have issued a bulletin to the troops.'

'Then tell him you've changed your mind.'

'I can't do that, Sunny. His presence at Mogilev will offer them great encouragement. You know how low their spirits have been lately, how morale has been slipping away. You read as many of the despatches as I do, I've seen you with them in your parlour. Anything we can do to encourage the men—'

'And you think an eleven-year-old boy can do that?' she asked with a bitter laugh.

'But he is not just any eleven-year-old boy, is he? He is the Tsarevich. He is the heir to the throne of Russia. He is a symbol—'

'Oh, I hate it when you talk about him like that!' she snapped, pacing across the room now in a fury, passing me by as if I was nothing more than a strip of wallpaper or an ornamental sofa. 'He's not a symbol to me. He is my son.'

'Sunny, he is more than that and you know it.'

'But Mother, I want to go,' said a small voice from the carpet, Alexei's, and he stared up at the Tsaritsa with honest, adoring eyes. Her own eyes, I noticed. They were very alike, the two of them.

157

'I know you do, my darling,' she said, leaning down for a moment and kissing his cheek. 'But it's not safe for you there.'

'I'll be careful,' he said. 'I promise you.'

'Your promises are all well and good,' she replied. 'But what if you should trip over? What if a bomb explodes near by and you fall? Or, God forbid, if a bomb should go off where you are?'

I felt a desperate urge to shake my head and sigh, thinking her the most over-protective of mothers. What if he should fall over? What a ludicrous thought, I decided. He was eleven years old. He should be falling over a dozen times a day. Yes, and picking himself up again.

'Sunny, the boy needs to be exposed to the real world,' said the Tsar, his voice growing more firm now as if he was resolved in his decision and would allow no further debate. 'All his life he has been cosseted in palaces and wrapped in cotton wool. Think of this: what if something should happen to me tomorrow and he had to take my place? He knows nothing of what it is to be Tsar. I barely knew anything of it myself when our dear father was taken from us, and I was a man of twenty-six. What hope would Alexei have in such circumstances? He spends all his life here, with you and the girls. It is time he learned something of his responsibilities.'

'But the danger, Nicky,' she implored, rushing to her husband now and taking his hands in hers. 'You must be aware of it. I have consulted on this most carefully. I asked Father Gregory what he thinks of the plan before I even came to you on it. So you see, I have not been as impetuous as you might think. And he told me that it was an ill-conceived idea. That you should reconsider—'

'Father Gregory tells me what I should do?' he cried, appalled. 'Father Gregory thinks he knows how to run this country better than I, is that it? That he knows more about how to be a good father to Alexei than the man who sired him?'

'He is a man of God,' she protested. 'He speaks to one greater than the Tsar.'

'Oh, Sunny!' he roared, turning away from her now, his voice filled with anger and frustration. 'I cannot have this conversation again. I cannot have it every day! It is enough, now, do you hear me? Enough!'

'But Nicky!'

'But nothing! Yes, I am father to Alexei, but I am father to many millions more than him and I have responsibilities towards their protection too. The boy will come with me to Mogilev. He will be taken care of, I assure you. Derevenko and Federov will be with us, so if anything should happen, then the doctors will be there to attend to him. Gilliard will come too, so that he does not fall behind in his studies. There will be soldiers and bodyguards to take care of him. And Georgy will not leave his side from the moment he wakes until the moment he falls asleep again at night.'

'Georgy?' cried the Tsaritsa, her face wrinkling in surprise. 'And who is Georgy, might I ask?'

'My dear, you have met him. Ten or twelve times at least.' He nodded in my direction and I gave a gentle cough and stood up, emerging from the shadows of the room and into her presence. She turned and stared at me as if she had not the least idea what I was doing there or why I was demanding her attention, before turning away

159

from me and marching up to her husband.

'If anything should happen to him, Nicky—'

'Nothing will happen to him.'

'But if anything does, I promise you . . .'

'You promise me what, Sunny?' he asked coldly. 'What is it that you promise me?'

She hesitated now, her face close to his, but said nothing. Defeated, she turned and stared coldly at me before looking down at her son and her face relaxed into happiness again, as if there was no more perfect or beautiful sight to be found anywhere in the world.

'Alexei,' she said in a gentle voice, stretching her hand out. 'Alexei, leave those toys and come with Mother, now won't you? It must be time for your supper.'

He nodded and stood up, took her hand, and followed her as she swept out of the room.

'Well?' asked the Tsar, staring at me, his voice chilly and angry. 'What are you waiting for? Go with him. Keep him safe. That's what you're here for.'

*　　　*　　　*

The Russian Army Headquarters—Stavka—were situated at the top of a hill, in what had been the provincial governor's house before he was forced to relocate in order to ensure that he still had a region to administer when the war was over. A large, sprawling mansion, it was set in several dozen acres of ground, with enough outside huts and cabins dotted around the landscape to accommodate all those military personnel who passed through.

The Grand Duke Nicholas Nicolaievich, who was almost permanently stationed at Stavka, occupied the second-finest bedroom in the building, a quiet chamber on the first floor that overlooked a garden where the governor had tried unsuccessfully to cultivate vegetables in the frozen earth. The best room, however, a large suite on the top floor of the house with an attached office and private bathroom, was kept free at all times for when the Tsar came to inspect the troops. The view from the latticed windows offered a tranquil vision of distant hills, and on quiet evenings it was sometimes possible to hear the water running in the nearby streams, offering the illusion that the world was at peace and we were living innocent, rural lives in the serenity of eastern Belarus. For the duration of our visit, the Tsar shared this room with Alexei, while I was given a bunk in a small ground-floor parlour, which I shared with three other bodyguards, including my friend Sergei Stasyovich, who was one of those whose responsibilities extended solely to the protection of the Tsar.

It was a joy to watch the Tsar and the Tsarevich together during this time, for I had never seen a father and son who revelled in each other's company quite so much. In Kashin, this kind of affection would have been frowned upon by all. The closest we came to any degree of filial warmth was the respect shown by my old friend Kolek towards his father Borys. But there was a natural warmth and friendliness between man and boy that made me envious of their relationship and it was only enhanced when they were removed from the austerity of palace life. I thought of Daniil often at such moments, and with regret.

The Tsar insisted from the start that Alexei not be treated as a child, but as the heir to the Russian throne. No conversation was considered too private or too serious for his ears. No sight was to be withheld from his eyes. When Nicholas rode out to visit the troops, Alexei rode alongside him, with Sergei and me and the other bodyguards following closely behind. At troop inspections, the soldiers would stand to attention and answer their Emperor's questions while the boy would stand quietly by his father's side, polite and attentive, listening to all that was said and digesting every word.

And when we visited the field hospitals, which we did frequently, he did not display any signs of squeamishness or horror, despite the terrible sights which were laid out before us.

At one particular encampment, our entire entourage stepped into a grey-canopied tent where a group of doctors and nurses were tending to perhaps fifty or sixty wounded soldiers, who lay in single beds pressed so close together that it almost seemed as if one long mattress had been stitched together for them to die upon. The smell of blood, decomposing limbs and rotting flesh lingered in the atmosphere and as we entered, I longed to run back outside to the fresh air, my expression contorting in disgust as my throat fought against a natural tendency to gag. The Tsar himself displayed no such signs of revulsion; nor did Alexei allow himself to be overcome by such sensory horrors. Indeed, looking in my direction as I coughed, I perceived a definite expression of disapproval on his face, which embarrassed me, for

162

he was just a boy, five years my junior, and was acting with more dignity than I could summon. Humiliated, I fought against my disgust and followed the Imperial party as they moved from bed to bed.

The Tsar spoke to each of the men in turn, leaning down close to their faces so that their conversation would have a semblance of privacy. Some of the men were able to whisper replies to him, others had neither the strength nor the composure to engage in conversation. All seemed thoroughly overawed that the Tsar himself was among them; perhaps they thought that in their fever they were simply imagining things. It was as if Christ himself had stepped inside the tent and begun to offer a benediction.

Halfway through the room, Alexei let go of the Tsar's hand, stepped across to the beds on the opposite side and began to talk to the men there in imitation of his father. He sat down beside them and I heard him telling them how far he had travelled, all the way from St Petersburg, to be with them that day. How his horse was a charger but we rode at a slow pace in case any danger came to him. He talked of small matters, inconsequential things that must have seemed tremendously important to him, but the patients appreciated the simplicity of his conversation and were charmed by him. As they reached the end of their respective lines, I noticed the Tsar turn to observe his son, who was placing a small icon within the hands of a man who had been blinded by an attack. Turning to one of his generals, he made a quiet remark that I could not hear, and the other man nodded and watched as the Tsarevich completed his

163

conversation.

'Is something the matter, Father?' asked Alexei, turning around and seeing that all eyes were now focussed on him.

'Nothing at all, my son,' said the Tsar, and I was sure that I could hear the words catch in his throat, so overwhelmed was he by the mixed emotion of sympathy for the men's suffering and pride at his son's forbearance. 'But come, it is time to leave now.'

*   *   *

I didn't see the Grand Duke Nicholas Nicolaievich, whose life I had saved and whose appreciation had brought me to my new life, until more than a week after we arrived at Stavka. When we did meet again, he had just returned from the Front, where he had been leading the troops with varying degrees of success, and had come back to Mogilev to consult with his cousin, the Tsar, and to plan the autumn strategy.

I had entered the house from the garden, where Alexei was constructing a fort among some trees, when I saw that great giant of a man marching along the corridor towards me. My initial instinct was to turn and run back outside, for his huge stature and girth suggested a most intimidating presence—almost more intimidating than the Tsar himself—but it was too late to make my escape, for he had seen me and was raising his hand in greeting.

'Jachmenev,' he roared as he came closer, practically blocking out the sunlight from the open doors. 'It is you, isn't it?'

164

'It is, sir,' I admitted, offering him a low, respectful bow. 'It's nice to see you again.'

'Is it?' he asked, sounding surprised. 'Well, I'm glad to hear it. So here you are then,' he added, looking me up and down to decide whether he still approved of me or not. 'I thought it might work out. I said to Cousin Nicky, there's a boy I met in this little shithole of a village, a very brave lad. Not much to look at it, it's true. Could do with a few extra inches of height and a few more pounds of muscle, but not a bad fellow all the same. Might be exactly who you're looking for to take care of young Alexei. I'm glad to see he listened to me.'

'You have my gratitude, sir, for the great change in my circumstances.'

'Yes, yes,' he said dismissively. 'Bit of a difference from . . . where was it we encountered each other?'

'Kashin, sir.'

'Ah yes, Kashin. Dreadful place. Had to hang the fool who tried to shoot me. Didn't want to do it, really, he was just a boy, but there's no excuse for such mischief. Had to be made an example of. You can understand that, can't you?'

I nodded, but said nothing. The memory of my part in Kolek's death was something I tried not to dwell on, for I felt tremendously guilty about how I had profited from it. Also, I missed his companionship.

'Friend of yours, was he?' asked the Grand Duke after a moment, sensing my reticence.

'We grew up together,' I said. 'He had strange ideas sometimes, but he was not a malicious person.'

'Not so sure about that,' he replied with a shrug. 'He did point a gun at me, after all.'

165

'Yes, sir.'

'Well, it's all in the past now. Survival of the fittest and all that. Speaking of which, where is the Tsarevich anyway? Aren't you supposed to be by his side at all times?'

'He's just outside,' I said, nodding my head in the direction of the small copse, where the boy was dragging some logs across the grass to aid in the construction of the walls of his fort.

'He's all right out there on his own, is he?' asked the Grand Duke, and I couldn't help but sigh in frustration. I had been attending to the Tsarevich for almost two months now and had never known a child who was wrapped in cotton wool quite as much as him. His parents behaved as if he might snap in two at any moment. And now the Grand Duke was suggesting that he could not be left alone for fear of injury. *He's just a boy*, I wanted to shout at them sometimes. *A child! Were none of you ever children?*

'I can go back out to him if you'd prefer it,' I replied. 'I was only stepping inside for a moment to—'

'No, no,' he said quickly, shaking his head. 'I daresay you know what you're doing. I don't make it my business to tell another man's servant how to do his job.'

I bristled a little at this characterization. The Tsar's servant. Was that what I was? Well, of course it was. I was hardly free. But still, it was an unpleasant thing to hear the words said aloud.

'And you have settled in to your new duties well?' he asked me.

'Yes, sir,' I replied truthfully. 'I am ... well, perhaps it's the wrong phrase, but I enjoy them

166

very much.'

'Not the wrong phrase at all, my boy,' he said, snorting a little and then blowing his nose on an enormous white handkerchief. 'Nothing better than a fellow who enjoys what he does. Makes the day go a lot quicker. And how's that arm of yours holding up?' he added, punching me so hard where the bullet had entered my shoulder that it was all that I could do not to let out a great scream of agony or punch him in return, an action which would have had dire consequences for me.

'Much improved, sir,' I replied through gritted teeth. 'There is a scar, as you predicted, but—'

'A man should have a scar,' he said quickly. 'I've got scars all over me, you know. My body's full of them. Naked, I resemble something that a cat's crawled over with untrimmed nails. I must show you some time.' I stared at him, astonished by the remark. The last thing I wanted was to be offered a tour of the Grand Duke's scars. 'There's not a man in this army who isn't scarred,' he continued, oblivious to my surprise. 'Take it as a mark of honour, Jachmenev. And as for the women ... Well, when they see it, I promise you it will take their fancy more than you would imagine.'

I blushed, innocent that I was, and looked down at the ground, quite silent.

'All the saints, boy,' he said, laughing a little. 'You've gone quite scarlet. You've been showing the scar to every whore around the Winter Palace already, have you?'

I said nothing and looked away. The truth was that I had done no such thing, that I remained as innocent of carnal pleasures as on the day when I was born. I had no interest in whores, although

167

they were accessible to me for they were a staple of palace life. Nor did I have any interest in women who did not require compensation for their charms. There was only one girl who attracted my attentions. But to reveal it would have been impossible, for it was so inappropriate an attachment that its revelation might have cost me my life. The last thing I was going to do was admit it to Nicholas Nicolaievich.

'Well, good for you, boy,' he said, slapping my arm once again. 'You're young. You might as well take your pleasures where you—Good God!'

The sudden change in his tone made me look up and I saw that he was not looking at me any more, but staring out of the window towards the garden, where the Tsarevich's fort was coming along nicely. Alexei himself was nowhere to be seen, however, and as I followed the direction of the Grand Duke's eyes, I caught sight of him, perhaps fifteen feet off the ground, sitting on a thick branch which extended from an oak tree.

'Alexei!' whispered the Grand Duke under his breath, the word filled with trepidation.

'Ho there!' shouted the boy from his vantage point, his voice reaching us now, delighted by how high he had climbed. 'Cousin Nicholas, Georgy, can you see me?'

'Alexei, stay where you are!' roared the Grand Duke, running out into the garden. 'Don't move, do you hear me? Stay exactly where you are. I'm coming for you.'

I followed him outside quickly, astonished by how seriously he seemed to be taking this matter. The boy had managed to get himself up the tree, it would hardly be any more difficult to get himself down again. And yet Nicholas Nicolaievich was sprinting towards the oak as if all our lives and the fate of Russia itself depended on our rescuing him.

It was too late, however. The sight of this monster of a man charging towards him was too much for the boy, who tried to stand up and descend the trunk—convinced, perhaps, that he had broken some unknown rule and would be wise to run away before being caught and punished—but he caught his foot in a branch and in a moment I heard a surprised cry emerge from his lips as he struggled to find purchase on one of the smaller branches and twigs beneath him before falling hard and noisily to the ground below, where he sat up, rubbed his head and elbow, and grinned at us both as if the entire thing had been a great surprise to him, but not an entirely unpleasant one.

I smiled back. He was fine, after all. It was boyish mischief. No harm had been done.

'Be quick,' said the Grand Duke, turning to look at me now, his face pale. 'Call the doctors. Get them here now, Jachmenev.'

'But he's fine, sir,' I protested, surprised by how seriously he was taking this accident. 'Look at him, all he did was—'

'Get them *now*, Jachmenev,' he roared, practically knocking me over in his anger, and this time I did not hesitate.

I turned, I ran, I summoned help.

And within a few minutes the entire household had come to a dramatic stop.

*   *   *

The evening came and went without dinner being

served; the night passed by without any entertainment being offered. Finally, just after two o'clock in the morning, I found an excuse to leave the room where the other members of the Leib Guard had gathered, each one staring at me more contemptuously than the last, and made my way back to my bunk, where I wanted nothing more than to close my eyes, fall asleep quickly and put the events of that horrible day behind me.

In the time between the accident and the early morning I had endured feelings of confusion, anger and self-pity, but was still ignorant as to why Alexei's fall was considered to be such a terrible disaster, for he displayed no outward sign of injury except for a few small bruises dotted along his elbow, leg and torso. Of course, I had begun to realize that the care which was extended towards the Tsarevich was not purely because of his proximity to the throne, but that something more serious lay at its heart. Looking back, I could recall conversations with the Tsar, with some of the guards, even with Alexei himself, where matters had been implied but not stated fully, and I cursed my stupidity for not having made further enquiries.

As I made my way along the corridors, feeling increasingly sorry for myself, a door to my left opened and before I could even turn my head in that direction to see who was inside, a hand had gripped my lapel and practically lifted me from the floor to pull me inside.

'How could you have been so stupid?' Sergei Stasyovich asked me, closing the door and spinning me around to face him. To my great surprise, I saw that the only other person in the room was Alexei's older sister, the Grand Duchess Marie, who was

170

standing with her back to a window, her face pale, her eyes red with tears. One of the guards had mentioned earlier that the Tsaritsa Alexandra had already arrived from St Petersburg, and upon hearing this I had felt a sudden burst of hope that she would not have come alone. 'Why weren't you watching him, Georgy?'

'I *was* watching him, Sergei,' I insisted, upset by how the entire world seemed to have decided that everything that had taken place was the fault of this poor *moujik* from Kashin. 'I was in the garden with him, he wasn't doing anything dangerous. I only stepped inside for a moment and was distracted by—'

'You should not have left him,' said Marie, stepping towards me. I offered her a low bow, which she waved away as if it was an insult. She was the same age as I—we had both turned seventeen a few days earlier—and had a porcelain beauty that turned men's heads whenever she walked into a room. To some, she was considered the great beauty of the Tsar's daughters. But not to me.

'This is what happens when amateurs are allowed within our ranks,' said Sergei, turning around in frustration and pacing the room. 'Oh, I'm sorry to say it, Georgy, it's hardly your fault, but you don't have the experience for such responsibility. It was quite ridiculous of Nicholas Nicolaievich to have recommended you. Do you know how long I have trained to protect the Tsar?'

'Well, as you're only two years older than me, I can't quite see the difference,' I said, for I was damned if I was going to be spoken down to by him.

'And he has been in the palace for eight years,'

171

snapped the Grand Duchess, stepping closer to me now, infuriated by this last remark. 'Sergei spent his youth in the Corps of Pages. Do you even know what that is?' She stared at me contemptuously and shook her head. 'Of course you don't,' she said, answering her own question. 'He was among 150 boys drawn from the court nobility and trained in the ways of the Leib Guard. And only the very finest members of the corps are assigned to protect my family. Every day he has learned what to look out for, where the dangers lie, how to prevent any tragedy from taking place. Do you have any idea how many of my ancestors and relatives have been murdered? Do you realize that my brother and sisters and I walk in the shadow of death at every moment of the day? All we have to rely on is our prayers and our guards. Sergei Stasyovich is the type of man we need around us. Not you, not you.'

She shook her head and looked at me pitifully. I found it quite extraordinary that her anger appeared to be divided between what had happened to her brother and what I had said about Sergei. What was he to her, after all, except just another member of the Leib Guard? For his part, the object of her defensiveness was fuming now by the window, and I watched her go to him and speak quietly before he shook his head and said *no*. I wondered whether Marie was not a little enamoured of him, perhaps, for he was a striking young man, tall and handsome, with piercing blue eyes and a shock of blond hair that made him seem more Aryan than Russian.

'I don't know what is expected of me,' I said finally, growing close to tears now in my distress. 'I've looked out for him all that I can since the moment I was appointed to my duties. It was an accident, why is that so hard to understand? Young boys have accidents.'

'Get some sleep, Georgy,' said Sergei quietly, turning around now and walking over to pat my shoulder in commiseration. I brushed his hand away, not wishing to be patronized by him. 'Tomorrow will be a busy day, no doubt. They will want to talk to you. It's not your fault, not really. The truth is that you should have been told before now. Perhaps if you had known . . .'

'Known?' I asked, my brow furrowing in confusion. 'Known what?'

'Go,' he said, opening the door and pushing me back out on to the corridor. I was about to argue further, but he was talking quietly with the Grand Duchess again. Feeling myself entirely surplus to their interests, I grew utterly frustrated with the situation and left quickly, not going to my bed as I had initially planned, but returning instead to the garden where these events had begun.

There was a full moon that night and I found myself standing in the same spot where I had been talking with the Grand Duke earlier in the afternoon, content now to be alone with my private thoughts and regrets. A gentle breeze was blowing outside and I closed my eyes in front of the open doors and let it wash over me, imagining that I was far away from here, in a place where so much was not expected of me. In the darkness, in the gloomy solitude of that corridor at Stavka, there was some element of peace to be found, a small respite from the drama which had engulfed us throughout the afternoon and evening.

I heard the footsteps marching along the corridor

for some time before I even thought to turn and look in their direction. There was an urgency to them, a determination that made me nervous.

'Who's there?' I called. Despite what Sergei and the Grand Duchess Marie might have thought, I had been trained over the previous few months in ever more ingenious ways to deal with a suspected assassin, but surely there could not be one here, at Army Headquarters of all places. 'Who's there?' I repeated, louder now, wondering whether I might yet have a chance to redeem myself in the eyes of the Imperial family before the sun rose. 'Make yourself known.'

As I said this, the figure finally emerged into the brightness of the moonlight and before I had a chance to catch my breath she was standing directly before me, raising her hand in the air, and with one sharp and determined motion, she struck me forcefully across the face. So taken by surprise was I by both the strength and the unexpected nature of the act that I fell out of my stance, tripping backwards and stumbling on to the floor, landing painfully on my elbow, but I made no cry, merely sat there, dazed and nursing my wounded jaw.

'You fool,' said the Tsaritsa, taking another step towards me, and I retreated a little, like a crab rearing backwards along a beach, although I didn't think that she intended to strike me again. 'You stupid fool,' she repeated, her voice devastated from anger and fear.

'Your Majesty,' I said, standing up now, but keeping a safe distance from her. There was a look of absolute terror in her eyes, a panic unlike any I had ever seen before. 'I keep telling people, it was an accident. I don't know how it—'

'We cannot *afford* accidents,' she shouted. 'What is the point of you if you do not look after my son? If you do not keep him from harm?'

'The point of me?' I asked, certain that I did not care for the expression, even if it did come from the Empress of Russia. 'I cannot keep my eyes on him at every moment of the day,' I insisted. 'He is a boy. He looks for adventure.'

'He fell from a tree, this is what they tell me,' she replied. 'What was he doing in a tree in the first place?'

'He climbed it,' I explained. 'The Tsarevich was building a fort. I expect he was looking for more wood and—'

'Why were you not with him? You should have been with him!'

I shook my head and looked away, unable to understand how she could think that I could possibly be always by the boy's side. He was an active fellow, no matter what they thought of him. He escaped me constantly.

'Georgy,' said the Tsaritsa, putting her hands to her cheeks now and holding them there for a moment as she exhaled lengthily. 'Georgy, you don't understand. I told Nicky that we should have explained it to you.'

'Explained it?' I asked, raising my own voice now, despite the difference in our rank, for whatever it was could be held back from me no longer. 'Explained what? Tell me, please!'

'Just listen,' she said, putting a finger to her lips for a moment and I looked around, waiting to hear something that might explain everything.

'What is it?' I asked. 'I hear nothing.'

'I know,' she said. 'It is silent now. There's not a sound. But in an hour's time, perhaps less, these corridors will echo with the sound of my son's cries as the first agonies begin. The blood around his wounds will fail to clot. And then he will start to suffer. And you might think that you have never heard such anguished cries, but . . .' She released a small, bitter laugh as she shook her head, 'they will be nothing, *nothing*, in comparison to what will follow.'

'It was not a heavy fall,' I protested, hearing the weakness of my words, for I had started to realize that there was a reason for such protectiveness.

'A few hours after that and the real pain will begin,' she continued. 'The doctors will not be able to stem the flow of blood, for his wounds are all internal, and it is impossible to operate upon him, for we cannot allow him to bleed even more freely. Having no natural release, the blood will flow into Alexei's muscles and joints, trying to fill spaces that are already full, expanding those injured areas ever further. He will start to suffer in ways that neither you nor I can possibly imagine. He will cry out. And then he will scream. He will scream for a week, perhaps longer. Can you imagine that kind of suffering, Georgy? Can you imagine what it must be like to scream for so long?'

I stared at her and said nothing. Of course I couldn't imagine it. The idea was beyond imagination.

'And throughout this time, he will drift in and out of consciousness, but mostly he will be awake to experience the pain,' she continued. 'His entire body will go into seizure and he will become delirious. He will be torn between nightmares, between screaming out in pain and praying for his father or me to help him, to relieve some of his suffering, but there will be nothing we can do. We will sit by his bedside, we will talk to him, we will hold his hand, but we will not cry, because we cannot be weak in front of the child. And this will last for who knows how long? And then do you know what might happen, Georgy?'

I shook my head. 'What?' I asked.

'Then he might die,' she said coldly. 'My son might die. Russia might be left without an heir. And all because you allowed him to climb a tree. Do you understand now?'

I knew not what to say. The boy was a haemophiliac; he had what they called the 'royal disease', an affliction I had overheard servants gossiping about but had never given much thought to. England's late queen, Victoria, the Tsaritsa's own grandmother, had been a carrier, and having married off most of her children and grandchildren to the princes and princesses of Europe, the ailment was a shameful secret in many regal courts. Including our own. They should have told me before this, I thought bitterly. They should have trusted me. For after all, I would sooner have put a knife through my own heart than cause the Tsarevich any suffering.

'Can I see him?' I asked and she smiled at me for a moment, her expression softening slightly, before she simply turned away and disappeared back into the shadows of the long corridor, in the direction of the Tsarevich's room. 'I want to see him!' I shouted after her, not even considering how inappropriate this was. 'Please, you must let me see him!'

But my cries fell on deaf ears. In a reversal of the earlier moments, the Tsaritsa's footsteps marched quickly away but grew quieter now, fading into the distance until I was left alone again, staring into the garden, desperate and grieving for my actions.

And it was at that moment that Anastasia came to me.

She had been listening to every word that had been said between her mother and me. She must have arrived in the carriages earlier, as I had hoped. She had come for her brother.

And, I thought, for me.

'Georgy,' she cried, her voice rising above a whisper and carrying across the tops of the hedgerows and bushes to land like music on my ears. I turned my face in the direction from which it had come and saw the flutter of her white dress behind the dark-green plants. 'Georgy, I am here.'

I looked around quickly to ensure that we were not being observed and ran outside. She was waiting for me behind a cluster of hedgerows, and when I saw her anxious face, I felt like weeping. Her brother was in his bed, terrified, preparing for weeks of agony, but none of it seemed to matter suddenly and I felt ashamed. For she was here before me.

'I hoped you'd come,' I said.

'Mother brought us,' she cried, falling into my arms. 'Alexei is . . .'

'I know,' I said. 'And it's my fault. It's all my fault. I should have . . . I should have taken more care. If I had known—'

'You weren't to know the dangers,' she insisted. 'I'm frightened, Georgy. Hold me, won't you? Hold me and tell me that everything will be all right.'

I didn't hesitate. I wrapped myself around her and pressed her face to my chest, kissing the top of her golden hair and resting my lips there, inhaling the sweet aroma of her perfume.

'Anastasia,' I said, closing my eyes, wondering how I had ever found myself in this position. 'Anastasia, my beloved.'

1953

I waited for Zoya in the window seat of a café opposite the Central School of Art and Design, glancing at my watch from time to time and trying to ignore the chatter of the people around me. She was already more than half an hour late and I was beginning to grow irritated. A copy of *The Caine Mutiny* lay open before me, but I couldn't concentrate on the words and eventually set it aside, picking up a teaspoon instead to stir my coffee as I tapped the table nervously with the fingers of my left hand.

Across the road, the staff and students from the college were wandering past, stopping and chatting with each other, laughing, gossiping, offering kisses, some attracting the disapproving frowns of passers-by due to the unorthodox nature of their clothing. A young man of about nineteen turned the corner and marched along the street as if he was trooping the colour, wearing a pair of drainpipe trousers, a dark shirt and waistcoat, all topped off with a knee-length, Edwardian jacket. His hair was slick with Brilliantine and turned up

179

at the front in an elegant quiff, and he strutted along as if the entire city was his alone. It was impossible not to stare at him, which was presumably the intention.

'Georgy.'

I looked around and was surprised to see my wife standing beside me; I had been so entranced by the goings on outside the college that I'd failed to notice her arriving. That, I considered in a moment of sadness, was something that would never have happened a year before.

'Hello,' I said, looking at my watch and instantly regretting the move, for it was an aggressive gesture, designed to indicate her lateness without having to articulate it. I was annoyed, that was true, but I didn't want to *seem* annoyed. I had spent most of the last six months trying not to *seem* annoyed. It was one of the things that was holding us together.

'I'm so sorry,' she said, sitting down with an exhausted sigh and divesting herself of hat and coat. She had cut her hair quite short a few weeks earlier in a style reminiscent of the Queen—no, the Queen Mother; I still hadn't grown accustomed to calling her that—and I didn't care for it, if I was honest. But then there was a lot that I didn't care for at the time. 'I got held up as I was leaving,' she explained. 'Dr Highsmith's secretary was away from her desk and I couldn't leave without making the next appointment. It took her for ever to get back, and when she did, she couldn't find her diary.' She shook her head and sighed, as if the world was simply too exhausting a place to countenance, before smiling a little and turning to me. 'The whole thing took for ever. And then the buses . . . well, anyway, what can I say? Except sorry.'

'It's all right,' I said, shaking my head as if none of it really mattered. 'I hadn't even noticed the time. Everything all right?'

'Yes, fine.'

'What can I get you?'

'Just a cup of tea, please.'

'Just tea?'

'Please,' she said brightly.

'You're not hungry?'

She hesitated for a moment, considering it, and shook her head. 'Not right now,' she said. 'I don't have much of an appetite today, for some reason. I'll just have tea, thanks.'

I nodded and went to the counter to order a fresh pot. Standing there, waiting for the water to boil and the leaves to be drenched, I watched her as she stared through the window, looking out towards the college where she had been teaching for about five years now, and tried not to hate her for what she had done to us. For what she had done to me. For the fact that she could show up late, without an appetite, which suggested to me that she had been somewhere else, with someone else, eating lunch with him and not with me. Even though I knew that this was not the case, I hated her for the fact that she had made me suspicious of her every move.

'Thanks,' she said, as I placed the cup down in front of her. 'I needed that. It's cold outside now. I should have brought a scarf. So how was your morning?'

I shrugged my shoulders, irritated by her cheerful demeanour and meaningless chit-chat, as if there

181

was nothing wrong in the world at all, as if our lives were as they had always been and would ever be. 'No different to usual,' I said. 'Boring.'

'Oh Georgy,' she said, reaching her hand across the table and placing it on top of mine. 'Don't say that. Your life isn't boring.'

'Well, it's not as exciting as yours, that's for sure,' I said, regretting the words immediately as she froze, trying to decide whether I had meant them to be quite as cutting as they had sounded; her hand remained flat on top of mine for a few seconds longer and then she removed it, looked out of the window and sipped her tea cautiously. I knew that she wouldn't speak again until I did. After over thirty years of marriage, there was very little she could do that I wasn't able to anticipate. She could surprise me, of course, she had proved that. But still, I knew her moves like no one else ever could.

'The new girl started,' I said finally, clearing my throat, introducing a safe topic for conversation. 'That's news, I suppose.'

'Oh yes?' she asked in a neutral tone. 'And what's she like?'

'Very pleasant. Eager to learn. Quite knowledgeable about books. She read Literature at Cambridge. Frightfully smart.'

Zoya smiled and stifled a laugh. *'Frightfully smart,'* she repeated. 'Georgy, how English you've become.'

'Have I?'

'Yes. You never would have used phrases like that when we first came to London. It's all those years of being surrounded by dons and academics in the library.'

182

'I expect it is,' I said. 'They do say that language changes as one becomes more assimilated into a different society.'

'Is she mousy?'

'Who?' I asked.

'Your new assistant. What's her name, anyway?'

'Miss Llewellyn.'

'Is she Welsh?'

'Yes.'

'And is she mousy?'

'No. Just because she chooses to work in a library doesn't mean that she's some sort of shrinking violet who can't bear to be spoken to in case she turns bright red, you know.'

Zoya sighed and stared at me. 'All right,' she said, shaking her head a little. 'I didn't mean anything by it. I was just making conversation.'

Irritability. Petulance. Anxiety. A subconscious desire to find something wrong in every phrase she employed. A need to criticize her, to make her feel bad about herself. I could hear it every time we spoke. And I hated the fact of it. This was not who we were supposed to be. We were supposed to love each other, to treat each other with respect and kindness. We had never been Georgy and Zoya, after all. We were GeorgyandZoya.

'She'll do fine,' I said, my tone a little lighter now, not wishing to increase the tension of the conversation. 'Things won't be the same without Miss Simpson, of course. Or Mrs Harris, I should say. But there we are. Life goes on. Times change.'

'Yes,' she said, reaching down for her handbag and taking out a copy of that morning's *Times* newspaper. 'Have you seen this?' she asked, placing it on the table in front of me.

'I've seen it,' I replied after only a slight hesitation. I made sure to read *The Times* every morning at the library, she was well aware of it. What surprised me was that *she* had seen it, for Zoya was not a person who particularly enjoyed reading about current affairs, particularly when so many of them in these days were bellicose in nature.

'And what do you think?'

'I don't think anything,' I said, picking the newspaper up and staring for a moment at the face of Josef Stalin in the photograph, the heavy moustache, the lidded eyes smiling back at me with fake cordiality. 'What do you expect me to think?'

'We should hold a party,' she said, her voice cold but triumphant. 'We should celebrate, don't you think so?'

'No,' I replied. 'What is there to rejoice over, after all? So he is dead. And after him, you think ... what? You think things will be as they once were again?'

'Of course not,' she said, taking the paper from me and looking at the photograph again for only a moment before folding it over and pressing it forcefully back into her bag. 'I'm just happy, that's all.'

'That he's gone?'

'That he's dead.'

I remained silent. I hated hearing such venom in her tone. Of course I was no admirer of Stalin; I had read enough about his actions to despise him. In the thirty-five years since leaving Russia I had remained well enough informed on the events that were taking place in my native land to feel relieved that I was no longer a part of them. But I could not celebrate a death, even his.

'Anyway,' I continued after a moment, 'I don't have long before I have to go back to work and I want to hear about your morning. How did it go?'

Zoya looked down at the table for a moment. She seemed disappointed that we were changing the subject so quickly; perhaps she wanted to engage in a long conversation about Stalin and his actions and his purges and all his multiplicity of crimes. She could have that conversation if she wanted, I had already decided in my head. Only not with me. 'It was fine,' she said quietly.

'Just fine?'

'It was a little more . . . complicated this time, I suppose.'

I considered this and hesitated before questioning her further. 'Complicated?' I asked. 'How so?'

'It's hard to explain,' she said, her forehead wrinkling a little as she thought about it. 'When we had our first appointment last week, Dr Highsmith seemed interested in very little other than my daily life and routines. He wanted to know whether I enjoyed my work, how long I had lived in London, how long we had been married. Very basic questions. The kind of things you might chat about at a party if you were talking to a stranger.'

'Did that make you uncomfortable?' I asked.

'Not particularly,' she said, shrugging her shoulders. 'I mean, there was a limit to how much I was willing to talk about, of course. I don't even know the man. But he seemed to recognize that in me. He challenged me on it quite early.'

I nodded. 'And how far back did you go?'

'Quite far, in different ways,' she admitted. 'I

185

talked about how things had been during the war, the years leading up to it after we first got here. About how long we had waited to become parents. I talked . . .' She hesitated now and bit her lip, but then looked up and spoke in a more determined voice; I wondered whether this was something Dr Highsmith had encouraged her to do. 'I talked a little about Paris.'

'Really?' I asked, surprised. 'We never talk about Paris.'

'No,' she said, her tone betraying a slight accusation. 'No, we don't.'

'Should we?'

'Perhaps.'

'What else?'

'Russia.'

'You spoke about Russia?'

'Again, only in the most general terms,' she said. 'It seemed strange to discuss such personal matters with a person I've only just met.'

'You don't trust him?'

She shook her head. 'It's not that,' she said. 'I do trust him, I think. It's just . . . it's curious, he doesn't really ask any questions as such. He just talks to me. We have a conversation. And then I find myself opening up to him. Telling him things. It's almost like a form of hypnosis. I was thinking about that earlier as I was waiting for his secretary to return and he put me in mind . . . he reminded me of—'

'I know,' I said, very quietly, almost in a whisper, as if the very mention of his name might summon the beast back from the afterlife. A snapshot of reminiscence exploded in my memory. I was seventeen years old again, freezing cold, dragging a body towards the banks of the Neva, ready to throw it into the depths. There was blood on the ground from the bullet wounds. A feeling in the air that the monster might yet spring back to life and kill us all. The room began to spin a little as the sensations of that evening returned to me and I trembled. This was not something I liked to think about. It was not something I ever allowed myself to remember.

'He has a very calming tone,' she replied, not acknowledging what I had said, not needing to. 'He puts me at my ease. I was afraid he'd be like Dr Hooper, but he isn't. He seems to genuinely care.'

'And did you talk about the nightmares?' I asked.

'Today we did,' she said, nodding. 'He began by asking me why I had come to see him in the first place. Do you know, I never even realized that last time he hadn't asked me that? You don't mind me telling you all of this, do you, Georgy?'

'Of course not,' I said, attempting a smile. 'I do want to know, but . . . only if you want to tell me. If he helps you, that's all that's important to me. You don't have to feel you have to tell me everything.'

'Thank you,' she said. 'I suppose there are some things that would sound odd if I repeated them to you out of context. Things that made sense in the moment, if you know what I mean. But anyway, I told him how I had been waking in the night so much recently, about the terrible dreams, about how they had just come upon me out of nowhere. It's ridiculous really, after all these years, that such memories should resurface.'

'And what did he say?' I asked.

'Not a lot. He asked me to describe them to him and I did. Some of them, anyway. There are others that I don't think I can trust him with yet. And then we started to talk about a lot of different things. We talked about you.'

'About me?'

'Yes.'

I swallowed. I wasn't sure that I wanted to ask this question, but there was no way around it. 'What did he want to know about me?' I asked.

'He just asked me to describe you, that was all. The type of man you are.'

'And what did you tell him?'

'The truth, of course. How kind you are. How thoughtful. How loving.' She hesitated for a moment and leaned forward a little. 'How you have taken care of me all these years. And how forgiving you are.'

I looked at her and could feel the tears begin to build behind my eyes. I wasn't angry now; I was feeling hurt again. Betrayed. I sought the correct words. I didn't want to attack. 'And you told him about . . . did you tell him?'

She nodded. 'About Henry? Yes. I did.'

I sighed and looked away. Even now, almost a year later, the name was enough to shatter my mood and my confidence. I could still hardly believe that it had happened, that after so many years together she could betray me with another man.

*   *   *

Arina introduced Zoya and me to Ralph at the end of summer. I hadn't known what to expect—it was the first time she had ever brought a boy home, after all—and the truth was that I rather dreaded

188

the prospect of meeting him. It wasn't just that it forced me to acknowledge the fact that my daughter was approaching adulthood; there was also the matter of facing up to my own increasing age. In my foolishness, I still thought of my life as being spread out before me like a flowerbed in springtime, a row of tulips about to burst into brilliant life, when really it was more like rose plants in autumn, when the leaves begin to blacken and wither and the decay of winter is all that remains of their lives. Lost among the filing systems of the British Library, I was quiet throughout the day as this sobering thought settled upon my brain, and when Miss Llewellyn asked me whether I was feeling all right, I could only pass off my gloom with an embarrassed smile and an honest explanation.

'I don't know,' I said. 'I have a rather unusual evening ahead of me, that's all.'

'Oh?' she said, her curiosity piqued. 'That sounds interesting. Going somewhere special?'

'Sadly, no. My wife has invited my daughter's young man to dinner. It's the first time I've had to sit through such an ordeal and I'm not looking forward to it.'

'I brought my bloke Billy to meet my parents a couple of months ago,' she said, shivering a little at the memory of it and wrapping her cardiganed arms around herself. 'It ended in the most terrible fight. My father threw him out of the house. Said he'd never speak to me again if I kept going with him.'

'Really?' I asked, hoping that my evening would not end in quite so dramatic a fashion. 'He didn't care for him then?'

She rolled her eyes as if the scene itself was too awful to describe. 'It was a lot of nonsense really,' she said. 'Billy said something he shouldn't have said, then my dad said something even worse. He likes to think of himself as a revolutionary, does my Billy, and Dad won't have any truck with that type of thing. A real old British Empire type, you know the sort. You should have heard the way they shouted at each other when the poor old King was brought into the conversation, God bless his soul. I thought the police would be called out over it! How old is your daughter anyway, Mr Jachmenev, if you don't mind my asking?'

'She's just turned nineteen.'

'Well then, this is just the start of it, I imagine. I'm sure there'll be a lot more dinners to look forward to in the future. You'll see. This bloke will be the first of dozens.'

This suggestion didn't offer me quite the relief that she had intended and I returned home a little later than usual that evening, having stopped at a local church to light a candle—*for as long as I live*—for it was August the twelfth and I had a promise to fulfil.

'Georgy,' said Zoya, turning around to stare at me as I walked through the door, her face flushed with anxiety. 'What kept you? I expected you half an hour ago.'

'Sorry,' I said, noticing how much effort she had gone to with both her dress and her appearance. 'You're looking well,' I added, mildly irritated that she had gone to so much trouble for a boy we didn't even know.

'Well don't sound so surprised,' she replied with an insulted laugh. 'I do try to make an effort every

190

now and then, you know.'

I smiled and kissed her. For years, phrases like this would have been brushed off as teasing and affectionate. Now there was an undercurrent of tension, a feeling that whatever we had managed to bury between us was not forgiven at all, and that the wrong word uttered at the wrong moment might, like with Miss Llewellyn's boyfriend and father, lead to the most calamitous dispute.

'Are you having a bath?' she asked me.

'Do I need one?'

'You have been working all day,' she replied quietly, biting her lip a little.

'Then I suppose I'd better,' I sighed, throwing my briefcase down where I knew she would be forced to pick it up and put it out of sight once I had gone. 'I won't be long. What time is he expected at, anyway?'

'Not till eight. Arina said they were going to have a drink after work but they'd be along after that.'

'He's a drinker, then,' I said, frowning.

'A drink, I said,' replied Zoya. 'Give him a chance, Georgy. You never know, you might like him.'

I doubted it, but lying in the bath a few minutes later, enjoying the peace and relaxation of the warm soapy water, I continued to ponder the unsettling fact that Arina had reached the age where her thoughts had turned to the opposite sex. It didn't seem like any time at all since she was a little girl. Or, for that matter, since she was a baby. Indeed, it felt like only a few short years since Zoya and I had suffered and despaired at the thought that we would never be blessed with a child of our own. My life, I realized, was slipping away. I was fifty-four years old now; how had that happened? Wasn't it only a few months since I had arrived at the Winter Palace and marched along gilded corridors behind Count Charnetsky for my first meeting with the Tsar? Surely it was earlier this year when I stole a moment for myself on board the *Standart* as the Imperial Family listened to a performance by the St Petersburg String Quartet?

No, I thought, shaking my head at my own foolishness and allowing my body to slip deeper into the bath. No, it wasn't. That all happened years ago. Decades.

Those days belonged to another lifetime entirely, an existence which was never spoken of any more. I closed my eyes and allowed my head to sink beneath the surface of the water. Holding my breath, the echo of the past filled my ears and memory and I was lost once again inside those terrible, wonderful years between 1915 and 1918, when the drama of our country played out before me. Removed from the world, I could feel once again the sharp bite of the winter air along the banks of the Neva as it nipped at my nose and made me gasp in shock, could picture the faces of the Tsar and Tsaritsa as clearly as if they were standing before me. And the scent of Anastasia's perfume filled my senses as if in a dream, followed by a blurred picture of the young girl with whom I had fallen in love.

'Georgy,' said Zoya, tapping on the door and looking inside, her presence immediately making me spring upwards once again, gasping for air as I ran the wet hair away from my forehead and eyes with my hands. 'Georgy, they'll be here soon.' She hesitated, perhaps unsettled by an unexpected expression of regret and sorrow upon my face. 'What is it?' she asked. 'What's wrong?'

'Nothing,' I said.

'It's not nothing. You're crying.'

'It's bathwater,' I corrected her, wondering whether it was possible that in fact the suds had mixed with my tears without my even noticing.

'Your eyes look red.'

'It's nothing,' I repeated. 'I was just thinking about something, that's all.'

'What?' she asked me, a note of anxiety in her voice as if she was afraid to hear the answer.

'Nothing important,' I said, shaking my head. 'Just someone I used to know, that's all. Someone who died a long time ago.'

*   *   *

There were moments when I hated her for what she had done. I never thought that I could have it in me to feel anything other than love for Zoya, but there were times, lying awake in bed beside her, my body feeling as if it would evaporate if I touched her, when I wanted to scream aloud in my frustration and hurt.

When it was over, when we were trying to repair our fractured lives, I dared to ask her why it had happened at all.

'I don't know, Georgy,' she said, sighing, as if it was unkind of me even to want an answer.

'You don't know,' I repeated, spitting out the words.

'That's right.'

'Well then. What am I supposed to say to that?'

193

'I never loved him, if that matters at all.'

'It makes it worse,' I said, not knowing whether this was true or not, but wanting to hurt her. 'What was it all for, after all, if you never loved him? At least that would have been something.'

'He didn't know me,' she said quietly. 'That made him different.'

'Know you?' I asked, frowning. 'What do you mean?'

'My sins. He didn't know my sins.'

'*Don't*,' I shouted, lunging towards her, my fury rising. 'Do *not* use *that* to justify what you have done.'

'Oh I'm not, Georgy, I'm not,' she said, shaking her head and crying now. 'It was just . . . how can I explain something to you that I don't understand myself? Are you going to leave me?'

'I would like nothing more,' I told her; a lie, of course. 'I would never have done this to you. Ever.'

'I know that.'

'Do you think that I'm not tempted? Do you think that I never look at women and want to make them mine?'

She hesitated, but finally shook her head. 'No, Georgy. I don't think you ever do. I don't believe you are ever tempted.'

I opened my mouth to argue with her, but how could I, after all? She was right.

'That is what makes you *you*,' she insisted. 'You are kind and decent, and I . . .' She paused and when she spoke again, enunciating every word, I had never heard her sound so determined. 'I am not.'

We stood in silence for a long time and a thought occurred to me, one so monstrous that I could not

194

even believe that I was suggesting it.

'Zoya,' I said, 'did you do it so that I *would* leave you?' She looked at me and swallowed, turning away, saying nothing. 'Did you think that if I left you, it would be a punishment of sorts? That you deserve to be punished?'

Silence.

'My God,' I said, shaking my head. 'You still think it was your fault, don't you? You still want to die.'

*   *   *

The front door opened at precisely eight o'clock and Arina stepped in first, a shy smile upon her face, the expression she had always worn as a child when she had done something mischievous but wanted her escapade to be discovered. She stepped over to Zoya and me and kissed us both, as she always did, and then, emerging from the dark shadows of the hallway stepped a young man, hat in hand, his cheeks a little flushed, clearly anxious to make a good impression. Despite myself, I found his nervousness endearing and had to concentrate in order to stop myself from smiling. It must have been a day for memories, for his disquiet reminded me of my nervousness when I was first introduced to Zoya's father.

'Masha, Pasha,' said Arina, indicating the young man, as if we couldn't see him standing there before us in all his awkwardness, 'this is Ralph Adler.'

'Good evening, Mr Jachmenev,' he said immediately, extending a hand for me to shake and stumbling over my name, although it sounded as if he had prepared his opening gambit many times before delivering it. 'It's a great honour to meet you. And Mrs Jachmenev, I'd like to thank you very much for the great honour of inviting me to your home.'

'Well, you're very welcome, Ralph,' she said, smiling too. 'We're delighted to meet you at last. Arina has told us a lot about you. Won't you come in and sit down?'

Arina and Ralph took their seats at the table and I sat opposite Ralph as Zoya finished preparing the food, which gave me an opportunity to examine him in more detail. He was of average height and build, with a mop of shocking-red hair, a fact which surprised me, but he was not a bad-looking boy, I supposed. As far as boys went.

'You're older than I expected you to be,' I said, wondering immediately whether Arina was only the latest in a series of girlfriends he had seduced.

'I'm twenty-four,' said Ralph quickly. 'Still a young man, I hope.'

'Of course you are,' said Zoya. 'Try being fifty-four.'

'Arina's only nineteen,' I said.

'Five years then,' he replied, as if this difference in age was neither here nor there, and cutting me off from offering any further observation on it. Every time he spoke he looked across at Arina for approval, and when she smiled, he smiled too. When she spoke, he watched her, and his lips parted slightly. I felt there was a part of him that wanted to lean towards me and explain, in an entirely academic fashion, that he really couldn't believe his luck that someone like her was interested in someone like him at all. I recognized the mixture of passions in his eyes: admiration, desire, fascination, love. I was pleased for my daughter, unsurprised that she could inspire such emotions, but it made me a little sad, too.

She was so young, I thought. I wasn't ready to lose her.

'Arina tells us that you're a musician, Ralph,' Zoya said as we ate the kind of dinner we usually only ate on Sundays. Roast beef and potatoes. Two different types of vegetables. Gravy. 'What do you play?'

'The clarinet,' he replied quickly. 'My father was a wonderful clarinettist. He insisted that my brother and sisters and I took lessons from the time we were very small. I used to hate it when I was a child, of course, but things change.'

'Why did you hate it?' I asked.

'I think it was the teacher,' he said. 'She was about a hundred and fifty years old and every time I played badly she would beat me at the end of my lesson. When I played well, she would hum along to accompany Mozart or Brahms or Tchaikovsky or whoever.'

'You like Tchaikovsky?' I asked.

'Yes, very much.'

'I see.'

'But your attitude must have changed eventually,' said Zoya. 'If you play for a living, I mean.'

'Oh, I wish I could say that I do,' he said, interrupting her quickly. 'Forgive me, Mrs Jachmenev, but I'm not a professional musician. Not yet, anyway. I'm still studying. I take my classes at the Guildhall School of Music and Drama, just off the Embankment.'

'Yes,' she said, nodding her head. 'Yes, I know of

197

it.'

'A little old to be still studying, aren't you?' I asked.

'It's an advanced course,' he explained. 'So that I can teach as well as play, should the need arise. I'm in my final year now.'

'Ralph plays with an orchestra outside of class too,' said Arina quickly. 'He's performed at the Christmas service in St Paul's for the last three years; last year he was even given a solo, weren't you, Ralph?'

'Really?' said Zoya, sounding impressed as the boy smiled and blushed to be the centre of so much attention. 'Then you must be very good.'

'I don't know,' he said, frowning as he considered this. 'I'm improving anyway, I hope.'

'You should have brought your clarinet with you,' she continued. 'Then you could have played for us. I played piano, you know, when I was a child. I've often wished we had the space here for one.'

'Did you enjoy it?'

'Yes,' she said and opened her mouth to say more, but then seemed to think better of it and became immediately silent.

'I never learned an instrument,' I said, filling the silence. 'I always wanted to, though. Had I been offered the opportunity, I might have studied the violin. I've always considered it to be the most elegant of musical instruments.'

'Well you're never too old to learn, sir,' said Ralph and the moment the line was out of his mouth he flushed scarlet with embarrassment, which was not helped by the fact that I was staring directly at him with the most serious expression I could muster, as if he had just insulted me terribly.

198

'I'm awfully sorry,' he said, spluttering out the words. 'I didn't mean to imply that—'

'That I'm old?' I asked. 'Well, what of it? I *am* old. I was only thinking about it earlier. You'll be old yourself one day. See how you like it then.'

'I simply meant that one can take up an instrument at any age.'

'It would be a comfort to me in my dotage, perhaps,' I suggested.

'No, not at all. I mean—'

'Georgy, don't tease the poor boy,' said Zoya, reaching across and taking my hand for a moment. Our fingers interlaced and I looked down at them, noticing how the skin on either side of her knuckles was starting to become a little more taut with age; for a moment I imagined I could see the blood and phalanges beneath, as if her hand was being made translucent by the passing years. We were both growing older and it was a depressing thought. I squeezed her fingers tightly and she turned to look at me, a little surprised, perhaps wondering whether I was trying to offer her reassurance or hurt her. The truth was that at that moment I wanted to tell her how much I loved her, how nothing else mattered, not the nightmares, not the memories, not even Henry, but it was impossible to speak such words. And not because Ralph and Arina were there. It was just impossible.

'Did your father attend the same school?' Zoya asked a moment later. 'When he was learning the clarinet, I mean?'

'Oh no,' he said, shaking his head. 'No, he never took any lessons in England after he arrived here. His father taught him when he was a child and he simply practised on his own after that.'

'After he arrived here?' I asked, picking up on the phrase. 'What do you mean by that? He isn't English, then?'

'No, sir,' he said. 'No, my father was born in Hamburg.'

Arina had told us quite a lot about her young man but this was something she had not mentioned before, and Zoya and I immediately looked up from our plates to stare at him, entirely surprised by this news. 'Hamburg?' I said a few moments later. 'Hamburg, Germany?'

'Ralph's father came to England in 1920,' explained Arina, her expression betraying a little nervousness, I thought.

'Really?' I said, considering it. 'After the Great War?'

'Yes,' said Ralph quietly.

'And during the other war, the one that followed it, he returned to the Fatherland, I suppose?'

'No, sir,' he replied. 'My father was vehemently opposed to the Nazis. He never returned to Germany, not since the day he left.'

'But the army?' I asked. 'Wouldn't they have—'

'He was interned for the duration of the conflict,' he explained. 'In a camp on the Isle of Man. We all were. My father and mother, our whole family.'

'I see,' I replied, considering this. 'And your mother, she's from Germany too?'

'No, sir, she's Irish.'

'Irish,' I said, laughing and turning to Zoya as I shook my head in disbelief. 'Well, this just gets better and better. I suppose that would explain the red hair.'

'I suppose,' he replied, but there was a resilience in his voice now which I admired. Zoya and I knew only too well what it had been like to be in England during the war with an accent that did not fit with our neighbours. We had been insulted and abused; I had found myself on the receiving end of violence. The work that I had done during those years had been conducted, in part, to affirm my solidarity with the Allied cause. But still, we were Russians. We were émigrés. And while this was difficult enough, I could scarcely imagine what it might have been like to have been a German family in England at the same time. I suspected that young Ralph had more steel in his bones than his nervousness around his girlfriend's parents implied. I imagined that he knew very well how to defend himself.

'That must have been difficult for you,' I said, aware of the understatement.

'It was,' he said quietly.

'You have brothers and sisters, I suppose?'

'One of each.'

'And did your family suffer?'

He hesitated before looking up and nodding, his eyes staring directly into mine. 'Very much,' he said. 'And not just mine. There were others there too. And there were many who were lost, of course. Those are not days that I like to remember.'

A silence descended on the table. I wanted to know more, but felt that I had asked enough. Telling us this much, I decided, was a testament to how much he cared for my daughter. I decided that I liked this Ralph Adler, that I would be his supporter.

'Well,' I said, refilling everyone's wine glass and raising mine before them in a toast. 'We all live here now, émigrés together. Russian, German, Irish, it doesn't matter. And we have all left people behind us and lost people along the way. Perhaps we should drink in memory of them.'

We clinked our glasses together and returned to our meals, a family of four already, not three.

* * *

Arina begged me to buy a television set so we could watch the coronation of the new Queen at home and I resisted at first, not because I was uninterested in the ceremony itself, but because I couldn't quite see the point of spending so much money on something that we would only use once.

'But we'll use it every day,' she insisted. 'Or I will anyway. Please, we can't be the only family on the street not to own one. It's embarrassing.'

'Don't exaggerate,' I told her, shaking my head. 'What is it that you want anyway, that we sit here every night, the three of us, staring at a box in the corner of the room and never speak to each other? Anyway, if everyone else has one, why can't you sit with one of the neighbours and watch the service there?'

'Because we should watch it together,' she told me. 'As a family. Please, Pasha,' she added, offering me the beseeching smile that never failed to win me over. And sure enough, the following Monday, only the afternoon before the Queen was due to make her way to Westminster Abbey, I finally relented and returned home with a new wedge-shaped Ambassador console, which fitted snugly into the corner of our small living room.

'But it's so ugly,' said Zoya, sitting on the sofa

202

while I tried to attach the wires correctly. At the showroom I had been momentarily seduced by the models on display and had chosen this particular receiver for its wooden surround, which was made from a similar material to our dining table. It was divided into two halves, a small twelve-inch screen resting comfortably above a similar-sized speaker, the two settings giving the box the appearance of an unfinished traffic light. Despite myself, I was quite excited by this new purchase.

'It's wonderful,' said Arina, sitting down beside her mother and staring at it in wonder as if it was a Picasso or a Van Gogh.

'It should be,' I muttered. 'It's the most expensive thing we own.'

'How much was it, Georgy?'

'Seventy-eight pounds,' I said, astonished even as I said the words that I could have spent so much money on something so essentially worthless. 'Over ten years, of course.'

Zoya uttered an old Russian oath beneath her breath but didn't offer any criticism; perhaps she was already seduced by the machine too. It took a little time for me to understand how to operate it, but I finally finished making all the connections and pressed the 'on' button and we watched, the three of us, as a small white circle appeared in the centre of the screen and then, two or three minutes later, spread out to fill the screen with a symbol for the BBC.

'Programmes don't start until seven o'clock,' explained Arina, who seemed content nevertheless to sit there staring at the test card.

The whole country had been given the following day off work and the streets were lined with so much bunting and decoration that the city appeared to have transformed itself into a circus overnight. Ralph arrived before lunchtime, laden down with cold meats, chutneys and cheese for sandwiches, and more bottles of beer than I thought strictly necessary.

'Anyone would think you were getting married, the way you're carrying on,' I said to Arina, who had been up since six o'clock, fussing about in great excitement, and had finally ended up sitting on the floor in front of the television in an attempt to get as close to the proceedings as possible. 'Is this what we're going to be like from now on, a family of baboons, transfixed by a flickering light emerging from a wooden box?'

'Oh, Pasha, shush,' she said, watching as the reporter in the studio repeated the same information over and over again and passed it off as news.

Zoya did not seem as interested as the young people in the events taking place, maintaining as much distance from the television set as was possible in our small living room, busying herself with small unnecessary jobs. But when the young Queen began her journey in the gold-crested carriage from the palace, looking out towards her people with a confident smile upon her face and waving with that particularly regal twist of the wrist, she pulled a seat over and began to watch silently.

'She's a pretty thing,' I remarked as Elizabeth ascended the throne, only to receive another shushing from my daughter, who thought nothing of commenting on every jewel, every tiara, every throne and every piece of ceremonial splendour which was displayed before us, but didn't want me to interrupt the proceedings with a single word.

'Isn't it wonderful?' she asked, turning to us then, her face lit up with delight at what she saw. I smiled at her, feeling uncomfortable, and glanced across at my wife, who was transfixed by the images on the television too and had, I thought, not even heard a word that our daughter had said.

'Ralph and I are going to the palace,' announced Arina when the ceremony was finally over.

'Why, for heaven's sake?' I asked, raising an eyebrow. 'Haven't you seen enough?'

'Everyone's going there, Mr Jachmenev,' said Ralph, as if it was the most obvious thing in the world. 'Don't you want to see the Queen when she steps out on the balcony?'

'Not particularly,' I said.

'You go,' said Zoya, standing up and stepping away from us, filling the sink with hot water and throwing the used plates into it forcefully. 'It's for the young people, not us. We couldn't stand the crowds.'

'Well, we better go now, Ralph, or we won't get a good place,' said Arina, grabbing his hand and dragging him away before he even had a chance to thank us for our hospitality. I could hear others on the street beyond, leaving their houses too, having watched the Coronation, and making their way along Holborn towards Charing Cross Road, and from there on to the Mall in the hope of getting as close to the Queen Victoria Memorial as possible. I listened to them for a few minutes before standing up and walking over to Zoya.

'Are you all right?' I asked.

'Yes.'

'Are you sure?'

'No.'

'Was it the ceremony?'

She sighed and turned around to look at me, our eyes meeting for a few seconds before she looked away.

'Zoya,' I said, wanting to take her in my arms, to hold her, to comfort her, but there was something that prevented me from doing so. This disruption in our marriage. She sensed it herself and offered an exhausted sigh, walking away from me without another word or touch and stepped towards the bedroom, where she closed the door behind her, leaving me alone.

*　　　*　　　*

I knew that something wasn't right long before she told me about it. This man, Henry, had arrived at the Central School, where Zoya worked, from America to teach for a year and they had quickly become friends. He was younger than her, in his late thirties, I think, and no doubt found himself lonely in a city where he knew no one and had no friends. Zoya was not the type to feel a responsibility towards people in this way—she typically eschewed any form of social interaction with her colleagues outside of the school itself— but for some reason, she took him under her wing. Soon they were taking their lunch together every afternoon and arriving back late for classes because they had found themselves so engrossed in conversation.

They went for a drink together every Thursday evening after work. I was invited along only once, and found him pleasant company, if a little trivial in his conversation and prone to self-importance, and then I was never invited again and no reference was made to this fact. It was as if my audition to join their little club had gone badly and they didn't want to hurt my feelings by mentioning it. I didn't mind particularly; if anything I liked the fact that Zoya had made a friend of her own, for she had never had very many of those, but still, the rejection smarted.

She'd come home and tell me all about Henry, the things he had done that day, the things he had said, how knowledgeable he was, how funny. He did a near-perfect impersonation of President Truman, she told me, and I wondered how Zoya even knew what President Truman sounded like in order to make the comparison. Perhaps I was being naive, but none of it bothered me in the least. In fact, I found her little obsession amusing and started to tease her about him from time to time, and she'd laugh and say that he was just a boy she got along with, that was all, it was hardly worth making a fuss over.

'He's hardly a boy,' I pointed out.

'Well, you know what I mean,' she said. 'He's so young. I'm not interested in him in that way at all.'

I remember that conversation well. We were standing in the kitchen and she was scouring a pot over and over, despite the fact that it had become entirely clean a few minutes earlier. Her cheeks had grown flushed as the exchange continued and she'd turned away from me, as if she couldn't bring herself to look me in the eye. I had only been teasing her, nothing more, in the way that she had always teased me about Miss Simpson, but it

207

surprised me that she had grown so coy, almost coquettish in response.

'I wasn't talking about you being interested in him,' I said, trying to laugh it off and ignore the sudden tension that had fallen between us. 'I was talking about him being interested in you.'

'Oh, Georgy, don't be ridiculous,' she said. 'The very idea.'

And then one day, she simply stopped talking about him entirely. She was still returning home from work at the usual time, still going for a drink with him once a week, but when I asked whether they had enjoyed a pleasant evening, she shrugged her shoulders as if she could barely remember any details of it and said that it had been fine, nothing special. She didn't even know why she bothered any more.

'And is he enjoying London?' I asked.

'Who?'

'Henry, of course.'

'Oh, I expect so. He doesn't really talk about it.'

'So what do you talk about?'

'Well, *I* don't know, Georgy,' she said defensively, as if she wasn't even present for their conversations. 'Work, mostly. Students. Nothing very interesting.'

'If he's not very interesting, then why do you spend so much time with him?'

'What are you talking about?' she asked, growing unexpectedly angry. 'I hardly spend any time with him at all.'

The entire thing began to strike me as quite bizarre, but even though there was a tiny voice at the back of my mind telling me that there was more to this than she was telling me, I chose to

208

ignore it. The idea seemed utterly impossible, after all. Zoya was in her fifties. We had been together for more than half our lives. We loved each other very much. We had been through an extraordinary amount of hardship and difficulty together. We had suffered and lost together and survived. And through it all there had always been the two of us; we had always been GeorgyandZoya.

And then the year ended and Henry went back to America.

At first, Zoya seemed a little hysterical. She came home from work and talked all night long, as if she was afraid that to pause for even a moment would allow her to consider everything that she had lost and break down entirely. She cooked elaborate meals and insisted on our taking expeditions at the weekends to the most ridiculous places—London Zoo, the National Portrait Gallery, Windsor Castle—behaving as if we were a pair of young lovers getting to know each other for the first time and not a married couple who had been together for their entire adult lives. It felt as if she was trying to get to know me again, as if she'd lost sight of me somewhere along the way but knew that I was worthy of her love, if she could only remember the reason why she had once felt that emotion for me.

The hysteria gave way to depression. She started to engage less and less in conversation with me, spurning all attempts on my part to talk or share details of our days. She went to bed early and never wanted to make love. She, who had always taken such pride in her appearance, particularly since she had unexpectedly won the position at the Central School and felt that she had to equal the

209

high fashion standards set by the other teachers and students, started to 'dress down', not caring if she went to classes in yesterday's clothes or with her hair more unkempt than it would previously have been.

Finally, unable to contain her deceit any longer, she sat beside me one evening and said that she had something she wanted to tell me.

'Is it about Henry?' I asked, surprising her, for he had left England more than five months before and his name had never been mentioned even once in our home during all that time.

'Yes,' she said. 'How did you know?'

'How could I not have known?' I said.

She nodded and told me everything. And I listened, and didn't grow angry, and tried to understand.

Not easy.

And then, a few weeks later, her nightmares began. She would wake in the middle of the night, covered in perspiration, breathing heavily and trembling with fear. Waking beside her—for we never slept apart, not even on our worst nights— I'd reach out for her and she'd jump with fright, failing to recognize me at first and then, the lights on, her fear subsiding, I would take her in my arms as she tried not to weep but to describe the images she had been confronted with in the darkness and solitude of her dreams.

Finally, our marriage at its lowest ever ebb, my wife unable to sleep, barely eating, and me filled with love and anger and hurt, she woke one day and said that this could go on no longer, that something had to change. I froze, thinking the worst. Imagining her leaving me alone, facing a life

210

without her.

'What do you mean?' I asked, swallowing nervously, preparing a speech in my mind that would forgive everything, everything, if she would only love me as she had before.

'I need to get some help, Georgy,' she said.

The *Starets* and the Skaters

For several days I felt an uncanny sensation that I was being followed. Leaving the palace for a walk along the Moika in the early evening, I would hesitate, stop and turn around, scanning the faces of the people walking quickly past me, convinced that one of them was watching me. It was a curious and disturbing feeling that, at first, I put down to paranoia brought on by my changed circumstances.

By now I was so happy in my new position with the Imperial Family that I could barely recall my past without fearing a return to it. When I did think of home there was a pricking of my conscience, but I ignored it and cast it quickly from my mind.

And yet I wasn't thinking of Kashin at all when it manifested itself once more in front of me. I was thinking of the Grand Duchess Anastasia, of the moments when we would meet on darkened corridors when I could spirit her inside one of the many hundreds of empty rooms in the palace to kiss her, to pull her close to me, to hope that she would suggest an even greater intimacy to quell my teenage lust. The previous evening I had quite forgotten myself, taking her hand as we embraced

211

and pushing it slowly along my tunic, down towards my belt, my heart racing with desire and the anticipation of the moment when she would pull away and say *No, Georgy . . . we can't . . . we can't . . .*

My mind was so filled with these thoughts and an urgent desire to return quickly to the solitude of my room that I barely glanced at the young woman standing wrapped in heavy shawls by the side of the Admiralty. She said something, a phrase I didn't hear as the wind blew around me, and in my selfishness I snapped irritably at her that I had no money to give her, that she should go to one of the soup kitchens that had sprung up around St Petersburg for food and warmth.

To my surprise she ran after me and I spun around just as she grabbed my arm, wondering whether she really thought that she could rob me of what little money I had, and even then I failed to recognize her immediately until she said my name.

'Georgy.'

'Asya!' I cried, astonished, delighted at first, staring at my sister as if she was an apparition and not a person at all. 'But I can't believe it. Is it really you?'

'It is,' she said, nodding, tears of joy forming as pools in her eyes. 'I have found you at last.'

'Here,' I said, shaking my head. 'Here, in St Petersburg!'

'Where I always wanted to be.'

I embraced her, pulled her close to me, and then a moment of great shame: the thought went through my mind, *What is she doing here anyway? What does she want of me?*

'Come over here,' I said, beckoning her towards the shelter of one of the colonnades. 'Step out of the cold, you look frozen. How long have you been here, anyway?'

'Not long,' she said, sitting beside me on a low stone bench hidden away from the noisy winds, where we might hear each other better. 'A few days, that's all.'

'A few days?' I replied, surprised. 'And you're only coming to me now?'

'I wasn't sure how to approach you, Georgy,' she explained. 'Every time I saw you, you were with groups of other soldiers and I was afraid to interrupt. I knew I would find you on your own sooner or later.'

I nodded, recalling the feeling that I had been watched and had felt annoyed by it.

'I see,' I said. 'Well, you have found me now.'

'At last,' she said, breaking into a smile. 'And how well you look! You are eating, I can tell.'

'But exercising too,' I said quickly, offended. 'My work here never ends.'

'You look healthy, that's all I meant. Life in the palace agrees with you.'

I shrugged my shoulders and looked out towards the square and the Alexander Column that had been one of my first sights of this new world, conscious that my sister looked extremely thin and pale.

'I nearly fainted when I first saw it,' she said, following my gaze.

'The palace?'

'It's so beautiful, Georgy. I've never seen anything like it before.'

I nodded, but tried to look unimpressed. I

wanted her to feel that this was a place where I belonged, that my life had always led me here.

'It is a home, like any other,' I said.

'But it's not!' she cried.

'I mean that on the inside, when you are with the family, they think of it as their home. One quickly grows accustomed to such wealth,' I lied.

'And have you met them yet?' she asked me.

'Who?'

'Their Majesties.'

I burst out laughing. 'But Asya,' I explained, 'I see them every day. I am companion to the Tsarevich Alexei. You knew that was why I was being brought here.'

She nodded and seemed lost for words. 'It was just . . . I didn't believe it could be true.'

'Well, it is,' I said irritably. 'Anyway, why are you here?'

'Georgy?'

'Sorry,' I said, regretting my tone immediately. It astonished me how much I wanted her to go away. It was as if I believed that she had come to take me home. But she represented a part of my life that was over for me now, a time that I wanted not only to move past but to forget entirely. 'I only meant, what good fortune has brought you to the city too?'

'None. Yet,' she replied. 'I couldn't stand it there without you, you see. In Kashin. I couldn't bear to be left behind. So I made my way here. I thought . . . I thought that perhaps you could help me.'

'Of course,' I said nervously. 'But how? What can I do for you?'

'I thought perhaps . . . well, they must want servant girls in the palace. There might be a position for me. If you spoke to someone.'

'Yes, yes,' I said, frowning. 'Yes, I'm sure there is. I could try to find out.' I thought about it, wondering who I should consult. I pictured my sister in a maid's uniform or the lesser clothing of a kitchen servant and for a moment it seemed like a happy thought. She would find as much ambition here as I had. I would have a friend; not one whose respect I craved, such as Sergei Stasyovich. Nor one whose affection I desired, such as Anastasia. 'Where are you staying, anyway?'

'I found a room,' she said. 'It's not much and I can't afford to stay there for too long. Do you think you could ask for me, Georgy? We could meet again then. Here, perhaps.'

I nodded and felt a sudden urge to be rid of her, to be back inside the unreal world of the palace and not out here having conversations with the past. I hated myself for my selfishness but could not seem to vanquish it.

'A week then,' I said, standing up. 'A week from tonight, at this time. Come again and I will have an answer for you. I wish I could stay longer now, but my duties . . .'

'Of course,' she said, looking saddened. 'But later tonight, perhaps? I could return and—'

'It's impossible,' I said, shaking my head. 'Next week. I promise. I will see you then.'

She nodded and embraced me once more. 'Thank you, Georgy,' she said. 'I knew that you would not let me down. It is either this or I return home. There is nowhere else for me. You will do what you can, won't you?'

'Yes, yes,' I snapped. 'Now I must be gone. Until next week, sister.'

And with that I hurried back into the square and

towards the palace, cursing her for coming here, bringing the past into a place where it did not belong. By the time I reached my room I had grown more tender again, however, and resolved that the following morning I would do what I could to help her. And by the time my door was closed, she had vanished from my mind entirely and my thoughts were once again with the only girl whose existence mattered to me at all.

*   *   *

Of the three main imperial dwellings—the Winter Palace in St Petersburg, the cliff-top citadel at Livadia and the Alexander Palace at Tsarskoe Selo—the last of these was my favourite of the Tsar's many residences. It was an entire royal village situated some sixteen miles south of the capital, and the court regularly travelled there by train—slowly, of course, so as not to cause any sudden jolting which might instigate another episode of the Tsarevich's haemophilia.

Unlike in St Petersburg, where I was quartered in a narrow cell along a corridor populated by other members of the Imperial guard, my place at Tsarskoe Selo was a tiny billet situated close to the Tsarevich's own bedroom, which was in turn dominated by a large *kiot* upon which an extraordinary number of religious icons had been placed by his mother.

'Good God,' said Sergei Stasyovich, poking his head around the door one evening as he passed along the hallway. 'So, Georgy Daniilovich, this is where they've put you, is it?'

'For now,' I said, embarrassed that he should find

me lying on my bed, half asleep, when the rest of the household was engaged in work. Sergei himself was red-cheeked and bristling with energy and when I asked him where he had spent the evening he shook his head and turned away from me, examining the walls and ceilings as if they contained matters of great importance.

'Nowhere,' he replied reluctantly. 'I took a turn around the grounds, that's all. A walk down towards the Catherine Palace.'

'You should have told me you were going,' I said, disappointed that he had not invited me to accompany him, for he was the closest thing I had to a friend and there were moments when I thought I might be able to confide some of my secrets in him. 'I would have joined you. Did you go alone?'

'Yes. No,' he added a moment later, correcting himself. 'I mean yes, I was alone. What does it matter anyway?'

'It doesn't matter at all,' I said, surprised by his behaviour. 'I only wondered—'

'You're lucky to have this room,' he said, changing the subject.

'Lucky? I think it must have been a broom closet in the past, it's that small.'

'Small?' he asked, laughing quickly. 'Don't complain about it. There are twenty of us stuck together in one of the great dormitories on the second floor. You try getting a night's rest when they're all coughing and farting and crying out for their sweethearts in their sleep.'

I smiled and shrugged at him, pleased that I was not forced to join the guards in such surroundings. This room could barely contain a bunk and a small

217

table for a jug and wash basin, but Alexei and I had grown close and he liked me to be near by, and the Tsar decreed that it should be so and therefore it was so.

The Tsaritsa, Alexandra, seemed less happy with the arrangement. Ever since the incident at Mogilev when Alexei had fallen from the tree and injured himself, I had been out of favour with the Empress. She passed me in the corridors without a word, even as I bowed low and humbled myself before her. When she entered a room where her son and I were together, she ignored me completely and directed all her remarks towards him. This in itself was not unusual—she stared through most of those who were neither blood relatives nor members of an illustrious family—but it was the manner in which her lip curled slightly when I was near by that made me realize the extent of her contempt. I believe she would have been happy to have seen me dismissed from the Royal Family's service entirely and sent home to Kashin—or further, perhaps, into a Siberian exile—but the Tsar remained a supporter of mine and so I managed to retain my place. Had it not been for his faith in me, my life might have followed an entirely different direction.

It was three nights later before I had company in my room again, but this time my visitor was not quite as welcome as Sergei Stasyovich. I was preparing for sleep when a tap came at my door, so quiet that I failed to hear it at first. When the knock sounded again, I frowned, wondering who could possibly require me at this late hour. It could not be Alexei, for he never bothered to knock. Perhaps ... I could hardly breathe for thinking

218

that it might be Anastasia. I sat up, swallowed nervously, and went to the door, opening it only a fraction and peering into the darkness of the corridor beyond.

At first, it seemed as if my ears had deceived me and there was no one out there. But then, just as I was about to close the door again, a man stepped forward out of the shadows, his long dark hair and black robes blending into the gloom of the hall so that for a moment only the whites of his eyes were visible.

'Good evening, Georgy Daniilovich,' he said in a clear voice, opening his mouth to reveal a set of yellow teeth in an approximation of a smile.

'Father Gregory,' I replied, for although I had never spoken to him before, I had seen him on many occasions, passing in and out of the Tsaritsa's suite of rooms. I had first laid eyes on him on my very first night at the Winter Palace, of course, when I had disturbed him while he incanted a blessing over the Empress's head and he had looked across at me and caught me in the terror of his glance.

'I hope it's not too late to call on you,' he said.

'I was in bed,' I replied, suddenly conscious that I had opened the door wearing only the loose-fitting vest and shorts that constituted my night-clothes. 'Perhaps this can wait until tomorrow?'

'But I don't think it can,' he said, smiling wider as if this was a tremendous joke and stepping forward, not so much pushing me out of the way as simply continuing into the room until I had no choice but to step aside. He stood with his back to me, remaining perfectly still while staring down at my bed, before turning his gaze to the narrow

219

window that overlooked the courtyard and standing there as if he had been turned to stone. Only when I had closed the door again and lit a candle did he turn around, but the flickering light of the single flame was so weak that it did little to improve my view of him.

'I'm surprised to see you,' I said, determined not to appear intimidated by him, despite the fact that I found him to be a menacing presence. 'Is there a message from the Tsarevich?'

'No, and if there was do you think I would bring it?' he asked, looking me up and down slowly. I began to feel self-conscious in my underwear and reached for my trousers, which I pulled on even as he watched me, never once turning his gaze away. 'We have so much in common, you and I, and yet we never speak to each other. It's terribly sad, don't you think? When we could be such friends.'

'I can't think why,' I replied. 'In truth, Father Gregory, I have never been a spiritual man.'

'But the spirit is inside all of us.'

'I'm not so sure.'

'Why not?'

'I grew up without the benefit of education,' I explained. 'We had to work hard, my sisters and I. We didn't have time to worship icons or say prayers.'

'And yet you call me Father Gregory,' he said thoughtfully. 'You respect my position.'

'Of course.'

'You know what others call me, don't you?'

'Yes,' I replied immediately, determined to show no emotion, neither fear nor admiration. 'They call you the *starets*.'

'They do,' he replied, nodding his head and

220

smiling a little. 'A venerated teacher. One who lives a wholly honourable life. Do you find the name appropriate, Georgy Daniilovich?'

'I'm not sure,' I said, swallowing nervously. 'I don't know you.'

'Would you care to?'

I had no answer to this and simply remained where I was, unable to move, wanting to separate myself from his presence but feeling that my legs were great weights, pinning me to the floor.

'They have another name for me,' he said, after a long silence had lingered between us, and now his voice was low and deep. 'You have heard that name too, I imagine.'

'Rasputin,' I said, the word catching in my throat as I said it.

'That is it. And do you know what it means?'

'It means a man of no virtue,' I replied, struggling now to keep my voice steady, for those dark, unblinking eyes of his were staring directly into my own and causing me to feel entirely unsettled. 'A man who makes himself familiar with many.'

'How polite you are, Georgy Daniilovich,' he said, smiling a little. *Makes himself familiar with many*. A very quaint phrase. What they mean is that I have relations with every woman I meet.'

'Yes,' I said.

'My enemies claim that I have ravished half the population of St Petersburg, do they not?'

'I have heard that.'

'And not just the women, but the young girls too. And the boys. They say I take my pleasures wherever I can find them.' I swallowed nervously and looked away. 'There are those who even have the temerity to suggest that I have taken the

221

Tsaritsa to my bed. And that I have penetrated each of the Grand Duchesses in turn, like a rutting bull. What do you think of that, Georgy Daniilovich?'

I looked back at him now, my lip curling in distaste. I felt an urge to strike him, to turn him from my room, but I was powerless beneath that dark gaze of his. A chill ran through my body and I considered running towards the door, flinging it open and fleeing along the corridor, anything to be away from this man. And yet I could not make that step. Despite how much his words disgusted me, I felt captivated by him, as if my legs would not obey me even if I commanded them to run. A silence lay between us for a minute, perhaps more, and he seemed to enjoy my discomfort, for he smiled to himself and laughed very low while he shook his head.

'My enemies are liars, of course,' he said finally, extending his arms as if he was about to embrace me. 'Fantasists, every one of them. Heathens. I am a man of God, nothing more, but they portray me as a fellow steeped in licentiousness. They are hypocrites too, for you've said it yourself, one moment I am an honourable man, the next I am without virtue. One cannot be a *starets* and Rasputin simultaneously, don't you agree? I don't allow such people to injure me, of course. Do you know why?'

I shook my head, but said nothing.

'Because I have been put on this earth for a greater purpose than they,' he explained. 'Do you ever feel like that, Georgy Daniilovich? That you have been sent here for a reason?'

'Sometimes,' I whispered.

'And what do you think that reason is?'

I thought about it and opened my mouth to reply, before changing my mind and closing it again. I had replied *sometimes* but in truth I had never considered the matter before; only when he asked me the question did I realize that yes, I did believe that I had been brought to this place for a purpose which I did not yet understand. The notion was enough to make me feel even more unsettled and when I looked up, the *starets* was smiling that horrible smile once again, the strangest detail of which was that, much as he repulsed me, I found it impossible to remove my eyes from his face.

'I said earlier that you and I are alike,' he said, the dark pools around his pupils swirling before me in the candlelight, as malevolent and destructive as the Neva in the heart of winter.

'I don't believe we are,' I said.

'But you are the protector of the boy and I am the guardian of the mother. Can't you see that? And why do we care for them so? Because we love our country. Isn't it true? You can't allow any harm to come to the boy, or the Tsar rules without an heir of his own issue. And at this time of crisis too. War is a terrible thing, Georgy Daniilovich, don't you agree?'

'I don't allow harm to come to Alexei,' I protested. 'I would lay down my life for him if I had to.'

'And how many weeks did he suffer at Mogilev?' he asked then. 'How many weeks did they all suffer—the boy, the sisters, the mother, the father? They thought he would die, you know that. You lay awake at night listening to his screams, just as we all did. How did they sound to you, like noise or

223

music?'

I swallowed. Everything he was saying was the truth. The days and weeks that had followed the Tsarevich's fall had been nightmarish. Never had I seen a person suffer as he had. When I was permitted to enter his chamber to talk to him I did not see the cheerful, lively boy with whom I had formed an almost fraternal connection. Instead, I found a skeletal child, his limbs twisted and contorted upon the bed, his face yellow, his skin soaked in a perspiration that would return no matter how often cold cloths were pressed to his face. I saw a boy who looked at me through eyes that recognized nobody but yet begged me to help him, an innocent who reached out with what little strength he had and screamed at me, imploring me to do something, anything, to take his torment away. I had never witnessed such distress, had never even believed that the agonies he suffered could exist. How he survived it, I did not know. Every day and night I expected him to succumb to the pain and allow himself to slip away. But he never did. He had a strength which was quite unexpected. It was the second time I had realized that yes, this boy could be a Tsar.

And through it all, through those three weeks of torture, the Tsaritsa, that good woman, had almost never left his side. She sat beside him, holding his hand, talking to him, whispering to him, encouraging him. We were not friends, she and I, but by God, I could recognize a loving and devoted mother when I saw one, all the more so for having never had one myself. By the time it was over and the relief finally came, by the time Alexei began to improve and his strength started to return, she had aged noticeably. Her hair had turned grey, her skin had become blotched with stress. That one incident, for which I had been entirely responsible, had altered her irreparably.

'If I could have helped him, I would have,' I told the *starets*. 'There was nothing I could do.'

'Of course not,' he said, extending his hands and smiling. 'But you must never blame yourself for what happened. Indeed, that is why I came to visit you tonight, Georgy. To thank you.'

I frowned and stared at him. 'To thank me?' I asked.

'But of course. Her Majesty, the Tsaritsa, has been much occupied with the health of her son of late. She is concerned that she might have appeared . . . unfriendly towards you.'

'I thought no such thing, Father Gregory,' I lied. 'She is the Empress. She may treat me as she wishes.'

'Yes, but we thought it important that you understand that you are valued.'

'We?'

'The Tsaritsa and I.'

I raised an eyebrow, surprised by the formulation. 'Well, gratitude is not necessary,' I said finally, confused by his meaning, unconvinced that the Tsaritsa had ever said any such thing or sent him on this mission at all. 'And please reassure Her Majesty that I will do everything in my power to ensure that no such incident ever takes place again.'

'You're not just a handsome boy, are you?' he asked quietly, taking a step towards me so that only a few inches separated us and my back was pressed against the wall. 'You're also a very loyal one.'

'I hope so,' I replied, wishing that he would leave.

'Boys your age are not always so loyal,' he said, stepping closer still, and now I could smell the foulness of his breath and feel his body beginning to press against my own. My stomach turned; I felt a sudden conviction that he had been sent to murder me, but instead he simply turned his head a little and smiled, a ghastly expression of doom, and held my gaze with those terrible eyes. 'You are loyal to the entire family,' he purred quietly, running a finger from the top of my shoulder along my arm. 'Here, you took a bullet for one,' he whispered, hesitating at precisely the spot where Kolek's bullet had passed through my shoulder. 'And here you would take a bullet for the boy,' he said, pressing the palm of his hand flat against my chest, my heart pounding quickly beneath his touch. 'But where will you be when the bullets come in the future?'

'Father Gregory,' I whispered, desperate for him to leave me now, 'please . . . I beg of you.'

'Where will you be, Georgy? When the doors open and the men step inside with their revolvers? Will you take the bullets then or will you be hiding like a coward in the trees?'

'I don't know what you're talking about,' I cried, confused by what he was saying. 'What men? What bullets?'

'You'd step in front of one for the girl, wouldn't you?'

'What girl?'

'You know what girl, Georgy,' he said, his hand flat against my abdomen now, and I waited for the knife to appear, for him to press it into my gut and twist it to kill me. He knew; that much was obvious. He had discovered the truth about Anastasia and me and had been sent to kill me for my indiscretion. I wasn't going to deny it. I already loved her and if that was to be my doom, then so be it. I closed my eyes, waiting for my flesh to be pierced and the blood to spill from the cavity, drowning my bare feet with its glutinous warmth, but second followed second and minute followed minute and nothing happened, no blade ripped me in two, and when I opened my eyes again, he was gone. It was as if he had just dissolved into the atmosphere, leaving no trace of his presence behind.

Perspiring, trembling with fear, I collapsed on to the floor and buried my head in my hands. The *starets* knew everything, of course he did. But who would he tell? And when they found out, what would become of me then?

*　　　*　　　*

The lady who was in charge of all domestic staff in the Winter Palace was the Duchess Rajisa Afonovna, and she had been surprisingly friendly to me since our first meeting, the day after my arrival in the city. Our paths crossed from time to time in the family quarters as she was an intimate of the Tsaritsa's, and when they did, she always greeted me cordially and stopped to converse, which many of her rank would never deign to do. So it was to her that I went the next morning to enquire on Asya's behalf for employment.

She maintained a relatively small office on the first floor of the palace. I knocked and waited for her to answer, before poking my head around the door and greeting her.

'Georgy Daniilovich,' she said, breaking into a smile and beckoning me to enter. 'This is a welcome surprise.'

'Good morning, Your Grace,' I replied, closing the door behind me and taking a seat where she indicated, next to her on a small sofa. I would have preferred the single armchair a few feet from there, but the chair indicated a position of superiority and I would not have dared. 'I hope I'm not disturbing you.'

'You're not,' she said, gathering up some papers before her and laying them carefully on a small table. 'If anything, I welcome the distraction.'

I nodded, surprised again by how pleasantly she treated me, in marked contrast to her friend, the Tsaritsa Alexandra, who took no notice of me at all.

'How are you anyway?' she asked. 'You are settling in well?'

'Very well, Your Grace,' I replied, nodding. 'I believe I am starting to understand my duties.'

'And your responsibilites too, I hope,' she said. 'For you have many of them. You have earned the trust of the Tsarevich, I hear.'

'Indeed,' I said, breaking into a fond smile at the mention of Alexei. 'He keeps me busy, if I may say that.'

'You may,' she said, laughing. 'He's an energetic boy, that's certain. He will be a great Tsar one day, all being well.' I frowned, surprised by her choice of words, and for a moment I thought I saw the beginnings of a blush on her cheeks. 'A great Tsar, most certainly,' she said then, correcting herself.

'But you must find it strange here, do you not?'

'Strange?' I asked, uncertain what she meant.

'Being so far from home. From your family. My own son, Lev, I miss him every day.'

'He doesn't live in St Petersburg, then?'

'Usually, yes,' she said. 'But he is . . .' She sighed and shook her head. 'He is a soldier, of course. He is fighting for his country.'

'Yes,' I said. It made sense. The Duchess was no more than forty years old; it made sense that she would have a son in the army.

'He can't be more than a couple of years older than you, actually,' she said. 'You remind me of him, in some ways.'

'I do?' I asked.

'A little. You have his height. And his hair. And his build. Actually,' she added, laughing a little, 'you might be brothers.'

'You must worry about him.'

'From time to time I get a full night's sleep,' she said with a halfsmile. 'But not often.'

'I'm sorry,' I said, sensing that she might be getting upset. 'I shouldn't be discussing this with you.'

'It's all right,' she said, shaking her head and smiling. 'Sometimes I am scared for him, sometimes I am proud. And sometimes I am angry.'

'Angry?' I asked, surprised. 'At what?'

She hesitated and looked away. She looked as if she was struggling to stop herself from saying what she wanted to say. 'At the direction he takes us in,' she said quietly, through gritted teeth. 'At the madness of it all. At his utter incompetence in military matters. He'll have us all killed before he's

229

done.'

'Your son?' I asked, her sentences making little sense to me.

'No, not my son, Georgy. He is nothing more than a pawn. But I have said too much. You came to see me. How can I help you?'

I hesitated, unsure whether I should pursue the conversation we had been having, but decided against it. 'I just wondered about the domestic help,' I said. 'Whether you needed another person on the staff.'

'You're not thinking of trading the Leib Guard for a set of apron strings, I trust?'

'No,' I said, laughing a little. 'No, it's my sister, Asya Daniilovna. She has ambitions towards service.'

'Does she indeed?' asked the Duchess, appearing interested. 'She is a girl of good character, I assume?'

'Irreproachable.'

'Well, there are always places here for girls of irreproachable character,' she said, smiling. 'Is she here in St Petersburg, or back in ... I'm sorry, Georgy, I forget where it is you are from?'

'Kashin,' I reminded her. 'The Grand Duchy of Muscovy. And no, she's not there, she's already ...' I hesitated and corrected myself. 'Forgive me,' I said. 'Yes, she's still there. But she would like to leave.'

'Well, I daresay she could be here in a few days if we send word to her. Write to her, Georgy, by all means. Invite her here and let me know when she arrives. I can most certainly find a position for her.'

'Thank you,' I said, standing up, uncertain why I had lied about Asya's whereabouts. 'You are too kind to me.'

'It's like I said—' She smiled, picking up her papers once again. 'You remind me of my son.'

'I will light a candle for him,' I said.

'Thank you.'

I bowed deeply and left the room, standing in the corridor outside for a few moments. A portion of me was delighted that I could return to my sister with such news, that I could be a hero to her once again. Another part of me felt angry that she was entering this new world of mine, a world that I wanted only for myself.

'You seem confused, Georgy Daniilovich,' said the *starets*, Father Gregory, who appeared before me so suddenly, so unexpectedly, that I let out a cry of surprise. 'Be at peace,' he urged quietly, reaching a hand out and holding my shoulder, caressing it slightly.

'I am late for Count Charnetsky,' I said, trying to pull away from him.

'An odious man,' he said, smiling, displaying his yellow teeth. 'Why go to him? Why not stay with me?'

And what unexpected, impossible-to-understand part of me felt a desire to say *Yes, all right*? I shrugged him off, however, and walked away without a word.

'You'll make the right decision in the end, Georgy,' he called after me, his voice echoing along the stone walls and reverberating in my head. 'You will put your own pleasures ahead of the desires of others. That is what makes you human.'

I broke into a run and within a moment the sound of my boots banging along the corridor drowned out what I knew was the truth behind his words.

*   *   *

Throughout the winter and early spring of 1916, I made it my business to ensure that the Tsarevich did not engage in any activities which might result in his receiving an injury; no easy task when confronted with a lively, eleven-year-old boy who saw no reason why he should be refused the same games and exercises that his sisters enjoyed. There were many occasions when he lost his temper with his minders, throwing himself on his bed and beating the pillows with his fists, so upset was he by the manner in which he was protected. Perhaps this frustration was exacerbated by the fact that he came from a family of sisters, and he was the Tsarevich, and yet only they could do the things that he most desired.

In the late winter, the Imperial Family went on a skating expedition together on a frozen lake near Tsarskoe Selo. The Tsar himself and his four daughters, along with the tutor Monsieur Gilliard and Dr Federov, spent the afternoon carving grand designs into the thick ice, while in the safety of the lake's surround, wrapped in furs and gloves and hats, sat the Tsaritsa with her son.

'Can't I just go out there for a few minutes?' he pleaded as the light started to dim and it became clear that the games would soon come to an end.

'You know you can't, my darling,' replied his mother, smoothing his hair down along his forehead with her hand. 'If anything should happen—'

'But nothing will happen,' he insisted. 'I promise, I shall take great care.'

'No, Alexei,' she said with a sigh.

'But it's so unfair,' he snapped, his cheeks burning with resentment. 'I don't see why I should be stuck over here, on this side of the lake, while my sisters are out there, having fun, and are allowed to do anything they want. Look at Tatiana. She's practically blue with the cold. And yet no one insists that she should step away and warm herself up, do they? Look at Anastasia. She keeps staring over in my direction. It's obvious that she wants me to join them.'

I was standing to the rear of the royal party and smiled a little to myself as he said this, for I knew that it was not her brother who Anastasia was looking towards, but myself. It was a continuing source of astonishment to me that we had managed to maintain the secrecy of our love affair over the course of almost a year. Of course, there was a great innocence to it all. We arranged clandestine meetings, wrote private notes to each other in a code of our own design, and when we saw to it that we could be alone together, we held hands and kissed and told each other our love would last for ever. We were wrapped up in each other and terrified that someone might learn of our romance, for discovery would mean certain separation.

'You make all these demands, Alexei,' said the Tsaritsa with an exhausted sigh as she filled a pewter mug with hot chocolate from a flask. 'But surely I don't need to remind you of the agonies you suffer when you have one of your falls.'

'But I won't *have* one of my falls,' he insisted

233

through gritted teeth. 'Am I to be treated like this for the rest of my life? Am I to be wrapped in cotton wool and never allowed to be happy?'

'No, Alexei, of course not. And when you are a man you may do as you wish, but for now it is I who make the decisions and they are in your best interests. Trust me on this.'

'Father,' said Alexei, turning to the Tsar now, who had skated alongside Anastasia to the side of the lake, where he was forced to overhear their argument. Their faces were pink with the cold, but they had been laughing and enjoying themselves, despite the freezing temperature. Anastasia smiled at me and I smiled a little in return, careful that my reply should not be noticed. 'Father, please let me skate for a little bit, won't you?'

'Alexei,' he said, shaking his head in sorrow, 'we have spoken about this.'

'But what if I don't go alone?' suggested the boy. 'What if I was to skate with someone on either side of me? Someone to hold my hands and keep me safe?'

The Tsar considered this for a moment. Unlike his wife, he was conscious of the other people who made up our party—the servants, extended family members, princes of noble families—and at such times he was always anxious that his son should not be perceived as a weakling who could not risk the most normal of activities. He was the Tsarevich, after all. It was important that he be seen as strong and masculine if the security of his position was to be maintained. Sensing his father's hesitation, the boy seized on the weakness immediately.

'And I'll only stay out there for ten minutes,' he continued, pleading his case. 'Fifteen at most.

Maybe twenty. And I'll go terribly slow. No faster than walking, if you like.'

'Alexei, you cannot,' began the Tsaritsa, before she was interrupted by her husband.

'Do you give me your solemn promise that you will go no faster than a walk? And that you will hold the hands of those who accompany you?'

'Yes, Father!' shouted Alexei in delight, jumping off his chair and—to everyone's shock—almost tripping over his own feet as he reached for a pair of skates. I jumped forward to catch him before he could fall to the ground, but he corrected himself in time and stood there, looking a little embarrassed by his tumble.

'Nicky, no!' cried the Tsaritsa immediately, standing up too and looking at her husband angrily. 'You cannot allow it.'

'His spirit must have some freedom,' replied the Tsar, looking away from her, unwilling to catch his wife's eye. I could tell how much he hated this kind of scene to be played out in front of others. 'After all, Sunny, you can't expect him to sit here all afternoon and not feel that he is being cheated.'

'And if he should fall?' she asked, her voice already crackling with tears.

'I won't fall, Mother,' said Alexei, kissing her cheek. 'I promise it.'

'You nearly fell getting off your chair!' she cried.

'That was an accident. There won't be any more.'

'Nicky,' she said again, appealing to her husband, but the Tsar shook his head. He wanted to see his son on the lake, I realized. And regardless of the consequences, he wanted the rest of us to see him there too. Husband and wife stared at each other, their mutual strengths competing in a power struggle. Palace gossip had it that theirs had been a love match when they had married just over two decades before—their union had come about against the inclination of both the Tsar's father, Alexander III, and his mother, the Dowager Empress Marie Fyodorovna, who resented the Tsaritsa's Anglo-German ancestry. Throughout all their years together he had never treated her with anything other than adoration, even when daughter after daughter had been conceived and a son had seemed like a distant possibility. It was only in recent years, since Alexei had been diagnosed with haemophilia, that their relationship had begun to disintegrate.

Of course, the other gossip, repeated around the whole country, was that the Tsar had been replaced in Alexandra's affections and in her bed by the *starets*, Father Gregory, but whether this was true or a slander I did not know.

'I'll take him out, Father,' said a quiet voice and I looked towards Anastasia, who was smiling that innocent, gentle smile of hers. 'And I'll hold his hand all the time.'

'There, you see?' said Alexei to his mother. 'Everyone knows that Anastasia is the best skater of all of us.'

'Not just you, though,' replied the Tsaritsa, sensing defeat but wanting to ensure a part for herself in the decision-making. 'Georgy Daniilovich,' she said, surprising me by turning around and knowing exactly where to find me, 'you will accompany my children also. Alexei, you're to stand between them and hold both their hands, is that understood?'

'Yes, Mother,' he said in delight.

'And if I see you let go even once, then I will call you back and you will not disobey me.'

The Tsarevich agreed to her terms and finished tying his laces as I made my way to the edge of the lake and swapped my heavy snow boots for the lighter blades of the skating shoes. I caught Anastasia's eye and she smiled coquettishly at me; what a perfect little plan she had orchestrated. We were set to dance out on the lake together in full view of everyone without raising a single person's suspicions.

'You're a fine skater, Your Highness,' I declared as the three of us skated slowly towards the centre of the lake, where the other skaters and the Grand Duchesses parted in order to give us room.

'Why, thank you, Georgy,' she replied haughtily, as if I was nothing more than a servant to her. 'You seem surprisingly unsure of yourself on the ice.'

'Do I?' I asked, smiling.

'Yes, have you not skated before?'

'Many times.'

'Really?' she asked in surprise as the three of us circled the circumference together, swishing left and right, keeping in time with each other, picking up the pace every so often until the shouts of the Tsaritsa from the edge forced us to slow down again. 'I didn't know you had enough free time to leave the palace for such frivolity. Perhaps your duties are not as onerous as I thought.'

'Not here, Your Highness,' I answered quickly. 'No, I meant back in Kashin, my home village. In the winter when the lakes froze over we would slide across them. Not on skates, of course. We had no money for such luxuries.'

'I see,' she said, enjoying the flirtation. 'You

skated alone, I assume?'

'Not always, no.'

'With your friends, then? The other slow-witted, thick-bodied boys with whom you were reared?'

'Not at all, Your Highness,' I grinned. 'Families in Kashin, like every other place in the world, are blessed with both daughters and sons. No, I would skate with the girls of my village.'

'Stop fighting, you two,' cried Alexei, who was concentrating on staying upright, for in truth, he was not a very good skater at all. He was also too young to recognize that this was no argument, but a continuing flirtation.

'I see,' said Anastasia after a few moments. 'Well, it has stood you in good stead, sliding across your lakes with those big, hard-working girls. I myself have been an accomplished skater for a number of years now.'

'I can tell,' I replied.

'Yes, you have met Prince Evgeny Ilyavich Simonov?'

'On occasion,' I said, recalling the handsome young scion of one of St Petersburg's wealthiest families, a fellow blessed with maple-coloured skin, a thick head of blond hair and the whitest teeth I had ever seen on any living being. It was well known that half the young women in society were in love with him.

'Yes, he taught me everything I know,' said Anastasia with a sweet smile.

'Everything?'

'Almost everything,' she conceded a few moments later, pursing her lips together as she looked at me, the closest we could come to a public kiss.

'Let's try a circle,' I said, looking down at Alexei.

238

'A circle?'

'Yes, we can spin around. Your Highness,' I continued, looking at Anastasia, 'you take my hand too, so we three create a ring together.'

She did as instructed and a moment later we were bonded together, skating this way and that in a small circle of three, a pleasurable dance that was interrupted only when the Tsaritsa began waving her arms in frustration at the edge of the lake and insisting that we return to safety. Sighing, wishing that the moment could continue for ever, I suggested that we should go back, but the moment that Alexei was safely returned to his mother's arms, Anastasia grabbed my hand again and, faster now, sped along the ice with me as I struggled to match her speed and maintain my equilibrium.

'Anastasia!' cried the Tsaritsa, who was more than aware how unseemly it was for us to be skating alone together like this, but the sound of the Tsar roaring with laughter at how I had nearly tipped over was enough to convince me that such an escapade would be permitted, for a few moments at least.

And so we skated. And the skate became a dance. We fell in line with each other, matching movement for movement, length for length. It lasted for no more than a few minutes, but it felt like an eternity. When I think back to Tsarskoe Selo and the winter of 1916, it is this that I remember most vividly.

The Grand Duchess Anastasia and I, alone on the ice, hand in hand, dancing to our own peculiar rhythms, as the red sun descended and darkened before us and her parents and sisters watched us from afar, ignorant of our passion, unaware of our

239

romance. Dancing in time with each other, a perfect combination of two, wishing that this moment might never end.

*   *   *

And now I must relate the great moment of shame in my life. I live with the memory of it by telling myself that I was young, that I was in love, not just with Anastasia but with the Imperial Family, with the Winter Palace, with St Petersburg, with the entire new life that had been so unexpectedly thrust upon me. I tell myself that I was drunk with selfishness and pride, that I did not want anyone else to become part of my new existence, that I wanted only to begin again. I tell myself all these things, but they are not enough. It was a sin.

Asya was waiting for me at the time that we had said; I suspected that she had been there for much of the afternoon.

'I'm sorry,' I told her, looking her directly in the eye even as I betrayed her. 'There's nothing here for you. I asked, but there's nothing that can be done.'

She nodded and accepted what I said without complaint. As she vanished into the night I told myself that she would be better off in Kashin, where she had friends and family, a home. And then I put her from my mind as if she had been nothing more than a distant acquaintance and not a sister who loved me.

I never saw or heard from her again. I must live with this memory, with this dishonour.

1941

I failed to notice the gentleman on the first three occasions when he appeared at the library, but on the fourth, Miss Simpson, who was much taken with him, pulled me aside with an exhilarated expression on her face.

'He's here again,' she whispered, clutching me by the arm and looking out into the body of the library, before turning back to me eagerly; I had never seen her quite so animated before. She had the feverish excitement of a child on Christmas morning.

'Who's here again?' I asked.

'*Him*,' she said, as if we had been engaged in a conversation about the fellow already and I was being deliberately obtuse by not acknowledging it. 'Mr Tweed, as I call him. You've noticed him, haven't you?'

I stared at her and wondered whether she was going mad; the war, after all, was playing havoc with everyone's mind. The constant bombings, the threat of bombings, the aftermath of bombings . . . it was enough to drive even the most rational soul towards lunacy. 'Miss Simpson,' I said, 'I have no idea what it is you're talking about. There's someone here who you've seen before, is that it? A troublemaker of some sort? I don't understand.'

She grabbed me, dragging me away from the desk where I had been working, and a moment later we were hidden behind a shelf of books, staring at a man who was sitting at one of the reading tables, his attentions entirely engaged

241

upon a large reference book. There was nothing particularly remarkable about him, other than the fact that he was dressed in an expensive tweed suit, hence Miss Simpson's name for him. I suppose he was a rather handsome fellow too, with dark hair swept and lacquered away from his forehead. His tan suggested that he was either not English or had spent a lot of time abroad. Of course, the most unusual thing of all was that a man of his age—he was in his late twenties—was in the library at the British Museum at two o'clock on a Thursday afternoon. He should, after all, have been in the army.

'Well, what about him?' I asked, irritated by my young colleague's enthusiasm. 'What has he done?'

'He's been in every day this week,' she said, nodding her head ferociously. 'Haven't you noticed him?'

'No,' I said. 'I don't make it a habit to notice young gentlemen who choose to use the library.'

'I think he must be sweet on me,' she said, giggling and looking back at him again with an appreciative smile. 'How do I look, Mr Jachmenev? Is my lippy all right? It's been months since I even had any and then this morning I found an old tube at the back of my dresser and thought *That's for luck*, so I put it on to cheer myself up. What about my hair? I have a brush in my bag. What do you think, should I give it a quick run-through?'

I stared at her and felt my sense of irritation growing. It wasn't that I was immune to the frivolity that some of the younger people engaged in from time to time; after all, in recent years daily life had become both more difficult and frightening for all of us. The last thing I wanted was to deny anyone a moment of fun on the rare occasions when one could be found. But there was a limit to how much jollity I could endure. It was, to put it plainly, annoying.

'You look fine,' I said, stepping away from her in an attempt to return to my work. 'And you'd look even better if you got on with your job and stopped wasting time with such silliness. Don't you have anything to be getting on with?'

'Of course I do,' she said. 'But come on, Mr Jachmenev, there's precious few men in London as it is and just take a look at him, he's gorgeous! If he's coming in here every day to see me, well, I'm not going to say no to him, am I? Perhaps he's just too shy to talk. There's an easy way around that, of course.'

'Miss Simpson, please, can't you—?'

But it was too late. She picked up a book from the shelf and began walking towards him. Despite my better instincts, I found myself watching out of a morbid desire to see what might happen next; there was always a certain voyeuristic thrill to be had from Miss Simpson's behaviour and, on occasion, I indulged in it. She swaggered across the floor, her hips swaying left and right with all the confidence of a film star, and when she reached him, she dropped the book purposefully to the ground, its hard covers crashing on the marble flooring with an enormous booming sound that echoed around the chamber, causing me to roll my eyes in my head. As she reached over to pick it up, she offered anyone who was near by a very clear view of both her posterior and the top of her stockings. It was almost indecent, but she was a pretty girl and it would have taken a stronger man than I to look away.

Mr Tweed reached for the book and I saw her laugh and say something to him, her fingers caressing the shoulder of his jacket for a moment, but he shrugged her off quickly and muttered a terse reply before replacing the dropped volume in her hands. Another question followed; this time he simply turned the front cover of his own book to display the title and she leaned over to look at it, offering him a clear view of her ample bosom. He seemed unmoved by the spectacle, however, and averted his eyes in a most gentleman-like fashion. From where I was standing, I could see that he had been engaged in a study of Gibbon's *Decline and Fall of the Roman Empire* and I wondered whether he was an academic or a professor of some sort. Perhaps he had an illness that prevented him from enlisting. There were any number of reasons why he might have been there.

It was not surprising that Miss Simpson was taking such an interest in him. A few years before, there would have been any number of young men passing through the library or the museum on any given day, but life had changed considerably since the outbreak of the war and the presence of an eligible young man at one of our reading tables, when so many of his number had been led away from the cities as if by a military Pied Piper, was certainly worthy of note. Our lives were governed by rationing, curfews, and the sound of the air-raid sirens every night. Walking along the streets, one was confronted by groups of two or three girls together, all nurses now, stepping quickly between makeshift hospitals and their digs, their faces pale, their eyes dark and hollow from lack of sleep and exposure to the broken, ripped-asunder bodies of their countrymen. Their white skirts were often flecked with scarlet but they seemed not to notice any more, or not to care.

For two years I had been expecting the library to be closed indefinitely, but it was one of those symbols of British life about which Mr Churchill maintained a stubborn defiance, and so we remained open to the public, often as a sanctuary for adjutants from the War Office, who sat in quiet corners of the reading room, consulting maps and reference books in an effort to impress their superiors with historically proven strategies for victory. We operated with a much smaller staff than before, although Mr Trevors was still with us, of course, for he was too old to enlist. Miss Simpson had come to us at the outbreak of hostilities; the daughter of some well-connected businessman, she had been given this position on account of the fact that she 'couldn't bear the sight of blood'. There were a couple of other assistants, none of whom were of fighting age, and then there was me. The Russian fellow. The émigré. The man who had lived in London for almost twenty years and was suddenly distrusted by almost everyone for one simple reason.

My voice.

'Well, he plays his cards close to his chest, that's for sure,' said Miss Simpson, returning to the desk where I was standing once again, having grown bored of observing her flirtation.

'Does he indeed,' I remarked, attempting to sound uninterested.

'All I did was ask him his name,' she continued,

245

ignoring my tone, 'and he said wasn't that very forward of me and I said, Well I call you Mr Tweed on account of the fact that you wear that gorgeous tweed suit every day. Present from your wife, was it, I asked him, or your girlfriend? *I'm afraid that would be telling*, he says to me then, all airs and graces, and I said I hoped he didn't think I was being inquisitive, only it's not so often we get the likes of him in here of an afternoon. *The likes of me?* he asks then. *What do you mean by that?* Well, I didn't mean any offence, I told him, only he seemed like a superior sort of chap, that was all, someone with good conversation, perhaps, and for what it was worth I was free myself later this evening and—'

'Miss Simpson, please!' I snapped, closing my eyes and rubbing my thumbs against my temples in irritation, for she was giving me a headache with her incessant prattle. 'This is a library. A place of erudition and learning. And you are here to work. It is not a forum for gossip or flirtation or silly chatter. If it's at all possible, could you kindly reserve your—'

'Well, pardon me and no mistake,' she snapped, standing tall with her hands on her hips as if I had just offered her the worst type of insult. 'Hark at you, Mr Jachmenev. Anyone would think I was after giving State secrets away to the Gerries, the way you carry on.'

'I'm sorry if I was abrupt,' I said with a sigh. 'But really, this is too much. There are two trolleys of books over there that have been waiting to be cleared since early morning. There are books left on tables that haven't been returned to their shelves. Is it really asking that much for you simply

246

to do your job?'

She glared at me for a moment longer and pursed her lips, sticking her tongue into the corner of her mouth before shaking her head and turning around, marching away with as much dignity and outrage as she could muster. I watched her for a moment and felt slightly guilty. I liked Miss Simpson, she meant no harm to anyone and was, for the most part, pleasant company. But I shuddered at the idea of Arina ever turning into a young woman like that.

'She's quite a piece,' said a quiet voice a few moments later and I looked up to see him, Mr Tweed, standing in front of me. I glanced down to take his book, but he wasn't holding any. 'A bit of a handful, I would imagine.'

'Her heart's in the right place,' I replied, feeling enough solidarity of the workplace to avoid criticizing her to a stranger. 'I suppose most of the young people have precious little to entertain themselves with these days. However, I do apologize if she was bothering you, sir,' I added. 'She's an excitable thing, that's all. I think she's flattered by your interest in her, if you don't mind me saying so.'

'My interest in her?' he asked, raising an eyebrow in surprise.

'The fact that you've been coming in every day to see her.'

'That's not why I've been coming in,' he said in a tone which made me look at him afresh. He had a curious air about him, one that implied that he was not perhaps the academic I had taken him for.

'I don't understand,' I said. 'Is there something I can—'

'It's not her I've been coming in to see, Mr Jachmenev,' he said.

I stared at him and felt my blood run cold. The first thing I tried to decipher was whether or not he had an accent. Whether he was an émigré, too. Whether he was one of us.

'How do you know my name?' I asked calmly.

'It is Mr Jachmenev, isn't it? Mr Georgy Daniilovich Jachmenev?'

I swallowed. 'What do you want?'

'Me?' He sounded a little surprised, but then shook his head and looked away for a moment before leaning in closer. 'I don't want anything. It's not me who wants your help. Who *needs* your help.'

'Then who?' I asked, but he said nothing, just smiled at me, the type of smile that—had she not been finally engaged upon her work in a separate part of the reading room—might have been the undoing of Miss Simpson.

*   *   *

The lightning war over London had been going on for months and had accelerated to the point where I thought it might drive us all mad. Every night we waited in terror for the wail of the air-raid sirens to begin—the anticipation was almost worse than the fact of them, for nobody could feel safe in the kinetic silence until they finally and inevitably began to sound—and when they did, Zoya, Arina and I would run towards the deep-level shelter at Chancery Lane, the two long parallel tunnels of safety which quickly filled with residents of nearby streets, to find a place to call our own.

248

There were only eight such shelters in the city, far too few for the number of people who needed to find refuge there, and they were dark, unpleasant places, stinking, noisy, fetid underground passages that, ironically, made us feel even less safe than we had in our own homes. Despite the strict rules regarding which shelter each enclave was supposed to go towards, people started to arrive at the stations in the early evening from the more distant areas of London, waiting outside in order to secure their own position, and there was often an unseemly rush to get through the doors when they opened. Unlike the popular legend which has built up over time, stoked by the flames of patriotism and the tranquillity of safe recollection, I can recall no cheerful moments in those shelters, few nights when there was any type of solidarity on display between us poor mice, driven underground by the overhead bombing. We rarely talked, we didn't laugh, we never sang songs. Instead, we gathered in small family groups, trembling, anxious, tempers fraying, occasional outbursts of violence pricking the fretful atmosphere. There was a constant terrifying sensation that at any moment the roof might collapse above our heads and bury us all in rubble-topped graves beneath the streets of the demolished city.

By the middle of 1941, the bombing had started to grow a little less frequent than six months previously, but one never knew the night, or the time of night, when the sirens might go off, a situation which left us in a constant state of exhaustion. Although everyone hated the sound of the bombs exploding, tearing down our neighbours' homes, creating deep chasms in the streets and killing those poor souls who failed to make it to the shelters on time, Zoya found them particularly agonizing. Any notion of firepower or slaughter was enough to send her spirits desperately low.

'How long can this go on?' she asked me one night as we sat in Chancery Lane, counting the minutes until we could emerge safely from our tomb to examine the damage of the previous night's bombing. Arina was asleep, half tucked inside my overcoat, seven years old by now, a child who thought the war was simply a normal part of life, for she could scarcely remember a time before it had been central to her world.

'It's hard to say,' I replied, wanting to offer her some notion of hope but unwilling to create false optimism. 'Not much longer, I think.'

'But haven't you heard anything? Has no one spoken to you and told you when we might—?'

'Zoya,' I said quickly, interrupting her and looking around to ensure that no one was listening, but it was too noisy for anything she said to be overheard. 'We cannot talk of that here.'

'But I can't take it any longer,' she said, her eyes filling with tears. 'Every night it's the same thing. Every day I worry about whether we will survive to see another morning. You have friends now, Georgy. You are important to them. If you could only ask them—'

'Zoya, be silent,' I hissed, my eyes narrowing as I glanced around quickly. 'I've told you. I know nothing. I can ask no one. Please . . . I know how difficult it is, but we cannot talk about these things. Not here.'

Arina shifted in my arms and looked up at me sleepily, her eyes half open, her mouth working slowly as her tongue flickered across her lips, her expression changing to ensure that both of us, mother and father, were still here to protect her. Zoya reached forward and kissed her forehead, smoothing the palm of her hand across her hair until the child returned to sleep.

'Do you ever think we came to the wrong place, Georgy?' she asked me, her voice quiet and resigned now. 'We could have gone anywhere when we left Paris.'

'But it's everywhere, my love,' I replied quietly. 'The whole world is caught up in this. There was nowhere we could have escaped it.'

My mind drifted back frequently to Russia during those long nights in the shelter. I tried to imagine St Petersburg or Kashin as they might exist after twenty years away from them and could not help but wonder how they were surviving the war, how their people were coping with this torture. I never thought of St Petersburg as Leningrad, of course, even though the newspapers referred to it as the Bolsheviks' city. I had never become accustomed to Petrograd either, the name the Tsar had inflicted on it during the Great War, when he feared that its original title was too Teutonic for a great Russian city, particularly when we were engaged in a war of boundaries with his German cousin. I tried to imagine this man Stalin, about whom I read so frequently, and whose face I distrusted. I had never met him, of course, but had heard his name discussed in the palace during the last year—along with those of Lenin and Trotsky—and it seemed curious that he had been the one to

251

survive and rule. The reign of the Romanovs had come to an end in an outpouring of repugnance at the autocracy of the Tsars, but it seemed to me that this new Soviet leadership differed from the old Russian empire in little but name.

Although I thought of them infrequently, I wondered how my sisters were coping with the war, whether they were even still alive to endure it. Asya would be in her mid-forties by now, Liska and Talya in their forties. They were certainly old enough to have sons—my nephews, who might be fighting on the Russian fronts, laying down their lives on European battlefields. I had often longed for a son and it hurt me to think that I would never know any of these boys, that they would never sit and share their experiences with their uncle, but this was the price I had paid for my actions in 1918: banishment from my family, eternal exile from my homeland. It was entirely possible that none of them were even alive any more, that they had grown old childless or had been murdered during the Revolution. Who knew what retaliation might have been visited upon them in Kashin, if news of my actions had reached that small, hopeless village.

Three bombings in particular had a great effect on my family. The first was the partial bombing of the British Museum, a place I considered a home of sorts. The library was left mostly intact, but parts of the main building were destroyed and subsequently closed down until they could be repaired again, at some unknown date in the future, and it grieved me to see such a magnificent building brought to this.

The second was the destruction of the Holborn

Empire, the cinema that Zoya and I had frequented on many occasions before the outbreak of the war, the place I associated almost entirely with my Greta Garbo obsession and the night that my wife and I had spent two hours lost in images and memories of our homeland during *Anna Karenina*.

The third was the most devastating of all. Our neighbour, Rachel Anderson, who had lived in the flat next to ours for six years and had been a friend and confidante to Zoya and a grandmother of sorts to Arina, was killed in a house in Brixton, where she had been visiting a friend, when they had failed to get to an air-raid shelter in time. Her body was not discovered for more than a week and in the meantime her absence had already left us fearing the worst. Her loss caused each of us great suffering, but most particularly Arina, who had seen Rachel every day of her life, and who had never known what it was to grieve before.

Unlike her parents, who knew only too well.

*   *   *

First, there were a series of letters, none of which contained any information that could possibly be considered important, but I translated them anyway, and looked for hidden meanings among the idioms. They were dated from over a year before and included details of troop activities which would have been long over by the time I sat down to render the Russian alphabet into English; most of the men whose movements had been directed by these letters were dead already. I worked carefully, reading each note from start to

253

finish in order to get a clear sense of their meaning before deciding how to decipher them. I wrote in a neat, clear script on white vellum paper which was provided for me by the War Office, using a black fountain pen of excellent quality which had been laid on the table before I arrived, and when I was finished, at almost the precise moment that I laid the pen down, the door opened and he stepped inside.

'The mirror,' I said, nodding in the direction of the glass which ran the length of one wall. 'You were watching me through it, I suppose?'

'Yes, Mr Jachmenev,' he replied with a smile. 'We like to observe. I hope you don't mind.'

'If I minded, I wouldn't be here, Mr Jones,' I said. 'It's not as if you made a great secret of it, anyway. I could hear you talking in there. It's really not very secure. I hope you don't use it for more important people than I.'

He nodded and gave me an apologetic shrug before taking a seat in the corner of the room and reading my pages carefully. He was wearing a different suit from the one he had worn in the library on the day he first introduced himself to me, but it was of equally good quality and I couldn't help but wonder how he was able to purchase it at a time when rationing was so strict. *Mr Tweed*, Miss Simpson had called him on that first afternoon. *Mr Jones*, he had introduced himself as a little later, offering no first name, a most unusual overture which implied that this was no more his real name than Miss Simpson's more fanciful offering. Not that it mattered. Whoever he was made no difference to me. After all, he wasn't the first person in my life who was pretending to be someone they were not.

'Your suit,' I said, watching him as he scanned my sentences, his expression changing from time to time as he drifted between approval and surprise.

'My suit?' he asked, looking up.

'Yes. I was just admiring it.'

He stared at me and the corners of his mouth turned up a little, as if he was unsure how to take the remark. 'Thank you,' he said, a note of suspicion in his tone.

'I wonder how such a suit is available to a young man. In these difficult times, I mean,' I added.

'I have a private income,' he replied immediately, the speed of his response suggesting to me that he didn't care to discuss it. 'These are very good,' he continued, stepping over to sit at the table beside me. 'Very good indeed. You've avoided the mistakes that most of our translators make.'

'Which are?'

'Translating every word and every phrase exactly as they appear on the page. Ignoring the differences in idiom from language to language. In fact you haven't translated them at all, have you? You've told me what every letter says. There's a keen difference.'

'I'm glad you appreciate it,' I said. 'But perhaps I can ask you something?'

'Of course.'

'Your Russian is obviously as good as mine is.'

'Actually, Mr Jachmenev,' he said with a smile, 'it's better.'

I stared at him, amused by his arrogance, for he was a good fifteen years younger than me and sported an accent which implied that he had been schooled at Eton or Harrow or one of the other

255

exclusive schools which made young gentlemen out of the sons of wealthy fathers. 'You're from Russia?' I asked in a disbelieving tone. 'You sound so . . . English.'

'That's because I am English. I've only been to Russia a few times. Moscow. Leningrad, of course. Stalingrad.'

'St Petersburg,' I said quickly, correcting him. 'And Tsaritsyn.'

'If you prefer. I've been as far west as the Central Siberian Plateau. As far south as Irkutsk. But that was purely for pleasure. Once I was even in Yekaterinburg.'

I had been looking back down at the letters as he spoke, enjoying the sight of Russian characters again, but at that word, at that most terrible of words, my head snapped up and I stared at him, examining his face for anything that might betray his own secrets.

'Why?' I asked.

'I was sent there.'

'Why Yekaterinburg?'

'I was sent there.'

I looked at him and felt a mixture of excitement and anxiety coursing through my veins. I couldn't remember when I had last encountered someone so entirely in control of their emotions; a young man who never perspired, never lost his temper and never said anything which he was not absolutely sure that he wanted to say.

'You have only visited Russia,' I said finally, for it seemed as if he was not going to speak again until I did.

'That's correct.'

'You've never lived there?'

'No.'

'But you believe your Russian is better than mine?'

'Yes.'

I couldn't help but laugh a little at the absolute certainty in his tone. 'Might I ask why?'

'Because it's my job to have better Russian than you,' he said.

'Your job?'

'Yes.'

'And what is your job exactly, Mr Jones?'

'To have better Russian than you.'

I sighed and looked away. The conversation was utterly pointless, of course it was. He wasn't going to tell me anything that he didn't want to. It would be simpler if I just waited for him to talk instead. He would say the same things, regardless.

'But having said that,' he added, lifting the letters once again and scattering them across the table, 'your Russian is excellent. I commend you. I mean it's not as if you've had anyone to practise it on these last twenty years, is it?'

'Haven't I?'

'Your wife, of course,' he said with a shrug. 'But you don't speak Russian at home. And you never speak it around your daughter.'

'How do you know what I speak at home?' I asked, feeling my temper begin to rise a little now; I hated the fact that he seemed to know so much about me. I had spent twenty years trying to protect my family's privacy and now this boy was sitting next to me telling me things that he should never have known. I wanted to know how had he discovered them. I wanted to know what else he knew about me.

257

'Am I wrong?' he asked, sensing my annoyance perhaps and softening his tone.

'You know that you're not.'

'And why is that, Mr Jachmenev? Why don't you speak your own language around Arina? Don't you want her to know her heritage?'

'You tell me,' I said. 'You seem to know everything else about me.'

Now it was his turn to smile. We sat there for what felt like a very long time but he said nothing in reply, simply shook his head and nodded.

'Really very good,' he repeated, tapping his index finger on the bundle of letters. 'I knew I'd found the right man. But I think next time we might offer you something a little bit more challenging, don't you?'

*   *   *

The experience of being Russian in London between 1939 and 1945 was not an easy one. There were many evenings when Zoya recounted stories to me of how, purchasing food in a grocer's or butcher's shop where she had been a customer for years, she was stared at with mistrust the moment her request betrayed her accent; of how the portions of rationed meat passed across the counter were always slightly smaller than those handed to the English women in front and behind her in the line. Of how the bottle of milk was always closer to its use-by date, the bread always a little more stale. Whatever friendliness and sense of belonging we had built up with our neighbours over more than twenty years among them, however much we thought we had assimilated ourselves into their country, seemed to dissipate almost overnight. It didn't matter to them that we were not German. We were not English, that was all that counted. We spoke differently, so we must be agents of the enemy, dispersed into the heart of their capital in order to discover their secrets, betray their families, murder their children. All around us was the stink of suspicion.

Whenever I stopped to read one of the propaganda posters that were liberally scattered around the walls of the city—careless talk costs lives; you never know who's listening; be like dad, keep mum—I understood why people stopped their conversations whenever they heard me speak and why they turned to look at me, their eyes opening wide as if I was a threat to their well-being. I began to hate speaking in shops or cafés, preferring to point to whatever I wanted and hoping that I could be served without the need for conversation. And when we were not avoiding the bombs in the air-raid shelters, Zoya and I spent every evening at home together, where we could talk freely without having to endure the intimidating stares of strangers.

Towards the end of 1941, I found myself walking home one evening with my spirits particularly low after a long and difficult day. The wife, daughter and mother-in-law of my employer, Mr Trevors, had been killed the night before, when Mrs Trevors' family home had been struck by a single bomb, dropped by a Luftwaffe aeroplane which had veered wildly off course. It was the worst luck imaginable—theirs was the only house in the street which was in any way damaged—and Mr Trevors had been distraught because of the tragedy. He'd wandered into the library in the late afternoon without any of us noticing and a short time later, I heard loud cries coming from his office. When I went inside, the poor man was seated behind his desk with an expression of utter devastation on his face, which changed to tears and howling when I attempted to comfort him. Miss Simpson followed me in a few minutes later and surprised me by taking full charge of the situation, finding whisky from I knew not where to settle his trembling, before taking him home and offering what little friendship he would allow at such a terrible moment.

Still unsettled by these events, I did something entirely out of character as I made my way home, stepping into a public house in desperate need of alcohol. The place was two-thirds full, mostly older men who were beyond the age of enlisting, women of all ages, and a few soldiers in uniform, home on leave. I barely gave any of them a second glance and walked directly to the bar, leaning up against it, glad for what little support it offered.

'A pint of ale, please,' I said to the barman, who was unfamiliar to me, despite the fact that this was as close to a local pub as Zoya and I had, but then we had rarely set foot in there.

'What was that?' he asked, his tone confrontational as he narrowed his eyes and looked at me with barely disguised contempt. It was difficult not to be aware of his thick arms as he wore the sleeves of his shirt rolled up towards the biceps, the suggestion of a tattoo peeping out from beneath the cuffs.

'I said I'd like a pint of ale,' I repeated, and this time he stared at me for ten, perhaps twenty seconds, as if he was considering whether or not to throw me out into the street, before finally nodding and walking slowly towards one of the pumps, where he poured a long draught into a glass, heavy with foam, and set it on the counter before me.

'Isn't that a bitter?' I asked, knowing full well that it would be better if I simply left the bar and went home. Zoya usually kept a few bottles of rationed ale hidden in a cupboard somewhere for emergency moments such as this.

'One pint of bitter,' said the barman, holding his hand out. 'As requested. That'll be sixpence, if you please.'

Now it was my turn to hesitate. I looked at the glass, the beads of perspiration clinging invitingly to the side, and decided that this was not the moment to protest. The hum of conversation around the room had already lessened, as if the other patrons were hoping that I might do something, anything, that would provoke a fight.

'Fine,' I said, reaching into my pocket and placing the exact change on the counter. 'And thank you.' I took my drink and sat down at an empty table, picking up a newspaper that a previous customer had left behind and scanning the headlines.

It was mostly war stories, of course. A series of quotes from a speech that Mr Churchill had given the afternoon before in Birmingham. Another that Mr Attlee had offered in support of the government. Short articles about bombings and the names of some of the people who had been killed, their ages and occupations, although nothing as yet about Mr Trevors' family; I wondered for a moment whether they would figure in the reports the following day or whether there were too many people killed to list them all. It was probably bad for public morale, anyway, to list the names of the dead every day. I was about to start reading a piece relating to a sporting event that barely interested me when I noticed two men walking down from the other end of the bar and sitting at the table next to mine. I glanced up—their drinks were half finished and I suspected they had been there for some time—but turned immediately back to my newspaper, unwilling to engage in conversation.

'Evening,' said one of the men, nodding at me, a fellow of about my own age with a pale complexion and rotten teeth.

'Good evening,' I replied, in a tone that I hoped would discourage further dialogue.

'Heard you at the bar, ordering your drink,' he said. 'Not from round here, are you?'

I looked up at him and sighed, wondering whether it would be in my best interests to simply stand up and leave, but decided not to allow myself to be intimidated by them.

'Actually, I am,' I replied. 'I live only a few streets away.'

'You might *live* only a few streets away,' he said, shaking his head, 'but you're not *from* here, are you?'

I stared at him and then towards his companion, who was a little younger, and rather simple looking, and nodded slowly. 'Yes, I am,' I replied calmly. 'I've lived here for nearly twenty years.'

'But you must be my age if you're a day,' said the man. 'Where were you for the twenty years before that, eh?'

'Do you really care?' I asked.

'Do I care?' he repeated with a laugh. 'Of course I bloody care, mate, or I wouldn't be asking you, would I? Do I care, he asks me,' he added, shaking his head and looking around as if the entire bar was his audience.

'It just seems like a rather dull question, that's all.'

'Listen, friend,' said the man, more forcefully now, 'I'm only trying to make conversation with you, that's all. I'm just being friendly, like. That's how we are here in England, you see. Friendly. Maybe you're not familiar with our ways, is that how it is?'

'Look,' I said, putting my glass down and staring him directly in the eye, 'if you don't mind, I'd prefer to be left in peace. I just want to enjoy my drink and read this newspaper, that's all.'

'Peace?' he said, crossing his arms in front of his chest and looking at his friend, as if he had never heard anything so extraordinary in all his life. 'Did you hear that, Frankie? This gentleman here says he wants to be left in peace. I daresay we'd all like to be left in peace, now wouldn't we?'

'Aye,' said Frankie, his head nodding up and down like a braying donkey. 'I know I would.'

'Only we none of us have any peace any more, do we?' he continued. 'What with all the trouble your lot have caused.'

'My lot?' I asked, frowning. 'And what lot would that be, exactly?'

'Well, you tell me. All I know is you're not an Englishman. You sound half-German to me.'

Now it was my turn to laugh. 'Do you really think that if I was German I would be sitting here, in a public house in the middle of London? Don't you think I would have been taken away and interned a long time ago?'

'Well, I don't know,' he replied with a shrug. 'They might have missed you out. You're a crafty lot, you Germans.'

'I'm not German,' I said.

'Well, that voice of yours tells me different. You didn't grow up in Holborn, I know that much for sure.'

'No,' I admitted. 'No, I didn't.'

'So what's all the secrecy about, then? Got something to be ashamed of, have you? Worried you might be caught?'

I looked around and hesitated before answering; there was a hum of chatter in the room, but I could tell that most ears were tuned to our conversation nevertheless.

'I'm not worried about anything,' I said eventually. 'And I'd rather not continue with this discussion, if it's all the same to you.'

'Then answer my question, that's all I want,' he said, his tone growing less patient with me now, more aggressive. 'Come on then, Mister, if it's not some big secret, then why can't you tell me where that accent of yours comes from?'

'Russia,' I said. 'I was born in Russia. Is that enough for you?'

He sat back for a moment and seemed almost impressed by this. 'Russia,' he repeated beneath his breath. 'Where do we stand on the Russians then, Frankie?'

'On their necks,' said the younger man, leaning forward and attempting to look threatening, which was difficult for him as he had an innocent, childlike expression, rather like a newborn lamb struggling to find its feet; I got the impression that when he was not being called upon to speak he was lost in a world of his own thoughts.

'Gentlemen, I think it's time for me to leave,' I said, standing up and walking away from them. They called after me that they were only being friendly, that all they wanted was to pass the time of day with me, but I ignored them and left the bar, aware that more than one set of eyes was focussed on me. I kept looking straight ahead, however, and turned on to the street which led towards my home. A few moments later, I heard footsteps behind meand my heart sunk. For twenty, thirty seconds I tried desperately not to turn around, but they were getting closer and closer. Finally, unable to stop myself, I looked back, just as the two men from the pub caught up with me.

'Where do you think you're going then?' asked the older one, pushing me against the wall and holding me there, his hand pressed around my throat. 'Going off to spill secrets to your Russian friends, are you?'

'Let go of me,' I hissed, breaking free of him for a moment. 'You've both been drinking. You're well advised to go back to it and leave me be.'

'Well advised, are we?' he asked, laughing as he looked at the younger man, before pulling his arm back and clenching his fist, ready to attack me. 'I'll give you well advised.'

That hand never made contact with my face. My left arm grabbed his right and, old habits, snapped it immediately as my own right fist pulled back, before sweeping forward with a low blow to the side of his jaw, sending him sprawling backwards

265

on the pavement, uttering an oath as he clutched his broken arm, which would not yet be hurting him, but growing numb and offering the sensation of great pain to come.

'He's broken my arm, Frankie,' he cried, the words dribbling down his chin like spilt beer. 'Frankie, he's only gone and broken my arm. Get him, Frankie. Sort him out.'

The younger man looked at me in astonishment—he had not expected such violence; nor had I—and I stared at him with a cold expression, holding his gaze for a moment before shaking my head, as if to tell him that any move on his part would be an ill-conceived idea. He swallowed nervously and I turned and walked away, maintaining a steady pace as I turned the corner, trying to ignore the sounds and threats that were following in my wake.

It had been years since I had been called upon to defend myself in such a way, but I had been trained well by Count Charnetsky and the movements came back to me quickly. But still, for all that, I felt a degree of shame for my actions and told Zoya nothing of the events of the evening when I returned home, talking to her instead of Mr Trevors' tragedy and the sympathy that Miss Simpson had offered him in his time of need.

*   *   *

My working hours remained unaltered. I arrived at the library at eight o'clock in the morning and left at precisely six. I spent much of my time behind the main desk, entering titles in the card system, as I had always done. When the tables became

266

particularly messy, I assisted Miss Simpson with clearing them. When there were difficult reference books which readers needed to source, I found them and delivered them into their hands as efficiently as possible.

But this was now a cover for my real responsibilities, which lay elsewhere.

If it was just an envelope which was to be delivered to me, a note would be placed in my jacket pocket as I walked to work, without my even noticing it, with a sentence scrawled on it. A phrase that meant nothing. *Don't forget we need milk, love Zoya*, written in a hand which was obviously not her own.

At the library, ensuring that no one was observing me, I would take a pencil and paper and look again at the words.

D for 4. F for 6. W is 23, which equals 5. N is 14, another 5. M, 13, which sums to 4. L, 12, therefore a 3. And finally Z, 26, 8.

Don't forget we need milk, love Zoya.
4655438
465-5438.

The book reference. Find the book, find the letter.

Read the letter.

Translate the letter.

Destroy the letter.

Deliver the meaning.

If there was more than a simple envelope, if it was a series of documents that needed to be examined, a man would pass me by as I left our flat in the morning, a different man every time, and he would bump into me and apologize, saying that he should have been looking where he was going.

When this happened, I would stop to buy a newspaper and some fruit at a corner shop near the museum. As I examined the fruit, searching for the least bruised apple, I would leave my briefcase on the floor beside me. When I lifted it again, it would be slightly heavier than it was before. Then I would buy the fruit and leave.

On occasion, the telephone would ring at the museum at precisely four twenty-two in the afternoon and I would answer it.

'Is that Mr Samuels?' a voice would say on the other end.

'There's no Mr Samuels here, I'm afraid,' I would reply, those exact words. No divergences. 'This is the library at the British Museum. Who are you looking for?'

'I'm so sorry,' was the reply. 'I think I must have the wrong number. It was the Natural History Museum I was after.'

'That's perfectly all right,' I would say, hanging up, and then, when I left work later, rather than walking directly home to my wife and child, I would take a bus towards Clapham and a car would be waiting for me on the corner of Lavender Hill and Altenburg Gardens to take me to see Mr Jones.

'A devil of a problem for you today, Mr Jachmenev,' he might say as I arrived. 'Think you can handle it?'

'I can but try,' I would reply with a smile, and he would lead me to a quiet room and lay a series of documents or photographs before me. Or perhaps he might introduce me to a roomful of stern men, none of whom would offer their names to me, but each of whom would pepper me with questions the

268

moment I walked through the door, and I would do my best to answer them with clarity and confidence.

On one occasion, I spent an entire night reading more than three hundred pages of telegrams and letters. Having imparted everything I had understood from them to Mr Jones, he appeared surprised by my reasoning and asked me to talk him through the logic of my translation once again. I did so, he thought about it a little more, and then summoned a car. Within the hour I was standing before Mr Churchill, who sucked on a cigar as I repeated to him what I had told Mr Jones earlier. He looked entirely displeased throughout my discourse, as if the whole direction of the war was changing and it was entirely my fault.

'And you're sure of this, are you?' he asked, stomping out the words at me with a heavy scowl.

'Yes, sir,' I said. 'Quite sure.'

'Well, it's very interesting,' he replied, drumming his chubby fingers on the table before him for a few moments before standing up. 'Very interesting and very surprising.'

'Indeed, sir,' I replied.

'Well done, Mr Jones,' he said then to my deliverer, checking his pocket-watch. 'But I must go now. Keep up the good work, there's a good fellow. Sound chap you have here, too. What's his name, anyway?'

'Jachmenev,' I said, even though the question hadn't been addressed to me. 'Georgy Daniilovich Jachmenev.'

He turned to stare at me, as if I had been entirely impudent to answer him when the question had been directed elsewhere, but finally he nodded and went on his way.

'A car will take you back to Clapham,' said Mr Jones then. 'I'm afraid you'll have to make your own way home from there.'

And so I did. Walking back in the moonlight, tired after a long day, I was nervous that at any moment the sirens would sound and Zoya, Arina and I would be separated.

Zoya smiled at me when I came through the door and prepared breakfast, placing it before me with a large pot of tea. She never once asked me where I had been.

The White Nights

The war was not going to our advantage.

As the riots in the streets evolved into attacks on the grain stores and municipal warehouses, the atmosphere surrounding the Imperial Family and its entourage began to change from arrogant confidence to frustration and concern. Through it all, however, the Tsar and Tsaritsa continued to divide their time between the palaces at St Petersburg, Livadia and Tsarskoe Selo and their leisure trips on board the *Standart*, as if the world was as it had ever been, and we poor disciples packed our belongings and followed them wherever they travelled.

At times it seemed as if they were entirely unaware of the mood among the people over whom they ruled, but as more news arrived from the Front regarding the number of Russian casualties, the Tsar resolved to quit the Winter

Palace entirely and replace his cousin, the Grand Duke Nicholas Nicolaievich, as head of the armed forces. To my surprise, the Tsaritsa offered little opposition to his decision, but then on this occasion he did not plan on permitting their son to accompany him.

'But is it entirely necessary?' she asked as the family gathered for a typically sumptuous meal; I stood alongside the butlers and servants in an unobtrusive line against the walls of the dining room, none of us allowing ourselves to breathe too loudly lest it upset the Imperial digestion. Naturally, I had positioned myself opposite Anastasia so that I could watch her as she ate; when she dared, she would glance in my direction and offer a tender smile that made me forget my tired legs. 'You mustn't put yourself in danger, Nicky. After all, you bear too many great responsibilities for that.'

'I understand that, but it's important that changes are made,' replied the Tsar, reaching for an elaborate samovar that stood on the table and refilling his cup slowly, narrowing his eyes as he watched the tea pour as if it might hypnotize him and spirit him away to a happier place. A moment later, he was using the tips of his fingers to massage his temples in a gesture of exhaustion. He had lost a great deal of weight in recent months, I noticed, and his thick, dark hair was advancing quickly towards grey. He seemed to be a man afflicted with a great and terrible burden, one that he might not be able to endure for much longer. 'England fears that we will pull our troops away from the action,' he continued in a tired voice. 'Cousin Georgie has said as much to me in a letter.

And as for France—'

'You told him we would do no such thing, of course?' interrupted the Tsaritsa, sounding appalled at the very idea.

'Of course I did, Sunny,' he replied irritably. 'But it's becoming difficult to put up a convincing argument. Most of the Russian Polish territories are now controlled by Cousin Willy and his German thugs, not to mention the Baltic regions.' I felt my eyes roll in my head as he said this; it struck me as extraordinary that the leaders of each of these countries bore such an intimate familial relationship to each other. It was as if the entire matter was nothing more than a childish game: Willy, Georgie and Nicky running around a garden, setting out their forts and toy soldiers, enjoying an afternoon of great sport until one of them went too far and they had to be separated by a responsible adult. 'No, I've made my mind up,' he said in a determined voice. 'If I place myself at the head of the army, then it becomes a message to both our allies and our enemies of the seriousness of my intentions. And it will be good for the men's morale, too. It's important that they see me as a warrior Tsar, a ruler who will fight alongside them.'

'Then you must go,' she replied with a shrug as she separated the meat of a lobster from its shell and examined it for imperfections, before allowing it the honour of being eaten by her. 'But while you are away—'

'You shall, of course, be at the helm of our constitutional duties,' he said, anticipating her question. 'As traditi gon dictates.'

'Thank you, Nicky,' she smiled, reaching across

and placing a hand on top of his for a moment. 'It pleases me that you have so much faith in me.'

'But of course I do,' he replied, not sounding terribly convinced by the wisdom of this decision, but knowing that it would be impossible to place anyone else in a position superior to his wife. The only other appropriate person was eleven years old and not yet ready for such responsibility.

'And anyway,' said the Tsaritsa quietly, looking away from her husband, 'I shall have my advisors near by at all times. I promise to listen carefully to your ministers—even Stürmer, whom I despise.'

'He's an effective Prime Minister, my darling.'

'He's a fop and a faint heart,' she snapped. 'But he is your choice and he will be offered every courtesy, as befits his office. And Father Gregory will never be far from my side, of course. His counsel will be invaluable.'

I noticed the Tsar freeze for a moment when she mentioned the *starets'* name, and a pulse in his jaw reflected his hostility to the idea of any influence that malevolent creature could extend, but if there were concerns or arguments that he wanted to make, he kept them to himself for now and simply nodded his head in resignation.

'Then you will be well served,' he offered quietly after a respectable pause, and no more was said on the subject.

'Not that I will be able to spend all my time on constitutional matters,' continued the Tsaritsa a few moments later, her voice betraying a little anxiety now, and I found myself turning my head slightly to look at her, as did her husband, who put down his cup and frowned.

'Oh?' he asked. 'And why is that?'

273

'I've had an idea,' she said. 'And I hope you'll think it a good one.'

'Well, I can't decide that until you tell me what it is, now can I?' he asked, smiling at her, although his tone suggested some impatience, as if he was dreading what his wife might be considering next.

'I thought I might do something to help the people too,' she said. 'You know I visited that hospital opposite St Isaac's Cathedral last week, don't you?'

'Yes, you mentioned it.'

'Well, it was horrible, Nicky, quite horrible. They don't have enough doctors or nurses to tend to the patients and they arrive, hundreds of them, throughout the day. And not just there, but all over the city. I'm told there are more than eighty hospitals scattered around St Petersburg now.'

The Tsar frowned and looked away from her for a moment; he didn't like to be confronted with the realities of the war he was fighting. The image of the young men arriving on stretchers was not one he liked to consider.

'I'm sure that everything that can be done for them is being done, Sunny,' he said finally.

'But that's just it,' she replied, leaning forward, her face flushed with excitement. 'There's always more that can be done. And I thought that I might be the one to do it. I thought I could help out as a nurse.'

For the first time that I could remember there was absolute silence in the Imperial dining room. Every member of the family sat as if they had been turned to stone, their knives and forks suspended in mid-air, staring at the Tsaritsa as if they could not quite believe what she had just said.

274

'Well, why are you all looking at me so?' she asked, turning from one face to another. 'Is it really so extraordinary that I would want to help these suffering boys?'

'No, of course not, my darling,' said the Tsar, recovering his voice. 'It's just . . . well, you have no training as a nurse, that's all. Perhaps you would be more of a hindrance to the good work which is being done there.'

'But that's just it, Nicky,' she insisted. 'I spoke to one of the doctors and he told me that it would take only a few days to train a lay person such as myself to assist in the basic tasks of nursing. Oh, it's not as if we would be performing operations or anything like that. We'd just be there to help out. To tend to wounds, to change dressings, even to clean up a little. I feel . . . you see, this country has been very kind to me since you brought me here all those years ago. And for every disrespectful cur who slanders my name, there are a thousand loyal Russians who love their Empress and would lay down their lives for her. This is my way of proving myself to them. Say I can do it, Nicky, please do.'

The Tsar tapped his fingers on the tablecloth for a moment as he considered her request, no doubt as surprised by his wife's sudden rush of philanthropy as the rest of us were. However, she appeared to be sincere, and finally he shrugged and offered a nervous smile, before nodding his head.

'I think it's a wonderful idea, Sunny,' he said. 'And of course you have my permission. Just be careful, that's all I ask. There are security arrangements that will have to be put in place, but if it's what you want, then who am I to stand in

275

your way? The people will see how devoted we both are to their welfare and to the success of the war effort. Only I must ask, you said "we", not "I". What did you mean by that?'

'Well, I shouldn't like to be there alone,' she said, turning towards the rest of the family now. 'I thought that Olga and Tatiana might join me too. They are of age, after all. And they can be of use.'

I turned to look at the Empress's two eldest daughters, who had both grown a little pale at the mention of their names. They said nothing at first, looking instead from their mother to their father, and then towards each other in dismay.

'Father?' began Tatiana, but he was already nodding his head furiously and appeared to have determined on his response.

'It's a magnificent idea, Sunny,' he said. 'And, my daughters, I cannot tell you how proud I am of you both that you would want to help out in this way.'

'But Father,' said Olga, who looked appalled at the idea, 'this is the first that either of us has heard of—'

'You make me very proud of you, my darling,' said the Tsar quietly, reaching across and taking his wife's hand. 'You all do. What a family I have! And if this doesn't stop the *moujiks* from debasing our names, then I don't know what will. It is actions like these that win wars, not fighting. Never fighting. You realize that, children, don't you?'

'What about me, Father?' asked Anastasia suddenly. 'Can I help too?'

'No, no, *Shvipsik*,' he said, laughing and shaking his head. 'I think you're a little too young yet to see such things.'

'I'm fifteen!'

'And when you are eighteen, like Tatiana, we can reconsider. If, God forbid, the war has not been won by then. But don't worry, we can find other ways for you and Marie to be of use. We will all help out. The entire family.'

I breathed a sigh of relief that Anastasia was not to be permitted to join her mother and sisters, for the entire thing struck me as a foolish if generous idea. A group of untrained nurses gathered in one hospital, surrounded by bodyguards, sounded like a method for disturbing the work that was being done there rather than assisting. Perhaps my sigh was too loud, however, for the Tsaritsa turned and stared at me—as she was generally loath to do—and her eyes widened in irritation.

'And you, Georgy Daniilovich,' she said, 'you have something to say on the matter?'

'I beg your pardon, Your Majesty,' I replied, blushing furiously. 'A throat tickle, that was all.'

She raised an eyebrow in distaste before turning back to her meal, and I caught Anastasia's eye, who was watching me and smiling as ever.

*   *   *

'It's all so horrible,' said the Grand Duchess Tatiana several weeks later, as she sat with Marie, Anastasia and Alexei in their private drawing room at the end of a particularly trying day. She looked pale and had lost weight since her nursing duties had begun; the dark bags beneath her eyes testified to early mornings and late evenings, while her discomfort in her chair suggested that her back was beginning to ache from spending long hours leaning over the beds of the injured soldiers. As the Tsarevich was present with his sisters, so was I, while Sergei Stasyovich completed our party, not standing to formal attention as was proper, but resting on the arm of one of the sofas close to the Grand Duchess Marie, rolling a cigarette casually as if he was not a servant of the Imperial Family at all, but an intimate. 'The hospitals are filled to capacity,' continued Tatiana, 'and the men are horribly injured, some with missing limbs or eyes. There's blood everywhere. Constant moaning and wailing. The doctors run about and shout their orders with no regard for rank whatsoever and their language borders on the profane. There are mornings when I wake up and wish that I might fall ill myself in order not to have to be there.'

'Tatiana,' cried Marie, outraged, for she had her father's sense of duty towards the soldiers and envied her older sisters their new responsibilities. She had pleaded with her mother to be allowed to join them as a nurse, but, as with Anastasia, her request had been denied. 'You shouldn't say such things. Think of the agonies our soldiers endure.'

'Marie Nicolaevna is right,' said Sergei, joining the conversation for the first time and staring at Tatiana with a look of pure distaste, an expression she had probably never seen on anyone's face before. 'Your disgust at the sight of blood is nothing compared to the suffering these men endure. And what's a little blood, after all? We're all filled with it, no matter what the colour.' I turned to look at him in surprise. It was one thing for us to be present at conversations such as this and even to offer a supportive comment from time to time, but to criticize one of the Grand Duchesses openly was an impertinence that could not go unanswered.

'I'm not saying that I suffer more than they do, Sergei Stasyovich,' replied Tatiana, her cheeks reddening noticeably as her anger rose. 'I would never suggest such a thing. I simply meant that it is not a sight that anyone should have to witness, that's all.'

'Of course not, Tatiana,' said Marie. 'That much is obvious. But don't you see? It's all very well for us to discuss these matters, wrapped up safely together in the Winter Palace, but think of the young men who are dying to ensure the continuance of our way of life. Think of them and tell me that you do not ache for them.'

'But sister, of course I ache for them,' she protested, raising her voice now in frustration. 'And I tend to their wounds and read to them and whisper in their ears and do all that I can to make them comfortable. Oh, it doesn't matter! You have misunderstood me entirely. And as for you, Sergei Stasyovich,' she added, turning to glare at him furiously, 'you might not speak with such arrogance if you found yourself at the Front rather than here.'

'Tatiana!' cried Marie, appalled.

'Well it's true,' she said, throwing her head back in a manner reminiscent of her mother. 'Who is he to speak to me in such a fashion, anyway? What does he know of the war, after all, when he spends his days following all of us around and practising his cross-steps and flèche attacks?'

'I know a little of it,' replied Sergei, narrowing his eyes as he glared at her. 'After all, I have six brothers fighting for your family's continuance. Or had, anyway. Three have been killed, one is missing in action, and the other two I have heard no news of in more than seven weeks.'

To her credit, Tatiana blushed a little at this remark and perhaps felt a little ashamed of herself. I noticed that when Sergei mentioned his dead brothers, the Grand Duchess Marie sat forward in her seat, as if she wanted to go to him and offer comfort. There were tears resting gently in her eyes—she looked very beautiful at that moment, the shadows cast by the fire flickering across her pale skin. Sergei noticed them too and the corners of his mouth turned upwards slightly in an appreciative smile. I was surprised to observe such intimacy between the two, and was moved by it.

'I don't mean that I would try to find a way *not* to go,' insisted Tatiana, looking across at each of us in turn, in order to ensure that we understood how seriously she meant this. 'I just wish that the war would end soon, that's all. Surely we all wish for that. Then we could go back to the way things used to be.'

'But things will never be as they were,' I heard myself say, and now it was my turn to be the recipient of her icy stare.

'And why do you say that, Georgy Daniilovich?'

'I only mean, Your Highness, that there are days and styles of living which are lost for ever. When the war is over, when peace has been restored, the people are going to demand more of their leaders than they did in the past. It's obvious. There will scarcely be a family in the land who has not lost a son in the fighting. Don't you think they will seek some recompense for their losses?'

'Recompense from whom?' she asked coldly.

'Why, from your father, of course,' I said.

280

She opened her mouth to reply, but it seemed that she was too shocked by the impertinence of what I had said to find the words to argue with me. The silence lasted for only a moment, however, before she turned away from me and threw her hands in the air in frustration.

'My sister just wants everything to go back to how it once was,' said Marie then, playing the role of peacemaker. 'And that's not such a terrible thing to wish for, after all. This was a wonderful country to grow up in. There were balls at the palace every night and wonderful parties. We all wish that things could have stayed like that for ever.'

I said nothing, but shot Sergei an amused glance, intended to mock her innocence and naivety. To my surprise, however, he did not return my smile, but glared at me instead as if he was insulted that I would dare to include him in some private joke against the Grand Duchess Marie.

'You should feel fortunate, Tatiana,' said Anastasia, speaking up now for the first time. 'It is a great honour for you to help the troops in this way. You are saving lives.'

'Oh, but I'm terrible at it,' she sighed, shaking her head. 'And the sight of all those lost limbs! You can't understand it, *Shvipsik*, unless you've seen it. Do you know that yesterday our mother assisted at an operation where a boy of seventeen had both his legs amputated? She stood there and witnessed it, helping out in whatever way she could. But the screams of the boy ... I swear I will hear that screaming again at my dying moment.'

'I only wish that I were a year or two older so that I could help out too,' said Anastasia wistfully, standing up and walking towards the window,

281

staring down into the courtyard below; I could hear the rush of the fountain as its water rose and fell and imagined that she was looking towards the nearby colonnades, where she had fallen into my arms for the first time and we had kissed. I longed for her to turn around and catch my eye, but she remained silent and strong, looking out beyond the walls of the palace itself.

'Well, you can take my place any time you want,' said Tatiana, standing up and brushing down the front of her skirts. 'I feel utterly miserable and intend to take a long bath. Goodnight,' she said, sweeping out of the room as if she had been the victim of a great insult, followed by Marie, who looked back as if she had one final comment to make, but thought better of it and left the room without another word.

A moment later Sergei left too, citing a forgotten task, and the night drew to a close. As Anastasia took Alexei to his room, I remained in the parlour for a few more minutes, turning off some of the lights, leaving only a few candles illuminated, anticipating the moment when she would return, when she would close the doors quietly behind her and find her way back into my open arms.

*　　　*　　　*

I had never experienced the White Nights and it was Anastasia's idea that I should see them for the first time with her. In truth, I had never heard of the phenomenon before and thought I was going mad when, restless and waking in the middle of the night, I opened my eyes to see bright daylight shining into my room. Thinking that I had slept through my usual early-morning awakening, I washed and dressed quickly and ran down the corridor towards the playroom, where Alexei could usually be found at that time, reading one of his military books or playing with some new toy.

The room was deserted, however, and as I made my way through the state rooms and the reception areas, finding each one as empty as the next, I started to panic and wondered whether I had slept through some great calamity that had occurred in the night. I was not far from the Tsarevich's own chamber, however, and when I ran inside, I was relieved to find the boy fast asleep in his bed, stretched across the covers, one bare leg extended over the side..

'Alexei,' I said, sitting down beside him and rousing him gently by the shoulder. 'Alexei, my friend. Come along, you should be up by now.'

He grunted and mumbled something indecipherable before rolling over; I could only guess what his mother would say if she arrived to kiss him goodbye before leaving for the hospital and found him still asleep so I shook him again, unwilling to allow him to return to his dreams. 'Alexei, wake up,' I insisted. 'You should be at your lessons.'

He opened his eyes slowly and stared at me as if he did not know who or where he was, before glancing over towards the window, where the light was streaming through the curtains.

'It's the middle of the night, Georgy,' he groaned, smacking his lips together and emitting an exaggerated yawn, stretching his arms out in exhaustion. 'I don't have to get up yet.'

'But it's not,' I said. 'Look how bright it is. Why,

it must be . . .' I glanced towards the clock which hung on his bedroom wall and was surprised to see that it was just past four o'clock. There was no possibility that we had all slept until the middle of the afternoon, however, so the only explanation could be that it was still early morning.

'Go back to bed, Georgy,' he muttered, turning over and falling immediately back to sleep with the ease of one whose conscience is clear.

Disoriented, I walked back towards my own room and returned to bed, although it was impossible to sleep in my confusion.

The following morning, however, I found myself alone with Anastasia as she finished her breakfast and she explained the phenomenon to me.

'We call it the White Nights,' she said. 'Haven't you ever heard of it?'

'No,' I said.

'I think it must be peculiar to St Petersburg. It has something to do with the fact that the city is situated so far to the north. Monsieur Gilliard explained it to us recently. The sun doesn't descend below the horizon at this time of the year for a few days, so the sky doesn't get dark. It gives the impression that it is daytime constantly, although I suppose there is more of a dusk-like feeling in the early hours of the morning.'

'How extraordinary,' I remarked. 'I was sure that I had overslept.'

'Oh, you wouldn't be allowed to oversleep,' she replied with a shrug. 'Someone would be sure to come and find you.'

I nodded, feeling slightly irritated by this remark, a sensation which was only alleviated when she stepped closer to me and, ensuring that there was no one in sight to observe us, kissed me lightly on the lips.

'You know, it's traditional for young lovers to walk along the banks of the Neva together during the White Nights,' she said, smiling flirtatiously at me.

'Is it indeed?' I asked, a grin beginning to spread across my face.

'It is. Some are even known to make plans for marriage then. It's just as curious a phenomenon as the White Nights themselves.'

'Well,' I said, extricating myself from her grip playfully, as if the idea of such a commitment was anathema to me, 'then I should be leaving.'

'Georgy!' she cried, laughing at me.

'I'm only teasing,' I said, taking her in my arms once again, although I did so nervously. Of the two of us, I was always the one more scared of getting caught; perhaps because I knew that my punishment for discovery would be far more severe than hers. 'But I think it's a little early for an engagement, don't you? I can only imagine what your father would say.'

'Or my mother.'

'Or her,' I agreed, grimacing, for while the concept of my ever being allowed to marry a daughter of the Tsar was a foolish one, there was a small part of me that believed that the Tsar himself would look more favourably on a love-match than the Tsaritsa would. It was neither here nor there, of course. Such an inappropriate match could never be made. A fact which neither Anastasia nor I liked to dwell upon.

'Still,' she said, skirting quickly past the awkwardness of the moment, 'you cannot be in St

285

Petersburg and not experience them. We should go out tonight.'

'We?' I asked. 'You don't mean we should go together?'

'Well, why not? After all, it might be bright out, but it will still be night-time. The household will be asleep. We could slip out, well disguised, and no one would ever know.'

I frowned. 'Isn't it a little risky?' I asked. 'What if we are seen?'

'We won't be,' she insisted. 'As long as we don't draw attention to ourselves, that is.'

I was unsure of the wisdom of the plan, but Anastasia's enthusiasm won me over, as did the idea of the two of us walking along the riverbank hand in hand, like any of the other young lovers who strolled together at night. We would be normal people for once. Not a Grand Duchess and a member of the Leib Guard. Not an anointed one and a *moujik*. Just two people.

Georgy and Anastasia.

Typically, the Imperial Family went to bed early, particularly now that the Tsar was quartered at Stavka and the Tsaritsa and her two eldest daughters were up by seven o'clock in order to be at the hospital an hour later. And so we decided to meet by the Alexander Column in Palace Square at three o'clock in the morning, when we were sure that no one would be awake to see us. I went to my bed at midnight as usual, but didn't sleep. Instead I read a few chapters of a book I had borrowed from the library, a volume of Pushkin's poetry that I had recently been reading in an attempt to educate myself; I didn't understand much of it, but did my best to concentrate. When it was time to leave, I

286

pulled on a pair of trousers, a shirt and an overcoat—not my typical guard's uniform—and crept downstairs and out into the peculiar bright night.

The square was quieter than I had ever seen it before, but there were still people passing through, their spirits raised by the late-night illumination. Groups of soldiers returning from some adventure ambled by noisily. Two prostitutes, young and rouge-faced, leered in my direction and offered me those sensual delights which were still unknown to me, but which I desired desperately. Drunks returning from some excess sought, sung and forgot the words of ancient songs in off-key voices. I spoke to no one, however, ignoring all advances, and waited silently in our agreed meeting place until I saw my darling emerge from behind one of the colonnades and raise a gloved hand in my direction. She was dressed in the most extraordinary outfit. A simple dress, with a *dusegrej* on top, the sleeveless, fur-lined jacket a second layer beneath the common person's *letnik*. A cheap pair of shoes. A headscarf. I had never seen her wear anything quite so lacking in jewels before.

'Good God,' I said, walking towards her and shaking my head, even as I tried to stop myself from laughing. 'Where on earth did you find those things?'

'I stole them from one of my maid's wardrobes,' she giggled. 'I'll replace them in the morning, she'll never know.'

'But why?' I asked. 'It's beneath you to wear such—'

'Beneath me?' she asked, surprised. 'Why, Georgy, you don't know me at all if you believe that I think that way.'

'No,' I said quickly. 'No, I didn't mean that. It's just—'

'There may be people who will recognize me,' she said, looking around and pulling her scarf closer about her head. 'It's unlikely, but nevertheless, it's not worth taking the risk. These clothes will help me blend into the crowd, that's all.'

I took her hand and pressed my lips to hers, my body curving against the contours of her own, my desire anxious to be recognized. 'You could never blend into any crowd,' I told her. 'Don't you know that by now?'

She smiled and bit her lip in that funny way of hers, shaking her head at my foolishness, but I could tell that she was pleased by the compliment.

A few minutes later, we were making our way along the side of the palace and on to the path that bordered the banks of the river. The night was warmer than most I had known; we could breathe without seeing clouds of unspoken words dissolving into the atmosphere before us and my trousers were not clinging to my legs with that damp sensation that characterized so many St Petersburg evenings. The first sight that greeted us was the vision of the half-completed Palace Bridge, whose construction had begun even before I had arrived in the city, but which had been halted by the war and stood as a stark reminder of how our progress had been stunted in recent years. Stretching from the front of the Hermitage and across to Vasilievsky Island, the enormous brick and steelwork supports stood in place on either side of the Neva, but there was no sign that the two would ever meet; instead they stretched out towards each other, like a pair of lovers separated by a great expanse of water. I caught Anastasia staring in their direction, her expression a little disheartened, and found myself hurting for her.

'You're looking at the bridge?' I asked.

She nodded but remained silent for a moment, imagining what might have been. 'Yes,' she said finally. 'Do you think they will ever complete it?'

'Of course,' I said, my confident tone masking my uncertainty. 'Some day. It can't stay like that for ever.'

'When it began I was perhaps eleven or twelve years old,' she recalled, smiling a little. 'Alexei's age. The construction law decreed that no work could be done on it between nine at night and seven in the morning, the time when, perhaps, you might consider it most suitable to work on such a project.'

'Really?' I asked, surprised by her knowledge of such things.

'Yes. And do you know why they did that?'

'No.'

'Because it would have kept me awake. My sisters and me that is. And my brother.'

I looked at her and laughed, sure that she was teasing me, but the expression on her face told a different story and I could only laugh again, amazed by the extraordinary life she lived.

'Well, you can sleep all you want now,' I said finally. 'There will be no workers, or any steel for that matter, until the war is over.'

'That day cannot come quickly enough,' she said as we continued to walk.

'You miss your father?'

'Yes, very much,' she admitted. 'But it's more than that. And it's not for the reasons my sister wants the war to end. I have no interest in balls or fine dresses or dancing or any of those trivialities which St Petersburg society treasures above all other things.'

'You don't?' I asked, surprised. 'I thought you might have enjoyed such entertainments.'

'No,' she said, shaking her head. 'I don't *dislike* them exactly, Georgy, it's not as simple as that. Sometimes they can be amusing. But you have no idea what life was like here before the war. My parents went to a different party every night of the week. Olga had just come out into society. They would have found her a husband soon. Some English prince, most likely. And they will, once the war is over, that much is certain. There's always talk of her being intended for Cousin David, the Prince of Wales.'

'Really?' I asked, surprised, for I hadn't thought that Olga was yet promised to any man. 'How long have they been in love?'

'In love?' she asked, turning to me and raising an eyebrow. 'Don't be ridiculous, Georgy, they're not in love.'

'Then how—?'

'Don't be naive. Surely you know how these things work. Olga is a beautiful young woman, don't you agree?'

'Well yes, of course,' I said. 'She has a more beautiful sister, however.'

Anastasia smiled and pressed her head to my arm as we continued to stroll along. The statue of the Bronze Horseman was on my left, looking for all the world as if it was ready to burst into a charge

290

and race towards the waterfront. 'Then she will need a husband,' she continued. 'She is the eldest daughter of the Russian Tsar, after all. She cannot marry just anyone.'

'No,' I agreed. 'No, I can see that.'

'And it has always been said that she and Cousin David would make a perfect match. He will be king one day, of course. When Cousin Georgie dies. That might not be for many years yet, of course, but then the throne will be his. And Olga will be Queen of England. Like our great-grandmother, Queen Victoria.'

I shook my head, confused by the associations between all the royal families of Europe.

'Is there anyone you're not related to?' I asked.

'I don't think so,' she replied in a perfectly serious tone. 'No one who matters, anyway. Cousin Georgie is King in England. Cousin Alfonso is King in Spain. Cousin Christian is King in Denmark. And then, of course, there is Cousin Willy, the Kaiser in Germany, but we are told not to refer to him as cousin any more. Not now that we are at war. But he was Queen Victoria's grandson, just as Mother was her granddaughter. Perhaps it is all a little strange. Do you think it odd, Georgy?'

'I'm not sure what to think,' I said. 'I can't keep track of all these names and the countries they rule over. I thought Prince Edward was the Prince of Wales.'

'Same person,' she said. 'David is his given name, Edward his regal name.'

'I see,' I said, not seeing at all.

'And if Olga is to be married to the Prince of Wales and become Queen of England, are Tatiana and Marie to suffer similar fates?'

'Of course,' she said, pulling her greatcoat tighter around her, for the night had grown cold now, even if the sun did still consent to give us light. 'They'll find some silly prince for both of them, I'm sure of that. No one as illustrious as Cousin David, perhaps. Tatiana might marry Cousin Bertie, I suppose. Mother proposed that idea last year and Father approved. Then they could be sisters in the English court, you see, which would be very convenient.'

'And what of you?' I asked quietly, stopping now and taking her arm to pull her around to face me. The tides of the river were flowing towards the banks and as she turned the wind lifted her hair away from her forehead, causing her to close her eyes slightly against the breeze, even as she put a hand to her neck to tie her headscarf more carefully.

'Me, Georgy?' she asked.

'Yes. Who are you to marry? Am I to lose you to some English prince? Or a Greek one? A Danish one? An Italian? At least let me know the nationality of my rival.'

'Oh, Georgy,' she said sadly, turning away from me, but I was not about to let her go so easily.

'Tell me,' I insisted, pulling her closer. 'Tell me now, so that I can prepare for my broken heart.'

'But it's you, Georgy,' she said, her eyes filling with tears as she reached forward to kiss me. 'It's you that I intend to marry. No one else.'

'But what can I offer you?' I asked, desperate with love and desire. 'I bring you no kingdom, you understand. No principality. No land over which to reign. I come without title or provenance, without

292

money or expectations. I am simply me. I am just Georgy. I am no one at all.'

She hesitated and looked deep into my eyes. I could see the sorrow there. The anguish. I knew that she cared nothing for my lack of prospects in the world, that I did not need to be of royal blood for her to love me. But still, this matter lay between us and divided us, like the tides of the Neva, separating the two unfinished sides of Palace Bridge. The war would end, the day would come, and the Tsar would decide. Another young man would arrive in St Petersburg. And he would be introduced to Anastasia and they would dance a mazurka together at the Mariinsky Palace while the whole of society watched them, and she would have little choice but to obey. And that would be the end of the matter. She would be betrothed to another. And I would be lost.

'There is one possibility,' she began, but before she could say anything further, we were interrupted and we both jumped in fright. So intent had we been on our conversation that we had lost track of everyone around us, and the sound of a man's voice next to me shocked us back into the real world.

'My apologies,' said the young man, a fellow of around my age, dressed in an outfit similar to my own. 'Could I trouble you for a match?'

I glanced at the unlit cigarette he held out towards me and patted the pockets of my coat for a light. Anastasia stepped out of my grip as I did so and retreated a little along the path, wrapping her arms around her body to protect herself from the cold as she looked down into the water. I located a small box of matches in my pocket and as the young man took one, I noticed his companion, a young peasant girl, staring at Anastasia. She was around the same age as my darling, no more than sixteen, with pretty features, spoiled only by a noticeable scar which ran along her left cheek from directly beneath her eye for perhaps two inches to a point below her cheekbone. The young man, who was handsome, with thick blond hair and an easy smile, lit his cigarette, smiled and thanked me.

'We'll all want to sleep tomorrow afternoon,' he said, glancing out towards the bright horizon.

'Probably,' I said. 'I keep thinking I should feel tired already and yet I don't. The light is playing tricks on me.'

'Last year I stayed up for the entire three days,' he said, taking a long drag from his cigarette. 'I was supposed to return to my regiment immediately afterwards, but I slept too long. I was nearly shot for it.'

'You're a soldier, then?' I asked.

'Was,' he said. 'I got shot in the shoulder and lost the use of this arm.' He nodded towards his left side. 'So they let me go.'

'Lucky you,' I said, smiling.

'Not so lucky,' he replied, shaking his head. 'I should be there, not here. I want to fight. And you?' he asked, looking me up and down to reassure himself that I was healthy. 'You are in the army?'

'On leave,' I lied. 'I have to return at the end of the week.'

He nodded and his expression seemed regretful. 'I wish you well, then,' he said, glancing towards Anastasia and smiling. 'I wish you both well.'

'And you,' I said.

'Well, enjoy your evening,' he added, turning to take his lover's hand, but she was staring at Anastasia with nothing short of awe upon her face, as if Mother Mary herself had descended from heaven to walk among us along the banks of the river. She knew who Anastasia was, of course, that much was obvious. And like most of the *moujik*s, she considered her to be appointed to her position by God himself. I held my breath, waiting to see whether she would cry out and betray us, but her dignity came to the fore and she shook her head to snap out of the daze, and instead simply reached forward and took Anastasia's right hand in her own, before sinking to her knees on the wet cobbles and pressing her fingers to it for a moment. I stared at this beautiful young woman, whose face had been terribly injured in who knew what way, pressing her lips against the pale, unblemished hand of the girl I loved, and felt a sudden rush of wonder for where I found myself. She looked up after a moment, and bowed her head.

'May I have your blessing?' she asked, and Anastasia's eyes opened wide in surprise.

'My . . . ?' she began.

'Please, Highness.'

Anastasia hesitated, but did not move. 'You have it,' she said, smiling gently as she leaned forward and embraced the girl. 'And for what little it is worth, I hope that it brings you peace.'

The girl smiled and nodded, took her injured soldier's hand, and they walked on without another word. Anastasia turned to me and smiled, her eyes filled with tears.

'It's getting cold, Georgy,' she said.

'Yes.'

'It's time to go back.'

I nodded and took her hand and we returned to the palace in silence, saying nothing further about the conversation we had been engaged in regarding Anastasia's marriage prospects. We had been born into different lives, it was that simple. We could no sooner change who we were than alter the colour of our eyes.

We separated as we entered Palace Square with one final, sorrowful kiss, and I made my way towards the doors which would lead to the staircase for my own room. Looking up towards the dark, unlit windows, I noticed a dark figure watching me from the third floor, but as I narrowed my eyes and blinked, trying to make out who was standing there, exhaustion caught up with me at last and the vision seemed to dissolve and disappear as if it had been nothing more than an illusion. I thought no more of it for now and went on my way to bed and to sleep.

1935

A moment of great happiness.

Zoya and I are sitting on our bed in the attic room of a lively Brighton boarding-house, enjoying a week's holiday, and she has just presented me with a new, finely tailored shirt as a birthday present. It's a rare thing for us to take a trip like this; our days and weeks and months are always filled with work, responsibilities, anxieties about money, so that extravagances such as vacations usually fall beyond our reach. But Zoya proposed that we leave London and take a short break together, somewhere we could enjoy long, lazy lunches in outdoor cafés without having to watch the clock, somewhere we could stroll along a beach hand in hand while children laughed and played on the pebbles and I had said *yes* without a moment's hesitation. *Yes*, let's do it. *Yes*, when can we leave?

Our trip coincided with my thirty-sixth birthday and that morning I woke with the realization that I had now spent more years away from my family in Kashin than I had ever spent with them, a thought that suffocated my otherwise cheerful mood with sensations of regret and shame. It was not often that I allowed the faces of my parents and sisters to reappear in my mind—I had been a poor son, there was no doubt of that, and an even worse brother—but they were with me that morning, crying out from some dark and distant chamber of my memory, embittered that I had found such unexpected happiness while they . . . well, I knew not what had become of them, other than a certainty that they were dead.

'I bought it in Harrods,' Zoya said, biting her lip a little in anticipation as I unwrapped the packaging and examined the gift; it was a shirt of unusual quality, the kind of luxury I would never have afforded for myself but was delighted to receive. 'You do like it, Georgy, don't you?'

'Of course I do,' I replied, reaching over to kiss her. 'It's very beautiful. But it's too much, really.'

'Please,' she said, shaking her head, anxious that I would not ruin her own pleasure by listing all the reasons why she should not have spoiled me. 'I'd never even set foot in Harrods before. It was quite

297

an experience, if I'm honest.'

I laughed when she said this, knowing how she would have planned the expedition weeks in advance, chosen the correct day when she could walk to Knightsbridge, select the gift, bring it home, inspect it, wrap it and hide it before I returned from work. I had never been inside the doors of the great department store myself, although I had walked past it on any number of occasions. I always felt a little apprehensive as I did so, however, sure that I would be turned away by some over-zealous doorman if I attempted to step inside, my inexpensive suit and émigré accent marking me out as one who had no business being on the inside. Zoya, on the other hand, was not intimidated by splendour; her avoidance of such stores stemmed from nothing other than common sense, for she would never have wasted her time longing for things that she couldn't have.

'Now my present, my present!' shouted Arina, toddling towards me with her arms outstretched, a small gift in her hands, also beautifully wrapped. She was grinning wildly but still uncertain on her legs, having only recently grown accustomed to standing and walking without assistance, delighted by her newly discovered independence. She hated it when we came too close, however, preferring the freedom to run where she wanted, regardless of danger. Our daughter did not want any safety nets.

'Another present!' I cried, sweeping her up in my arms and lifting her off the ground, her legs flying out in the air as she rejected the embrace and pushed me away, demanding to be returned to the floor immediately. 'What a lucky man I am! But what could it be?'

I unwrapped the package slowly and removed the gift from the tissue paper, staring at it for a moment, unsure what it was that I was looking at, and then recognizing it an instant later and drawing a deep breath of surprise, truly astonished by what I was holding in my hands. I looked across at Zoya and she smiled, a little nervously I thought, as if she wasn't quite sure how I might react to such a reminder of my past. Lost for words and worried that I might betray my emotions with some ill-chosen phrase, I said nothing for now but stepped over to the window instead, turning my face away from my family as I allowed the sunlight to illuminate this treasure.

My daughter had given me a snow globe, its base no bigger than the palm of my hand, a white plastic dome with a glass hemisphere constructed on top. At its centre stood an awkward model of the Winter Palace in St Petersburg, its frontage a dark blue where it should have been pale green, the roof statues nowhere to be seen, the Alexander Column missing from the square in front; but despite its deficiencies, the building was unmistakable to my eyes. Indeed, it would have been immediately recognizable to anyone who had ever lived or worked within its gilded walls. I held my breath as I stared at it, as if worried that to breathe on it might cause its collapse, and narrowed my eyes to examine the small white grooves that represented the windows of the three-floored palace.

And the memories flooded back.

I pictured the Tsarevich, Alexei, sprinting away from the colonnades, running along the edges of the quadrangle while a member of the Leib Guard gave chase, terrified that the boy might fall and injure himself.

I saw his father in the first-floor study, consulting with his generals and Prime Minister, his beard flecked with grey, his bloodshot eyes betraying their anxiety at the dispiriting news emerging from the Front.

In a room above, I imagined the Tsaritsa kneeling at her prie-dieu, the *starets* standing before her, muttering some dark incantation beneath his breath as she prostrated herself before him, not like an Empress at all, but like a common *moujik*.

And then, emerging from a door of the inner courtyard, a young man, a peasant from Kashin, lighting a cigarette as he stood in the cold air, rejecting the company of a fellow guard, for he wanted to be alone with his thoughts, to consider how he could possibly stifle the overwhelming love that he was feeling for one who was entirely beyond his reach, a liaison he knew to be utterly impossible.

I shook the globe and the collection of snowflakes which had been resting peacefully on its base rose upwards in the water, floating gently towards the roof of the palace before descending slowly, and the characters in my memory emerged from their hidden places and looked towards the skies, their hands outstretched, smiling at each other, together once again, wishing that these moments might never end and the future might never come.

I turned to Zoya, moved by the gift which had, of course, been purchased by her and not by our one-year-old daughter. 'It's hard to believe,' I said, my voice betraying a sudden rush of emotion.

'I found it in a jewellery store on the Strand,' she said, stepping over to the window too and laying her head gently on my shoulder as I held the globe out between us. The snow continued to fall; the palace continued to stand; the family continued to breathe. 'There was a whole shelf of them,' she told me. 'Different places in the world, of course. The Coliseum. The Tower of London. The Eiffel Tower.' She hesitated for a moment before looking up at me again. 'But I didn't choose it, Georgy, I swear it. I let Arina look at all of them and she picked the one she liked the best. She picked St Petersburg.'

I stared at her in surprise and couldn't help but smile. 'It's just so unexpected,' I said, shaking my head. 'It's been . . .' I thought about it for a moment and calculated the time in my head. 'It's been almost twenty years, can you believe that? I was so young then. Just a boy.'

'But you're still young, Georgy,' she said with a laugh, running her hand through my hair. It was such a delight to see her so happy. Those were joyous years, with our little Arina, the most unexpected gift of all, by our sides. 'And anyway, I'm growing old alongside you,' she added. 'I'll be getting wrinkles soon. Turning into an old woman. What will you think of me then?'

'What I have always thought of you,' I replied, kissing her, putting my arms around her as I held on to the globe carefully before we were separated by our daughter, who was pushing her way between us, determined to be part of our happy number.

'Father,' she said, sounding so serious now, the way she always did when she had a question she considered to be of the highest importance.

'Whose present is the best, mine or Mother's?'

'I like them both equally,' I said, refusing to choose one over the other. 'And I love you both equally too,' I added, picking her up and kissing her, holding her tight, wrapping her closely in my embrace, refusing to let her go.

*   *   *

When we first came to London, we rented a small flat in Holborn, where we had the misfortune of living next door to a tedious, middle-aged civil servant who leered at Zoya whenever he passed her on the street but glared at me as if I was beneath his contempt. On the few occasions that I attempted conversation with him, he behaved in an abrupt fashion, as if my accent was enough to convince him that I was unworthy of his time.

'Can't you do something about her crying?' he shouted one morning as I closed our front door behind me, blocking my way as I tried to ascend the steps to the street.

'Good morning, Mr Nevin,' I replied, determined to be polite in the face of his rudeness.

'Yes, yes,' he said quickly. 'That child of yours. She keeps me awake at nights. It's ridiculous. When are you going to do something about it?'

'I'm sorry,' I said, not wishing to antagonize him any further, for his cheeks were crimson with rage and he had black circles beneath his eyes from sleep deprivation. 'But she is only a few weeks old. And,' I added, laughing a little, hoping that this might appeal to his humanity, 'we are new at this, after all. We're trying our best.'

'Well, your best isn't good enough, Mr Jackson,'

302

he snapped, poking a gnarly finger at me that, fortunately for him, did not make contact with my chest; I was tired, too, and my patience might have snapped if he had touched me. 'A man needs his sleep, I've lived here for—'

'It's Jachmenev,' I said quietly, feeling my own anger beginning to build now.

'What's that?'

'My name,' I said. 'It's not Mr Jackson, it's Mr Jachmenev. But you may call me Georgy Daniilovich, if you like. We are neighbours, after all.'

He remained silent for a moment, staring at me as if he wasn't sure if I was deliberately trying to provoke him or not, before throwing his hands in the air and marching off, leaving a few jingoistic comments flying through the air to remember him by.

It was an irritation, of course—the man was a boor, but neither Zoya nor I had any desire to fall out with our neighbours. However, the matter was resolved happily a few months later when he moved out in a fit of pique and his flat was taken over by a widow in her mid-forties, Rachel Anderson. And rather than being irritated by our daughter, she seemed utterly charmed by her, a reaction which naturally endeared her to a pair of proud parents, and we quickly became friends.

She regularly volunteered to babysit for us, and as our friendship grew, so did our trust in her, and we took her up on her offer. She was alone and lonely, that was easy to see, and enjoyed playing grandmother to Arina, a surrogate perhaps for the children and grandchildren that she had been denied.

'A stroke of luck for us that Rachel likes babies,' I said to Zoya as we strolled towards the Holborn Empire one evening, enjoying the romance of being alone again, if only for a few hours. 'I can't imagine leaving Arina in the care of our previous neighbour, can you?'

'Definitely not,' said Zoya, whose initial reluctance to spend an entire evening away from home had dissipated almost immediately when we had left the flat. 'Still, you are sure you want to go to the pictures, aren't you?'

'We can go somewhere else if you want,' I replied, for all that mattered to me was that we would spend some time together. When I had seen what was playing at the Empire I had made the suggestion without fully thinking it through, immediately realizing that it was either the best idea I had ever had, or the worst.

'No, no,' she said, shaking her head. 'I'm looking forward to it. I think. Aren't you?'

'Yes,' I replied eagerly. I will make a confession: I had been to the cinema only three times before that night, but each time it was to see Greta Garbo. The first occasion had been five years earlier, when I had wandered alone into the Empire, not knowing what was playing, and watched the actress as Anna Christie, a former prostitute trying to improve her lot in life. I saw her again two years later, playing Grusinskaya, the fading ballerina of *Grand Hotel*, which charmed me less. But she won me over again the following year as the Swedish queen, Christina, and now I was back for a fourth visit, with Zoya by my side, to see her play a part close to my heart, Anna Karenina.

Those two simple words were enough to

transport me back twenty years. Looking at them printed in large black letters above the cinema's facade, I could feel the ache in my bones still from Count Charnetsky's endless training sessions and my own disorientation at trying to find my way back to my room in a palace which was still unfamiliar to me.

He's the one who was shot in the shoulder, isn't he? Tatiana had asked, looking across at me, welcoming this brief respite from her lessons.

No, I heard it was someone terribly handsome who saved Cousin Nicholas's life, replied Marie, shaking her head.

It is him, said Anastasia quietly, meeting my eyes.

The cinema was full that night, the air already filled with cigarette smoke, the theatre noisy with the chatter of courting couples and single romantics, but we found two seats together on the balcony and settled back in contentment as the lights faded and the buzz of conversation began to diminish. A newsreel was shown first and we saw images of a hurricane hitting the coast of Florida, destroying everything in its path. A man called Howard Hughes, we were told, had just set a new airspeed record of 352 miles per hour, while America's president, Mr Roosevelt, was shown at the Black Canyon, between the states of Arizona and Nevada, preparing to open the Hoover Dam. The newsreel ended with a five-minute film of the German chancellor, Herr Hitler, parading through the streets of Nuremberg, inspecting the army and delivering speeches at rallies attended by tens of thousands of German citizens. The audience gasped at the devastation of the hurricane, cheered at the antics of Mr Hughes, talked loudly over the oration of Mr Roosevelt, but sat in rapt silence as the chancellor addressed the masses, shouting at them, screaming at them, pleading, imploring, insisting, demanding, as if he was only too aware that his speech would be heard even five hundred miles away in the Holborn Empire and he wanted to hypnotize every member of the audience with his ferocious battle cries, despite the fact that they could not understand a single word he said.

Zoya and I understood enough German, however, to grasp the essence of what Hitler was saying. And we sat a little closer to each other as he roared, but said nothing.

When he finally left the screen, the film began and the train carrying Anna and the Countess Vronskaya pulled in at the Moscow station, emitting huge clouds of smoke which parted gradually to reveal Garbo—Anna Karenina—her large, clear eyes perfectly centred on the screen, the dark mink of her hat and coat in stark contrast to her simple, flowing curls.

'The way she looked!' I enthused to Zoya afterwards, smitten by the performance as we walked home. 'The passion in her eyes! And Vronsky's eyes too, for that matter. They didn't even need to speak a word, they just looked at each other and were overwhelmed by their passions.'

'You thought that was love?' she asked quietly. 'I saw something else.'

'What?'

'Fear.'

'Fear?' I repeated, staring at her in surprise. 'But they don't fear each other at all. They are meant for each other. They know it from the very first moment they meet.'

'But their expressions, Georgy,' she said, her voice rising a little in frustration at my simple view of the world. 'Oh, they're only actors, I know, but didn't you see it? To me it felt as if they looked at each other in absolute horror, as if they knew that they couldn't possibly control the chain of events set in place by that simple, inevitable meeting. The lives they had lived until that moment had come to an end. And then it didn't matter what happened next, their destinies were already decided.'

'You have a very bleak way of looking at things, Zoya,' I said, not entirely pleased by her reading of the scene.

'What was it that Vronsky said to Anna later on?' she asked, ignoring my remark. '*You and I are doomed . . . doomed to unimaginable despair. Or bliss . . . unimaginable bliss.*'

'I don't remember that line from the novel,' I remarked.

'Don't you? Perhaps it's not there. It's been so many years since I read it. Still, I feel that I know this woman.'

'But you're nothing alike,' I said, laughing.

'Aren't we?'

'Anna does not love Karenin,' I pointed out. 'But you do love me.'

'Of course I do,' she replied quickly. 'I didn't mean that.'

'And you would never commit an infidelity, as Anna does.'

'No,' she said, shaking her head. 'But her sadness, Georgy. Her realization when she steps off the train that her life is already over, it's only a matter of enduring the time ahead until she reaches the end . . . that doesn't seem familiar to you at all?'

I stopped in the street, turning to her with a frown clouding my face. I couldn't decide how to respond to this. I needed time to consider what she had said; time to understand what it was that she was trying to tell me.

'It doesn't matter anyway,' she said finally, turning around now and smiling. 'Look, Georgy, we're home.'

Inside, we found that Arina was already asleep, and Rachel assured us that our daughter was quite simply the most wonderful child that she had ever had the good fortune to spend an evening with, something which we already knew, but delighted in hearing anyway.

'I haven't been to the picture house in years,' she said as she put her coat on for the short walk next door. 'My Albert, he took me there all the time when we were courting. We saw all sorts of things, we did. Charlie Chaplin, he was my favourite, though. You like his films, do you, loves?'

'We've never seen him,' I admitted. 'We know of him, of course, but—'

'Never seen a Charlie Chaplin?' she asked, outraged. 'You want to keep an eye out for the next one. I'll babysit again for you then, happily. He's the best, is old Charlie. I knew him well when he was a boy, you see. Grew up in Walworth, didn't he? Right round the corner from me. Can you believe it? I used to see him running around as a lad, all short trousers and parlour tricks, never giving anyone a moment's peace. I lived round on Sandford Row, and my Albert, he were from Faraday Gardens. Everyone knew each other back then and old Charlie, well he were famous even as a lad for his nonsense. Made good, though, didn't he? Look at him now. A millionaire over in America with all the nobs at his beck and call. It's hard to believe it, I swear it is. Who was in that film you saw tonight, then? Never seen a Charlie Chaplin? I never heard the like of it!'

'Greta Garbo,' said Zoya with a smile. 'Georgy's half in love with her, didn't you know it?'

'With Greta Garbo?' asked Rachel, pulling a face that suggested she'd just noticed an unpleasant odour. 'Oh, I can't see it myself. She has a terrible manly quality, I've always thought.'

'I am not "half in love with her" at all,' I said, blushing at the suggestion. 'Really, Zoya, why would you say such a thing?'

'Look at him, Mrs Anderson,' she replied, laughing brightly. 'He's embarrassed.'

'He's gone redder than a prize tomato,' she said, laughing too, and I stood there, looking away from them and frowning in my humiliation.

'A lot of nonsense,' I said, marching over to my armchair and sitting down, pretending to read the newspaper.

'Well, what was it like, anyway?' asked Rachel, looking over at my wife. 'This Greta Garbo film of yours. Any good?'

'It reminded me of home,' said Zoya quietly, in a tone that made me glance across at her, examining the wistful expression on her face.

'And that's a good thing, is it?' asked Rachel.

Zoya smiled, before nodding and letting a great sigh escape her lips. 'Oh yes, Mrs Anderson,' she said. 'That's a good thing. A very good thing indeed.'

Before Arina was born, there had been some discussion at the factory where Zoya was employed as a sewing machinist that she was going to be promoted to the position of supervisor. The hours would have been no easier, of course—long working days from eight o'clock in the morning until half past six at night, with only a half-hour break at lunchtime—but the pay would have been much improved, and rather than sitting at her machine throughout the day, she would have had the freedom to move around the factory floor.

That possibility came to an end, however, when she became pregnant.

We told no one our news for almost four months—we had suffered too many losses by that point in our lives to believe that we would ever become parents—but eventually, she started to show and our doctor reassured us that yes, on this occasion the pregnancy had taken and there was no reason to believe that we would suffer another miscarriage. Almost immediately, Zoya made the decision not to return to the factory after the birth, but to devote her time instead to bringing up our daughter, a moot point anyway, given that her employers did not allow young mothers to return to work until their children were of school-going age. And while this put a greater strain on our finances, which were now reduced to my single salary, we had saved our money carefully over the previous few years and, in recognition of my new responsibilities, Mr Trevors granted me a small pay rise immediately following Arina's birth.

It was a surprise, therefore, when I returned

home one evening to find a large sewing machine standing in the corner of our living room, its heavy metal casing glaring defiantly at me as I walked through the door, and my wife clearing a space to the right of it for a small occasional table on which to rest her fabric, needles and pins. Arina was watching intently from her chair, her eyes wide, captivated by this unusual activity, but she clapped her hands together joyfully when she saw me and pointed towards the machine, shouting loudly in delight.

'Hello there,' I said, divesting myself of my hat and coat as Zoya turned to face me with a smile. 'What's going on here?'

'You're not going to believe it,' she replied, kissing me on the cheek and sounding thrilled by whatever development had taken place during the day, her tone betraying a certain anxiety at the same time that I would share her happiness. 'I was making Arina's breakfast this morning when there was a knock on the door. And when I looked through the window, I couldn't believe my eyes. It was Mrs Stevens.'

Zoya tended to grow nervous whenever there was an unexpected knock on the front door. We had few friends and it was unusual for any of them to call around unannounced, so any disturbance to our typical routine caused my wife to feel uneasy, as if something terrible was about to take place. Rather than open the door immediately, she always walked towards the window and pulled the net curtain a little to the side to get a better view of who had come calling, for it was possible from that position to see the back of our visitor, while he or she remained unaware that they were being observed. It was a habit that never left her. She never felt safe, that was the problem. She always believed that some day, somehow, someone would find her. That they would find all of us.

'Mrs Stevens?' I asked, raising an eyebrow. 'From Newsom's?'

'Yes, she took me completely by surprise. I thought that perhaps there was some discrepancy in my final pay packet and she had been sent around to fix it, but no, it was nothing like that. At first she said that she wanted to stop by to see how I was and how Arina was, which of course I didn't believe for a minute. And then, after having a cup of tea and making me feel entirely uncomfortable in my own home, she finally said that they are suffering a shortage of machinists at the factory just now, there aren't enough to fill all their orders anyway, and they wondered whether I would be interested in doing some work from home.'

'I see,' I replied, nodding as I looked across at the machine, aware how this particular interview was certain to end. 'And you said yes, of course.'

'Well, I didn't see any reason why not. They're offering very generous wages. And a man from Newsom's will deliver everything I need once a week and collect my work at the same time, so I don't need to go anywhere near the factory. It'll help us to have more money coming in, won't it?'

'Yes, of course,' I said, considering it. 'Although I'd like to think I could take care of all three of us.'

'Oh, I know you can, Georgy. I only meant—'

'She must have been sure of your response if she brought the machine with her too.'

Zoya stared at me in bewilderment for a moment, before bursting out laughing. 'Oh

Georgy,' she said, shaking her head, 'you don't think Mrs Stevens carried it here all the way from the factory, do you? Why, I could barely drag it across the floor. No, one of the workmen came with it this afternoon, after I had agreed. He left only a short while ago.'

Perhaps it was wrong of me, but I wasn't entirely happy with the arrangement. It seemed to me that our home was our home, it was not a place that should be turned into a sweatshop, and that these new arrangements had been made without my even being consulted. But at the same time I could see how happy Zoya was, that this work would provide a break from playing with Arina all day long, and realized that it would be churlish of me to stand in her way.

'It's all right, Georgy, isn't it?' she asked me then, sensing my ambivalent feelings on the subject. 'You don't mind?'

'No, no,' I replied quickly. 'If it makes you happy.'

'It does,' she said assertively. 'I feel flattered that they even thought of me. And besides, I like earning my own money. I promise, there will be no work in the evenings. You won't have to put up with the noise of the machine when you get home from the library. And if I buy some fabric of my own, then I can make clothes for Arina too, which will be a great bonus.'

I smiled and said that I thought it was a very fine idea, and then, to my surprise, Zoya spent the rest of the evening working on the machine, examining the various patterns which had been sent with it for her to begin before the man from Newsom's returned the following week. I watched as she concentrated on her task, her eyes narrowing a little as she followed a line of stitching along a piece of fine, pale cotton, snipping off the edge of the thread and lifting the arm of the machine before tying off the knot. At home, this would have been considered a menial job, a task for *moujiks*, but here in London, almost two thousand miles and twenty years away from St Petersburg, it was a task which gave my wife pleasure. And for that, if nothing else, I was grateful.

*   *   *

When we did have an evening visitor, it was usually Rachel Anderson, who knocked on our door once or twice a week and spent an hour in our company in order to relieve her loneliness. We both enjoyed her visits, for she was a kind soul who came as much to play with Arina—who adored her—as she did to see us, a fact which inevitably endeared her to Zoya and me.

That year, as Christmas approached, we all sat together in our front parlour listening to a concert on the wireless. Arina was asleep in my arms, her tiny mouth half open, her eyelids flickering slightly as she dreamed, and I felt an almost overwhelming sensation of well-being at this happy home life which had been gifted to me. Zoya was sitting next to me, her head resting against a cushion as we listened to Tchaikovsky's Fourth Symphony. Our fingers were interlaced and I could see that she was lost in the music and the memories it conjured up for her. Glancing across at Rachel, I caught her gaze in the candlelight, and although she was smiling at our small family, her expression was one of almost unbearable sorrow.

'Rachel,' I asked, concerned for her, 'are you feeling all right?'

'I'm fine,' she reassured me, shaking her head and attempting a smile. 'Absolutely fine.'

'You don't look fine. You look as if you're about to burst into tears.'

'Do I?' she asked, raising her eyes for a moment as if to stem any sudden tide. 'Well, perhaps I do feel a little emotional.'

'Tchaikovsky can provoke strong sensations,' I said, hoping that I had not embarrassed her. 'When I listen to this movement, my head is filled with recollections of old Russian folk songs. I can't help but feel nostalgic for it.'

'It's not the music,' she replied quietly. 'It was the three of you.'

'What about us?'

She laughed and looked away. 'I'm just being an old softie, that's all. You just seem so content, all of you, sitting there like that, all snug in each other's company. It puts me in mind of my Albert. It makes me think of what might have been.' She hesitated, before offering an apologetic shrug. 'It would have been his birthday today, you see. His fortieth birthday. We most likely would have been enjoying a right knees-up tonight, had things worked out differently.'

'Rachel, you should have said,' said Zoya, standing up and going over to sit next to her, placing an arm around her shoulder and kissing her cheek. Her great empathy always came to the fore at moments like this, when she saw another soul in torment; it was one of the things I loved about her. 'I expect you think about him a lot.'

'Yes, every day,' she admitted. 'Even though it's been more than twenty years since he died. They buried him in France, did I ever tell you that? I used to think that made it worse, as I couldn't just stroll down to see him and put flowers on his grave like anyone else. There've been days when I've wanted nothing more than to fill a little flask of tea and stroll down to sit where I knew he was near by, but I can't do that. Not here. Not in London.'

'Haven't you ever gone over?' I asked her. 'It's not a long trip from Dover.'

'I've been eight times, luvvie,' she said with a smile. 'I might go again in a year or so if I can afford the crossing. He's buried in Ypres, in a cemetery called Prowse Point. Rows and rows of neat white tombstones, all lined up together, all covering the bodies of the dead boys. The whole place is so immaculately kept. It's almost as if they're trying to pretend there's something, I don't know, clean about the way they died. When there isn't. The purity of that place is a lie. That's why I've always wished that he was here, in some graveyard with overgrown trees and hedgerows and a few field mice running through it. Somewhere more honest.'

'He was a foot soldier?' I asked. 'An officer?'

'Oh no,' she said, shaking her head. 'No, Georgy, he wasn't grand enough to be an officer. Wouldn't have wanted it either. He was with the Somerset Light Infantry. Just one of the boys—nothing special, I suppose. Except to me. He died at the end of 1914, quite early on, really. He hardly got to see any action at all. Sometimes I think that was a blessing,' she added, considering it. 'I've always felt sorry for those poor boys who died in '17 or '18.

The ones who spent the last few years of their lives fighting and suffering and witnessing God only knows what horrors. At least my Albert . . . at least he didn't have to go through any of that. He went to his reward quite early on.'

'But you still miss him,' said Zoya quietly, taking Rachel's hand in her own, and the older woman nodded and gave a deep sigh, trying to hold back the tears.

'I do, luvvie,' she said. 'I miss him every day. I think of all that we might have been together, you see. All the things we might have done. Sometimes it makes me terrible sad, and other times, it makes me so angry with the world that I could scream. Those bloody politicians. And God. And the war-mongers—Asquith and the Kaiser and the Tsar, all of them buggers.' Zoya bristled a little at the reference, but made no comment. 'I hate them for taking him from me, you see. A lad like him. A young lad. With everything to live for. But who am I talking to, after all? You must have suffered during the war, too. You had to leave your homeland. I can't even imagine what that was like.'

'They weren't easy days for anyone,' I said hesitantly, unsure whether this was a safe subject for conversation.

'I lost my entire family in the war,' said Zoya, surprising me that she should talk of her past at all. 'All of them.'

'Oh, luvvie,' said Rachel in surprise, leaning forward and rubbing her hands now. 'I didn't know that. I always thought that maybe you'd just left them behind you in Russia. You never speak of them, I mean. And there's me, bringing up all those bad memories for you.'

'That is what wars do,' I said, anxious to change the subject. 'They take our loved ones from us, separate families, create untold misery. And for what? It's hard to see.'

'It's coming back, you know,' she said then, the seriousness of her tone surprising me.

'Coming back?' I asked.

'War. Can't you feel it? I can. I can almost smell it.'

I shook my head. 'I don't think so,' I said. 'Europe is . . . stirring, that's for sure. There are troubles and enmities, but I don't believe there will be another war. Not in our lifetime. No one wants to go through what we all went through last time.'

'Don't you think it's ironic,' she replied, considering this, 'that all those boys conceived in a great outpouring of love and lust when the Great War came to an end will be just the right age to fight when the next one begins? It's almost as if God created them for no other reason than to fight and die. To stand before the rifles and swallow the bullets that fly towards them. It's a joke, really.'

'But there won't be a war,' insisted Zoya, interrupting her. 'As Georgy says—'

'Such a waste,' Rachel said with a sigh, standing up and reaching for her coat. 'Such a terrible waste. And I don't mean to contradict you, Georgy, not in your own home, but you're wrong, I'm afraid. It's coming all right. It'll be here before too long. Just wait. You'll see.'

The Neva

The note was placed under the door of my room and slid so far along the floor that it almost disappeared beneath the bed. Only my name was printed on the exterior—*Georgy Daniilovich*—in a fine Cyrillic handwriting. It was rare for me to receive communications in this way; typically, any changes to the schedule of the Leib Guard were passed from Count Charnetsky to the divisional leaders, who in turn informed each man under their command. I was curious to open it, but surprised to find nothing but an address and a time printed neatly on the card inside. No instructions or clue as to who might have sent the note. No details of why my presence was required. The entire thing was a mystery which, at first, I put down to Anastasia, but then I recalled that she was due to attend a dinner at Prince Rogesky's house later that evening with her family, so she could hardly have been arranging a secret assignation. Still, my interest was piqued, my evening was free and my spirits were good, so I went to the bath-house and washed myself thoroughly, before dressing in my finest non-military clothes and leaving the palace to make my way to the proposed address.

The night was dark and cold and the streets thick with snow, so deep that I was forced to lift my boots high above the mounds as I trawled slowly along them. As I walked, my hands buried in my pockets, I found it impossible to ignore the propaganda posters pasted on the walls and lampposts of the central city. Images of Nicholas and Alexandra, disgraceful images, naming them as plunderers of the land, tyrants, despots. Portraits of the Tsaritsa as a whore and a she-wolf, some where she was surrounded by a harem of young, tumescent men, others where she was lying prone and exposed beneath the lusty gaze of the dark-eyed *starets*. The posters had become a regular feature of the city and were torn down by the authorities every day, only to reappear as quickly as they were removed. To be discovered with any in your possession was to risk death. I wondered how the Tsar and his wife could bear to see themselves depicted in so obscene a fashion as they passed through the streets. He who had spent months and sacrificed his health leading the army in an attempt to protect our borders. She who was at the hospital every day, tending to the sick and the dying. The Tsaritsa was no Marie Antoinette and her husband no Louis XVI, but the *moujiks* seemed to look at the Winter Palace as a second Versailles and my heart was heavy as I wondered where all this discord might end.

The address on the card led me to a part of the city I rarely visited, one of those curious areas which housed neither palaces for princes nor hovels for peasants. Nondescript streets, small shops, beer taverns, nothing that suggested anything extraordinary might be taking place here that required my attendance. I wondered for a moment whether the note had been intended for me at all. Perhaps someone had meant to put it beneath the door of a fellow involved in one of the numerous secret societies that plagued the city. Someone involved in politics. Perhaps I was being

320

led towards a covert meeting designed to cause further upheaval against the Romanovs and I would be taken for a traitor by them all. I almost considered turning away and heading back to the Winter Palace, but before I could decide for sure, the house that I was searching for appeared before me. I stared cautiously at the unimposing black door, behind which lay someone who wanted me to visit.

I hesitated, surprised by my own anxieties, and knocked quickly upon the wooden frame. I had been invited here, I told myself. The note had been addressed to me. There was no immediate answer, however, so I removed my right glove to knock again more loudly. But at that same moment the door swung open and I stood face to face with a dark-clothed figure, who stared at me for a moment as he tried to identify my face in the darkness of the night, before breaking into a delighted, hideous smile.

'You came!' he roared, reaching out and placing both hands on my shoulders. 'I knew you would! Young men are so easily led, don't you agree? I could have told you to throw yourself into the depths of the Moyka and you would be lying dead on the riverbed by now.'

I struggled beneath the weight of those great hands and tried to shrug them off, but without success; he pressed down with such determination that it felt like a test of his strength and my endurance. 'Father Gregory,' I said, for it was he who had opened the door—the monk, the man of God, the *moujik* who had made a whore of the Russian Empress. 'I didn't realize it was you who had invited me here.'

'Why, would you have come quicker if you had?' he asked, grinning. 'Or not come at all, perhaps? Which would it have been, Georgy Daniilovich? Not the latter, surely. I won't believe that for a moment.'

'It's a surprise, that's all,' I said truthfully, for as uncomfortable as I felt around him, and as much as he repulsed me, it was impossible not to be simultaneously fascinated by him, for his was a consistently intoxicating presence. Whenever I saw him, I found myself in a state of near paralysis. In this, I was not alone. Everyone hated him, but no one could keep their eyes off him.

'You came and that is all that matters,' he said now, ushering me through the door. 'Come inside, it's cold outside and we can't have you becoming sick, can we? I want to introduce you to my friends.'

'But what am I doing here?' I asked, following him as he walked along a dark corridor towards the rear of the house, where a room entirely illuminated by red candles could be glimpsed in the background. 'Why did you invite me?'

'Because I enjoy the company of interesting people, Georgy Daniilovich,' he roared, seemingly enchanted by the sound of his own voice. 'And I consider you a very interesting person.'

'I don't know why,' I said.

'Don't you? You should.' He stopped for a moment and turned to smile at me, revealing two rows of yellow teeth. 'I like anyone who has something to hide, and *you*, my young delight, are filled with secrets, are you not?'

I stared into those deep-blue eyes of his and swallowed nervously.

'I have no secrets,' I said. 'None at all.'

'Of course you do. Only a dullard has no secrets and I don't think you're one of those, are you? And anyway, we are all hiding something. Every one of us. Our betters, our equals. Those who have not had our advantages. No one likes to reveal their true selves; we would fall upon each other if we did. But you are a little different from most, I agree with you on that. For you seem utterly incapable of hiding your secrets. I can't believe that I'm the only one who has noticed. But please, this is not why I brought you here,' he added, turning back and continuing along. 'Such talk can wait. Come and meet my friends. I think you will enjoy each other.'

I told myself that I should turn and leave, but he had disappeared into the red-candled room by now and there was no force on earth that could have stopped me from following him inside. I knew not what I might encounter when I stepped through the door. A small gang of fellow *starets*, perhaps. Or the Tsaritsa. It was impossible to guess. And as much as I tried to imagine it, the sight that greeted me when I entered was strange, unexpected and immediately intoxicating.

The room was filled with low sofas, each upholstered in deep shades of scarlet and purple, and dominated by expensive rugs and tapestries that looked as if they might have been delivered from the bazaars of Delhi. Spread across the room, lying on the sofas and chaises longues, were perhaps a dozen people, each one dressed more provocatively than the last. A woman whom I knew to be a countess and a former intimate of the Empress, who had earned her displeasure after a troubled visit to Livadia when she had dared to kick the Tsaritsa's malevolent terrier, Eira. A prince of the royal blood. The daughter of one of St Petersburg's most notorious sodomites. Four or five younger people, perhaps my own age, perhaps a little older, whom I had never seen before. Some prostitutes. A young boy of quite extraordinary beauty whose face was smeared with rouge and lipstick. Most of them were in a state of undress, their shirts open, bare feet on display, some clothed in nothing but their undergarments. One of the prostitutes, visible through the mist which clouded the room and took hold of my senses, causing me to feel immediately drowsy and anxious for more, was seated on the sofa with a boy's head in her lap; he was completely naked and his tongue lapped at her body like a cat at a saucer of milk. I stared at the tableau before me, my eyes wide in a mixture of revulsion and desire, the one urging me to run, the other pressing me to stay.

'Friends,' roared Father Gregory, spreading his arms wide and silencing the room immediately. 'My most dear friends, familiars and intimates, may I introduce a delicious young man whose acquaintance I have been lucky enough to make. Georgy Daniilovich Jachmenev, late of the village of Kashin, a miserable shithole in the centre of our blessed country. He displayed great loyalty to his royal family, if not, it is fair to say, to his oldest friend. He has been in St Petersburg for some time now, but has never, I think, learned to enjoy himself. I mean to change that tonight.'

His guests stared at me with a mixture of boredom and disinterest, continuing to drink from their wine glasses and take deep breaths from the bubbling glass pipes that passed between them, their conversation starting up again now in a low, whispered murmur. They had a dead look in their eyes, every one of them. Except Father Gregory. He was fiercely alive.

'Georgy, aren't you glad that I invited you?' he asked me quietly, placing an arm around my shoulder and pulling me towards him as he stared across at the woman and the boy, watching them as they began to move and groan in rhythm with each other. 'It's so much better here than at that dreary old palace, wouldn't you agree?'

'What do you want with me?' I asked, turning to look at him. 'Why did you ask me here?'

'But my dear, it was you who wanted to come,' he said, laughing in my face as if I was a fool or a halfwit. 'I didn't take your hand and lead you through the streets, did I?'

'I didn't know who sent the card,' I replied quickly. 'Had I known—'

'You knew perfectly well, but you didn't care,' he said, smiling at me. 'It's foolish to lie to oneself. Lie to others, by all means, but not to yourself. Anyway, come, my young friend, don't be angry with me. We don't allow temper here, only harmony. Have a glass of wine. Relax. Let yourself be entertained. You might like it here, Georgy Daniilovich, if you allow yourself to forget who you think you are and be who you truly want to be. Or should I call you Pasha? Would you prefer it if I did?'

I opened my eyes wide. No one had called me that name in years, and even then it had only been my father. 'How did you hear that name?' I asked. 'Who told you that?'

'I hear many things,' he cried, raising his voice suddenly but causing none of his guests to stir in surprise or fright; his tone trembled with righteousness and dread as he spoke. 'I hear the voices of the peasants in the field, crying out for justice and equality. I hear the sound of Matushka, crying at night over her diseased son. I hear it all, Pasha,' he cried, his voice piteous now and craven, his face crumpled in pain as he leaned closer to me. 'I hear the sound of her breath as she turns and sees the vehicle, ready to run her down, to take her life. I hear the cries of the sinners in hell, begging for release. I hear the laughter of the saved as they turn their faces away from us in Paradise. I hear the stomp of the soldiers' boots as they enter the room, the rifles in their hands, prepared to shoot, prepared to kill, prepared to martyr—' He stopped there and buried his face in his hands. 'And I hear you, Georgy Daniilovich Jachmenev,' he said, taking his hands away from his face and pressing them to either side of my own, his fingers warm and soft against my cold cheeks. 'I hear the things that you say, the things you try so desperately not to hear.'

'What things?' I asked, my voice emerging almost too quietly to be heard. 'What do I say? What do you hear?'

'Oh, my dear boy,' he said, shaking his head. 'You say, *What has happened? Who was shooting?*'

'Here, drink some of this,' said a voice to my right, interrupting us, and I turned to see the prince standing there, a glass of dark-red wine in his hand. I could think of no good reason to refuse it and brought it to my mouth immediately, swallowing it down in one mouthful.

326

'Very good,' said Father Gregory, smiling at me and stroking my cheek in a fashion which made me want to lay it closer against his hand and sleep. 'Very good, Pasha. Now sit down, won't you? Let me introduce you to my friends. I think there will be some here who can give you pleasure.' He reached across to a shelf as he said this, took another pipe and held it over a flame; his hand did not seem to notice or care about the pain of the burn. 'You will partake of this too, Georgy,' he said, handing it to me. 'It will relax you. Trust me,' he whispered. 'You do trust me, Pasha, don't you? You trust your friend Gregory?'

There was only one response to this. I was hypnotized by it all. I could feel hands reaching out from the sofa behind me, stroking my body. The prostitute. The boy. Inviting me to join them in their play. Across the room, the countess was watching me and caressing her breasts, which she revealed to me without embarrassment. Before her, the prince had sunk to his knees. The other young men and women whispered to each other, and smoked, and drank, and looked at me, and looked away, and I felt my body drift as if it was an unnecessary encumbrance as I allowed myself to fall, to become one with the room, to unite with their merry party, and when my voice came, it did not sound like mine at all, but like the sigh of another, a person I did not know, speaking from a distant land.

'Yes,' I replied. 'Yes, I trust you.'

*   *   *

As 1916 drew to a close, St Petersburg felt like a

327

volcano preparing to explode, but the palace and its inhabitants remained blissfully unaware of the unrest which circulated through the streets and we all continued with our regular routines and customs as if nothing was wrong. In early December, the Tsar returned from Stavka for a few weeks and an atmosphere of joy and even frivolity lingered over the Imperial Family, until, that is, the afternoon when the Tsar finally discovered that his beloved daughter was engaged in an illicit relationship with one of his most trusted Leib Guards. And then it seemed as if the war had moved from the German borders, the Russian borders, the Baltic borders, the Turkish borders, and concentrated its fury entirely on the second floor of the Winter Palace.

Neither Anastasia nor I ever discovered for sure who betrayed this long-held secret to the Tsar. The rumour went about that some mischief-maker had written an anonymous note and left it on the desk in Nicholas's study. Another was that the Tsaritsa had learned of it from one of the gossiping maids, who had seen evidence of it herself. Yet a third, entirely untrue, involved speculation that Alexei had observed a clandestine kiss and told his father about it, although the boy would never have done such a thing. I knew him well enough for that.

The first I knew of the discovery came late one evening when I was leaving the Tsarevich's room and could hear a storm brewing further along the corridor, where his father's study was located. On any other occasion I might have stopped to try to overhear the reason for the commotion, but I was tired and hungry and continued on my way, only to be grabbed by the arm, entirely by surprise, and dragged into a reception room, where the door was quickly closed and locked. I spun around, startled, to face my kidnapper.

'Anastasia,' I said, delighted to see her, convinced in my arrogance that she had been overcome by her desire for me and had waited until she knew that I would be passing. 'You have an adventurous side tonight.'

'Stop it, Georgy,' she replied quickly, releasing me from her grasp. 'Haven't you heard what's happened?'

'Happened?' I asked. 'Happened to whom?'

'Marie,' she said. 'Marie and Sergei Stasyovich.'

I blinked and thought about it. I was tired that evening, my mind was not working as quickly as it might have, and I failed to understand immediately what she meant.

'Marie, my sister,' she explained quickly, seeing the lack of comprehension on my face. 'And Sergei Stasyovich Polyakov.'

'Sergei?' I asked, raising an eyebrow. 'Well, what about him? I haven't seen him this evening, if that's what you mean. Wasn't he to be part of your father's retinue this afternoon when he attended the Peter and Paul Cathedral?'

'Listen to me, Georgy,' said Anastasia, snapping at me in my stupidity. 'Father has found out about them.'

'About Marie and Sergei Stasyovich?'

'Yes.'

'But I don't understand,' I said. '*What* Marie and Sergei Stasyovich? There is no Marie and Sergei Stasyovich, is there?' I heard the sentence even as it came out of my mouth and the explanation became suddenly clear. 'No!' I cried, my mouth opening wide and my eyes opening even wider in surprise. 'You don't mean—'

'It's been going on for months now,' she said.

'But I can't believe it,' I replied, shaking my head in astonishment. 'Your sister is an Imperial Grand Duchess, a daughter of the royal blood. And Sergei Stasyovich . . . well, he's a pleasant enough fellow and good-looking, I suppose, if you like that sort of thing, but she would hardly fall for . . .' I hesitated and chose not to complete that sentence. Anastasia raised an eyebrow at me and, despite the concern on her face, could not help but smile a little. 'Of course it's possible,' I ventured then. 'What was I thinking of?'

'Someone told Father,' she replied. 'And he's furious. Simply furious, Georgy. I don't think I've ever seen him so upset.'

'It's just . . . I can't believe that Sergei never told me,' I said, shaking my head. 'I thought we were friends, after all. In fact, he's about the closest friend I have here.' As I said these words, my mind was suddenly filled with images of the last boy I had called my closest friend. The boy I had grown up with from infancy to manhood. The friend whose blood remained on my hands.

'Well, have you told him about us?' she asked, stepping away from me now and pacing the floor in concern.

'No, of course not. I would never trust him with such an intimacy.'

'Then he must feel the same way about you.'

'I suppose so,' I said, and despite the hypocrisy of it, I couldn't help but feel slightly aggrieved. 'And what about you?' I asked. 'Did you know that this had been going on?'

330

'Of course I did, Georgy,' she replied, as if the answer was obvious. 'Marie and I tell each other everything.'

'And you never told me?'

'No, it was a secret.'

'I didn't think we had secrets,' I said quietly.

'Didn't you?'

'We are all hiding something,' I muttered to myself, looking away from her for a moment. She stared at me, looking directly into my eyes, with as much intensity as the *starets* had on that terrible night some weeks before. The association, the memory, was like a knife being plunged through my heart and I grimaced and felt ashamed. 'And what about us?' I asked eventually, trying to recover my composure. 'Does Marie know about us?'

'Yes,' she admitted. 'But I promise you, Georgy, she won't tell anyone. It's our secret.'

'Marie and Sergei Stasyovich were your secret too. And that got out.'

'Well *I* didn't tell Father,' she said angrily. 'I would never do that.'

'And what about Olga and Tatiana? Did they know about Marie and Sergei? Do they know about us?'

'No,' she said, shaking her head. 'These were things that Marie and I spoke about at bedtime. They were nothing more than the secrets we shared with each other.'

I nodded and believed her. Despite the fact that there were hundreds of rooms in each of the Imperial Family's palaces, the two elder sisters, Olga and Tatiana, always shared a bedroom with each other for company, as did Marie and

Anastasia. It was not surprising that each pair of sisters should have their own secrets and intimacies.

'Well, what's happened?' I asked, recalling the shouting that I had heard emerging from the Tsar's study a little earlier. 'Do you know what's going on up there?'

'Marie was dragged into my father's study by Mother an hour ago. When she came back she was nearly hysterical with tears. She could hardly talk to me, Georgy, she could barely speak. She said that Sergei Stasyovich was being sent into exile to Siberia.'

'Siberia?' I asked, inhaling quickly. 'But it can't be.'

'He is to go tonight,' she said. 'They are never to see each other again. And he is lucky, she said. He might have been executed for it, had their relationship gone deeper.'

I narrowed my eyes and stared at her and she blushed, a deep shade of scarlet. Despite the fact that we had been connected to each other for so long, nothing sexual had yet taken place between us, save the romance of our endless kisses.

'They called in Dr Federov,' she said quietly, her cheeks reddening even more as she mentioned his name.

'Dr Federov?' I asked. 'But I've never seen him summoned for anything other than to protect the health of your brother. Why did they need him?'

'He examined her,' she replied. 'My parents instructed him to discover whether or not ... whether or not she had been violated.'

My mouth fell open in surprise; I could scarcely imagine the horror of it. Marie had only turned seventeen a few months before. To be subjected to such a humiliating examination at the hands of the aged Federov, and with her parents in the next room—I assumed that they were in the next room, anyway—was an experience so ghastly that it didn't bear thinking of.

'And she . . . ?' I began, hesitant to say the words.

'She is innocent,' insisted Anastasia, a ferocity appearing in her eyes now as she looked up at me again, determined to hold my gaze.

I nodded and considered this for a moment before checking my timepiece. 'And Sergei Stasyovich,' I asked. 'Where is he? Has he left yet?'

'I think so,' she said, sounding confused. 'I'm not sure. Georgy, you can't go looking for him. It will go badly for you if you are seen to sympathize.'

'But he's my friend,' I said, reaching for the door handle. 'I have to.'

'He's not so much your friend that he told you what was happening.'

'That doesn't matter,' I said, shaking my head. 'He will be in pain right now. I can't let him go without speaking to him. I betrayed a friend once before and it is all that I can do to endure the shame of it. I won't do it again, no matter what you say.'

She stared at me and looked as if she wanted to make further protest, but could recognize an equal determination in my face and so finally nodded, but looked anxious nevertheless.

'We must be careful from now on,' she said as I opened the door. 'I couldn't bear it if they found out. If you were sent away from me. No one can ever know.'

I rushed over and held her in my arms and she

began to weep, half for us, I suspected, and half for her sister's broken heart.

'No one will know,' I confirmed, already worried because *someone* already did.

I found Sergei Stasyovich just as he was leaving the palace, held under guard by two other young officers, friends of both of ours, with whom we had got drunk on many leisure evenings. They looked miserable to have been entrusted with this task. I begged them for a few minutes alone with my friend and they agreed, stepping away from us so that we could say our goodbyes.

'I can't believe it,' I said, staring at his tired, unhappy face. He wore a haunted expression, as if he could not quite believe that the events of the previous few hours had taken place at all.

'Try, Georgy,' he replied with a smile.

'But do you really have to leave us? Won't they . . .' I looked across at our friends, his guards. 'Won't they set you free somewhere along the way? You could go anywhere. You could start a new life.'

'They cannot,' he said, shrugging his shoulders. 'It would be more than their lives were worth. There will be someone at the other end to receive me. He will write to the Tsar. These are their orders, after all. And I cannot disobey. I'm sorry to be saying goodbye to you, Georgy,' he added, his voice catching a little in his misery. 'I don't know if I have been much of a friend to you—'

'Or I to you,' I said quickly.

'Perhaps we have both had our minds elsewhere, yes?' He smiled at me and I felt myself grow pale. He knew, of course. He knew of me what I had not had the wit to realize of him. 'Just be *careful*,' he insisted, lowering his voice as he looked around nervously. 'He will wait for his moment. And he will cut you down, as he did me.'

'He?' I asked, frowning. 'He who?'

'Rasputin!' he hissed, pulling me to him now and wrapping me in a bear hug. 'The author of my misfortunes. Rasputin knows everything, Georgy,' he whispered into my ear. 'He treats us all as if we are nothing more than players in his endless games. From the Tsar and the Tsaritsa right down to the insignificant people like us. He has toyed with me for months.'

'In what way?' I asked as we separated.

He shook his head and offered a bitter laugh. 'It doesn't matter. It shames me to think of it. But this is not a man who you want to know your secrets,' he added. 'This is not a man at all, I think. He is a devil. I should have killed him when I had the chance.'

'But you could never do such a thing,' I said, appalled. 'Not without cause.'

'And why not? What will my life be now without her? What will hers be without me? He's up there right now, I promise you, laughing at us both. In my foolishness I believed he would not betray us if . . . if . . .'

'If what, Sergei?'

'If I did what he asked of me. I should have killed him, Georgy. I should have slit his throat from ear to ear.'

I looked up towards the palace windows, half expecting to see the dark shadow that I had observed there on more than one occasion in the past, but there was no sign of Father Gregory now. I wished that I could see the note that was left for the Tsar, examine the envelope, the letter paper, the handwriting. I could picture it perfectly.

The perfect Cyrillic handwriting.

'I must go,' said Sergei, looking across at the guards, who had brought three horses around now. 'We won't meet again. But think of what I have said. My life is over now. Mine and Marie's. But yours and Anastasia's . . . you still have time.'

I opened my mouth, ready to protest, but I did not know what he meant. And so I said nothing more, simply watched as he rode away from the palace towards his lonely, desperate future.

Father Gregory. The monk. The *starets*. Rasputin. Call him what you will. His hand was in this business, of course it was. He had manipulated Sergei Stasyovich in who knew how many ways. And finally my friend had said no and had turned against him. And this was his reward.

I had already tried, unsuccessfully, to block the events of that night from my mind. In truth, I remembered little of it. The alcohol. The drugs. The potions he had given me. The other players in his tableau. I could not even remember everything that I had done. Except that I was ashamed of it. Except that I regretted it. Except that I wished to God that I had never picked up that envelope off the floor of my bedroom.

The only thing that was important to me now was Anastasia. I could not allow him to do to us what he had done to Sergei Stasyovich and Marie. I could not allow him to separate us. And so I admit it. I confess it now, once and for all. I became the man I never thought I would be. I determined that he would not destroy us both.

*   *   *

336

Finding enemies of Father Gregory was not difficult; they were legion. His influence over every section of society was quite extraordinary. During the years that he had spent in St Petersburg, he had gained enough power to remove both ministers and prime ministers from their offices. His uncontrollable lust had brought him to the centre of more marital breakdowns than could be counted. He had incurred the enmity of the ruling classes for turning the people against the autocracy, for while the great ladies of society, including the Tsaritsa herself, might have been swayed by his hypnotic and seductive control, the *moujik*s in the towns and villages of Russia were not.

The wonder was not that there were so many people willing to kill him; the wonder was that he lasted so long in the first place.

The days following the revelation of Marie and Sergei Stasyovich's affair were anxious ones. I was driven half crazy with worry that the *starets* would find some reason to inform the Tsar of my own relationship with his youngest daughter. Combined with this, I was saddened by the loss of my friend and concerned for Anastasia, who was tending to her grieving and disgraced sister and seemed to be suffering an equal amount of pain.

It seemed impossible that I could continue with such an existence, constantly terrified of every knock at my door, afraid to walk the corridors of the palace in case I ran into my tormentor. And so, a few evenings after Sergei's exile, without stopping to consider the consequences of my actions, I went to the armoury and took a pistol from the racks, and waited until dark before making my way to the house that I had visited not three weeks before, on the evening when I had debased myself for the *starets'* pleasure. I was concerned that I would be seen and so disguised myself well, wearing a heavy cloak that I had purchased from a stall the day before, a hat and muffler, a long scarf. No one would have recognized me or taken me for anything other than a busy merchant, making his way quickly through the streets, aiming for nothing more than to get home and out of the cold. Even to walk those streets again, even to hear the sound of my hand knocking on that black wooden door-frame filled me with shame and remorse; I could feel my gorge rise at the memories of what I had done and what I had tried so desperately to forget. My innocence had been lost, I no longer knew whether I was even worthy of Anastasia's love.

My hands trembled not just with the frost in the air but with the fear of what I was planning to do, and I kept one hand tightly gripped to the pistol concealed within my greatcoat as I waited for my enemy to appear. Would I shoot him where he stood, I wondered? Would I allow him to say one last prayer, to beg forgiveness, to supplicate himself before whatever god he held dear, in the way that he had forced so many to supplicate themselves before him.

I heard footsteps growing louder on the corridor within and my heart raced with anxiety, my slick fingers sticking on the pistol trigger, and I thought that no, if I was to do it at all, I should do it when he appeared, before he knew what was happening and could seduce me to mercy. To my surprise,

338

however, it was not he who opened the door, but the prostitute whose pleasures I had indulged in a few weeks before. She wore a vacant expression on her face, not recognizing me at first, and I could tell that she was either drunk or had lost her reason from who knew what concoction.

'Where is he?' I asked, my voice deep and dreadful as I committed myself to my final purpose.

'Where is who?' she replied, unmoved by either my appearance or my determination. I was only one of many the *starets* had brought here. Dozens, probably. Hundreds.

'You know who,' I insisted. 'The priest. The one they call Rasputin.'

'But he's not here,' she sighed, then shrugged her shoulders and offered a drunken laugh. 'He's left me all alone,' she added in a dreamlike tone.

'Then where is he?' I demanded, reaching forward and shaking her by the shoulders; she grew angry then and stared at me with hate in her eyes, before thinking better of it and smiling.

'The prince came for him,' she said with a shrug.

'The prince? What prince? Tell me his name!'

'Yusupov,' she said. 'It was hours ago now. I don't know where they went.'

'Of course you do,' I said, curling my free hand into a fist and showing it to her without remorse. 'Tell me where they've gone or I swear to you—'

'I don't know,' she said, spitting out the words. 'He didn't tell me. He could be anywhere. What are you going to do anyway, Pasha?' she continued in a mocking tone. 'You think you can hurt me? Is that really what you want to do to me?'

I stared at her, shaken that she recognized me

after all, but I said nothing, simply spun around in the street so that I didn't have to look at her.

'The Moika Palace,' I said quietly, thinking of Felix Yusupov's home. It was the most likely place for them to have gone; after all, the Moika was infamous for its parties and debauched behaviour. It was a place, I thought, where Father Gregory would feel very much at home. I looked at the whore one last time and she began to speak again, to taunt me, but I heard not a word of it, turning away from her and heading in the direction of the river.

I made my way towards the banks of the Moika River and crossed at Gorokhovaya Ulitsa, passing the bright lights of the Mariinsky Palace as I made my way towards the Yusupov home. The river was mostly frozen over, the ice crashed up against itself by the walled banks, freezing in great white-peaked caps, like a snowy mountain range as viewed from above. I encountered not a single soul on that long, chilly walk; all the better, I realized, for the outcome of my actions could only result in my own death—particularly if the Tsaritsa was to hear of them. There were many who would applaud me for what I was planning to do, of course, but they would be a silent majority, unwilling to stand behind me if I was brought to trial. And if I was found guilty, then I would necessarily end my story as his final victim, swinging from a tree in the woods outside St Petersburg.

Finally, the Moika Palace rose up before me. I was pleased to see that there were no guards patrolling the grounds. Perhaps ten, fifteen years earlier, there would have been dozens parading the forecourt, but not any more. It was a sign of how far the ruling classes had fallen. The idea that the palaces might not even last another year was in common parlance. In the meantime, the wealthy were living their debauched lives while they still could, drinking their wine, gorging on their meat, sodomizing their whores. Their end was coming and they knew it, but they were too drunk to care.

I made my way to the rear of the palace and was about to try one of the doors when I heard a gunshot from within. Startled, I stood there as if I had been turned to stone. Had it really been a gunshot or was I imagining things? I swallowed nervously and looked around, but there was no one in sight. I could hear voices shouting, laughing, inside the palace the sound of people hushing others, and then to my horror another gunshot. And another. And another. Four in total. I looked around and just at that moment a great light illuminated me as the door opened and an unknown man threw himself upon me, his arm around my neck, the blade of his knife pressing against the skin of my throat.

'Who are you?' he hissed. 'Tell me quick or you die.'

'A friend,' I stuttered, desperate to get the words out without extending my throat too far, lest the knife bury itself in my neck.

'A friend?' he said. 'You don't even know to whom you are speaking.'

'I'm . . .' I hesitated. Should I identify myself as the Tsar's man? Or an intimate of Rasputin's? An enemy, perhaps? How could I know whose body controlled this arm?

'Dmitri, no,' came a second voice and a man

emerged from the palace whom I recognized immediately as Prince Felix Yusupov. 'Let him go. I know this boy.' I was released immediately but held my ground, running a hand across my throat, searching for any cuts, but I was unharmed. 'What are you doing here?' he asked me. 'I know you, don't I? You're the Tsarevich's bodyguard.'

'Georgy Daniilovich,' I said, acknowledging this.

'Well, what do you want here? It's late. Has the Tsar sent you?'

'No,' I said quickly, shaking my head. 'No one sent me. I came of my own volition.'

'But why? Who are you looking for?'

The man who had held me a moment before came around in front of me and I stared at him with murderous intent. I had seen him on a few occasions in the past, a tall, unhappy-looking fellow. A Grand Duke, I thought, or perhaps a Count. He glared at me, daring me to challenge him. 'Answer him,' he snapped. 'Who were you looking for?'

'The *starets*,' I admitted. 'I looked for him at his home and he wasn't there. I thought he might be here.'

Prince Yusupov stared at me in surprise. 'Rasputin?' he asked quietly. 'And why were you looking for him?'

'To kill him!' I shouted, no longer caring who knew it. I was damned if I was going to be a pawn in any more of their games. 'I came to murder him and I'll do it, even if I have to take both of you first.'

The Prince and his companion looked at each other and then back at me, before bursting out laughing. I felt like shooting them both on the spot. What did they take me for, some child having a tantrum? I was here to kill the *starets* and I was damned if I would leave without doing so.

'And why, young Georgy Daniilovich, would you want to do that?' he asked.

'Because he is a monster,' I said. 'Because if he is not destroyed, then the rest of us will be.'

'The rest of us will be anyway,' said the Prince with a disaffected smile. 'There's nothing any of us can do to stop that. But as for the mad monk . . . well, I'm afraid you're too late.'

I didn't know whether I felt relief or dismay. 'He is gone then?' I asked, imagining him fleeing along the streets back into the arms of his whores.

'Oh, yes.'

'But he was here?'

'He was,' admitted the Prince. 'I brought him here earlier tonight. I gave him wine. I gave him cakes. I laced them with enough cyanide to kill a dozen men, let alone some stinking *moujik* from Pokrovskoye.'

I stared at him and opened my eyes wide in surprise. 'Then he is dead?' I asked, astonished. 'You have already killed him?'

The two men exchanged another look and shrugged almost apologetically. 'You would think so, wouldn't you?' he asked, smiling at me. His manner was not that of one who had attempted murder and I wondered whether he might be drunk or out of his senses too. 'But it had no effect on him. He is not human, you see,' he added, as if this was a simple fact of life, something of which every civilized person was aware. 'He is the devil's creature. The cyanide did not kill him.'

'Then what did?' I asked, a chill running through

my veins.

'This,' replied the Prince with a smile, removing his pistol from inside his tunic, and sure enough, smoke was still snaking from the tip. I immediately recalled the sound of gunfire that had almost led me to run away from the Moika not ten minutes before.

'You shot him,' I said flatly, chilled by the reality of the words, despite the fact that it had been my intention anyway.

'Of course. I'll show you if you like.'

He led the way back inside the palace and we walked a short distance to a dark corridor, illuminated on either side by tall white candles. In the centre of the floor, lying face-down, was the unmistakable figure of Father Gregory, his black cloak spread around him, his arms splayed out in a cartoonish pose, his long hair stringy and filthy on the marble floor.

'I decided that if poison couldn't do the job, then bullets would,' said the Prince as I stepped closer to the corpse and looked down. 'I put one in his stomach, one in his leg, one in his kidneys and one in his chest. Someone should have done it years ago. Perhaps we wouldn't all be in the mess we are now if someone had.'

I was barely listening to him, but staring at the body instead. I was glad that someone else had done the job and wondered for a moment whether I would have had the fortitude to commit so heinous a crime. I felt no happiness though, no satisfaction that he was gone. Instead, my head was filled with nausea and revulsion and I realized that I wanted nothing more than to be back in the safety of my palace bed, for however much longer it was to be mine. No, given the choice I would have been in the arms of my love, my Anastasia, but for now that was impossible.

'I'm glad you did it,' I said to the Prince, turning to reassure him, lest he kill me too for witnessing the crime. 'He deserved everything he—'

I didn't get to finish the sentence for at that moment a sound emerged from Father Gregory's body, his eyes opened wide, and he began to laugh, to screech, to emit a sound that was more animal than human. I gasped as his mouth fixed into a horrendous smile, his lips parting to show his yellow teeth and dark tongue. I wanted to scream or run, but could do neither. Within a second, the Prince discharged a bullet into his heart. His body jumped, collapsed and slumped.

Now he was dead.

*   *   *

Within the hour he was gone. We carried him, the three of us, to the banks of the Neva and threw him in. He sank quickly, his awful face staring up at us as he receded into the black depths, his eyes still open as we took our last sight of him.

That night was one of the coldest in memory and the river froze over for almost a week.

When the ice began to thaw a little and Rasputin's body was discovered, his arms were extended from his sides, his hands curled into claws, the nails white with scrapings of ice. He had tried to get out. He still hadn't been dead. He had clawed away at the thick ice for who knew how long. The cyanide hadn't killed him, four of the Prince's bullets, drowning. None of it had worked.

I don't know what it was that took him in the end. All that mattered was that he was gone.

1924

We found work easily in London; both Zoya and I were settled with respectable positions within a few weeks of our arrival from Paris, enough to keep food on our table, enough to keep our minds from dwelling too long on the past. My interview with Mr Trevors took place on the same morning that Zoya was offered employment at Newsom's textiles factory, which specialized in the production of women's undergarments and nightwear. The next morning, and every morning that followed it, she left our small flat in Holborn at seven o'clock, dressed in the grey, drab uniform of the shop floor, a similarly dowdy cloth cap covering her hair, not a strand or a stitch or a thread able to diminish her beauty by the slightest degree. Her tasks were monotonous and she rarely had an opportunity to use any of the skills she had perfected in Paris, but she took pride in her work nonetheless. A part of me felt that she was wasting her talents engaged in such menial work, but she seemed content with her position and sought no greater opportunities for now.

'I like being in the factory,' she said whenever I suggested this. 'There are so many people there, it's easy to become lost. Everyone has a single, simple task to undertake and everyone does it quietly and without fuss. No one pays any attention

346

to me. I like that. I don't want to stand out. I don't want to be noticed.'

Sometimes when she came home, however, she complained about how hard it was to endure the chatter of the other women, for her station was situated at the centre of a long row of machinists who opened their mouths when the whistle blew in the morning and barely closed them again until they were safely back home at the end of the day. There were eight women to her left, a further six to her right, with five rows both behind and in front of her. The conversation of the workers was enough to give anyone a headache, but, if nothing else, at least it distracted from the incessant buzz and hum of the sewing machines.

There was a great deal more interest in our accents in England than there had been in France, where the presence of different nationalities had become the norm after the war. The fact that we had spent more than five years in the French capital meant that our enunciation had developed a curiously hybrid tone, located somewhere been St Petersburg and Paris. We were regularly asked where we came from and when we replied, truthfully, there was often a raised eyebrow and sometimes a cautious nod of the head. But we were treated civilly by most people for, after all, this was 1924 and we were between the wars.

Zoya became an object of interest for a young woman named Laura Highfield, who operated the machine next to hers. Laura was a dreamer and found the fact that Zoya had been born in Russia and had spent so many years of her life in France to be both romantic and exotic, and she quizzed her relentlessly on her past, with little satisfaction.

On one particular evening in late spring, when a week's worth of snowfall lay on the ground to remind me of home, I finished work early at the library and strolled towards the factory to meet Zoya and take her to dinner at one of the inexpensive cafés that lined her route home. As we were leaving, Laura caught sight of us together and called my wife's name, waving her arms frantically at her as she ran towards us.

There must have been two or three hundred women emerging from the gates at that same moment, all lost in chatter and gossip, but the great sound from the factory horn that repeatedly signalled the end of the working day sent me into a peculiar reverie. It reminded me very much of the horn that would echo from the Imperial train as it traversed the Russian countryside, transporting the Tsar's family on their endless pilgrimages throughout the year. It sounded once and I pictured Nicholas and Alexandra seated in their private salon, their gold crests emblazoned on the thick carpet as the train brought them from St Petersburg to the Palace of Livadia for their spring holiday; it sounded again and there was Olga studying her languages as we travelled to Peterhof in May; again, and I saw Tatiana lost in one of her romantic novels as the train roared onwards in June towards the Imperial yacht and the Finnish fjords; again, and I thought of Marie, staring out towards the hunting lodge in the Polish forest; once more, and there was Anastasia, desperately trying to attract her parents' attention as they returned to the Crimea; one final time, and it is November now and the train is making its way at a snail's pace towards Tsarskoe Selo for the winter,

348

under strict instructions from the Empress not to exceed fifteen miles an hour, lest the Tsarevich Alexei suffer another of his traumas with the jostling of the buffers along the tracks. So many memories, all rushing towards me, every one reborn by the sound of a klaxon sending a group of workers home to their families.

'You look distracted,' Zoya said as she took my arm and rested her head against my shoulder for a moment. 'Is everything all right?'

'Perfectly fine, *Dusha*,' I said with a smile, kissing the top of her head lightly. 'Just some silliness on my part, that's all. I thought for a moment—'

'Zoya!'

The voice calling from behind made us turn around to where Laura was dashing towards us, a group of women following her. They were going for a cup of tea, she told Zoya, looking me up and down judgementally as she spoke; did she want to join them?

'I can't,' she said, failing to introduce me and rushing us along. 'Sorry. Some other time, perhaps?'

'Friends of yours?' I asked, surprised by how quickly she was trying to get away from them.

'They try to be,' she said. 'We just work together, that's all.'

'I can go home if you want to go for tea with them,' I said. 'We don't know many people in London, after all. It might be nice to have—'

'No,' said Zoya quickly, interrupting me. 'No, I don't want that.'

'But why not?' I asked, surprised. 'Don't you like them?'

She hesitated and her face took on a certain

349

anxiety before she replied. 'We shouldn't make friends,' she said finally.

'I don't understand.'

'*I* shouldn't make friends,' she said, correcting herself. 'They don't need to be involved with me. That's all.'

I frowned, unsure what she meant by this. 'But I don't understand,' I said. 'What harm could it do, after all? Zoya, if you think that—'

'It's not safe, Georgy,' she snapped, her words rushing out quickly as her temper flared. 'It will do her no good to befriend me. I'm bad luck. You know that. If I get too close . . .'

I stopped in the middle of the street and stared at her in amazement. 'Zoya!' I cried, taking her by the arm and turning her round to face me. 'You can't mean it.'

'Why can't I?'

'No one is bad luck,' I said. 'The idea is preposterous.'

'To know me is to suffer,' she replied, her voice deep and grave, her eyes darting back and forth as her forehead wrinkled into a painful furrow of lines. 'It doesn't make sense, Georgy, I know it doesn't, but it's true. You must see the truth of it. I don't want to be close to Laura. I don't want her to die.'

'To die?' I cried, turning to glare quickly at a man who had pushed past me, my sudden fury enough to make me want to chase after him and challenge him. I might have done it, too, had Zoya not grabbed my elbow tightly and forced me to look at her.

'I am a person who should not be alive,' she said, her words dissolving the crowds around us into

350

dust so that there were only the two of us left alone in the world, my heart racing at the expression of utter belief and unhappiness on my wife's face. 'He saw it in me,' she continued, looking away now and focussing on the tall banks of snow which were building behind us. I could hear the laughter of children as they kicked their way through the mounds and made snowballs to throw at each other, the shouts of dismay as they buried their small hands in the flurry to numb their fingers. '*Poor child*, he said. *They all come to harm when they are near you, do they not?*'

'Zoya,' I said, shocked, for she had never mentioned this to me before. 'I don't . . . how could you . . .'

'I don't want friends,' she hissed. 'I don't need anyone. Only you. Think of it. Think of them all. Think of what I did. It never ends, does it? They're the price that I pay for life. Even Leo—'

'Leo!' I could scarcely believe that she was mentioning his name. Neither of us had forgotten him, of course—we would never forget him—but, like everyone else, he was a part of the past. And Zoya and I, we buried the past, deep. We never spoke of it. It was how we survived. 'What happened to Leo was nobody's fault but his own.'

'Oh Georgy,' she said quietly, laughing a little and shaking her head. 'To be as simple-minded as you. What a joy that must be.'

I opened my mouth to contradict her, not insulted by what she had said but devastated. For she was right. I was simple-minded, a virtual half-wit when it came to arguing this subject with her. I wanted to express my love for her but it seemed so empty, so trivial, compared to what she was saying.

351

I had no words left.

'But look!' she cried a moment later, clapping her hands together in delight as she spotted her favourite café opening its doors along the street, her sudden enthusiasm, reflected in the darkening night, reminding me of the innocent girl with whom I had fallen in love. It was as if the last few minutes of our conversation had not even taken place. 'Oh, they're open again, I thought they had closed for ever. Let's go in, Georgy, can we? We can have our dinner there.'

She ran out on to the road so quickly, without looking in either direction, that she just missed being hit by a bus that sounded its horn violently at her as she ran past. My heart jumped in horror as I pictured her being crushed under its wheels, but as it drove on I could see her stepping quickly into the warmth of the café, entirely oblivious to the just-avoided accident.

*   *   *

Five months later, she made her first suicide attempt.

The day started much like any other, except for the fact that I was suffering from a sick headache and complained of it over breakfast; it was an unfamiliar sensation to me for I almost never became ill. I had woken from a colourful and dramatic dream, the type you hope to retain in your memory for later consideration, but which quietly slips away and dissolves, like sugar in water. I decided that it must have involved a marching band or percussion orchestra, for the migraine, a dull pounding in my forehead that blurred my vision and sapped my energy, was present from the moment that I opened my eyes, and threatened to get worse as the morning progressed.

Zoya was still wearing her nightgown during breakfast, unusual in itself, for she typically dressed for work while I was taking my bath. Her boiled egg with toast was missing too and she sat opposite me with a distant expression on her face, ignoring the cup of tea that I'd placed before her.

'Is everything all right?' I asked her, almost resenting having to speak, for it only provoked the drum-beats behind my eyes. 'You're not feeling ill too, are you?'

'No, I'm fine,' she said quickly, offering a half-smile and shaking her head. 'I'm just running late, that's all. I feel quite tired this morning. I suppose I should get ready.'

She stood up and went into the bedroom to change. As I sat there, there was a part of me that recognized something different and awkward in her behaviour, but my head was pounding so badly that I didn't feel able to ask her about it. The window was open and I could tell that it was a brisk, chilly morning; all I wanted was to go out on to the street and begin my walk to work, in the hope that the fresh air would clear my head by the time I reached Bloomsbury.

'I'll see you this evening,' I said, walking into the bedroom to offer her a kiss goodbye. I was surprised to find her still sitting on the bed, staring at the blank wall before her. 'Zoya?' I asked, frowning, 'what on earth's the matter? Are you sure you're all right?'

'I'm fine, Georgy,' she replied, standing up and

reaching into the wardrobe to retrieve her uniform.

'But you were just sitting there,' I said. 'Is there something on your mind?'

She turned to look at me and I could see her forehead wrinkling slightly as she struggled with something that she wanted to say. Her lips parted and she drew a breath, but then hesitated, shook her head and looked away.

'I'm just tired, that's all,' she said finally, with a shrug of her shoulders. 'It's been a long week.'

'But it's only Wednesday,' I said, smiling at her.

'A long month, then.'

'It's the sixth.'

'Georgy . . .' she sighed, her tone growing irritable and frustrated.

'All right, all right,' I said. 'But maybe you should get some rest. This isn't to do with . . .' It was my turn to hesitate now; the subject was a difficult one and not ideally suited to the early hour of the morning. 'You're not worried about . . .'

'About what?' she asked defensively.

'I know you were disappointed on Sunday,' I said. 'On Sunday afternoon, I mean, when—'

'It's not that,' she said quickly, looking a little flushed, I thought, as she turned away and smoothed down her uniform on its hanger. 'Honestly, Georgy, not everything is to do with that. I knew it wouldn't be this month anyway. I could tell.'

'You seemed to think it might be.'

'Then I was wrong. If we are to be blessed . . . then it will happen at the right time. I can't continue to focus on it. It's too much for me, Georgy, can't you see that?' I nodded. I didn't want us to argue and even the effort of holding this conversation at all was affecting my headache so badly that I thought I might be sick. 'What time is it anyway?' she asked me a moment later.

'A quarter past seven,' I said, glancing at my watch. 'You'll be late if you don't hurry up. We'll both be late.'

She nodded and reached forward to kiss me, smiling a little as she did so. 'Then I'd better hurry along,' she said. 'I'll see you this evening. I hope your headache disappears soon.'

We parted and I went to the front door of the flat, but before I could open it, I heard her walking quickly through the kitchen towards me; as she grabbed me by the arm, I turned around and she threw herself into my arms. 'I'm so sorry, Georgy,' she said, the words muffled as she buried her face in my chest.

'Sorry?' I asked, pulling away from her a little and smiling in confusion. 'Sorry for what?'

'I don't know,' she said, puzzling me even further. 'But I do love you, Georgy. You know that, don't you?'

I stared at her and laughed. 'But of course I know it,' I said. 'I feel it every day. And you know that I love you too, don't you?'

'I've always known it,' she replied. 'At times, I don't know what I ever did to deserve such kindness.'

On any other occasion I would have happily sat down with her and listed her attributes, the dozens of ways I loved her, the hundreds of reasons why, but the dead thumping behind my forehead was growing worse by the minute so I simply reached down, kissed her softly on either cheek, and said that I had better get some air quickly or I would collapse with the pain.

She watched me as I climbed the steps towards the street, but when I turned back to wave, the door was already closing behind me. I stood there and stared at the frosted glass, through which I could make her out as she stood pressed up against it, her head bowed slightly. She held that pose for five, perhaps ten seconds, then walked away.

Contrary to what I had hoped, I was feeling even more unsettled by the time I arrived at the library, but I made an effort to ignore my pain and continue with my duties. By eleven o'clock, however, the pain had spread to my stomach and limbs and I became convinced that I must have picked up a bug somewhere, which would not be cured by a long day of activity. It was not a busy day, though—we had no acquisitions to catalogue and the readers' room was unusually quiet—so I knocked on Mr Trevors' door and explained my situation. The combination of my pale, perspiration-tinged face and the fact that I had not taken a day's sick leave in all the time that I had been employed there ensured that he sent me on my way without complaint.

Leaving the library, I couldn't face the walk back to Holborn and took a bus instead. Its movement as it shuddered along Theobald's Road towards our home made me feel even more ill and I worried that I might either vomit on the floor in front of me or be forced to jump off the moving bus to spare my disgrace. At the end of my journey, however, lay the only thing of any interest to me at that moment—my bed—and I focussed on it andtried to ignore the suffering which was threatening to overwhelm me.

Finally, at half past eleven, I walked carefully down the steps towards our flat and opened the door, letting myself in with a great sigh of relief. It felt strange to be in the flat alone—Zoya was almost always here when I was at home—but I poured myself a glass of water and sat at the table, thinking of nothing in particular as I took a few cautious sips, hoping that it might help to settle my stomach.

Taking that day's *Times* from my briefcase, I glanced at the headlines for a moment and my eyes were taken by a report about the uprising in Georgia. The Mensheviks were battling the Bolsheviks for independence, but their struggle appeared to be failing. I was well aware of the numerous insurgencies and uprisings that were taking place throughout the various parts of the empire and of the number of states that were striking out for sovereignty. I usually read *The Times* during my tea break at the library and paid special interest to any story which related to my homeland, but I had paid particular attention to this one in recent weeks on account of the Menshevik leader, Colonel Cholokashvili, who had been part of a delegation sent to Tsarskoe Selo during 1917 to report to the Tsar on the progress of the Russian armies at the front. He was younger than the other representatives at the palace, and I had been fortunate to engage in a brief conversation with him when he was leaving and he had said to me that guarding the life of the Emperor and his heir was of as much importance as safeguarding our borders during the war. His words had been of particular importance to me at

357

the time, for I had become worried that I was forsaking my true duties by remaining in the employ of the Imperial Family when tens of thousands of young men my own age were dying in the Carpathian mountains or on the battlefields of the Masurian Lakes.

By the time I finished the article, I found that both my headache and stomach upset had begun to subside a little, but I thought I would spend the day in bed nevertheless and hopefully wake up feeling fully restored.

I opened the door to the bedroom and stared.

Lying across the bed was Zoya, her eyes closed, her arms spread out from her sides, blood seeping from a pair of deep wounds which had been etched across her wrists, a reddish-black puddle blending into the blanket beneath her. I stood at the doorway, frozen, horrified, experiencing the most curious sensation of incomprehension and impotence. It was almost as if my brain could not fully assimilate the scene that was presented to it, and because of that was unable to offer instruction to my body as to how to respond. Finally, however, with a great animal roar that emerged from the pit of my stomach, I ran towards the bed and lifted her in my arms, tears streaming down my face as I looked into her eyes and shouted her name over and over in a desperate bid to revive her.

Within a few seconds, her eyelids flickered slightly; her pupils focussed on my own for a moment before she looked away and an exhausted sigh escaped her lips. She did not welcome my presence; she did not want to be saved. I ran to the wardrobe, grabbed a pair of scarves from a shelf and brought them back to the bed, locating the place on each arm where the knife had entered and binding the wounds tightly, cutting off the flow of blood. A deep cry was coming from Zoya's mouth now as she begged me to leave her alone, to let her be, but I could not, I would not, and having secured her arms, I ran out on to the street and down to the end of our row of houses, where, to our good fortune, a doctor's surgery was located. I must have looked like a lunatic as I ran inside, wild-eyed, my shirt, arms and face covered with Zoya's blood, and a middle-aged woman sitting in the reception area let out a terrible scream, perhaps mistaking me for a crazed murderer intent on doing them harm. But I had enough wits about me to explain to the nurse what had happened and to ask for help, to demand it, and now, quickly, before it was too late.

In the days that followed, I often wondered about the headache and stomach bug which affected me on that day. It was so unusual for me to have suffered from them and yet, had I been in my usual good health, I would have remained at the library of the British Museum for the entire day and been widowed by the time I returned home.

*   *   *

Considering the life that I have lived, the people I have known, the places I have seen, it is unusual for me to be intimidated by someone simply because he holds a position of authority, but Dr Hooper, who took care of Zoya while she was in hospital, awed me slightly and made me anxious of appearing foolish in his company. He was an elderly gentleman, cocooned inside an expensive tweed suit, with a neatly trimmed Romanov beard, piercing blue eyes and a trim athletic body unusual in a man of his age and rank. I suspected that he terrified the doctors and nurses under his charge and did not suffer fools gladly. It annoyed me that he did not see fit to talk to me during the weeks when my wife was recovering from her injuries at the hospital; whenever I passed him on the corridor and attempted to converse with him, he begged off on the grounds that he was too busy for me at that moment and referred me to one of his juniors instead, none of whom seemed any more informed about my wife's condition than I was myself. The day before I was due to take her home, however, I phoned his secretary in advance and begged for a meeting with the doctor prior to his signing her out. And so, three weeks after I had discovered Zoya bleeding and dying on our bed, I found myself seated in a large, comfortable office on the top floor of the psychiatric wing, staring across at this most senior doctor as he examined my wife's file carefully.

'Mrs Jachmenev's physical injuries have healed perfectly well,' he announced finally, setting the file aside and looking across at me. 'The wounds she inflicted on herself were not deep enough to lacerate the arteries. She was lucky with that. Most people don't know how to finish the job correctly.'

'There was an awful lot of blood,' I said, hesitant to relive the experience but feeling that it was necessary that he know the full story. 'I thought . . . when I found her, that is . . . well, she was very pale and—'

'Mr Jachmenev,' he said, holding up a hand to silence me, 'you've been in here two, three times a day since your wife was admitted, have you not? I've been impressed by your attentiveness. You might be surprised by how few husbands bother to visit their wives, regardless of the reasons for their admission. But during that time you must have noticed an improvement in her condition. There's really no need for you to worry about any of her physical problems any more. There might be a slight scarring on her arms, but it will fade in time and become barely noticeable.'

'Thank you,' I said, a sigh of relief escaping from me. 'I must admit that when I found her, I immediately thought the worst.'

'Of course you know my speciality, however, and I am more concerned with her mental scars than her physical ones. As you know, every attempted suicide must be thoroughly evaluated before we can allow the perpetrator to return home.' *The perpetrator.* 'For their sake as much as anything else. I've spoken quite extensively to your wife over the last few weeks in an attempt to find the root cause of her behaviour and I must be honest with you, Mr Jachmenev, she does give me cause for concern.'

'You mean she might try this again?'

'No, I don't think that's likely,' he said, shaking his head. 'Most survivors of suicide attempts are too ashamed and shocked by their actions to try a second time. Most, you understand, don't really mean it in the first place. It is, as they say, a cry for help.'

'And you think that's what it was?' I asked hopefully.

'If she meant it, she would have found a gun and shot herself,' he replied, as if this was the most obvious thing in the world. 'There's no way back from that. People who survive want to. That's in her favour to begin with.'

I wasn't so convinced of this in Zoya's case; after all, as far as she had been concerned I was not going to return home for another six hours at least. She would never have survived the bleeding for that long, regardless of which veins she had cut. And where, after all, would she have found a gun? Perhaps, I considered, Dr Hooper was judging us all by the standards of his own armoury. He looked for all the world like a man who spent his weekends rifle in hand, slaughtering all forms of wildlife in the company of minor royalty.

'And in your wife's case,' he continued, 'I think the shock of the attempt, coupled with her feelings towards you, might prevent such a recurrence anyway.'

'Her feelings for me?' I asked, raising an eyebrow. 'She wasn't thinking of me when she did this thing, though, was she?'

The words were unworthy of me, but, like Zoya's, my own mood had swung from positive to hideously bleak over recent weeks. There were nights when I lay awake, thinking of nothing other than how close she had been to death and how I could possibly have survived without her. There were days when I berated myself for not recognizing her suffering and coming to her aid. There were times when I pressed my fists against my forehead in frustration, angry that she thought so little of me that she could cause me so much suffering.

'You mustn't think that this is about you,' said Dr Hooper finally, seeming to read my mind as he stepped around from the desk now and sank into an armchair beside me. 'It's not about you at all. It's about her. It's about her mind. Her depression. Her unhappiness.'

I shook my head, unable to take it in. 'Dr Hooper,' I said, choosing my words carefully, 'you must understand, Zoya and I have a very happy marriage. We rarely argue, we love each other very much.'

'And you've been together . . .'

'We met when we were teenagers. We married five years ago. They have been happy times.'

He nodded and made a church steeple out of his hands, pointing his fingers towards the heavens, and breathed heavily as he considered this.

'You have no children, of course,' he said.

'No,' I replied. 'As you know, we have suffered a number of miscarriages.'

'Yes, your wife has spoken to me of that. Three, is that correct?'

I hesitated for a moment at the memory of these three lost babies, but finally nodded my head. 'Yes,' I said, coughing to clear my throat. 'Yes, it has happened three times.'

He leaned forward and looked me directly in the eye. 'Mr Jachmenev, there are a number of things which I am not at liberty to discuss with you, things that Zoya and I have spoken about in confidence, under the auspices of doctor and patient, you understand?'

'Yes, of course,' I said, frustrated at not being told exactly what was wrong with her when it was I, above all others, who wanted to help her. 'But I am her husband, Dr Hooper. There are certain things—'

'Yes, yes,' he said quickly, dismissing this as he leaned back. I felt that he was examining me carefully—analysing me, even—as if he was trying to decide for himself how much he could permit me to know and how much he should leave out. 'If I was to say that your wife is a very unhappy woman, Mr Jachmenev,' he said finally, 'you would no doubt understand.'

'I would have thought that was obvious,' I said, my voice low and angry, 'considering what she did.'

'You may even think that she is disturbed in her mind.'

'You don't think she is?' I asked.

'No, I don't think that either explanation entirely covers what is wrong with Zoya. Such words are too simplistic, too facile. Her problems lie deeper, I think. In her history. In the things that she has witnessed. In the memories that she has repressed.'

It was my turn to stare at him now and I could feel myself growing a little more pale, unsure what he was getting at. I could not imagine for a moment that Zoya would have confided the details of our past—of her past—to him, even if she did trust him. It seemed like an entirely uncharacteristic gesture on her part. And I couldn't help but wonder whether he knew that there was something he wasn't seeing, and that I might tell him if guided along that path. Of course, he did not know me; he did not realize that I would never betray my wife.

'Such as what?' I asked finally.

'I think we both know the answer to that, Mr Jachmenev, don't you?'

I swallowed and set my jaw; I was not going to admit to this either way. 'What I want to know,' I

364

said, a note of determination entering my tone, 'is whether I should continue to be worried about her, whether I should be watching over her throughout the day. I want to know whether something like this might ever happen again. I have to work every day, of course. I cannot be with her constantly.'

'It's hard to say,' he replied, 'but on consideration, I don't think you have very much to worry about. I will be undertaking further sessions with her, of course, on an out-patient basis. I think I can help her come to terms with the things that cause her suffering. Your wife labours under the illusion that the people closest to her are in danger, you realize that, don't you?'

'She's mentioned it to me,' I admitted. 'Only briefly. It's something that she keeps locked inside herself.'

'She's talked about these miscarriages, for example,' he said. 'And about your friend, Monsieur Raymer.'

I nodded and looked down for a moment, acknowledging the memory. *Leo*.

'Your wife must be made to see that she is not responsible for any of these things,' he said, standing up now to indicate that our interview was at an end. 'That is down to me, of course, during our out-patient sessions. And down to you, in your life together.'

*   *   *

Zoya was already dressed and waiting for me when I entered the ward, sitting on the side of her bed, neat and prim in a simple cotton dress and overcoat that I had brought for her the day before.

365

She looked up and smiled as she saw me walking towards her and I smiled too, taking her in my arms, pleased that the great bandages that covered the healing wounds on her arms were hidden to me by the sleeves of the coat.

'Georgy,' she said quietly, breaking down in tears as she saw what must have been a mixed expression on my face. 'I'm so sorry. I didn't mean to hurt you.'

'It's all right,' I said—a curious choice of words, for of course it was anything but all right. 'At least you can leave here now. Everything will be fine, I promise you that.'

She nodded and took my arm as we left the ward. 'Are we going home?' she asked me.

Home. Another strange word. Where was it, after all? Not here in London. Not Paris, either. Home was many hundreds of miles away, a place to which we could never return. I wasn't going to lie to her by saying yes.

'Back to our little flat,' I said quietly. 'To close the door behind us and be together, as we were always meant to be. Just the two of us. GeorgyandZoya.'

The Tsar's Signature

That it should end like it did, in a railway carriage in Pskov, still astonishes me.

We didn't celebrate the arrival of 1917 with the same degree of festivity or merriment as we had previous years. The Tsar's household was in such disarray that I even considered leaving St

Petersburg and returning to Kashin, or perhaps heading westward in search of a new life entirely; only the fact that Anastasia would never have left her family—and that I never would have been permitted to take her with me anyway—prevented me from doing so. But tension surrounded all of us who were part of the Imperial entourage. The end was in sight, it was just a question of when.

The Tsar had spent much of 1916 with the army, and in his absence, the Tsaritsa had been left in charge of political matters. While he maintained his position at Stavka, she dominated the government with a strength and single-mindedness that was as impressive as it was misguided. For of course she spoke not with her own voice, but in the words of the *starets*. His influence had been everywhere. But he was dead now, the Tsar was away, and she was alone.

News of Father Gregory's death had reached the Winter Palace within a day or two of that terrible December evening when his body, poisoned and bullet-ridden, had been thrown into the River Neva. The Empress had been distraught, of course, and relentless in her insistence that his murderers be held to account for their crimes, but recognizing the vulnerability of her own position, she quickly began to internalize her distress. I watched her sometimes as she sat in her private sitting-room, staring blankly out of the window while one of her waiting women chattered on about some unimportant piece of palace gossip, and I could see in her eyes the determination to go on, to rule, and I admired her for it. Perhaps she was not so much Rasputin's pawn, after all.

When the Tsar returned for a brief Christmas

visit, however, the Tsaritsa insisted that Felix Yusupov be brought to justice, but as he was a member of the extended Imperial Family the Tsar claimed that there was nothing he could do.

'You are more in thrall to these hangers-on and bloodsucking leeches than you are to God,' she cried within hours of his reappearance, an afternoon when we were all shocked by how unwell Nicholas looked. It was as if he had aged ten, perhaps fifteen years since we had last seen him in August. He looked as if one more drama to face would be enough for him and he would happily pass out and die.

'Father Gregory was not God,' insisted the Tsar, massaging his temples with his fingers and looking around the room in search of support. His four daughters were pretending the argument was not taking place; their attendants were retreating into the shadows of the room, as was I. Alexei was watching from a seat in the corner; he was almost as pale as his father, and I wondered whether he had not injured himself earlier in the day and told no one. It was sometimes possible to tell when the internal bleeding had started: the panicked, desperate look on the boy's face, the desire to sit perfectly still to ward off approaching trauma, were familiar sights to those of us who knew him well.

'He was God's representative,' shouted the Tsaritsa.

'Is that so?' asked the Tsar, looking across at her now angrily, fighting to maintain his composure. 'And I thought that *I* was God's representative in Russia. I thought that *I* was the anointed one, not some peasant from Pokrovskoye.'

'Oh, Nicky!' she cried in frustration, throwing herself into a chair and burying her face in her hands for a moment, before standing up and marching over to him again, addressing him as if she was his mother, the Dowager Empress Marie Fedorovna, and not his wife. 'You cannot allow murderers to go free.'

'I do not want to,' he said quickly. 'Do you think that is what I want from Russia? From my own family?'

'They are hardly your family,' she interrupted.

'If I punish them, it is as if I am saying that we approved of Father Gregory's influence.'

'He saved our son!' she cried. 'How many times did he—'

'He did no such thing, Sunny,' he said. 'Blessed heaven, how he had you in his grasp!'

'And is that why you hated him so much?' she asked. 'Because I believed in him?'

'Once, you believed in me,' he replied quietly, looking away from her now, his face scored with so much misery that I almost forgot that he was the Tsar at all and believed that I was looking at a man no different to myself. How grateful I felt at that moment that no one knew of my own involvement in Rasputin's death; had that been revealed, the weight of the Tsar's anger would have undoubtedly been turned in my direction and I might have found myself walking to the gallows before nightfall as a sop to his wife's distress.

'But I do believe in you, Nicky,' she said, softening her tone now and reaching out to him. But he misunderstood the move, I think, and backed away from her, leaving her standing in the centre of the floor with her arms outstretched to

369

him. 'All I ask is—'

'Sunny, the people hated him, you know that,' he insisted.

'Of course I know it.'

'And you know why.'

She nodded and said nothing, perhaps aware at last that her five children were observing the scene, even if they pretended that nothing untoward was taking place. I glanced towards Anastasia, who was seated on a sofa, crocheting, her fingers moving carefully in and out of the fabric as she watched her parents argue. I wanted to run to her, to take her away from that terrible place that seemed to be crumbling down around us. Thoughts of Versailles entered my mind again, but I pushed them aside; I knew only too well how that story had ended.

'Father Gregory was my confessor, nothing more,' said the Tsaritsa finally, in an injured voice. 'And my confidant. But I can live without him, Nicky, you must believe that. I can be strong. I *am* strong. With you away while this hateful war continues—'

'And then there's that,' snapped the Tsar, throwing up his arms. 'It's too much, can't you see it? This power that you have. You must allow others to—'

'It is traditional for the Tsaritsa to be in charge of policy while the Tsar is away,' she replied haughtily, raising her head in a regal fashion. 'There is precedent. Your mother did so, as did hers, and hers before her.'

'But you go too far, Sunny. You know you do. Trepov tells me—'

'Ha! Trepov,' she cried, practically spitting out the name of the Prime Minister. 'Trepov hates me.

370

Everyone knows that.'

'Yes,' cried the Tsar, laughing bitterly. 'Yes, he does. And why does he?'

'He doesn't understand how to run a country. He doesn't understand where strength comes from.'

'And where does it come from, Sunny, can you tell me that?' he asked, lunging towards her now angrily. They had not seen each other in months, the depth of their passion and love was well known to all, it ran through the daily letters they sent to each other, but here they were, apparently hating each other, fighting as if the whole world had conspired to rip them apart. 'It comes from the heart! And the head!'

'What do you know of my heart?' she screamed, and each of her daughters ceased their sewing as she shouted this and looked at their parents in fright. I glanced towards Alexei, who seemed ready to burst into tears. 'You who have none!' she continued. 'You who can think only from his head! When did you last care for what I felt in my heart?'

The Tsar stared at her, saying nothing for a moment, and then shook his head. 'Trepov insists,' he said finally, with a defeated shrug. 'You cannot be in charge any more when I am gone.'

'Then you must not go!'

'I have to go, Sunny. The army—'

'Can survive without you. The Grand Duke Nicholas Nicolaievich can be reinstated.'

'The Tsar must be at the head of the army,' he insisted.

'Then I remain in charge.'

'You cannot.'

'You will allow a man like him to dictate to you?' she asked, astonished. 'You will allow anyone to dictate anything to you? You who claim to be God's anointed one?'

'*Claim* to be?' he asked, his eyes opening wide in astonishment. 'What is this *claim*? Are you now saying that it is not what you believe?'

'I am asking whether this is where we are now, that is all. You say you would not be told what to do by a peasant from Pokrovskoye, but you drop like a cur before a bastard from Kiev. Explain the difference to me, Nicky. Explain it as if I was some ignorant, ill-educated *moujik*, and not the granddaughter of a Queen, the cousin of a Kaiser and the wife of a Tsar.'

The Tsar walked over behind his desk and sat down, hiding his eyes behind his hand for a few moments before looking up again, an expression of doom haunting his face. 'The Duma,' he said finally. 'They demand that they are given proper parliamentary rights.'

'But how can there be any parliament within an autocracy?' she asked. 'The terms are mutually exclusive.'

'That, my dear Sunny,' replied the Tsar with a bitter laugh, 'is rather the crux of the thing, don't you think? There can't be. But I can't fight two wars at once, either. I won't do it. I don't have the strength for it. And neither does the country. No, I shall return to Stavka in a few days, you will go to Tsarskoe Selo with the family, and Trepov will look after political matters in my absence.'

'If you do this, Nicky,' she said quietly, 'then there will be no palace to return to. I can promise you that.'

'Things will . . .' he said, his entire body slumped in his chair. 'Things will resolve themselves. It will

372

just take time, that's all.'

The Tsaritsa opened her mouth to say more, but, sensing that she had been defeated, merely shook her head and stared at her husband with pity in her eyes. Looking around the room, she focussed on each of her children in turn, her gaze darkening and softening from face to face, only brightening up when she locked eyes with her youngest child, Alexei.

'Children,' she said. 'Come with me, won't you?'

The five Romanovs stood immediately, but the Tsaritsa extended both her hands in the air, the palms stretched out flat, and shook her head; it was that rarest of occasions when she deigned to acknowledge the presence of lesser mortals in the room.

'Just my children,' she said in a forceful voice. 'The rest of you, stay here. With the Tsar. He may have need of you.'

She led the way out towards her own private sitting room and I watched as the children followed her. Anastasia turned her head in my direction as she left, her eyes meeting mine, and she smiled nervously, a smile that I returned, hoping that she would find something there to offer her comfort. A few moments later, the women who acted as companions to each of the Imperial Grand Duchesses left the room and the bodyguards took up their positions outside the doors, until there was only the Tsar and me left together. There was a part of me, in my youthful foolishness, that wanted to stay and talk to him, to offer some consolation or solace, but it was not my place to do so. I hesitated for only a moment before turning to leave. He looked up as I walked away, however, and called me back.

'Georgy Daniilovich,' he said.

'Your Majesty,' I replied, turning around to face him and offering a deep bow. He stood up from his seat and stepped towards me slowly. It shocked me to see the difficulty with which he walked. He was not even fifty years old, but the events of recent years had turned him into an old man.

'My son,' he said, barely able to look me in the eye after the scene that I had witnessed. 'He is well?'

'I think so, sir,' I replied. 'He does not engage in any dangerous activity.'

'He looks pale.'

'The Tsaritsa has insisted on his staying indoors ever since the *starets* was murdered,' I said. 'He has seen no daylight at all, I think.'

'Then he is a prisoner here?'

'Of sorts,' I agreed.

'Well, we are all prisoners here, Georgy,' he said with a halfsmile. 'Wouldn't you say so?'

I said nothing in reply, and when he turned his back on me, I took this as my cue to leave and began to walk towards the door.

'Don't go, Georgy,' he said, turning around again. 'If you please. There's something I need you to do for me.'

'Anything, sir.'

He smiled. 'You should never say that until you know what is required of you.'

'I never would,' I replied quickly. 'But you are the Tsar. So I say again: anything, sir.'

He stared at me, bit his lip for a moment in a style reminiscent of his youngest daughter and smiled.

'I need you to leave Alexei,' he said. 'I need you to stop being his protector. For a little while, at least. I need you to come with me.'

*   *   *

I wondered whether I had imagined the knock but then it came again, more urgently; I climbed out of bed and stepped towards the door, opening it carefully so the creak would not disturb others along the corridor. Without a word she pushed past me and before I knew it was standing in my room.

'Anastasia,' I said, looking outside for a moment to make sure that she hadn't been followed. 'What are you doing here? What time is it?'

'It's late,' she said, her voice betraying her anxiety. 'But I had to come. Close the door, Georgy. No one can know I'm here.'

I shut it immediately and reached across for the candle that I kept on the windowsill. As the wick took light I turned around and noticed that she was wearing her nightdress and gown, an outfit which may have covered her entire body but nevertheless offered a distinct erotic charge, suggesting as it did the proximity of bedtime and intimacy. She was staring at me too and only then did I realize that I was dressed even more improperly than she, in nothing but a pair of loose-fitting shorts. I blushed—invisible, I hoped, in the candlelight—and retrieved my trousers and shirt as she turned around to offer me some privacy.

'I'm decent now,' I said when I was dressed. She turned again but seemed to have lost her train of thought somewhat, as had I. There was nothing I wanted more than to take her in my arms, remove my clothing once again, and her nightgown, and wrap my body around hers in the warmth of the blankets.

'Georgy . . .' she began, but then shook her head and looked as if she might cry.

'Anastasia,' I said, 'what is it? What's the matter?'

'You were there today,' she said. 'You saw it. What's going to happen, do you know? There are so many terrible rumours going around.'

I took her hand and we sat side by side on the edge of my bed. After the Tsaritsa had taken Anastasia and her siblings from the parlour earlier in the day, I had sought her out in order to tell her of my conversation with her father, but she had spent the afternoon under the tutelage of Monsieur Gilliard and I had not been able to find a suitable excuse to go to her when her lessons were over.

'Olga says that everything is coming to an end,' she continued, her voice filled with desperation. 'Tatiana is nearly hysterical with worry. Marie hasn't been the same since Sergei Stasyovich left. And as for Mother . . .' She offered a small, angry laugh. 'They hate her, don't they, Georgy? Everyone hates her. The people, the government, Trepov, the Duma. Even Father seems to—'

'Don't say that,' I said quickly. 'You must never say that. Your father adores the Tsaritsa.'

'But all they ever do is fight. He was not home from Stavka a few hours and you saw what took place. And now he is going back tomorrow. Will this war ever end, Georgy? And why have the people turned on us so?'

I hesitated to answer. I loved her desperately, but

could think of any number of reasons why the Imperial Family had found themselves in this position. Of course, the Tsar had made many mistakes in the way he had pursued his aggression against the Germans and the Turks, but that was as nothing compared to how the subjects he claimed to love were treated. We in the royal household travelled from palace to palace, we stepped on board lavish trains, we disembarked from sumptuous yachts; we ate the finest food, wore the most luxurious suits and gowns. We gambled and played music and gossiped about who would marry who, which prince was the most handsome, which debutante the most flirtatious. The ladies dripped with jewels that they wore once and discarded; the men decorated their impotent swords with diamonds and rubies and dined off caviar, getting drunk every night on the finest vodka and champagne. Meanwhile, the people outside the palaces were desperate for food, for bread, for work, for anything which might make them feel more human. They shivered in the frost of our Russian winter and counted the members of their families who would not survive until spring. They sent their sons to die on battlefields, while a woman they considered more German than Russian controlled the lives of the people. They watched as their Empress consorted like a whore with a peasant they despised. They tried to express their anger through demonstrations, riots and a free press, and were cut down at every turn. How often had the hospitals been filled with their wounded and dying, after the Tsar's men had sought to ensure the pre-eminence of the autocracy? How many journeys to the graveyards

377

had they made? These were the things I wanted to tell her, the explanations I wanted to give, but how could I, when she had never known any life other than the one of extraordinary privilege into which she had been born? She who was destined to marry a prince some day and spend her life as an object of veneration. And who was I to offer such explanations anyway, when I had spent two years among these people, enjoying their luxuries, revelling in this fantasy that I was one of them and not simply a retainer, a disposable lieutenant who could be despatched to any corner of Russia on the whim of an autocrat?

'Things will resolve themselves,' I whispered, echoing her father's earlier words as I took her in my arms, while not believing them for even a moment. 'There is a cycle of disillusionment and—'

'Oh Georgy, you don't understand,' she cried, pulling away from me. 'Father has ordered the entire family to Tsarskoe Selo. He says that he will be staying at Stavka for the remainder of the war, that he will fight on the front line if he has to.'

'Your father is an honourable man,' I said.

'But the rumours, Georgy ... you know what I am referring to?'

I hesitated. I knew exactly what she meant, but I did not want to be the first to say the words that were bouncing off every gold-encrusted wall in the palace and every filthy street in St Petersburg. The phrase that every minister, every member of the Duma and every *moujik* in Russia seemed to want to hear.

'They say ...' she continued, swallowing a little as she struggled to get the words out, 'they say that

378

Father . . . what they want is for him to . . . Georgy, they say that he will have to renounce the throne.'

'That will never happen,' I said automatically and she narrowed her eyes, trembling before me.

'But you don't even seem surprised,' she told me. 'You've heard of this, then?'

'I've heard it said,' I admitted. 'But I don't think . . . I can't imagine it will ever come to pass. My God, Anastasia, there has been a Romanov on the throne of Russia for three hundred years. No mortal man can remove him. It's unthinkable.'

'But what if you're wrong?' she asked. 'What if he is no longer Tsar? What will happen to us then?'

'Us?' I asked, wondering who this 'us' was. She and I? Her brothers and sisters? The Romanov family?

'Nothing can happen to you,' I said, smiling to relieve the tension. 'You are a Grand Duchess of the Imperial line. What on earth do you think—'

'Exile,' she whispered, the word like a curse on her tongue. 'There is talk that we will be sent into exile, all of us. My whole family. Turned out of Russia like a group of unwanted immigrants. Sent to . . . who knows where.'

'It won't come to that,' I said. 'The Russian people would not allow it. There is anger, yes. But there is also love. And respect. Here in this room, too. Whatever happens, my darling, I will be there with you. I will protect you. No harm will ever come to you, not while I'm around.'

She smiled a little, but I could see that she remained anxious and she moved slightly away from me on the bed, as if considering whether she might not return to her own room now, before she was discovered. To my shame, I found myself

379

entirely aroused by her presence in such an intimate setting, and had to struggle with every demon in my body not to take her in my arms and push her on to the mattress, smothering her body with my kisses. *She would let me*—I thought that, too. *If I asked her, she would let me.*

'Anastasia,' I whispered, standing up now and turning away from her so that she might not see the expression of desire on my face. 'It's fortunate you came here tonight. There's something I need to tell you.'

'There was nowhere else I wanted to be,' she said, softening now. 'At least when we are at Tsarskoe Selo there will be more opportunities for us to be together. That is one good thing.'

'But I won't be at Tsarskoe Selo,' I said quickly, determined that the simplest thing to do was to say the words and be damned. 'I can't come with you. The Tsar has relieved me of my duties with regard to your brother. He wishes me to return to Stavka with him.'

The silence in the room seemed to last for an eternity. Finally I turned around and saw her expression. A thin streak of pale-blue moonlight was piercing my window, dividing her face in two.

'No,' she said finally, shaking her head. 'No.'

'There's nothing I can do,' I said, feeling the tears spring up behind my eyes. 'He has ordered me and—'

'No!' she cried again, and I looked towards the door anxiously lest she be overheard and her presence here discovered. 'You can't mean it. You can't leave me on my own.'

'But you won't be on your own,' I explained. 'Your mother will be there. Your sisters, your brother. Monsieur Gilliard. Dr Federov.'

'Monsieur Gilliard?' she cried, appalled. 'Dr Federov? What use are they to me? It's you that I need, Georgy, you. Only you.'

'And I need you too,' I cried, rushing towards her and covering her face with kisses. 'You're all that matters to me, you know that.'

'But if it's true, then why are you leaving me?' she cried. 'You have to say no to Father.'

'To the Tsar? How can I?' I asked. 'He commands, I obey.'

'No, no, no,' she said, bursting into tears. 'No, Georgy, please . . .'

'Anastasia,' I said, swallowing hard in order to make myself sound as rational as possible, 'whatever happens over these weeks, I will return to you. Do you believe that?'

'I don't know what to believe any more,' she said, the tears streaming down her face now. 'Everything has gone wrong. Everything is disintegrating around us. Sometimes I think that the world has gone mad.'

A loud noise went up from outside the palace and we both jumped. Startled, I ran to the window and saw a crowd of five hundred, perhaps a thousand people, marching towards the Alexander Column with banners proclaiming the pre-eminence of the Duma, shouting at the Winter Palace with murderous intent in their eyes. *It won't be tonight*, I thought then. *But soon. It will happen soon.*

'Listen to me, Anastasia,' I said, returning to her and taking her by both arms and staring into her eyes. 'I want you to tell me that you believe me.'

'I can't,' she cried. 'I'm so frightened.'

'Whatever happens, wherever you go, wherever they take you, I'll find you. I'll be there. No matter how long it takes. Do you believe that?' She shook her head and wept, but this was not enough for me. 'Do you believe me?' I insisted.

'Yes,' she cried. 'Yes, I believe you.'

'And may God strike me dead if I let you down,' I said quietly.

She stood away from me then, stared at me one final time, then turned and was gone from the room, leaving me alone, perspiring, scared, tormented.

It would be almost eighteen months before I saw her again.

*   *   *

The Imperial train, which had once been so full of life and excitement, seemed empty and desolate. The Imperial Family were not there, most of the Leib Guard were absent, there were no tutors, doctors, chefs or string quartets fighting for attention. The Tsar, seated behind the desk in his private carriage, was shrunken, leaning forward over a set of papers that were spread out before him, but not, I thought, reading any of them. It was March 1917, two months since we had left St Petersburg.

'Sir,' I asked, stepping forward and looking at him anxiously. 'Sir, are you all right?'

He looked up slowly and stared at me, as if he did not know who I was for a moment. A thin smile appeared on his face, then vanished just as quickly.

'I'm fine,' he said. 'What time is it?'

'Almost three o'clock,' I replied, glancing at the

ornate clock on the wall behind him.

'I thought it was still morning,' he said quietly.

I opened my mouth to reply, but could think of no suitable response. I wished that Dr Federov was there, for I had never seen the Tsar look so ill before. His face was grey and had aged considerably. The skin on his forehead had become dry and flaky, while his hair, usually so lustrous and shiny, had grown greasy and lank. The air in the study was stale and I felt so claustrophobic that I immediately walked to a window to open it.

'What are you doing?' he asked, looking across at me.

'Letting some air in,' I said. 'Perhaps you'd feel better if—'

'Keep it closed.'

'But don't you find it stuffy in here?' I asked, placing my hands on the base of the window and preparing to raise it.

'Keep it closed!' he shouted, startling me, and I turned around immediately to look at him.

'I'm sorry, Your Majesty,' I said, swallowing nervously.

'Have things changed so much here that I have to give an order twice?' he snapped, his eyes narrowing as he stared at me with the look of a fox preparing to take a rabbit. 'If I say keep it closed, then you will keep it closed. Is that understood?'

'Of course,' I replied, nodding my head. 'I apologize, sir.'

'I'm still the Tsar,' he added.

'You will always—'

'I had a dream earlier, Georgy,' he said, looking away from me now and addressing an invisible

383

audience; his tone had changed in an instant from anger to nostalgia. 'Well, it wasn't so much a dream as a memory. The day that I became Tsar. My father wasn't even fifty when he died, did you know that? I didn't think my turn would come for . . .' He shrugged his shoulders and considered it. 'Well, for many years anyway. There were some who said I wasn't ready. But they were wrong. I had been preparing for that moment all my life. It's a curious thing, Georgy, to be able to fulfil one's destiny only when one loses one's father. And I was devastated after my father died. He was a monster, of course. But still, I took his death hard. You never knew your father, did you?'

'I did, sir,' I replied. 'I told you about him once.'

'Oh yes,' he said, waving me away. 'I forgot. Well, my father was a very difficult man, there's no doubt about that. But he was nothing compared to my mother. God save you from a mother like mine.'

I frowned and looked over at the open door which led towards the train's corridor. It was empty still and I wished that someone would appear and relieve me. I had never heard the Tsar speak in this way before, and I hated hearing his voice so filled with self-pity and disillusionment. It was as if he had turned into one of those morose drunks that one encounters on the street late at night, full of resentment towards those they think have destroyed their lives, desperate for someone to listen to their melancholic stories.

'I married Sunny only a week after he died,' he continued, tapping his fingers on the desk before him rhythmically. 'It seems like a different time entirely. When we entered Moscow to be crowned,

384

the crowds . . . they came from all over Russia to see us. They loved us then, you see. It doesn't seem so very long ago, but it is, I suppose. More than twenty years. It's hard to believe, isn't it?'

I smiled and nodded, although in truth it seemed like a very long time to me. I was only eighteen years old, after all, and had never known a Russia without Nicholas II at the head of it. Twenty years was more than a lifetime—more than my own, anyway.

'You shouldn't be here today,' he said a moment later, standing up and staring at me. 'I'm sorry I brought you.'

'Would you like me to leave, sir?' I asked.

'No, that's not what I meant.' His voice suddenly rose and became plaintive. 'Why do people continually misunderstand me? I only meant that it was unfair of me to bring you to this place. It's only because I trust you. Can you understand that, Georgy?'

I nodded, unsure what he wanted of me. 'Of course,' I replied. 'And I'm grateful for it.'

'I thought that if you had saved the life of one Romanov named Nicholas, then perhaps you would have it in you to save another. A superstitious fancy. But I was wrong, wasn't I?'

'Your Majesty, no assassin will come near you while I am here.'

He laughed at this and shook his head. 'That wasn't what I meant either,' he said. 'Not what I meant at all.'

'But you said—'

'You can't save me, Georgy. No one can. I should have sent you to Tsarskoe Selo. It's beautiful there, isn't it?'

I swallowed and was about to suggest that he still could—after all, that was where Anastasia was—but I held my tongue. This was no time to desert him. I might have been a boy, but I was man enough to know that.

'Sir, you seem distressed,' I said, stepping towards him now. 'Is there anything . . . perhaps if we were all to leave this place? The train has been standing here for two days now. We're in the middle of nowhere, sir.'

He laughed at this and shook his head as he settled on to a settee. 'The middle of nowhere,' he repeated. 'You're right about that.'

'I could send one of the soldiers to the nearest town for a doctor.'

'Why would I want a doctor? I'm not ill.'

'But sir . . .'

'Georgy,' he said, massaging the dark rings beneath his eyes with his fingers, 'General Ruzsky will be coming back here in a few minutes. Do you know why he is visiting me?'

'No, sir,' I replied, shaking my head. The General had spent most of the afternoon with the Tsar. I had not been present for any of their conversations but had heard raised voices through the woodwork and then, finally, silence. When the General had left, he had rushed off with an expression that betrayed both anxiety and relief. I had left the Tsar alone with his thoughts for almost an hour since then, but had grown concerned for him and had stepped inside to see whether there was anything he needed.

'He's bringing some papers for me to sign,' he said. 'When I sign these papers, a great change will take place in Russia. Something that I never

386

imagined could possibly happen. Not in my lifetime.'

'Yes, sir,' I replied, a standard response, for even when the Tsar spoke in such a way it was considered ill-mannered to question him. One was obliged to wait for him to offer more information.

'You have heard about the Winter Palace, of course?'

'No, Your Majesty,' I said, shaking my head.

'It has been taken,' he said, smiling a little. 'The government. Your government. *My* government. They have taken it from me. It's under the rule of the Duma now, I am told. Who knows what will become of it? A few years from now and it will be a hotel, perhaps. Or a museum. Our state rooms will be souvenir shops. Our parlours will be used to sell tea-cakes and seed-buns.'

'That could never happen,' I said, shocked to imagine the palace under the control of anyone but him. 'It is your home.'

'But I have no home any more. There's no place for me in St Petersburg, that's for sure. If I was even to think about going back—'

A tap on the door interrupted his speech and I glanced towards it, then back at the Tsar; he sighed heavily before nodding and I stepped across to open it. General Ruzsky was standing on the other side with a heavy parchment in his hand. A thin man with grey hair and a bushy black moustache, he had been coming and going from the train ever since we had stopped here a couple of days earlier and had never once acknowledged me, despite the fact that I had been on hand throughout most of his dealings with the Tsar. Even now he brushed past me without a word and stepped quickly into

387

the study, nodding quickly at Nicholas before placing the document before him. I turned to leave, but as I did so, the Tsar looked over and raised his hand.

'Don't go, Georgy,' he said. 'I think we will need a witness to this. Isn't that so, General?'

'Well ... yes, sir,' replied the General gruffly, looking me up and down as if he had never seen such a poor specimen of humanity before. 'But I hardly think a bodyguard is the appropriate person, do you? I can fetch one of my lieutenants.'

'It doesn't matter,' said the Tsar. 'Georgy will do just as well. Sit down,' he said to me and I took a seat in the corner of the carriage, doing my best to remain inconspicuous. 'Now, General,' he said finally, scanning the document carefully, 'it says everything that we agreed upon?'

'Yes, sir,' replied Ruzsky, taking a seat now too. 'All it requires is your signature.'

'And my family? They will be kept safe?'

'Currently they are being protected by the army of the provisional government at Tsarskoe Selo,' he said carefully. 'No harm shall come to them, I promise you that.'

'And my wife,' said the Tsar, his voice breaking a little. 'You guarantee her safety?'

'But of course. She is still the Tsaritsa.'

'Yes, she is,' replied the Tsar, smiling now. 'For now. I note, General, that you say they are "being protected". Is that a euphemism for being imprisoned?'

'Their status has yet to be decided, sir,' replied the General, and I found myself shocked by his response. Who was he to speak to the Tsar like this? It was outrageous. And I hated the idea of

Anastasia being watched over by any members of the provisional government. She was an Imperial Grand Duchess, after all, the daughter, the granddaughter, the great-granddaughter of God's anointed ones.

'There is one other matter,' said the Tsar after a long pause. 'Since we last spoke, I have had a change of mind on one thing.'

'Sir, we have discussed this,' said the General in a tired voice. 'There is no way that—'

'No, no,' said the Tsar, shaking his head. 'It's not what you think. It relates to the succession.'

'The succession? But you have already decided on that. You will abdicate in favour of your son, the Tsarevich Alexei.'

I shot forward in my seat at these words and it was all that I could do not to let out a cry of horror. Could it really be so? Was the Tsar about to renounce his throne? Of course he was, I realized quickly. I had known it would come to this. We all had. I had just been unwilling to face up to it.

'We ... and by "we" I mean my immediate family—my wife, my children and I—' said the Tsar, 'we will be sent into exile after the instrument is invoked, will we not?'

The General hesitated for only a moment, but then nodded his head. 'Yes, sir,' he said. 'Yes, it will be impossible to guarantee your safety in Russia. Your relatives in Europe, perhaps . . .'

'Yes, yes,' said the Tsar dismissively. 'Cousin Georgie and that lot. I know they'll look after us. But if Alexei were to be Tsar, then he would be forced to remain behind in Russia? Without his family?'

'Again, that is the most likely outcome.'

389

The Tsar nodded. 'Then I wish to add a clause to the document. I wish to renounce not only my own claim to the throne, but also that of my son. The crown can pass to my brother Michael instead.'

The General sat back and stroked his moustache for a moment. 'Your Majesty,' he said, 'do you think that is wise? Does the boy not deserve a chance to—'

'The boy,' snapped the Tsar, 'as you very clearly state it, is just a boy. He is only twelve years old. And he is not well. I cannot allow him to be separated from Sunny and me. Make the change, General, and I will sign your document. Then perhaps I will have a little peace. I deserve at least that much after all these years, don't you agree?'

General Ruzsky hesitated for only a moment before nodding his head and scratching away at the page while the Tsar stared out of the window. I focussed my eyes directly on him, hoping that he would perhaps feel my gaze and look towards me, so that I might offer some small semblance of support, but he did not turn back until the General muttered something to him. He quickly took the paper, looked it over and signed it.

We all remained very still after this, until the Tsar stood up.

'You may leave now,' he said quietly. 'Both of you, please.'

The General and I made for the door and closed it behind us.

Inside, the last Tsar was left to his thoughts, his memories and his regrets.

1922

My Parisian employer, Monsieur Ferré, was not pleased with my continued absences from work, but he waited until the last customer had left the shop before taking me aside to make his displeasure clear. He had been behaving in a disgruntled fashion throughout the day, offering a series of sarcastic comments about my time-keeping and refusing to allow me my regular afternoon break on the grounds that he had been too lenient with me as it was. I tried to engage him in conversation in the late afternoon, but he brushed me aside with the ease that one swats a fly hovering around one's head and stated quite flatly that he had no time for me at that moment, that he was completing his monthly accounts and would speak with me later in the evening, when the store was closed. Not looking forward to our conversation, I busied myself in the history section of the bookshop at the appointed time and pretended to be so engrossed in my work as not to hear him when he called my name. Finally, he marched around the corner, discovered me shelving a series of volumes on the history of French military costume, and practically spat on the ground in irritation.

'Jachmenev,' he said, 'didn't you hear me calling for you?'

'My apologies, sir,' I replied, standing up and brushing the dust of the books off my trousers; my knees buckled slightly beneath me as I tried to right myself, for the gaps between the stacks were astonishingly narrow. Monsieur Ferré made a point of keeping as much stock as possible on the premises, but the result of this was that the books were crammed too tightly together upon the shelves, and the proximity of the bookcases made it almost impossible for more than one person to inspect them at any one time. 'I was absorbed in what I was doing,' I added, 'but there was—'

'And if I had been a customer, what then?' he asked in a belligerent tone. 'If you had been alone in the shop, hidden away like a teenage boy perusing a volume of Bellocq, then any petty thief might have run away with the day's takings, simply because you find yourself unable to concentrate on more than one task at a time.'

I knew from experience that it was pointless to argue with him, that it would be better if I simply allowed him to express his anger and rid himself of it before mounting my defence. 'I'm very sorry, sir,' I said finally, attempting to sound contrite. 'I'll try to pay more attention in future.'

'It's not just about paying attention, Jachmenev,' he said irritably, shaking his head. 'This is exactly what I wished to talk to you about. You will admit, will you not, that I have been more than fair in my dealings with you during these last few weeks?'

'You've been extremely generous, sir, and I'm very grateful for it. As is my wife.'

'I've allowed you to take as much time away from your duties as you needed to get over your . . .' He hesitated, unsure how to phrase this correctly; I could tell that he was uncomfortable at even being drawn into such a conversation. 'Over your recent difficulties,' he said finally. 'But I am not a charitable organization, Jachmenev, you must understand that. I cannot afford to maintain an employee who comes and goes at the drop of a hat, who does not fulfil his hours as contracted, who leaves me alone in the shop when I have so many other matters to attend to—'

'Sir,' I said quickly, stepping forward a little, anxious that he should not dismiss me from my position, which would have been one further blow during an already difficult time. 'Sir, all I can do is apologize for how unreliable I have been of late, but I really do think that the worst is over now. Zoya is back on her feet, she's returning to work herself on Monday. If you could see your way to giving me another chance, I promise that I will give you no cause to reprimand me again.'

He glared at me and looked away for a moment, nibbling at his lower lip with his front teeth, a habit he always indulged in when faced with a difficult decision. I could tell that his instinct was to fire me, that it had even been his intention to do so, but my words were winning him over and he was wavering in his final judgement.

'You will agree, sir,' I added, 'that I have been entirely reliable to you over the last three years of my employment?'

'You've been an excellent assistant, Jachmenev,' he replied in frustration. 'That's why this whole matter has been so disappointing to me. I've spoken very highly of you to friends of mine, you know, other businessmen here in Paris. Men who have a very low opinion of Russian émigrés in general, I might add. Men who see the lot of you as revolutionaries and trouble-makers. I've told them that you have proved yourself to be one of the most reliable workers I have ever had the good fortune to employ. I don't want to let you go, young man, but if I am to keep you on—'

'Then you will have my absolute assurance, sir,' I said, 'that I will be here on time every morning and will remain at my post throughout the day. One more chance, Monsieur Ferré, that's all I ask. I promise you will have no cause to regret your decision.'

He thought about it a little more, before wagging his fat little finger at me. 'One more chance, Jachmenev, that is all. You understand me?'

'I do, sir.'

'I have every sympathy for you and your wife, it's a terrible thing you've been through, but that's neither here nor there. If you give me any reason to speak to you like this again, then that will be the end of things between us. In the meantime, you can work a few extra hours tonight to make up the time. Some of these shelves are a disgrace. I walked around earlier and noticed the alphabetical system has collapsed almost entirely. I could find nothing I was looking for.'

'Yes, sir,' I said, bowing my head slightly, an old habit which I had yet to lose when faced with a figure of authority. 'I'll be happy to sort things out. And thank you. For the second chance, I mean.'

He nodded and I turned back to my work in relief, for the job at the bookshop was an enjoyable one and I found it stimulating to be surrounded by so much scholarship and erudition. More importantly, however, I could not afford to lose the small income that it provided us with. What little savings we had built up since our arrival in Paris more than three years before had been reduced considerably by medical expenses over the

394

previous five weeks, since Zoya's miscarriage, not to mention the temporary loss of our second income, and I dreaded to think what might become of us if I was dismissed from my position. I resolved to give Monsieur Ferré no further cause to think badly of me.

*   *   *

The first I knew of Leo's arrest was when Zoya appeared, ashen-faced, in the bookshop late one afternoon in November, when the weather had turned bracingly cold and the trees were already denuded of their leaves. I was standing behind the counter, examining a series of anatomical textbooks that Monsieur Ferré had inexplicably purchased at auction a few days before, when the small bell above the door rang and I instinctively shuddered, waiting for the icy breeze to blow through the shop and nip at my ears and nose. Looking up, I was surprised to see my wife stepping towards me, her coat wrapped tightly around her body, a scarf she had knitted herself hanging loosely around her neck.

'Zoya,' I said, relieved that my employer had gone home for the day, for he would not have been happy to see me receiving personal visitors. 'What's the matter? You're as white as a ghost.'

She shook her head, hesitating for a moment as she recovered her breath, and my mind swam with the possibilities of what could be wrong. It was almost three months now since she had lost the baby and although her spirits were still low, she had started to find happiness in our daily lives once again. Only a few nights earlier, we had made love for the first time since our loss; it had been gentle and affectionate and I had held her in my arms afterwards, where she had remained perfectly still, looking up to kiss me tenderly from time to time, the tears finally coming to an end, replaced by the promise of hope. I dreaded to think that she had become ill once more, but seeing me staring at her in increasing panic she dismissed my worries quickly.

'It's not me,' she said. 'I'm fine.'

'Thank God,' I replied. 'But you look so distressed. What can have—?'

'It's Leo,' she said. 'He's been arrested.'

I opened my eyes wide in surprise but couldn't prevent a smile from passing across my face, wondering what fresh trouble our dear friend had managed to involve himself in now, for he was no stranger to drama or excitement. 'Arrested?' I asked. 'But why? What on earth has he done?'

'It's beyond belief,' she said, and I could tell by the look on her face that this was a much more serious matter than I had originally thought. 'Georgy, he has killed a gendarme.'

My mouth fell open and I felt my head grow a little dizzy at the words. Leo and his girlfriend Sophie were our two closest friends in Paris, the first companions we had found there. We had shared countless dinners with them, got drunk on too many occasions, laughed and joked and, above all, argued about politics. Leo was a dreamer, an idealist, a romantic, a revolutionary; he could be witty and frustrating, passionate and irritable, flirtatious and generous. There was no end of adjectives to describe this extraordinary man, no shortage of occasions when Zoya and I had left his company half in love with him or swearing that we would never see him again. He was everything that youth was about: a man of poetry, art, ambition and determination. But he was not a murderer. He had not a single strain of violence in him whatsoever.

'But it's not possible,' I said, staring at her in amazement. 'There must be some mistake.'

'There are witnesses,' she said, sitting down now and burying her face in her hands. 'Quite a few, it would seem. I don't know exactly what happened. Only that he is being held in the gendarmerie and there is no possibility of his being released.'

I steadied myself against the counter and considered this quietly for a few moments. It was almost impossible to believe. The idea of such violence was repugnant to me and, I was sure, to him also. He preached a gospel of pacifism and understanding, even if his revolutionary ideas sometimes allowed him to get carried away with historical precedents of proletarian savagery. I was sure that I had left such things behind me in another place, another country.

'Tell me what happened,' I said. 'Tell me everything you know.'

'I know very little,' she replied, the catch in her voice implying that she too had hoped that events like this would no longer be part of our lives. 'It was only an hour ago. Sophie and I were at work as usual, we were completing two dresses that needed to be ready by the end of the day, stitching a lace trim to attach to the collars, when a man entered the shop, very tall, very serious. I didn't know what to think when I saw him first. We can go a whole month sometimes, Georgy, and never see a man walk through our doors at all. I'm ashamed to admit it, but when I saw him, when I noticed the seriousness of his expression, the determination of his glance, I thought ... I thought for a moment ...'

'That we had been discovered?'

She nodded, but said nothing more of this for now. 'I stared at him in surprise, and started to ask whether we could help him with something, but he simply pointed a finger at my face, so high that it reminded me of a gun, and I thought for a moment that I was going to faint.

' "Sophie Tambleau?" he asked, looking across at me, and I said nothing for a moment, so unnerved was I by the situation. "Are you Sophie Tambleau?" he repeated, and before I could say anything, Sophie herself came forward, a blend of curiosity and concern upon her face.

' "I'm Sophie Tambleau," she said. "How can I help you?"

' "You can't," he replied. "I've been sent with a message for you, that's all."

' "A message?" she asked, laughing a little and looking at me. I started to smile too in relief, but the situation was extraordinary. Who ever sent messages to us?

' "You are the common-law wife of Leo Raymer?" Sophie shrugged. Of course the phrase was farcical, but she nodded and admitted that she was. "Monsieur Raymer is being held at the gendarmerie on the Rue de Clignancourt. He has been arrested."

' "Arrested?" she cried and the man said yes, that he had killed a gendarme earlier that afternoon and that he had been taken into custody awaiting

398

trial and had asked that someone get a message to Sophie to tell her of what had taken place.'

'But Leo!' I asked, amazed by what she was telling me. '*Our* Leo? How on earth could he have killed someone? Why would he do such a thing?'

'I don't know, Georgy,' she said, standing up now and pacing the floor in frustration. 'I don't know anything other than what I've just told you. Sophie's gone directly to see him. I said that I would come and find you and that we would follow her there. That was all right, wasn't it?'

'Of course,' I said, reaching for the shop keys, ignoring the fact that I was not due to close the store for another hour at least. 'Of course we must go, our friends are in trouble.'

We stepped out into the street and I locked the door behind me, cursing myself for forgetting my gloves that morning as the wind was so strong that I could feel my cheeks growing pink with the cold after only a few moments. As we made our way quickly down the street, my thoughts were almost entirely with my dear friend, locked in a cell somewhere for a horrible crime; but still, I could not help but feel as relieved as Zoya had been that it was Sophie whom the gentleman had come looking for, and not us.

It had only been four years since we had left Russia. I still believed that one day, they would catch up with us.

*   *   *

We were not allowed to visit Leo, nor would any of the gendarmes tell us anything about the circumstances which had led to his incarceration.

The elderly desk sergeant looked at me with utter disdain when he heard my accent and seemed loath to answer any of my questions, simply grunting and shrugging his shoulders at every enquiry I made, as if it was beneath his dignity to answer me. It was rare for either Zoya or me to encounter any racially motivated hostility within the city—after all, the war had seen to it that Paris was filled with people of all nationalities—but from time to time a certain resentment was evident in those elderly French citizens who did not like the fact that their capital had been invaded by so many exiled Europeans and Russians.

'You're not family,' the sergeant said, barely glancing up at me as he spoke, but continuing to fill in the letters of his crossword. 'I can tell you nothing.'

'But we are friends,' I protested. 'Monsieur Raymer was a witness at my wedding. Our wives work together. Surely you can—' At that moment, a door opened to my left and Sophie emerged, white-faced, desperately trying to stem her tears, followed by another gendarme. She seemed surprised to see us waiting for her, but grateful, and attempted a brief smile before walking towards the door.

'Sophie,' said Zoya, following her as she stepped outside into the darkness; night had fallen and mercifully the wind had diminished. 'Sophie, what's going on? What's happened? Where is Leo?'

She shook her head as if she could scarcely find the words to explain what had taken place, so we led her across the street to a nearby café, where we ordered three coffees and she finally summoned

400

the strength to recount what she had been told.

'It's the most ridiculous thing,' she said. 'An accident, that's all. A stupid accident. But they say that because it was a gendarme who was killed—'

'Killed?' I asked, struck by the brutality of the word, its sharp unpleasant sound. 'By Leo? But it's impossible! Tell me what happened exactly.'

'He went out this morning as usual,' she began with a sigh, as if she could not believe that a day that had begun in so banal a fashion could end so dramatically. 'He left the flat early, hoping to get a good position for his easel. With this terrible weather, there have been fewer opportunities for portrait painters. Most people don't want to sit on a chair in a windy street for thirty minutes while he captures their likeness. He went towards Sacré-Coeur, where there were sure to be many tourists. We have been struggling a little for money lately,' she admitted. 'Not enough to worry unnecessarily, you understand, but we couldn't afford to lose a day's pay. It's been difficult.'

'It's difficult for everyone,' I said quietly. 'But you could have always come to us if you needed help, you know that, don't you?' It was wrong of me to say this. The truth was that if Leo or Sophie had asked Zoya or me for assistance, we would not have been in a position to offer any. Suggesting otherwise was an arrogance that was unworthy of me. Zoya knew as much and glanced in my direction, frowning a little, and I bowed my head, embarrassed by my bravado.

'It's kind of you to say that, Georgy,' said Sophie, who most likely knew very well that our financial position mirrored their own almost exactly. 'But we hadn't quite got to the point where we needed to rely on the charity of our friends.'

'Leo,' said Zoya softly, reaching across and placing her hand flat on Sophie's own hand, which had begun to tremble slightly even as we sat there. 'Tell us about Leo.'

'There were more people at Sacré-Coeur than he might have expected,' she continued. 'Quite a few of the artists had set up their easels and everyone was trying to persuade a tourist into sitting for them. There was an old lady sitting on the grass, feeding the birds—'

'In this weather?' I asked, surprised. 'She would freeze to death.'

'You know how resilient these old crones are,' she replied with a shrug. 'They sit there, summer and winter, rain or shine. They don't care about the weather.'

It was true. I had observed on more than one occasion the number of elderly Parisians who spent their mornings and afternoons sitting along the grassy banks in front of the Basilica, scattering stale bread for the birds to eat. It was as if they believed that without their help, the avian world would face extinction. On one occasion not three weeks before, I had watched a man of perhaps eighty years of age, a wizened old creature whose face was a patchwork of lines and wrinkles and creases, sitting with his arms outstretched while a group of birds settled upon him. I sat there, staring at him for almost an hour, and during all that time he remained utterly motionless; had his arms not been extended as they were, I would have taken him for a corpse.

'Another artist,' continued Sophie, 'somebody new to Paris, someone Leo had never met before, arrived and decided that he wanted to position himself exactly where this old woman was seated. He asked her to move; she said no. He told her he wanted to paint there; she told him to go and soak his head. There were harsh words, I think, and then this man reached down and attempted to lift the woman from her rightful place, dragging her to her feet, ignoring her cries of protest.'

'Where was he from?' asked Zoya, and I looked at her, surprised by the question. I suspect she was hoping that he did not hail from our own country.

'Spain, Leo thinks,' she replied. 'Or Portugal, perhaps. Anyway, he saw this sacrilege taking place and you know what Leo is like, he cannot bear to witness such a lack of courtesy.'

It was true. Leo was notorious for tipping his cap at elderly women on the street, charming them with his wide smile and friendly airs. He held out seats for them at cafés and assisted them with their bags when they were walking in the same direction as he was. He saw himself as a representative of the ancient order of chivalry, one of the last men in 1920s Paris who subscribed to that antique society.

'He went over and grabbed the Spaniard, twisting him around and remonstrating with him for his treatment of the woman. A fight broke out, of course. There was pushing and shoving and name-calling—who knows what level of childishness. And they were very loud. Leo was shouting at the top of his voice, calling his opponent every name that he could think of, and from what I am told, the Spaniard gave as good as he got. Things were about to turn even nastier when they were interrupted by a gendarme, who separated them, an action which caused Leo to grow even angrier.

He accused the young policeman of siding with a foreigner against one of his own countrymen and a dispute broke out over that remark. And you know what he's like when he's confronted by authority. I daresay he lashed out, started spouting his opinions about *les gardiens de la paix*, and before anyone could take control of the situation, Leo had punched both the Spaniard in the nose and the gendarme in the face, one after the other.'

'Good God,' I said, trying to imagine his clenched fist smashing into the snout of one man and then pulling back, preparing to strike the other. Leo was a strong fellow; I would not have wanted to be the recipient of either of those blows.

'Of course, after he did that,' said Sophie, 'the gendarme had no choice but to arrest him, but Leo tried to get away from him, perhaps to make a run for it, by pushing him to one side. Unfortunately, the young policeman slipped as he was pushed and lost his footing on the steps. A moment later he had tumbled down fifteen, twenty steps to the next break in the staircase, and he landed heavily, cracking his skull against the stone. By the time Leo ran down to assist him, his eyes were already focussed on the heavens. He was dead.'

We sat in silence and I looked across at Zoya, whose face was pale, her jaw set tightly as if she was afraid of how she might react to this if she allowed her emotions to be displayed. Any thought of violence, of death, of the moment when a life came to its end was enough to disturb her emotions and unsettle her, to drag the terrible memories back to the forefront of her mind. Neither of us spoke. Instead we waited for Sophie, who appeared more calm now that she was laying out the story for us, to continue.

'He tried to run away,' she said finally. 'And of course that only made things worse. He got quite far, too, I think. He ran along the Rue de la Bonne and across into St Vincent, then turned back on himself, heading towards the St Pierre de Montmartre—'

I drew a breath at this; my first home in Paris had been there, and the flat that Zoya and I had shared since our wedding was on the Rue Cortot, not far from the St Pierre; I wondered whether Leo had been hoping to find a safe haven with us.

'—but by then there were six, perhaps seven gendarmes in pursuit of him, whistles blowing on every street, and they tackled him down, knocking him off his feet and sending him to the ground. Oh, Zoya,' she cried, reaching out to her friend. 'They beat him badly, too. One of his eyes is sealed shut and his cheek is almost purple with bruising. You would hardly recognize him if you saw him. They say it was necessary to restrain him, but it can't have been.'

'It was a terrible accident,' said Zoya firmly. 'Surely they can recognize that? And over something so trivial, too. The Spaniard, he was as much to blame.'

'They don't see it like that,' Sophie said, shaking her head as the tears began again, a great depth of sobbing emerging from her very heart, her previously stilled emotions vanquished at last by the realization of what had taken place. 'They see it as murder. He is to stand trial for it. He could be jailed for years—for his entire life, perhaps. Certainly his youth will be gone if he is ever released. And I cannot live without him, do you

405

see that?' she added, raising her voice hysterically. 'I will not live without him.'

I could see the café owner looking at us suspiciously, hoping that we would leave soon. He cleared his throat audibly and I nodded at him, threw a few francs on the table and stood up.

Zoya and I took Sophie back to our flat, where we gave her two large draughts of brandy and sent her to our bedroom to rest. She went without protest and fell asleep quickly, although we could hear her tossing restlessly in the bed.

'He can't go to jail,' said Zoya, when there were just the two of us together again. We were sitting at our small kitchen table, trying to think of a way to help them both. 'It's unthinkable. Surely there must be some way to save him?'

I nodded, but said nothing. I was concerned for Leo, of course I was, but it was not the prospect of his being sent to jail that worried me. It was something worse than that. He was responsible for the death of an officer of the French police force, after all. Accident or not, such matters were not taken lightly. The punishment could be more severe than either my wife or Leo's were currently willing to consider.

*　　　*　　　*

The trial of Leo Raymer began three weeks later, in the second week of December, and lasted a mere thirty-six hours. It began on a Tuesday morning and by Wednesday lunchtime the jury had returned their verdict.

Sophie had stayed in our apartment for a few days after the incident took place, but she went

406

home after that, saying that it was pointless to sleep on our couch and be under our feet every evening when she had a perfectly good, if lonely, bed not four streets away. We allowed her to leave with minimal protest, but spent every evening with her nevertheless, either in her flat or ours, or, if we could afford it, in one of the cafés that were dotted around the nearby streets.

Initially, she appeared to be close to hysteria about the sequence of events which had taken place; then she grew stronger and more optimistic, determined to do everything she could to secure Leo's release. Soon after that, she grew depressed, and then angry at her boyfriend for causing all of this trouble in the first place. By the time the trial began, she was exhausted by her emotions, and had grown dark-eyed from lack of sleep. I became concerned as to how she would react if the trial did not have a happy resolution.

I begged Monsieur Ferré for a day off on the Tuesday that the trial began and was unfortunate in that I appeared to have caught him at a bad moment, for he threw his pen down on the table, a splash of ink bouncing in my direction that caused me to jump back, and stared at me, breathing heavily through his nose.

'A day off during the week, Jachmenev?' he asked me. '*Another* day off? I thought that we had reached an understanding, you and I.'

'We have, sir,' I replied, not expecting him to react so violently to my simple request. I had been a model employee since my reprimand and thought that he would happily allow me to be absent from work for a single day. 'I'm sorry to ask for it, only—'

'Your wife must realize that the world does not—'

'This is not about my wife, Monsieur Ferré,' I said quickly, growing angry that he would have the audacity to criticize Zoya. 'This has nothing to do with what happened all those months ago. I think I told you about my friend? Monsieur Raymer?'

'Ah, the murderer,' he said with a half-smile. 'Yes, I remember. And of course I've read about the case in the papers.'

'Leo is no murderer,' I replied. 'It was a terrible accident.'

'In which a man died.'

'Just so.'

'And not just a man, but a man whose responsibility it was to protect the citizenry. Your friend will find it difficult to secure his release, I imagine. Popular opinion is against it.'

I nodded and tried to control my emotions; he was only repeating what I already knew. 'May I take the day off or not?' I asked, looking up and fixing my gaze to his, holding it there for as long as I dared, until finally he broke away and threw his hands in the air in a gesture of surrender.

'Fine, fine,' he said. 'You may take one day off. Unpaid, of course. And if there are reporters at the courthouse, as there will no doubt be, do not tell them that you work in this establishment. I don't want my bookshop associated with such a sordid business.'

I agreed to his terms, and on the morning that the trial began accompanied Zoya and Sophie to the courthouse, where we took our seats in the gallery, aware that every eye was turned in our direction. I could tell that it made Zoya uncomfortable and I took her hand in mine, squeezing it twice for luck.

'I don't like all this attention,' she said quietly. 'A reporter asked me on the way in to identify myself.'

'You're not obliged to tell them anything,' I replied. 'Neither of us is. And remember, they're really not interested in us at all. It's Sophie they want.'

I felt callous making such a remark, but it was the truth, and I wanted to reassure my wife that we were safe. Perhaps if she believed it, then I would believe it too.

The courtroom was full of interested spectators and it was not long before there was an audible intake of breath around the pews, as a door opened and Leo was led in, surrounded by several gendarmes. He scanned the room quickly in search of us, and when he found us, he offered a brave smile which I was certain masked the anxiety he felt inside. He looked more pale and thin than the last time I had seen him—the night before the incident, when we had sat in a bar together, just the two of us, drinking too much red wine; the night he had told me that he planned to ask Sophie to marry him on Christmas Day, a fact that she was still unaware of—but he held himself bravely, looking straight ahead when the charge was read and answering in a clear voice when he asserted his plea of 'not guilty'.

The morning was filled with a series of tedious legal discussions between the judge, the prosecutor and the court-appointed lawyer who was representing our friend. In the late afternoon, however, it grew more interesting as several witnesses were called to the stand, including the elderly woman whom the Spaniard had tried to remove from her place. She sang the praises of Leo, of course, and blamed the gendarme for the accident—as well as the Spaniard himself, who was unnecessarily harsh in his condemnation of Leo, perhaps on account of his wounded ego. A few others made an appearance, men and women who had been on the steps of Sacré-Coeur at the time of the incident and had given their names to the investigators. A lady who had been only inches from the dead man when he fell. The doctor who had first examined him. The coroner.

'It went well, don't you think?' Sophie asked me that night and I nodded my head, believing there was nothing to be lost with this supportive lie.

'Some of the testimony was helpful,' I admitted, stopping short of adding that most of it portrayed Leo as being impetuous and bullying in the way that he had behaved, his impulsive conduct leading to the death of an honest and innocent young man.

'It will all go well tomorrow,' said Zoya, hugging her as we parted that night. 'I am sure of it.'

We fought later, the first time that Zoya and I had ever raised our voices to each other. Although I had every intention of going to the courthouse, I made the mistake of mentioning that Monsieur Ferré would likely be very angry with me for taking a second day away from the bookshop, and she misinterpreted my concern for our future as selfishness and a lack of consideration for our friends, a charge that upset and wounded me.

Later that night, having made up after our fight—so strange to remember, we both shed tears, so unaccustomed to argument were we—we lay in bed together and I urged Zoya to prepare herself for what was to come, that this matter might not end as we would wish it.

She said nothing in reply, simply turned over to sleep, but I knew that she was not so naive as to fail to recognize the truth in my warning.

*   *   *

We sat in the same seats the next day and on this occasion the courtroom was at full capacity to hear Leo's testimony. He began nervously, but soon his familiar strength returned to him and he gave a performance of remarkable oratorical prowess that made me wonder for a moment whether in fact he might yet save himself. He portrayed himself as a hero of the people, a young man who could not stand by and watch an elderly woman—an elderly *French*woman, he pointed out—insulted and mistreated by a guest of his country. He spoke of how much he admired the work of the gendarmes, and said that he had seen the young man lose his footing and had in fact reached out a hand to save him, not push him, but it was too late. He had fallen. The courthouse sat in absolute silence as he spoke, and when he descended the stand he glanced towards Sophie, who smiled at him anxiously; he smiled back, before resuming his seat between the officers sent to guard him.

The last witness, however, was the young policeman's mother, who told the court of his movements that morning and portrayed her son— quite properly, perhaps—as a saint in waiting. She spoke proudly and with dignity, giving in to tears only once, and by the end of her testimony I knew that there was little hope.

An hour later, the jury returned, announced a

verdict of guilty to murder, and as the court broke into spontaneous applause, Sophie jumped to her feet and immediately fainted, leaving Zoya and me to carry her out into the hallway.

'It can't be, it can't be,' she said in a daze as she came back to consciousness on one of the cold stone benches that lined the exterior walls. 'He is innocent. They can't take him from me.'

Zoya was in tears now too and the two women hugged each other, trembling violently. I could feel a spring rising behind my own eyes too. It was too much for me. I stood up, unwilling to allow them to see me break down.

'I'll go back inside,' I said quickly, turning my back on them. 'I'll find out what happens next.'

Stepping back into the courtroom, I had to fight my way through to a position where I could see for myself what was taking place. Leo was on his feet, a gendarme on either side of him, white-faced, looking for all the world as if he could not believe what had happened, certain that he would be released at any moment with the apologies of the court. But that was not to be.

The judge banged his gavel on the bench for silence and proceeded with the sentencing.

When I emerged from the courtroom a few moments later, I was sure for a moment that I was going to be sick. I ran quickly outside to gather as much air into my lungs as possible, and as I did so, the full horror of what I had just heard came home to me and I had to place my hand against the wall to steady myself, lest I collapse entirely and disgrace myself.

Zoya and Sophie, a few feet away from me, turned and stopped crying for a moment, staring at

412

me.

'What is it?' asked Sophie, running towards me. 'Georgy, tell me! What has happened?'

I shook my head. 'I can't,' I said.

'Tell me!' she repeated, shouting now. 'Tell me, Georgy!' She slapped my face, once, twice, three times, hard. She clenched her hands into fists and pummelled my shoulders, and I felt nothing, just stood there as Zoya pulled her away. 'Tell me,' she was continuing to scream, but the words were lost in such misery and sobbing that they were all but unintelligible.

'Georgy?' asked Zoya, looking towards me and swallowing nervously. 'Georgy, what is it? We have to know. You have to tell her.'

I nodded and looked at her, unsure how to put such a thing, such an unspeakable thing, into words.

*   *   *

The execution took place early the following morning. Neither Zoya nor I was there to witness it, but Sophie was permitted to spend thirty minutes with her lover before he was brought to the courtyard and guillotined. I was shocked—beyond shocked—to learn that this was to be his punishment, that an instrument of death that I associated with the French Revolution was still in use, more than a century later, for those sentenced to death. It seemed barbaric. None of the three of us was able to believe that such a punishment could be meted out to our young, handsome, funny, vibrant, impossible friend. But there was no escaping it. The sentence was handed down and carried out within twenty-four hours.

Paris held no more beauty for us after that. I offered my resignation in writing to Monsieur Ferré, who tore up my letter without reading it and told me that it did not matter what it said, I was dismissed anyway.

It didn't matter.

Sophie came to see us only once before she left the country, thanking us for what we had done to help her, promising to write when she arrived at wherever it was that she was going.

And Zoya and I decided to leave Paris for good. It was her decision, but I was happy to acquiesce.

On our last night in the city, we sat in our empty flat, staring out of the window towards the spires of the many churches that littered the streets.

'It was my fault,' she said.

The Journey to Yekaterinburg

When I went to bed that night in one of the small cots that lined the walls of the guards' carriage, I was sure that I would find it impossible to sleep. The day had grown chaotic as the Tsar had sunk into a silent depression, and those of us who formed his entourage were embarrassed and disconsolate. I am not too proud to admit that I wept as I placed my head on the pillow, for my emotions were in a heightened state, and although I did eventually close my eyes, my dreams were tormented and I woke several times in the night, disoriented and upset. As the hours passed, however, I settled into a deeper slumber, and when

414

I opened my eyes again, not only had the night vanished, but most of the morning too. I blinked and waited for the events of the previous day to dissolve as dreams do, but rather than fade away in confusion, they clarified and reasserted themselves and I realized that it was all true and that the unimaginable had actually happened.

Sunlight seeped through the windows. I glanced around to see who else was sharing the carriage with me and was surprised to discover that I was entirely alone. This part of the train was almost always filled with other members of the Leib Guard, sleeping, trying to sleep, dressing, talking, arguing. For it to be so serene was disconcerting. An eerie quiet surrounded me as I climbed out of bed slowly, pulled on my shirt and trousers and looked warily out at the cold, endless forest that stretched for hundreds of miles on either side of the train.

Marching quickly through the dining car, the games saloon and the carriages which were the private domains of the Grand Duchesses, I made my way to the Tsar's private study, where the previous afternoon he had signed away his own birthright and that of his son, and knocked on the closed door. There was no response from within and I leaned closer to it, my ear to the wood, straining to hear any conversation inside.

'Your Majesty,' I called, determined still to address him by this title as I knocked again. 'Your Majesty, can I assist you with anything?'

There was no answer, so I opened the door and stepped inside to discover the room as empty as my sleeping quarters had been. I frowned and tried to imagine where the Tsar might be; he spent every morning locked away in his private study working on his papers. I couldn't imagine that would have changed, even in the new circumstances in which we found ourselves. There were still letters to be written, after all, papers to be signed, decisions to be made. Now more than ever it was important that he looked to his business. Looking back along the corridor to ensure that no one was coming, I stepped over to his desk and rifled quickly through the papers that remained there. They were complicated, political documents that meant nothing to me and I turned away from them in frustration, before noticing that the portrait of the Tsar's family which always stood on the desk had been removed from its frame, leaving nothing but the silver casing behind. I stared at the empty frame for a moment and picked it up, as if it might offer me some clues as to the Tsar's whereabouts, but replaced it a moment later and decided that I should disembark immediately.

The train had not moved since the night before, and as I jumped off, my boots crunched loudly on the stones beside the sleepers. Further along I could make out the figure of Peter Ilyavich Maksy, another member of the Leib Guard, who had been part of the Tsar's retinue since before I had first come to St Petersburg; we had never got along well and for the most part I avoided him. Another former member of the Corps of Pages, he resented my presence on the Imperial staff; he had been particularly incensed when I had been relieved of what he considered my 'babysitting' duties in respect of the Tsarevich and been brought here as part of the Tsar's retinue. Still, he appeared to be the only person left, so I had little choice but to

416

talk to him.

'Peter Ilyavich,' I said, striding up to where he stood, trying not to be unsettled by the disgruntled manner in which he stared at me as I walked along, as if I was nothing more than a minor irritation in his morning. He held his cigarette in his mouth for a long time before allowing himself one final drag and tossing it to the ground, where he stamped it underfoot.

'My friend,' he said, nodding at me, his voice laden with sarcasm. 'Good morning.'

'What's going on?' I asked. 'Where is everyone? The train is deserted.'

'They're all up front,' he said, glancing along the tracks towards the foremost carriage. 'Well, those who are left, anyway.'

'Left?' I asked, raising an eyebrow. 'What do you mean, left?'

'Didn't you hear?' he asked me. 'Don't you know what happened last night?'

I began to feel a great sense of dread build within me, but didn't want to anticipate what he meant. 'Just tell me, Peter,' I pleaded. 'Where is the Tsar?'

'There is no Tsar any more,' he said with a shrug, as if this was the most natural thing in the world. 'He's gone. We're free of him at last.'

'Gone?' I asked. 'But gone where? You don't mean—'

'He has renounced the throne.'

'I know that much,' I snapped. 'But where—'

'They sent a train for him in the middle of the night.'

'Who did?'

'Our new government. Don't tell me you slept through it! You missed a wonderful show.'

I felt an immediate rush of relief—he was alive, then, which meant it was unlikely that any harm had come to his family either—but this was quickly replaced by a desire to know where he had been taken.

'Why do you care, anyway?' Peter asked me, narrowing his eyes and reaching forward to brush some dust off my collar, an aggressive action from which I reeled back.

'I don't care,' I lied, sensing how the world had changed overnight, where the new dangers lay. 'I'm just interested.'

'Interested in what's happened to Romanov?'

'I want to know, that's all,' I insisted. 'I went to bed and . . . I don't know, I must have been exhausted. I slept through it. I didn't hear any train.'

'We are all exhausted, Georgy,' he said, shrugging his shoulders. 'But it's over now. Things will be better from now on.'

'What train was it?' I asked, ignoring the obvious pleasure he was taking in the Tsar's abdication. 'When did it come?'

'It must have been two, three o'clock in the morning perhaps,' he said, lighting another cigarette. 'Most of us were asleep, I suppose. I wasn't. I wanted to watch as they took him away. The train came from St Petersburg, it stopped a mile or so along this rail. There were a group of soldiers on board with a warrant for the arrest of Nicholas Romanov.'

'They arrested him?' I asked, perplexed, but refusing to rise to the bait of his mocking name for the Tsar. 'But why? He had done what they asked of him.'

'They said it was for his own protection. That it would not be safe for him to return to the capital. There are riots everywhere there, it's a mess. The palace is infested with people. The shops are being broken into in search of bread and flour. There's anarchy throughout the city. His fault, of course.'

'Spare me your editorial,' I hissed, furious now and grabbing him by the collar. 'Just tell me where they took him.'

'Hey, Georgy, let me go!' he cried, staring at me in surprise as he wrenched himself free from my grasp. 'What's the matter with you, anyway?'

'The matter with me?' I asked. 'The man we have served has been taken into custody and you stand here smoking cigarettes like it's any other morning.'

'But it's a glorious morning,' he said, clearly astonished that I did not share his sentiments. 'Haven't you longed for this day?'

'Why didn't they take this train?' I asked, ignoring his question and looking around at the Imperial transport, all fifteen carriages of it, which was stranded on the line now. 'Why send a different one?'

'Romanov is not to be allowed his luxuries any more,' he told me. 'He's a prisoner, you understand? He owns nothing. He has no money. This train does not belong to him. It belongs to Russia.'

'Until yesterday, he *was* Russia.'

'But this is today.'

I had half a mind to challenge him there and then, to wrestle him away from where he stood and punch him four square in the nose, daring him to retaliate, in order that I could take out my anger

419

on him, but it was pointless.

'Georgy Daniilovich,' he said, laughing as he shook his head. 'I don't believe it. You really are the Tsar's bitch, aren't you?'

I curled my lip in distaste at the remark. I knew that there were those among the Imperial entourage who despised the Tsar and all that he stood for, but I felt a loyalty to the man that could not be assuaged. He had treated me well, there was no question of that, and I would not deny him now. Regardless of the consequences.

'I am his servant,' I said. 'Until my dying day.'

'I see,' he muttered, looking down at the dust beneath his feet and kicking the ground with the toe of his boot. I looked away from him, desiring no further conversation, and stared into the distance, towards the north, towards St Petersburg. There was no way that they would have taken him back there. If the riots were as bad as Peter Ilyavich had said then he would be torn limb from limb in the centre of Palace Square, and the Bolsheviks could not afford such a public blood-letting so early in their revolution. I turned back to Peter, determined to get more answers, but he was gone. Looking up towards the foremost carriage, I could make out the sound of different voices talking together loudly, arguing, but not so distinctly that I could hear what they were saying. To the left of the train I noticed two cars that had not been there the previous afternoon—more Bolsheviks, I presumed—and felt a sudden rush of anxiety for what might be about to happen.

I had been reckless with what I had said to Peter Ilyavich; he was reporting me, even then.

Swallowing nervously, I turned around and began

to walk slowly towards the back of the train, increasing my stride as the final carriage came into sight. Looking over my shoulder I could see no one there, but I knew that I had only a few moments before they came for me. Who was I, after all, other than some lucky *moujik* who had made a strange success of his life? They might keep the Tsar alive—he was a prize, after all—but what was I? Just someone who had saved one Romanov and protected another.

The forest opened up before me to my left; I crossed the tracks and leapt directly into the conurbation of firs and pines, cedars and larches that stood tightly packed together in the dense woodland. Through the rush of my breathing and the sweeping of the branches, I was sure that I could hear the voices of the soldiers following me, their rifles in their hands, determined to hunt me down. I hesitated for a moment and gasped for breath—yes, it was true, they were coming. I had not just imagined it.

I was no longer a member of the Leib Guard; that portion of my life had ended. Now I was a fugitive.

*   *   *

It was almost October by the time I returned to St Petersburg. It was difficult to know whether I was still in danger, but the thought of being captured and murdered by the Bolsheviks was enough to keep me one step ahead of anyone whom I thought might be pursuing me. So I had chosen not to return immediately to the city, preferring to lie low in towns along the way instead, sleeping wherever I

421

could find a sheltered, secluded spot, swimming in streams and rivers to rub the stink from my body. I allowed my hair to grow long and a rough beard to cover my face, until I was almost unrecognizable as the youthful, eighteen-year-old soldier I had been at the end of the Romanov dynasty. My arms and legs became muscular from constant activity and I learned to kill animals, to skin and gut them, to cook them on an open fire, sacrificing their lives to save my own.

From time to time I stopped in small villages and was offered labouring work for a few days in exchange for food and a bed. I would quiz the farmers for political news, and it surprised me that a provisional government which so prided itself on belonging to the people allowed so little detail of its activities to be made public. From what I could discover, a man named Vladimir Ilyich Ulyanov—known to all as Lenin—was now in charge of Russia, and, in direct contrast to the Tsar, had moved his headquarters from St Petersburg to the Kremlin in Moscow, a place that Nicholas had always detested and had rarely visited. He had been crowned there, of course, like all the Tsars who preceded him, and I couldn't help but wonder whether this tradition had been in Lenin's mind as he chose his new seat of power.

When I finally returned, St Petersburg—or Petrograd, as it had been officially renamed—had changed considerably, but it was still recognizable to me. The palaces along the Neva had all been closed down, and I wondered where the princes and counts and dowager duchesses had made their new homes. They were related to royal families all across Europe, of course. Doubtless some had fled towards Denmark; others to Greece. The more resilient might have travelled across the continent and sailed for England, as the Tsar himself had planned to do. They were not here, however. Not any more.

Where once the banks of the river would have been dominated by horse-drawn carriages, transporting their wealthy occupants to skate on the frozen lakes or to enjoy merry evenings at each other's mansions, they were now empty, save for the peasants rushing along the pavement, desperate to get home, to escape the cold and eat whatever scraps of food they had managed to gather during the day.

It was freezing that winter, I remember that much. The air in Palace Square was so frosty that every time the wind blew, it bit at my cheeks and ears and the tip of my nose, forcing me to dig my nails into the palms of my hands to stop myself from crying out loud. I stood in the shadows of the colonnades looking at my former home, thinking how different things had been when I had first arrived here two years before, so naive, so innocent, so desirous of an existence different to the one that I had endured in Kashin. What would my sister Asya make of me now, I wondered, huddled up as I was against a wall, my arms wrapped around myself for warmth?

She would think it my just reward, perhaps.

I knew nothing of what had happened to the Imperial Family and had learned precious little as I'd travelled from village to village along the way. I assumed that they had been held for a short time and then sent into exile, Anastasia's worst fear, transported across the continent to England, where King George would no doubt have welcomed them with a familial embrace and wondered what on earth he was supposed to do with these Romanovs who expected so much from him.

Of course, it was Anastasia's face that lingered in my mind throughout every day, as I continued my journey and during the nights, when I tried to sleep. I dreamed of her and composed letters and sonnets and all manner of foolish poetry in my head. I had sworn to her that I would never desert her, that whatever happened, I would be there. But it had been almost nine months since we had last seen each other on the night that she had visited me in my room at the Winter Palace, distraught about her family's unhappiness. We hadn't imagined that that would be goodbye, but the Tsar had chosen to leave early the following morning, before his family had risen, and it had been my duty to accompany him. I could only imagine how upset Anastasia must have been when she had woken and discovered me gone.

Did she dream of me as I dreamt of her, I wondered, as I lay in barns and stables, peering through the cracks in the wooden beams above me at the stars above? Was she falling asleep at the same time, perhaps, staring at the crackling bursts of silver in a London sky, wondering where I was, imagining that I was lying out under the same night sky as she, whispering her name, begging her to believe in me? Those were difficult days. If I could have written, I would have done so, but where to write to? If I could have seen her, I would have walked across deserts, but where to go? I had no clues and only here, only in St Petersburg—yes, it would always be St Petersburg to me, never Petrograd—could I find someone to answer my questions.

I had been back almost a week when I found the clue I needed. I'd picked up a few roubles that afternoon helping to unload barrels of grain into the storeroom of a new government-sponsored warehouse and had decided to treat myself to a hot meal, the kind that I rarely allowed myself to indulge in. Sitting by the fire in a warm, cosy saloon, eating a bowl of *shchi* and drinking vodka, trying to enjoy a few simple pleasures for once, to be a young man again, to be Georgy, I noticed a fellow a few years older than me sitting at the table next to mine, who became more and more drunk as the night wore on. He was clean-shaven and wore the uniform of the provisional government, a Bolshevik through and through. But something about him told me that I had found what I was looking for.

'You look unhappy, friend,' I said and he turned and stared at me for a moment, examining my face carefully, as if deciding whether I was worth bothering with.

'Ah,' he said, waving his hand in the air. 'I was unhappy, it is true.' He lifted the bottle of vodka in his left hand and smiled at me. 'But not any more.'

'I understand,' I said, raising my own glass to him. '*Za vas.*'

'*Za vas,*' he said, draining his glass and pouring another.

I waited a few moments and moved across to sit opposite him. 'May I?' I asked.

He regarded me warily for a moment, then shrugged. 'As you please.'

425

'You're a soldier,' I said.

'Yes. And you?'

'A farmer.'

'We need more farmers,' he said with drunken determination, banging his fists on the table before him. 'That's how we get richer. Through grain.'

'You're right,' I said, pouring more vodka for us both. 'Thanks to you, the soldiers, we will all get richer in time.'

He exhaled loudly and shook his head, an expression of utter disillusionment on his face. 'Don't fool yourself, my friend,' he said. 'No one knows what they're doing. They don't listen to people like me.'

'But things are better than they were, are they not?' I asked, smiling, for even though he was dissatisfied with his lot, his allegiances most likely lay with the revolutionaries. 'Better than when we lived under the Ts— under Nicholas Romanov, I mean.'

'You speak the truth,' he said, reaching across to shake my hand as if we were brothers. 'No matter what else happens, we are all better off for those changes. Bloody Romanovs,' he added, spitting on the floor, which led to a cry from the bartender to act in a proper fashion or be thrown out on to the street.

'So what is the matter?' I asked. 'Why do you look so unhappy? Is it a woman, perhaps?'

'I wish it was a woman,' he replied bitterly. 'Women are the least of my worries right now. No, it's nothing, my friend. I won't bore you with it. I had expected something from a petty bureaucrat in Lenin's government today but was disappointed, that's all. And so I'm drowning my sorrows to get over it. I will still be disappointed tomorrow, of course, but it will fade.'

'You'll have a hangover, too.'

'That will also fade.'

'You are close to Lenin?' I asked, sure that I could find out what I wanted by flattering him.

'Of course not. I've never met him.'

'Then how—'

'I have other connections. There are men in positions of power who hold me in great esteem.'

'I'm sure there are,' I said, anxious to be agreeable. 'It is men like you who are changing this country.'

'Tell that to my petty bureaucrat.'

'Can I ask you . . .' I hesitated, anxious not to appear too desperate for information. 'Are you one of those heroes who were responsible for the removal of Romanov? If you were, say so now that I might buy you more drinks, for all of us poor *moujik*s owe you a debt of gratitude.'

He shrugged his shoulders. 'Not really,' he admitted. 'The paperwork, perhaps. That is all I had to do with it.'

'Ah,' I said, my heart leaping within my chest. 'Do you think they will ever be allowed to return here?'

'To Petrograd?' he asked, frowning. 'No, no. Definitely not. They would be torn asunder. The people would never stand for it. No, they are safer where they are.'

I breathed a sigh of relief and attempted to disguise it as a cough. This at least was my first sure sign that they were alive, that *she* was alive.

'They will be unused to the climate there,' I said, laughing in order to win his confidence. 'They say the winters there are cold, but they are nothing like they are here.'

'In Tobolsk?' he said, raising an eyebrow. 'I don't know anything about that. But they will be taken care of. The Siberian Governor's house may not be a palace, but it's a finer home than you or I will ever know. People like that know how to survive. They're like cats; they always land on their feet.'

It was all that I could do not to let out a cry of surprise. So they weren't in England, after all. They hadn't even left Russia. They had been taken to Tobolsk, beyond the Urals. Deep within Siberia. It was far away, of course. But I could turn around. I could go there. I could find her.

'Of course, that is not common knowledge, my friend,' he said, not sounding like he cared particularly whether I told anyone or not. 'Where they are being held, I mean. You must not say that to anyone.'

'Don't worry,' I said, standing up and throwing a few roubles on the table to pay for both our dinners and drinks as I left; he had earned that much, at least. 'I have no intention of talking to anyone about this.'

*   *   *

When I left St Petersburg I travelled east, passing through Vologda, Vyatka and Perm before arriving in the Siberian plains. It had now been more than a year since I had last laid eyes on Anastasia and almost as long since the Tsar had become Nicholas Romanov. I arrived lean and hungry, but driven forward by a desire to see her again, to protect her. My body was wasted from my long journey and had I been in possession of a looking glass, I swear that

428

I would have appeared a decade older than my true age, which was not yet twenty.

The journey had been fraught with difficulty. I had succumbed to a fever just outside Vyatka but was fortunate enough to be taken into the home of a farmer and his wife, who nursed me back to health and listened to my delirious ramblings and didn't hold them against me. On my last night in their home, I was sitting by the fire and the farmer's wife, a strong woman named Polina Pavlovna, placed her hand on top of mine, surprising me for a moment with the intimacy of the gesture.

'You must be careful, Pasha,' she said to me, for on my first or second day there I had been asked what my name was and in my delirious state, unable to remember, I had offered that hated pet-name of my childhood. 'There is danger in what you do next.'

'What I do next?' I asked, for during my restoration to health I had told them that I was travelling back to my own family, who lived in Surgut, in order to help with the farming. 'But I see no dangers there.'

'When Luka and I first met, we did not have the approval of my father,' she whispered to me. 'But we cared nothing for it, our love was strong enough. But his father was a poor man, a person no one thought much of one way or the other. It is different for you.'

I swallowed nervously, unsure how much I might have betrayed during my illness. 'Polina—' I began.

'It's all right,' she said, smiling at me. 'It's only me that you told. And I haven't told a soul. Not even Luka.'

I nodded and looked out of the window. 'Do I have much further to travel?' I asked.

'It will be weeks,' she said. 'But they will be well. Of this, I am sure.'

'How can you know that?' I asked.

'Because their story does not end in Tobolsk,' she said quietly, looking away from me with a mournful expression on her face. 'And the Grand Duchess, the one you love, her story has much left in it yet.'

I didn't know what to say to this and so remained silent. I wasn't the type to believe in superstition or the foresight of old women. I hadn't believed it from the *starets* and I was not going to believe it from a farmer's wife in Vyatka, although I hoped that what she was saying was the truth.

'The Tsar travelled through here once, you know,' she told me before I left. 'When I was just a young girl.'

I frowned, for she was an elderly woman. I could scarcely believe it.

'Not your Tsar,' she said, laughing a little. 'His grandfather. Alexander II. It was only a few weeks before he was killed. He came and went like a burst of lightning. The whole town came out to see him and he barely looked at any of us, simply charged past on his steed, and yet everyone felt as if they had been touched by the hand of God. It's hard to imagine now, isn't it?'

'A little,' I conceded.

*　　　*　　　*

I left the following day and was fortunate enough to remain healthy for the rest of my journey, arriving in Tobolsk in early July. The town was full of Bolsheviks, but no one gave me a second glance. They were not looking for me any more, I realized. Who was I, after all, except a retainer, a nobody. Any intention they might have had of tracking me down after the Tsar had been arrested had long since vanished.

Locating the Governor's house was easy and I arrived there late in the afternoon, expecting to find it heavily surrounded by guards. I wasn't entirely sure what I would do when I arrived. There was a part of me which had been considering simply asking to see the Tsar—or Nicholas Romanov, if they insisted—at which point I could offer to stay with the family as a servant and thereby see Anastasia every day until they were sent into exile.

However, the house was not exactly as I had imagined. There were no cars outside and only one soldier, who was leaning up against the fence, offering a deep yawn to the world. He watched me as I approached and narrowed his eyes irritably, but showed no sign of concern. Nor did he even bother to stand up straight.

'Good evening,' I said.

'Comrade.'

'I wondered . . . I believe this is the Governor's residence?'

'And what if it is?' he asked me. 'Who are you?'

'My name is Georgy Daniilovich Jachmenev,' I said. 'A farmer's son from Kashin.'

He nodded and turned his head for a moment, spitting on the ground. 'Never heard of you,' he said.

'No, I don't expect you would have. But your

431

prisoner has.'

'My prisoner?' he asked, smiling a little. 'And what prisoner would that be?'

I sighed. I didn't feel like playing games. 'I've travelled a long way to be here,' I said. 'All the way from St Petersburg, in fact.'

'From Petrograd, you mean?'

'If you like.'

'On foot?' he asked, raising an eyebrow.

'Much of it, yes,' I admitted.

'Well, what do you want here?'

'Until last year, I worked at the Imperial Palace,' I explained. 'I worked for the Tsar.'

He hesitated before answering. 'There is no Tsar,' he said sharply. 'You might have worked for the former Tsar.'

'The former Tsar, then. I thought . . . I wondered whether I could pay my respects.'

He frowned. 'Of course you can't,' he said. 'What are you, Jachmenev, stupid? You think we let anyone in to see the Romanovs?'

'I am no threat to anyone,' I said, extending my arms to show that I held no hidden weapons or secrets. 'I simply want to offer myself in service to them.'

'And why would you do that?'

'Because they were good to me.'

'They were tyrants,' he said. 'You're crazy to want to be with them.'

'Still, it's what I want,' I replied quietly. 'Is it possible?'

'Anything is possible,' he said with a shrug. 'But you're too late, I'm afraid.'

My heart skipped a beat; it was all I could do to stop myself from grabbing him by the lapels and demanding to know what he meant by that remark.

'Too late?' I asked carefully. 'In what way?'

'I mean they're not here any more,' he said. 'The Governor is in residence once again. I can ask for an audience with him, if you wish.'

'No, no,' I said, shaking my head. 'No, that won't be necessary.' I felt like sitting on the ground and burying my head in my hands. Would this torment never end? Would we never be reunited? 'I . . . I hoped to see them,' I said.

'They haven't been taken far from here,' he said. 'Perhaps you could go after them.'

I looked up at him hopefully. 'They haven't?' I asked. 'Where are they?'

He smiled and opened his hands, and I knew immediately that this information would not come cheap. I reached into my pockets and extracted every rouble I had. 'I can't negotiate,' I said, handing it over. 'You can search me if you want to. This is everything I have. Everything in the world. So please . . .'

He looked at his hand, counted the coins and put them in his pocket; then, before walking away, he leaned over and whispered one word in my ear.

'Yekaterinburg.'

*   *   *

And so I turned and walked once more, this time south-west towards the town of Yekaterinburg, somehow already knowing that this would be the end of my journey and that I would find Anastasia at last. The villages I passed through along the way—Tavda, Tirinsk, Irbit—reminded me a little of Kashin, and I rested at some of them, hoping to

433

talk with some of the farmers. But it was no use, they seemed suspicious of me and reluctant to talk. I wondered whether they knew who had travelled through their villages before me, whether they had even seen them. If they had, they said nothing about it.

It took me almost a week to arrive.

Here, the locals were even more anxious than any of the others that I had met on my journey, and I knew for certain that I had reached my destination. It didn't take long to find someone who could point me in the right direction. A large house at the corner of the town, surrounded by soldiers.

'A very wealthy merchant owns it,' the one helpful man who I encountered explained to me. 'It was taken away from him by the Bolsheviks. No one is allowed to enter.'

'This merchant,' I asked, 'where is he now?'

'Gone. Paid off. His name was Ipatiev. They took it from him. We locals still call it the Ipatiev house. The Bolsheviks call it the house of special purpose.'

I nodded and walked in the direction he had indicated.

She would be there, I knew it. They would all be there.

1919

Perhaps this will sound quaint or old-fashioned, but Zoya and I took rooms in separate houses on the hills of Montmartre in Paris, with opposing views so that we could not even wave to each other before we went to sleep at night or blow a kiss as the last action of the day. From hers, Zoya could look out towards the white-domed basilica of Sacré-Coeur, where the national saint had been beheaded and had died a martyr for his country. She could watch the crowds ascending the steep steps towards the three-arched entryway, hear the chatter of the people as they passed beneath her window walking to and from their places of work. From mine, I could see the peaks of St Pierre de Montmartre, the birthplace of the Jesuits, and if I strained my neck, I could observe the artists setting up their easels in their street studios every morning in the hope of earning enough francs for a humble dinner. We had not intended to surround ourselves with quite so much religion, but the rents were cheap in the *dix-huitième* and two Russian émigrés were able to blend in without comment in a part of the city already swarming with refugees.

The war was drawing to a close during those months as peace treaties began to be signed in Budapest, Prague, Zagreb and then, finally, in a railway carriage in Compiègne, but the previous four years had seen tens of thousands of Europeans flooding into the French capital, driven there by the advance of the Kaiser's men into their homelands. Although those numbers were dwindling by the time we arrived, it was not difficult to pretend that we were simply two more exiles who had been forced westwards, and no one ever questioned the truth of the stories we had prepared.

When we first arrived in the city after a painful and seemingly endless passage from Minsk, I made the mistake of assuming that Zoya and I would be living together as man and wife. The idea had been much in my mind as the countryside of my birth began to pass me by and be replaced by cities, rivers and mountain ranges I had only read about, and in truth I was both anxious and aroused by the thought of it. I spent much of the journey choosing the correct words with which I might introduce the subject.

'We need only take a small flat,' I proposed, ten miles outside of Paris, hardly daring to look at Zoya for fear that she would recognize the disquiet in my face. 'A living area with a kitchen attached. A small bathroom, if we're lucky. A bedroom, of course,' I added, blushing terribly as I said the words. Of course, Zoya and I had yet to make love, but it was my fervent hope that our life in Paris would provide not just independence and a new beginning, but an introduction to the pleasures of the sensual world as well.

'Georgy,' she said, looking across at me and shaking her head. 'We cannot live together, you know that. We are unmarried.'

'Of course,' I replied, my mouth so dry that my tongue was sticking uncomfortably to my palate. 'But these are new times for us, are they not? We know no one here, we have only each other. I thought perhaps—'

'No, Georgy,' she said, determined and biting her lip gently. 'Not that. Not yet. I cannot.'

'Then ... then we will marry,' I suggested, surprised that I had not considered this idea earlier. 'But of course, that is what I meant all along. We will become husband and wife!'

Zoya stared at me, and for the first time since she had fallen into my arms a week before, she let out a laugh and rolled her eyes, not to suggest that I was a fool, but at the foolishness of my suggestion.

'Georgy, are you asking me to marry you?' she said.

'Yes, I am,' I replied, beaming with pleasure. 'I want you to be my wife.' I tried to kneel down, as tradition demanded, but the space between the benches in the railway compartment was too small to make the movement graceful and while I managed finally to prostrate myself on one knee, I was forced to turn my head to look at her. 'I have no ring to offer you yet,' I said. 'But you have my heart. You have every part of me, you know that.'

'I know it,' she said, pulling me up and pushing me back to my seat gently. 'But are you asking so that we might ... so that ...'

'No!' I said quickly, embarrassed that she could think so badly of me. 'No, Zoya, not that. I am asking you because I want to spend my life with you. My every day and night. There is no one else for me in this world, you must know that.'

'And there is no one else for me either, Georgy,' she said quietly. 'But I cannot marry you. Not yet.'

'But why not?' I asked, trying to overcome the note of petulance which was creeping into my voice. 'If we love each other, if we are promised to each other, then—'

'Georgy ... think, please.' She looked away, having practically whispered these words to me, and I felt immediately ashamed of myself. Of course, how could I have been so insensitive? It was unconscionable of me to have even suggested the union at such a time, but I was young and drenched in love and desired nothing more than to be with this woman for ever more.

'I am sorry,' I said quietly, a few moments later. 'I didn't think. It was thoughtless of me.' She shook her head and I could see that she was close to tears. 'I won't ... I won't speak of this matter again. Until the appropriate time, that is,' I added, for I wanted to be clear that this was a subject which would not be forgotten. 'I have your permission, Zoya, to speak of it again? At a future date?'

'I will live in hope of it,' she replied, her smile returning now.

In my mind, I considered that we were now engaged and my heart filled with happiness at the thought of it.

And so we arrived at the hills of Montmartre and knocked on doors in search of rooms for rent. We had no bags, we had no clothing other than the rags on our backs. We had no belongings. We had little money. We had arrived in a strange country to start our lives over again, and every possession that we acquired from that moment forward would reference this new existence. Indeed, we had brought nothing at all from our old lives, except each other.

But that, I believed, would surely be enough.

We celebrated Christmas twice that winter.

In mid-December, our friends Leo and Sophie extended an invitation to us to join them for a meal on the twenty-fifth, the traditional day of Christian celebration, in their flat near the Place du Tertre. I was concerned at how Zoya would cope with such festivity and suggested that we ignore Christmas entirely and spend the afternoon walking the banks of the Seine, just the two of us, enjoying the rare peace that the day would offer.

'But I want to go, Georgy,' she told me, surprising me with her enthusiasm. 'They make it sound like so much fun! And we could do with a little fun in our lives, couldn't we?'

'Of course,' I said, pleased by her response, for I wanted to go too. 'But only if you're sure. It may be a difficult day, our first Christmas since leaving Russia.'

'I think,' she replied slowly, hesitating for a moment and considering the matter carefully, 'I think perhaps it would be a good idea to spend it with friends. There will be less time to dwell on unhappy things then.'

In the five months that we had been living in Paris, Zoya's personality had started to change. Back in Russia, she had been lively and amusing, of course, but in Paris, she had begun to let her guard down more and was free with her enthusiasms. The alteration suited her. She remained entirely unspoiled, but had become open to the pleasures that the world had to offer, although our financial state, pitiful as it was, ensured that we could take advantage of little of it. However, there were moments, many moments, when her grief resurfaced, when those terrible reminiscences stormed the barricades of her

439

memory and brought her low. During those times she preferred to be left alone and I do not know how she fought her way through the darkness. There were mornings when we met for breakfast and I found her pale, her eyes ringed with dark circles; I would enquire after her health and she would shrug off my questions, saying that it was hardly worth discussing, that she had simply been unable to sleep. If I pushed to know more, she would shake her head, grow angry with me and then change the subject. I learned to allow her the space to confront these horrors by herself. She knew that I was there for her; she knew that I would listen whenever she wanted to talk.

Zoya had met Sophie at the dressmaker's shop where they were both employed and they had quickly become friends. They made simple, plain dresses for the women of Paris, working in a store which had provided functional clothing throughout the war. Through Sophie, we became acquainted with her painter boyfriend Leo, and the four of us made up a regular quartet for dinner or Sunday-afternoon strolls, when we would cross the Seine in a spirit of great adventure and wander through the Jardin du Luxembourg. I thought Leo and Sophie were terribly cosmopolitan and rather idolized them, for they were no more than a couple of years older than us but lived together in unapologetic harmony, betraying their passion even in public with frequent displays of affection that I confess embarrassed but excitedme.

'I've cooked a turkey,' Sophie announced that Christmas Day, placing a strange-looking bird on the table before us, part of which seemed to have been in the oven for too long, while the rest remained curiously pink, an extraordinary trick that made the entire dish appear quite unappetizing. However, the company being what it was and the wine flowing as it did, we cared not for such niceties and we ate and drank all night long, Zoya and I looking away whenever our hosts exchanged their long, expressive kisses.

Afterwards we lay on the two sofas in their living room, talking art and politics, while Zoya rested her body against my own and allowed me to place an arm around her shoulders, pulling her closer towards me, the warmth of her skin adding to my own, the scent of her hair, typically lavender, perfumed earlier with one of Sophie's fragrances, quite intoxicating.

'Now you two,' said Leo, warming to his favourite topic, 'you came from Russia. You must have been steeped in politics all your life.'

'Not really,' I said, shaking my head. 'I grew up in a very small village that had no time for such things. We worked, we farmed, we tried to keep ourselves alive, that was all. We didn't have time for debates. They would have been considered great luxuries.'

'You should have made time,' he insisted. 'Especially in a country such as yours.'

'Oh, Leo,' said Sophie, pouring more wine, 'not this again, please!' She scolded him, but with good humour. Whenever we spent an evening together, the conversation always turned to politics eventually. Leo was an artist—a good one, too—but like most artists he believed that the world he re-created on his canvases was a corrupt one, which needed men of integrity, men like himself, to step to the fore and reclaim it for the people. He was a young man, of course, his naivety attested to that, but he hoped to put himself forward for election to the Chamber of Deputies one day. He was an idealist and a dreamer, but indolent too, and I doubted whether he would ever summon the necessary energy for a campaign.

'But this is important,' he insisted. 'Each of us has a country that we call our own, am I right? And as long as we are alive it isour responsibility to try to make that country a better place for all.'

'But better how?' asked Sophie. 'I like France the way it is, don't you? I can't imagine living anywhere else. I don't want it to change.'

'Better as in more fair to everyone,' he replied. 'Social equitability. Financial freedom. The liberalization of policy.'

'What do you mean by that?' asked Zoya, her voice cutting through the atmosphere, for she had neither Sophie's drunken enthusiasm nor Leo's antagonistic self-righteousness. She had also been quiet for some time, her eyes closed, not sleeping but apparently relaxed in the warmth of the room and the luxury of the alcohol. All three of us looked at her immediately.

'Well,' replied Leo with a shrug, 'only that it makes sense to me that every citizen has a responsibility to—'

'No,' she said, interrupting him, 'not that. What you said before. About a country such as ours.'

Leo thought about it for a moment and finally shrugged his shoulders, as if the whole thing was perfectly obvious. 'Ah, that,' he replied, propping himself up on one elbow as he warmed to his topic. 'Look, Zoya, my country, France, she spent centuries under the oppressive weight of a

442

disgusting aristocracy, generations of parasites who sucked the lifeblood out of every simple, hardworking man and woman in the land, stole our money, acquired our land, kept us in starvation and poverty while they indulged their own appetites and perversions to excess. And eventually we said "Too much!" We resisted, we revolted, we placed those fat little aristocrats in the tumbrils, we drove them to the Place de la Concorde, and swish!' He passed the flat of his hand quickly down through the air, mimicking the blade descending. 'We cut off their heads! And we took back the power. But my friends, that was nearly one hundred and fifty years ago. My great-great-great-grandfather fought with Robespierre, you know. He stormed the Bastille with—'

'Oh, Leo,' cried Sophie in frustration, 'you don't know that. You always say it, but what proof do you have?'

'I have the proof that he told his son the stories of his heroism,' he replied defensively. 'And those stories have been passed down from father to son ever since.'

'Yes,' said Zoya—a certain chill entering her tone, I thought—'but what has that got to do with Russia? You are not comparing like with like.'

'Well, *pffft*," said Leo, exhaling a whistle through his lips. 'I only wonder why it took Mother Russia so much longer to do the same thing, that's all. For how many centuries were peasants like you— forgive me, both of you, but let us call things what they are—forced into a pathetic existence just so the palaces could remain open, the balls could continue to be thrown? The *season* could take place?' He shook his head as if even the concept of such things was too much for him. 'Why did it take you so long to throw out your autocrats? To reclaim the power of your own land? To cut off their heads, as it were? Not that you did that, of course. You shot them, as I recall.'

'Yes,' replied Zoya. 'We did.'

I don't recall how much I had drunk that night— a lot, I suspect—but I sobered up immediately and wished that I had recognized the direction in which the conversation was going. Had I enjoyed such foresight, I might have changed the topic more quickly, but it was too late now and Zoya was sitting erect, the blood draining from her face as she stared at him.

'You stupid man,' she said. 'What do you know about Russia anyway, other than what you read in your newspapers? You cannot compare your country with ours. They are entirely different. The points you make are facile and ignorant.'

'Zoya,' he replied, surprised by her antagonism but unwilling to concede the point—I liked Leo very much, but he was the type who always believed that he was correct on such matters and looked with surprise and pity on those who did not share his views—'the facts are not in dispute. Why, one has only to read any of the published material to see how—'

'You would consider yourself a Bolshevik then?' she asked. 'A revolutionary?'

'I would side with Lenin, certainly,' he said. 'He is a great man. To come from where he has come and achieve all that he has achieved—'

'He is a murderer,' replied Zoya.

'And the Tsar was not?'

'Leo,' I said quickly, placing my glass on the table

444

before me, 'it is impolite to speak this way. You must understand, we were brought up under the rule of the Tsar. There are many people who revered him, who continue to revere him. Two of them are in this room with you. Perhaps we know more about the Tsar and the Bolsheviks and even Lenin than you do, as we lived through those times and did not simply read about them. Perhaps we have suffered more than you can understand.'

'And perhaps we shouldn't talk about such things on Christmas Day,' said Sophie, refilling everyone's glasses. 'We're here to enjoy ourselves, aren't we?'

Leo shrugged and sat back, happy to let the subject drop, positive in his arrogance that he was right and that we were too foolish to see it. Zoya said very little more that evening and the celebration ended in tension, the handshakes a little more forced than usual, the kisses a little more perfunctory.

'Is that what people think?' Zoya asked me as we walked back towards our separate rooms. 'Is that how they recall the Tsar? In the way that we think of Louis Seizième?'

'I don't know what people think,' I said. 'And I don't care about it. What matters is what we think. What matters is what we know.'

'But they have corrupted history, they know nothing of our struggles. They see Russia in such simplistic terms. The privileged as monsters, the poor as heroes, everyone is the same. They talk in such idealistic ways, these revolutionaries, but have such naive theories. It's too funny.'

'Leo is hardly a revolutionary,' I said, trying to laugh it off. 'He's a painter, nothing more. He likes to think that he can change the world, but what does he do each day, after all, except paint portraits for fat tourists and drink the money away in pavement cafés, spouting his opinions to anyone who will listen? You shouldn't concern yourself with him.'

It was easy to see that Zoya remained unconvinced. She spoke little for the rest of our walk and allowed me no more than a chaste kiss on the cheek as we parted, as a sister might offer her brother. As I watched her step through her front door, I guessed that she would have a difficult night ahead of her, her mind filled with all the things that she wanted to say, all the anger that she wanted to express. I wished that she would invite me in, just to share her troubles with her, nothing more. To be a partner in her anger. For I felt it too.

We celebrated our second Christmas thirteen days later, on January the seventh, and returned the compliment by inviting Leo and Sophie to a café, where we offered to buy them dinner. There was no possibility of us preparing a meal in either of our homes—our landladies would never have permitted it—and anyway, I was embarrassed that Zoya and I did not live together and would not have enjoyed being a guest in her home or inviting her as a guest to mine. I wondered whether Leo and Sophie talked about our living arrangements and was sure that they did. Indeed, Leo had once referred to me in a moment of exuberant drunkenness as his 'innocent young friend' and I had been offended by the implication of purity that accompanied it, an allegation which did nothing to improve my self-esteem. On another occasion, he

446

offered to bring me to a particular house he knew to rectify my problem, but I brushed the suggestion away and went home to satisfy my lust alone, before I could be tempted by his offer.

'But I don't understand,' said Sophie, taking her hat off and shaking out her long dark hair as we sat down. 'A second Christmas?'

'It is the traditional Russian Orthodox Christmas,' I explained. 'It's got something to do with the Julian and Gregorian calendars. It's all very complicated. The Bolsheviks would have the people conform to the rest of the world, and there's a certain irony in there somewhere, but those of us who are traditionalists think differently. Hence, a separate Christmas Day.'

'Of course,' said Leo with a charming smile. 'Heaven forbid that you should accede to the Bolsheviks!'

Zoya and Leo had not spoken since the earlier incident and the memory of their argument hung over the table like a cloud, but the fact that we had extended the invitation at all implied that we did not wish to lose their friendship and so, to his credit, Leo was the first to sue for peace.

'I think I owe you an apology, Zoya,' he said after two glasses of wine and a noticeable elbow in the ribs from Sophie to spur him into action. 'Perhaps I was a little rude to you on Christmas Day. *Our* Christmas Day, that is. I was probably a little drunk. Said some things I should never have said. I had no right to speak about your native country in the way that I did.'

'No, you shouldn't have,' she replied, but without any aggression in her tone. 'But at the same time, I should not have reacted quite as I did in your

447

home either, that is not how I was brought up, and I think I owe you an apology too.'

I noticed that neither of them was conceding that their points of view were incorrect, nor were they actually apologizing, simply lingering under the impression that they owed each other an apology, but I did not want to restart the argument by pointing either of these things out.

'Well, you're a guest in our country,' he said, smiling widely at her, 'and as such it was wrong of me to speak as I did. If you'll permit me?' He raised his glass in the air and we lifted ours to join him. 'To Russia,' he said.

'To Russia,' we replied, clinking glasses together and taking mouthfuls of wine.

'*Vive la révolution*,' he added beneath his breath, but I think only I heard that comment and of course I let it go.

'I do wonder all the same why you never speak of it,' he said a moment later. 'If it was such a wonderful place, I mean. Oh now, don't look at me like that, Sophie, it's a perfectly reasonable question that I ask.'

'Zoya doesn't like to talk about it,' Sophie replied, for she had tried on more than one occasion to solicit confidences from her new friend about her past, but had finally given up.

'Well, what about you then, Georgy?' asked Leo. 'Can't you tell us a little bit about your life before you came to Paris?'

'There's so little to tell,' I replied with a shrug. 'Nineteen years of living on a farm, that's all. It's not the stuff of anecdotes.'

'Well, where did you two meet then? You said you were from St Petersburg, Zoya, didn't you?'

'In a train compartment,' I said. 'The day we both left Russia for the last time. We were sitting opposite each other, there was no one else there, and we started talking. We've been together ever since.'

'How romantic,' said Sophie. 'But tell me this. If you have two Christmas Days, then surely you must be given two sets of presents. Am I right? And I know you bought her perfume for the first Christmas Day, Georgy. So what about it, Zoya? Did Georgy give you something else today?'

Zoya looked across at me and smiled and I nodded, happy for her to tell them. She laughed then and looked at them, a wide grin spreading across her face. 'Yes, of course he did,' she said. 'But didn't you notice?'

And with that she extended her left hand to show them my gift. I wasn't surprised that they had failed to notice it before. It must have been the smallest engagement ring in history. But it was all that I could afford. And what mattered was that she was wearing it.

*   *   *

We were married in the autumn of 1919, almost fifteen months after we had fled Russia, in a ceremony so lacking in grandeur that it would have seemed almost pathetic had we not compensated for its paucity with the intensity of our love.

Brought up to revere a strict, unswerving doctrine, we wanted nothing more than the blessing of the Church to sanctify our union. However, there were no Russian Orthodox churches to be found in Paris and so I suggested

449

marrying in a French Catholic church instead, but Zoya would not hear of it and seemed almost angry when I made the suggestion. I myself had never been particularly spiritual, although I did not question the faith in which I had been reared, but Zoya felt differently and saw rejection of our creed as a final step away from our homeland and one that she was not prepared to make.

'But where then?' I asked her. 'You surely don't believe that we should return to Russia for the ceremony? The danger alone would—'

'Of course not,' she said, although I knew very well that there was a part of her that longed to return to the country of our births. She felt a connection to the land and to the people that I myself had quickly shrugged off; it was an indelible part of her character. 'But Georgy, I would not feel truly married if the proper ceremonies did not take place. Think of my father and mother, how they would feel if I rejected our traditions.'

There was no argument that could be made against this and so I began the process of trying to locate a Russian Orthodox priest in the city. The Russian community itself was small and scattered and we had never made any attempts to assimilate ourselves into it. Indeed, on one occasion when a young Russian couple entered the small bookstore where I worked as an assistant, I heard their voices immediately—the music of their language as they spoke to each other in our native tongue summoned pictures and memories that made me dizzy with longing and regret—and I was forced to excuse myself and retreat to the alley behind the shop on the pretence that I felt suddenly ill, leaving my employer, Monsieur Ferré, irritated at having to serve the couple himself. I knew that most of my fellow émigrés lived and worked in the Neuilly district in the *dix-septième* and we avoided it deliberately, not wishing to become part of a society which could lead to potential danger for us.

I was subtle in my detective work, however, and was finally introduced to an elderly man by the name of Rakhletsky, living in a small tenement house in Les Halles, who agreed to perform the ceremony. He told me that he had been ordained a priest in Moscow during the 1870s and was a true believer, but he had fallen out with his diocese after the 1905 Revolution and relocated to France. A loyal subject of the Tsar, he had strongly opposed the revolutionary priest, Father Gapon, and had tried to dissuade him from marching on the Winter Palace that year.

'Gapon was belligerent,' he told me. 'An anarchist portraying himself as the workers' champion. He broke the conventions of the Church, marrying twice, challenging the Tsar, and still they made a hero of him.'

'Before they turned on him and hanged him,' I replied, a naive boy patronizing an elderly man.

'Yes, before that,' he admitted. 'But how many innocent people died because of him on Bloody Sunday? A thousand? Twice that amount? Four times?' He shook his head, appearing half regretful and half furious. 'I could not stay after that. He would have ordered me to be killed for my disobedience. It has always astonished me, Georgy Daniilovich, that those who are most repulsed by autocratic or dictatorial rule are among the first to eliminate their enemies once they take on the mantle of power themselves.'

451

'Father Gapon never achieved any power,' I pointed out.

'But Lenin did,' he replied, smiling at me. 'Just another Tsar, don't you think?'

I did not take his political views to Zoya, although she would have agreed with them, because I thought it wrong to bring such memories to our wedding day. I wanted simply to present Father Rakhletsky as just another exile, forced out of his home by the advance of the Kaiser's forces. It had taken me this long to find the man, I did not want any problems that might postpone our marriage any longer than necessary.

The ceremony took place in Sophie and Leo's flat on a warm Saturday evening in October. Our friends had generously offered the use of their home for the service and acted as witnesses on the day. Father Rakhletsky spent an hour alone in the small apartment earlier in the afternoon, consecrating their living room as a holy place, a procedure he said was 'highly unorthodox but extremely pleasurable', a turn of phrase which amused me.

It saddened me that I could not provide a more elaborate wedding day for my bride, but it was all that we could do to remain on the right side of poverty. Our jobs did not pay very much money, enough to cover our rent and to feed ourselves, that was all. Zoya ensured that we both saved a few francs every week in case an emergency presented itself and we were forced to flee Paris, but still we could afford very little in the way of luxury. Between them, Zoya and Sophie made her wedding gown in the dressmaker's shop after trade ended each day; Leo and I wore our best shirts and

452

trousers. On the day, I thought we had put together a charming display, despite our limited means.

Father Rakhletsky had not met Zoya before the ceremony, and when she entered the living room on my arm that evening her face was covered by a simple veil that masked her beauty and charm. He beamed happily at us, as if we were his children, or a favoured nephew and niece, and his joy at performing one more wedding in his life was easy to see. Sophie and Leo stood on either side of us, delighted to be part of this unusual experience. I believe it struck them as terribly modern and unconventional to be getting married in such a way and in such a place. Romantic too, perhaps.

We exchanged simple rings and then I took Zoya's left hand in my right as we accepted lighted candles in our free hands, holding them aloft while the priest recited the incantations over our heads. When he gave the signal, Sophie and Leo reached across to the tables on either side of them and took the small, simple crowns which Zoya had created from a combination of foil and felt, and placed them simultaneously atop our heads.

'The servants of God, Georgy Daniilovich Jachmenev and Zoya Fedorovna Danichenko,' sang the priest, holding his hands a few inches above our heads, 'are crowned in the name of the Father, and of the Son, and of the Holy Spirit.' I felt a great happiness enter my body when he spoke those words and clutched Zoya's hand in my own; I could scarcely believe that our lives were finally being joined together.

After this, the Gospel was read and we drank from the common cup, promising to share everything in our lives from that moment on, our joys as well as our sorrows, our triumphs alongside our burdens. When we had completed our pledges, Father Rakhletsky led us around the table, upon which was placed the Gospel and the cross, to symbolize the word of God and our redemption. We walked together in a circle for the first time as a married couple and then stood before the priest once again while he recited the final blessing, imploring me to be magnified as Abraham, to be blessed as Isaac, to multiply as Jacob had, to walk in peace and work in righteousness, then beseeching Zoya to be magnified as Sarah, glad as Rebecca, to multiply as Rachel had, to rejoice in her new husband and to fulfil the conditions of the law, for so it is well pleasing unto God.

And with that, the ceremony ended and our married life began.

Sophie and Leo burst into spontaneous applause, and Father Rakhletsky appeared surprised by their informality but not disturbed by it. He congratulated us both, shaking my hand heartily and reaching forward to offer my bride a kiss just as she lifted her veil.

He stopped at that moment, pulled short and reeled back, a sudden and unexpected movement which made me think that he had suffered some sort of seizure or heart attack. He muttered a phrase under his breath—I did not hear it—and hesitated for so long that Sophie, Leo and I could only stare at him as if he had gone entirely mad. His eyes were locked with Zoya's and, rather than looking away in confusion or embarrassment, she held his gaze, lifting her chin and offering him not her cheek to kiss, but her hand. A moment later, he returned to the present, took the hand hastily, kissed it, and backed away from us both without ever actually turning his back on us. His face betrayed his confusion, his astonishment and his utter disbelief.

Despite having promised to stay and dine with us after the ceremony, he gathered his belongings quickly and left, with only a few final words for Zoya, offered in the privacy of the hallway outside the flat.

'What a curious man,' said Sophie as we ate in some style an hour later, washing the food down with an extraordinarily good bottle of wine which our friends had provided.

'I think it must have been a long time since he had seen anyone quite so beautiful as your Russian bride,' said Leo, at his most charming and flirtatious, his neck-tie undone and hanging loosely around his open collar. 'He looked at you, Zoya, as if he was sorry that he hadn't married you himself.'

'I thought he looked like he had seen a ghost,' added Sophie.

I turned to my wife and she caught my eye for a moment before shaking her head slightly and returning to the conversation. I could not wait until we were alone, but not for the reason that you might imagine. I wanted to know what had been said between the priest and Zoya in the hallway before he left.

*   *   *

Leo and Sophie's second gift to us was the use of their flat as a honeymoon residence, three nights of togetherness while they relocated to mine and

Zoya's former rooms for the duration of our stay. It was thoughtful of them, for we were to move into our own flat shortly, but it was not due to be ready until the middle of that week and of course we did not wish to be separated from each other so soon after our marriage.

'He knew you,' I said to Zoya after Leo and Sophie left us that evening.

'He knew me,' she replied, nodding her head.

'Will he speak of it?'

'To no one,' she said. 'I am sure of it. He is a loyalist, a true believer.'

'And you believed him?'

'I did.'

I nodded, having no choice but to rely on her judgement. It was a curious moment of panic and had not gone unnoticed by any of us, but it was over now, we were a married couple. I took Zoya by the hand and led her to the bedroom.

Afterwards, wrapping my body around hers as we attempted to sleep, unaccustomed to the warmth and slickness of two naked forms entwined in rough blankets, I closed my eyes and ran my fingers along her legs, her perfect spine, the length of her body, saying nothing, ignoring the way she wept in my arms, trying to control her own shaking as she considered the day and the wedding and the memories of those who had not been present to help us celebrate.

The Ipatiev House

Up close, the Ipatiev house did not seem particularly intimidating.

I stared at it from my hiding place, a few feet into the tightly packed woodland that bordered the merchant's home, and tried to imagine what was taking place within its walls. A cluster of larch trees provided a convenient place for me to observe the house while remaining hidden from view; their overhanging branches and dense forestation offered some protection from the cold, although I regretted not being in possession of a heavier coat or the thick woollen gloves given to me by Count Charnetsky on my first days in St Petersburg. Before me was a small, grassy area where I could lie down and rest when my legs became too weary, and, further along again, several feet of thick hedgerow which led to a gravel driveway that ran parallel to the front of the house.

Somewhere over there, I told myself, the Imperial Family were gathered as prisoners of the Bolshevik government; somewhere over there was Anastasia.

A dozen soldiers came and went throughout the afternoon, leaning against the walls as they smoked and talked and laughed in friendly groups. A football, of all things, appeared for half an hour and they stripped to their shirtsleeves and tried to score goals against each other, the gate acting as one set of posts, the opposite wall as another. Almost all of them were young men in their mid-twenties, although the soldier in charge, who appeared from time to time to spoil their game, was a man in his fifties, of small, muscular stature, with narrow eyes and an aggressive demeanour. They were Bolsheviks, of course; their uniforms attested to that. But they went about their duties in a casual manner, as if the exalted status of their prisoners was a fact to which they were deliberately indifferent. Times had changed considerably since the abdication of the Tsar. Over the course of my eighteen-month odyssey from the railway carriage in Pskov to the house of special purpose in Yekaterinburg, I had grown to realize that people no longer treated the Imperial Family with the respect and deference that had always been their due. If anything, people competed with each other to offer the most obscene insult, publicly condemning the man they once considered to have been appointed to his throne by God. Of course, none of them had ever come face to face with the Tsar; if they had, they might have felt differently towards him.

What surprised me most, however, was the utter lack of security. Once or twice I stepped away from my hiding place and wandered along the road, passing by the open gates, taking care not to make eye-contact with anyone and receiving only the most disinterested of glances from the soldiers standing in the driveway. To them I was just a boy, an impoverished *moujik*, not worth wasting their time on. The gates remained open throughout the day; a car came and went on a number of occasions. The front door was never closed, and through the wide windows of a ground-floor parlour I could see the guards when they gathered together for meals; given such lax protection, I wondered why the family didn't simply come downstairs and flee into the village beyond. Late in the afternoon of my first day's vigil my eyes were cast towards one of the upstairs windows when a figure appeared suddenly to close the curtains and I knew immediately that the shadow belonged to none other than the Tsaritsa herself, the Empress Alexandra Fedorovna. And despite our often combative relationship, my heart leapt when I saw her because it was proof, if proof were needed, that my journey had been successful and I had found them at last.

As night fell, I was preparing to return to the village to find a warmer place to sleep when a small dog came charging from the front door and I could hear raised voices—a girl's and a man's— arguing in the hidden darkness behind the oak frame. A moment later the girl stepped out on to the driveway, looking left and right with an irritated expression on her face, and I recognized her immediately as Marie, the third of the Tsar's four daughters. She was calling out for the Tsaritsa's terrier, which by now had left the grounds, run across the road and was safely ensconced in my arms.

She walked quickly down the driveway, calling the dog's name repeatedly, causing the pup to bark back at her in reply; when he did so she looked in the direction of the woods, hesitating for only a moment before crossing the road and walking directly towards me.

'Where are you, Eira?' she shouted, coming closer and closer until she was only a few feet away from me in the darkness of the forest. Her tone grew more nervous now as she sensed that she was not alone. 'Are you in here?' she asked tentatively.

'Yes,' I said, reaching forward and grabbing her by the arm, pulling her quickly into the bushes where she fell directly on top of me. She was too startled to scream, and before she could recover her voice I pressed my hand across her mouth, holding her tightly as she struggled in my arms. The dog fell to the ground and stood barking at us both, but when I turned to glare at him he stopped immediately and pawed the ground, whimpering in dismay. Marie's head turned a little, her eyes opening wide when she saw her captor, and I could feel her body relax as she recognized me. I told her to stop struggling, not to scream, and that if she promised to do so I would remove my hand. She nodded quickly and I released her.

'I beg your pardon, Your Highness,' I said quickly, offering a deep bow as she stepped back so that she would know I meant her no harm. 'I pray that I didn't hurt you. I couldn't risk you screaming and alerting the guards, that's all.'

'You didn't hurt me,' she said, turning to the dog and whistling at him to stop him from whining. 'You surprised me, that's all. But I'm not sure I can believe who I'm looking at. Georgy Daniilovich, is it really you?'

'Yes,' I said, smiling at her, delighted to be in her company once again. 'Yes, Your Highness, it's me.'

'But what are you doing here? How long have you been hiding in these trees?'

'It would take too long to explain,' I said, glancing quickly back towards the house to make sure that no one was looking for her yet. 'It's good to see you again, Marie,' I added, unsure whether this was too intimate a remark but meaning it from

460

the depths of my heart. 'I've been searching for your family for . . . well, for a long time now.'

'It's good to see you too, Georgy,' she said, smiling, and I thought I could see tears forming in her eyes. She had grown thin since I had seen her last; her cheap dress was too big for her and hung off her frame in a shapeless fashion. And even in the shadows of the woods I could easily make out the dark circles under her eyes that indicated a lack of sleep. 'You're like a wonderful vision from the past, and sometimes I've felt that those days were just a trick of my imagination. But here you are. You found us.' Her emotion was evident and without warning she threw her arms around my neck and hugged me to her, a gesture of friendship, nothing more, but one I appreciated greatly.

'Are you well?' I asked, pulling away from her at last and smiling as widely as she was, moved by the warmth of our reunion. 'Is anyone hurt? How is your family?'

'You mean how is my sister?' she asked, smiling. 'How is Anastasia?'

'Yes,' I said, blushing slightly, surprised that she could read me so easily. 'So you know, then?'

'Oh yes, she told me a long time ago now. But don't worry, I haven't spoken about it to anyone. After what happened to Sergei Stasyovich . . .' She looked up quickly and her eyes darted back and forth in the darkness. 'He's not here too, is he?' she asked, her tone filling with excitement and hope. 'Oh, please tell me you've brought him with you—'

'I'm sorry,' I said, interrupting her. 'I haven't seen him. Not since the day he left St Petersburg.'

461

'The day he was sent away, you mean.'

'Yes, since then. He hasn't written to you?'

'If he has, his letters have been denied to me,' she said, shaking her head. 'I pray every day that he is well and that he will find me. I imagine that he is searching, too. But I can't believe you're here, my dear old friend. Only . . . now that you are here, what is it you want?'

'I want to see Anastasia,' I said. 'I want to do what I can to help your family.'

'There's nothing you can do. There's nothing anyone can do.'

'But I don't understand, Your Highness. You just walked out of there a few moments ago. The soldiers didn't come after you. Do they even care if you stay?'

'I told them I was looking for my mother's dog.'

'And they didn't mind? They just allow you to leave?'

'Why wouldn't they?' she asked. 'Where could I go, after all? Where could any of us go? My family is all inside. Mother and Father are upstairs. They know I will be back. They give us as much freedom as we want, except the freedom to leave Russia, of course.'

'That will happen soon,' I said. 'I'm sure of it.'

'Yes, I think so too. Father says we will go to England. He writes to Cousin Georgie almost every day to tell him of our plight, but there has been no reply. We don't know whether the letters are even being despatched. You haven't heard anything of this, I suppose?'

'Nothing at all,' I said, shaking my head. 'Only that the Bolsheviks are waiting for the right moment to get your family out of the country.

462

They don't want you here, that's for sure. But I think they intend to wait until it is safe for you to leave.'

'I wish that would be soon,' she said. 'I don't want to be a Grand Duchess any more, my father doesn't want to be Tsar. We don't care for any of that. They're just words, after all. All we want is to leave and have our freedom restored to us.'

'That day will come, Marie,' I said. 'I am sure of it. But please, you must tell me, when can I see Anastasia?'

She looked back towards the house, where one of the soldiers had stepped outside and was looking around, yawning in the night air. We stayed silent as he stood there, lit a cigarette, smoked it and then returned indoors.

'I'll tell her you're here,' she said. 'We share a room still. We will talk of it all night, I promise you that. You're not leaving soon, are you?'

'I'll never leave,' I told her. 'Not without your family.'

'Thank you, Georgy,' she said, smiling and looking down at the ground for a moment, staring at Eira, who was watching us silently now. 'But look, there's a group of cedar trees opposite,' she said, pointing away from the house into the darkness of the path. 'Go down there and wait. I'll go back indoors and tell Anastasia where you are. It might be only a few minutes before she joins you or it might be hours before she can leave, but wait for her and I promise you that she will come.'

'I'll wait all night if I have to,' I said.

'Good,' she said. 'She will be so happy to see you. And now I'd better go back before they come looking for me. Wait for her by the cedar trees,

Georgy. She'll be out before long.'

I nodded and she picked up the Tsaritsa's dog and ran across the road, looking back only for a moment as she went indoors again. I waited until I was sure that no one was watching, then stood up, brushed the dirt from my clothes and walked quickly along the path in the direction she had indicated, my heart beating faster in the hope of seeing Anastasia again.

*   *   *

When I awoke, it was already daylight. I opened my eyes and looked up at the glimpses of pale-blue sky which could be seen between the branches of the trees overhead, and for a moment I was at a loss as to where I was. An instant later the events of the previous evening came flooding back and I sat up, startled, immediately tormented by a great pain along the base of my spine, brought on no doubt by the uncomfortable position in which I had been sleeping.

I had waited for Anastasia by the cedar trees for hours, but had finally succumbed to sleep. At first I worried that I might have missed her entirely, but quickly shrugged off this concern, for if she had been able to leave the house then she would no doubt have discovered me in my hiding place and woken me up. I stood up and paced back and forth for a few minutes, trying to ease my pain by massaging my lower back with my hand; I immediately felt pangs of hunger in my stomach, for I had not eaten in more than a day.

Making my way back along the road, I hesitated outside the walls of the Ipatiev house and looked towards the upper windows, but could hear no voices inside. Passing by the front gate, however, I noticed a young soldier changing the tyre of a car and approached him cautiously.

'Comrade,' I said, nodding in his direction.

He glanced up, shielding his eyes from the sunlight as he looked me up and down with barely concealed disdain. 'Who are you?' he asked quickly. 'What do you want here, boy?'

'A few roubles, if you have it,' I said. 'I haven't eaten in days. Anything you can spare would be most appreciated.'

'Go beg somewhere else,' he replied, waving me away. 'What do you think this is, anyway?'

'Please, comrade,' I said. 'I might starve.'

'Look,' he said, standing up and wiping his hand across his forehead, leaving a long, dark oil stain streaked above his eyes. 'I've told you—'

'I could do that for you, if you like,' I said. 'I can change a tyre.'

He hesitated and looked down at the ground for a moment as he considered it. I suspected that he had been trying to complete this job for some time and was getting nowhere with it. A jack and a wheel wrench were lying beside the car, but the wheel nuts had not even been removed yet. 'You can do this?' he asked.

'For the price of a lunch,' I said.

'You do it right and I'll give you enough for a plate of borscht,' he said. 'Be quick about it, though. We may need this car later on.'

'Yes, sir,' I said, watching as he marched away and left me alone in the driveway.

I crouched down and examined the mess that he had made of the job so far, picking up the jack and propping it under the frame to lift the car. Unaccustomed to such mental stimulation I quickly became engrossed in my work. Indeed, so lost was I in my thoughts that I didn't even hear the footsteps as they approached me. And then, when my name was uttered in an awed whisper, I jumped in surprise, the wrench slipping between my fingers and grazing the knuckles of my left hand. I cursed and looked up, and the furious expression on my face immediately dissipated.

'Alexei,' I said.

'Georgy,' he replied, looking back towards the house now to make sure that he was not being observed. 'You came to see me.'

'Yes, my friend,' I said, and this time it was I who could feel tears behind my eyes. I had not realized quite how much I cared for this boy until he was no longer part of my life. 'Can you believe I'm here?'

'You have a beard,' he said.

'It's not much of one, though, is it?' I asked, rubbing the stubble irritably with my hand. 'Certainly not as impressive as your father's.'

'You look different.'

'Older, probably.'

'Skinnier,' he said. 'And paler. You don't look well.'

I laughed and shook my head. 'Thank you, Alexei,' I said. 'I could always rely on you to make me feel better about myself.'

He stared at me for a moment as if trying to decipher what I meant by this, but then his face broke into a wide smile as he realized that I was only teasing him. 'Sorry,' he said.

'How are you?' I asked. 'Are you holding up all right? I saw your sister yesterday, you know.'

466

'Which one?'

'Marie.'

'*Pffft,*' he said, blowing an unpleasant noise through his lips and shaking his head. 'I hate my sisters.'

'Alexei, don't say that, please.'

'But it's true. They never leave me alone.'

'Still, they love you very much.'

'Can I help you change the tyre?' he asked, looking down at the half-completed job before me.

'You can watch,' I said. 'Why don't you sit over there?'

'Can't I help?'

'You can be in charge,' I told him. 'You can be my supervisor.'

He nodded, satisfied, and took a seat on a large boulder that stood behind him, just the right height for him to sit and talk to me as I worked. It occurred to me that he didn't seem particularly surprised to find me there, working like this. He didn't even question it. It was simply another part of his day.

'You're bleeding, Georgy,' he said, pointing at my hand.

I looked down and, sure enough, there was a thin line of blood clotting above my knuckles from where the wrench had injured me. 'That was your fault,' I said, grinning at him. 'You surprised me.'

'And you said a bad word.'

'I did,' I admitted. 'We won't speak of it again.'

'You said—'

'Alexei,' I said, frowning.

I picked up the spanner and continued to work on the tyre in silence for a moment, anxious to talk to him but wary of asking my questions too quickly in case he ran back inside to tell the others of his discovery.

'Your family,' I said finally. 'They are all in the house?'

'They're upstairs,' he said. 'Father is writing letters. Olga is reading some silly novel. Mother is giving my other sisters their lessons.'

'And you?' I asked. 'Why aren't you at your lessons too?'

'I am the Tsarevich,' he said with a shrug. 'I chose not to partake.'

I smiled at him and nodded, feeling a sudden wave of sorrow for his predicament. The boy didn't even realize that he was the Tsarevich no longer, that he was just Alexei Nicolaievich Romanov, a boy with as little money or influence as me.

'I'm glad you're all well,' I said. 'I miss our days at the Winter Palace.'

'I miss the *Standart*,' he said, for the Imperial yacht had always been his favourite of all the royal residences. 'And I miss my toys and my books. We have so few here.'

'But you have been well since you came to Yekaterinburg?' I asked. 'You haven't suffered any injuries?'

'None,' he said, shuddering a little at the thought of it. 'Mother doesn't let me out often. Dr Federov is here too, just in case, but I've been quite well, thank you.'

'I'm glad to hear it.'

'And you, Georgy Daniilovich, how have you been? Do you know that I am thirteen years old now?'

'I know,' I said. 'I remembered your birthday last August.'

468

'In what way?'

'I lit a candle for you,' I replied, recalling the day when I had walked for almost eight hours in order to find a church where I might mark the Tsarevich's birth. 'I lit a candle and prayed that you were well and uninjured and that God would keep you safe from harm.'

'Thank you,' he said, smiling. 'It's my fourteenth birthday next month. Will you do the same thing then?'

'Yes, of course,' I said. 'Every year on August the twelfth I will do it. For as long as I live.'

Alexei nodded and looked around the courtyard. He seemed lost in thought and I said nothing to disturb him, simply got on with my work.

'Will you be able to stay here, Georgy?' he asked finally.

I looked across at him and shook my head. 'I don't think so,' I said. 'One of the soldiers said that he would give me a few roubles if I changed this tyre.'

'And what will you do with them?'

'Eat.'

'Will you come back afterwards? We don't have anyone to protect us, you know.'

'The soldiers protect you now,' I said. 'That's what they're here for, isn't it?'

'That's what they tell us, yes,' he replied, his brow furrowing a little as he considered it. 'But I don't believe them. I don't think they like us at all. I know I don't like them. I hear them saying terrible things all the time. About Mother. About my sisters. They show us no respect. They forget their place.'

'But you must listen to them, Alexei,' I said,

469

anxious for his safety. 'If you are good, then they will treat you well.'

'You call me Alexei now?'

'I apologize, sir,' I said, bowing my head. 'I meant Your Highness.'

He shrugged his shoulders as if it didn't matter, not really, but I could tell that he was utterly confused by his new status.

'You have sisters too, don't you Georgy?' he asked me.

'I did have,' I said. 'I had three. But I don't know what's become of them. I haven't seen them in a long time.'

'So between us we have seven sisters and no brothers.'

'That's right.'

'Strange, isn't it?' he asked.

'A little bit,' I said.

'I always wanted a brother,' he said quietly, looking down at the stony ground. He picked up a few pebbles from the driveway and tossed them back and forth between his hands.

'You never told me that,' I said, surprised to hear him say such a thing.

'Well, it's true. I always thought it would be nice to have an older brother. Someone to look out for me.'

'Then he would have been the Tsarevich, not you.'

'I know,' he said. 'It would have been wonderful.'

I frowned, surprised to hear him say that.

'And you, Georgy, did you ever want one?'

'Not really,' I said. 'I never thought about it. I had a friend once, Kolek Boryavich—we grew up together. He was like a brother to me.'

470

'And where is he now? Is he fighting in the war?'

'No,' I said, shaking my head. 'No, he died.'

'I'm sorry to hear it.'

'Yes, well, it was a long time ago.'

'How long?'

'More than three years.'

'That's not so very long.'

'It seems like a lifetime,' I said. 'Anyway, you have no brother, Kolek Boryavich is dead, but you and I are alive. Perhaps I could be like an older brother to you, Alexei. What would you think of that?'

He stared at me and frowned. 'But it's impossible,' he said, standing up now. 'You're just a *moujik*, after all. I am the son of a Tsar.'

'Yes,' I said, smiling. He didn't mean to hurt me, poor boy. It was simply the way that he had been brought up. 'Yes, it's impossible.'

'But we can be friends,' he said quickly, sounding as if he knew that he had said something he shouldn't have and regretted it. 'We'll always be friends, Georgy, won't we?'

'Yes, of course,' I said. 'And when you leave here, we will remain great friends for ever. I promise it.'

He smiled at me again and shook his head. 'But we'll never leave here, Georgy Daniilovich,' he said in a calm, measured tone. 'Don't you know that?'

I hesitated, quite unsettled by the certainty in his voice, and tried to think of something I could say to reassure him, but as I opened my mouth I glanced towards the house once again and could see Marie walking quickly towards us.

'Alexei,' she said, taking him by the arm, 'there you are. I was looking for you.'

471

'Marie, look, it's Georgy Daniilovich.'

'I can see that,' she replied, looking me directly in the eyes for a moment before turning back to her brother. 'Go indoors,' she said. 'Father is asking for you. And don't tell him who you were talking to, do you understand me?'

'But why not?' asked Alexei. 'He will want to know.'

'We can tell him later, just not now. We'll save it as a special surprise. Trust me, can't you?'

'All right,' he said, shrugging his shoulders. 'Goodbye then, Georgy,' he said, thrusting his hand out in the formal manner that I had seen him extend to generals and princes; I grasped it tightly and shook it, smiling at him.

'Goodbye, Alexei,' I said. 'I'll see you later, I'm sure.'

He nodded and ran back indoors.

When he was gone, Marie turned back to me. 'I'm sorry, Georgy,' she said. 'I told her. And she wanted to come, of course. But the soldiers were playing cards all night. She couldn't come downstairs.'

'And where is she now?' I asked.

'She's with Mother. She's desperate to see you. I was able to get out. I was coming to the cedars to find you. She said to tell you that she'll come tonight. Very late. She promises that no matter what happens, she'll come tonight.'

I nodded. To wait another half a day seemed like torture, but then I had waited this long, more than eighteen months. I could wait just a little longer.

'All right,' I said. 'Over there.' I pointed towards the clump of trees where we had talked the previous evening. 'I'll wait there from midnight and—'

'No, later than that,' she said. 'Come around two o'clock tomorrow morning. Everyone will be asleep by then. She'll come to you, I promise.'

'Thank you, Marie,' I said.

'Now you should leave here,' she insisted, looking around anxiously. 'If Mother and Father see you ... well, it's best that as few people as possible know that you're here.'

'I'll go,' I said, ignoring the fact that I hadn't yet finished tightening the wheel nuts on the new tyre. 'And thank you again.'

She reached forward and kissed my cheeks before returning to the house. I watched her leave, feeling terribly grateful to her. I had never known her all that well while I served her family but she had been kind to me, and Sergei Stasyovich had loved her. I looked around and considered waiting for the soldier to return and pay me my roubles, but there was no sign of him and I suddenly felt a great desire to be away from that place.

I turned to leave and was exiting the gates when I heard the sound of feet running quickly along the gravel behind me. I turned and saw Alexei, who showed no sign of slowing down, so I opened my arms and he ran into them, embracing me tightly, his arms wrapped around my neck as I lifted him off the ground.

'I wanted you to know,' he said, his voice choked up as if he was trying to stop himself from crying, 'I wanted you to know that you can be my brother if you like. As long as you let me be yours.'

He separated himself from me then and looked me directly in the eye, and I smiled and nodded. I opened my mouth to say yes, that I would be proud to be his brother, but my assent was all he needed; within a moment he had turned around and disappeared back into the house, into the heart of his family.

*   *   *

Every minute dragged.

I had no watch, so stepped inside a small café in the village to ask the time. Ten past two. A half a day to wait. It seemed impossible. I paced up and down the streets, growing more and more anxious and emotional with every second. I spent what seemed like hours wandering the streets aimlessly, before going back to the café to check the time once again.

'What do you think I am, boy, a clock?' shouted the man behind the counter. 'Go bother someone else with your questions.'

'Please,' I said. 'Can't you just—'

'It's almost three o'clock,' he snapped. 'Now get out of here and don't come back.'

Three o'clock! Not even an hour had passed.

It seemed as if God was smiling on me a few moments later, however, because just as I turned the corner my eyes caught a glint of something sparkling at my feet. I narrowed my eyes to try to see what it was, but try as I might, I couldn't locate it again and so retraced my steps until I caught the sparkle once more. Following it carefully, I pulled a clip from the dirt, and attached to it was a handful of banknotes—not many, but more than I had seen in a long time. Some unfortunate villager must have lost them in the dirt; it might have been only a few minutes before, it might have been

474

weeks, there was no way of knowing. I looked around to see whether anyone had seen me, but no one was looking in my direction so I stuffed the money into my pocket, thrilled by my good fortune. I could have handed it to a soldier, of course; I could have found the town council and allowed it to be returned to its rightful owner, but I did neither of those things. I did what anyone in my impoverished and starving position would have done: I kept it.

'It's a quarter past three,' roared the café owner when I stepped inside again. This time, I held a bank note in the air to make sure he knew that I was not simply there to bother him. 'Ah,' he said, smiling, 'that makes all the difference.'

I sat down, ordered a meal and something to drink and tried not to watch the minutes go by on the clock. Now that my eighteen-month journey was at an end, now that Anastasia and I were finally to be reunited, a single question loomed in my mind: what would I do when we were together again?

It wasn't as if the Bolsheviks were just going to allow her to leave the Ipatiev house and come with me. Even if they did, where would we go? No, we might be reunited for only a few minutes, an hour if we were lucky, and then she would have to return to her family. And what would I do after that, return every night to see her? Plan one clandestine meeting after another? No, there had to be a more sensible solution.

Perhaps I could save them, I thought. Perhaps I could find a way to get the entire family out, to smuggle them across Russia and northwards to Finland, where they could make their escape for

England. There were bound to be sympathizers along the way who would protect the Imperial Family, who would lie for them, who would die for them if necessary. And if I was successful, surely the Tsar could not refuse me his daughter's hand, despite the difference in our ranks. The idea seemed a brave one, but for the life of me, I could think of no way to accomplish it. The soldiers were all armed with rifles, while all I had to my name were a few banknotes found in the street. The Bolsheviks and the new People's Government were hardly likely to let their most prized assets simply flee the country to create a Russian court in exile. No, they would hold on to them for ever, they would keep them in seclusion, hide them away from the world. The Tsar and Tsaritsa would have no court any more, they would spend the rest of their lives under guard in Yekaterinburg. Their son and daughters would grow old here. They would be kept hidden for the rest of their lives, never allowed to marry or bear children, and the Romanov dynasty would come to a natural end. Another fifty, perhaps sixty years and they would be gone.

It was unthinkable, but the most likely explanation. Even to consider it left me in a state of depression. The hours went by, the sun set, I left the café and roamed the streets again, walking an hour in one direction in order for it to take me another hour to return again. I didn't grow tired, for tonight I was entirely alert. Nine o'clock came and went, ten o'clock, eleven o'clock. Midnight approached. I could wait no longer.

I went back.

If the house did not seem particularly oppressive during the daytime, it adopted a different characteristic at night, for the speckled shadows of the moon falling down upon the walls and fences that surrounded it unsettled me. The guards who had worked in shifts, casually walking up and down the driveway, apparently taking little notice of who was observing their movements, were now nowhere to be seen. The gate was unlocked and a lorry stood in the centre of the driveway, its cargo—if it had one—hidden from view by a tarpaulin sheet. I hesitated on the grass opposite, looking around nervously as I wondered what was taking place inside. After a few minutes, wary of the soldiers returning and finding me standing there, I made my way across to the cluster of trees where I had told Marie that I would wait and hoped that Anastasia would soon emerge to find me.

It was not long before the lights in the ground-floor parlour were turned on and what appeared to be the entire complement of soldiers entered the room. They were not wearing their Bolshevik uniforms now, but had changed into the simple clothing of local farmers. Their rifles were slung over their shoulders as ever, but rather than splitting up as I expected—some to sleep, some to work, some to watch—they took their seats around the table and turned their attention to an older man, a soldier who seemed to be in charge, who was on his feet talking while the rest sat silently and listened.

A moment later, I heard an unexpected sound on

the gravel of the driveway. I crouched further back into the woodland, while raising my head to try to see who had emerged. It was dark, however, and the lorry stood in my way, so I could distinguish no one in the distance except the guards in the parlour. I held my breath and yes, there it was again—feet walking carefully upon the stones, crunching them underfoot.

Someone had left the house.

I squinted and tried desperately to see whether it was Anastasia, but was loath to call out her name, even in a raised whisper, in case I was wrong and my presence was discovered. There was nothing I could do but wait. My heart pounded inside my chest and despite the chill of the hour a line of perspiration broke out across my forehead. Something felt wrong. I wondered whether I should take a chance and make my way across the road, but before I could decide, the guards stood up in unison and extended their right arms forward into the centre of the room, placing their hands on top of each other's in a great pile before lifting them off once again and standing very quietly in a row. Two of the men, the one who had been speaking and one other, left the parlour; through the half-open front door I watched them ascend the staircase that ran through the centre of the house.

Glancing again towards the driveway, I hoped to identify the person who had come outside, but all was silence now. Perhaps it had just been the Tsaritsa's terrier, I reasoned. Or another animal. Perhaps I had only imagined it. No matter; if there was someone there a moment before, he or she was gone now.

A light went on in an upstairs window and I turned quickly to look in its direction. I could hear voices from above, a low murmur, and then a shadow appeared through the pale curtain of a group of people standing as one, huddled together, then separating and making their way, one by one, towards the door.

I moved quickly to my left and peered through the trees at the staircase. A moment later the Grand Duchess Olga appeared, followed by a small group whose identities I had difficulty making out in the darkness, but who I was convinced must be her brother and sisters, Marie, Tatiana, Anastasia and Alexei. I saw them only briefly before they turned a corner and vanished. All five of them were being separated from their parents to be taken elsewhere, I decided. They were young, after all. They had committed no crimes. Perhaps they were being permitted to leave.

But no, the hallway stood empty for only a minute before the Tsar and Tsaritsa appeared and began to make their way down the stairs too, walking slowly as they supported each other, apparently both lacking strength, followed by two soldiers who led them in the same direction as their children had gone.

Absolute silence followed. The remaining soldiers in the parlour stood up and left the room slowly, the final one turning off the light, and then they too turned the corner and disappeared out of sight.

At that moment, I felt utterly alone. The world seemed a perfectly silent and peaceful place, save for the light rustle of the leaves overhead, stirred by the summer breeze. There was a certain beauty to the place, a civilized expectation that all was well in our country and all would be well, now and ever after, as I closed my eyes and allowed my mind to drift away in the silence. The Ipatiev house was in darkness. The family had vanished. The soldiers had disappeared. Whoever had been walking along the gravel driveway was out of sight and earshot. I was all alone, scared, uncertain, in love. I felt an overwhelming rush of exhaustion that hit me suddenly with the force of a hurricane; I thought I should simply lie down on the grass, close my eyes, go to sleep and hope that eternity would come. It would be very easy to lie down now, to offer my soul into the hands of God, to allow the hunger and deprivation to catch up with me and take me to a place of peace, where I could stand before Kolek Boryavich and say *I'm sorry*.

Where I could kneel before my sisters and say *I'm sorry*.

Where I could wait for my love to come to me and say *I'm sorry*.

Anastasia.

For one final moment, the world was in perfect silence.

And then the shots rang out.

First one, suddenly, unexpected. I jumped. My eyes opened. I stood, frozen to the spot. Then, a few moments later, a second, and now I gasped. Then a series of shots, as if every gun that every Bolshevik owned was being discharged. The noise was tremendous. I couldn't move. A bright light flashed on and off a thousand times to the left of the staircase as the guns sounded. My mind raced with possibilities that crashed together. It was so

480

unexpected that I could do nothing but stay where I was, unable to move, wondering whether the entire world had just come to an end.

It took fifteen, twenty seconds perhaps before I was able to breathe again, and just as I did so my feet found purchase on the ground and I tried to stand up. I had to see, I had to go there, I had to help them. Whatever was happening. I lifted myself up, but before I could move a great commotion sounded in the trees before me and a body threw itself at me, flattening me, sending me falling to the ground, dazed for a moment, wondering what had happened. Had I been shot? Was this the moment of my death?

But that foolishness lasted only a moment and I scrambled backwards, straining in the darkness to see who was lying next to me. I stared and gasped.

'Georgy,' she cried.

1918

It was a moment I had never conceived of in my imagination. I, Georgy Daniilovich Jachmenev, the son of a serf, a nothing, a nobody, crouched in a thicket in the darkness of a freezing-cold Yekaterinburg night, holding in my arms the woman I loved, the Grand Duchess Anastasia Nicolaevna Romanova, the youngest daughter of His Imperial Majesty, the Emperor Tsar Nicholas II and the Tsaritsa, Alexandra Fedorovna Romanova. How had I got here? What extraordinary fate had taken me from the log huts of Kashin into the embrace of one of God's anointed? I swallowed nervously, my stomach performing revolutions of its own within my body as I tried to understand what had happened.

In the distance, the lights of the Ipatiev house were being turned on and off and I could hear the conflicting sounds of angry shouting and manic laughter emerging from within. Narrowing my eyes, I saw the Bolshevik leader standing in an upstairs window, opening it, leaning out and stretching his neck in an almost obscene manner to observe the panorama from left to right, before shivering in the cold, closing it once again, and disappearing from sight.

'Anastasia,' I whispered, forcefully pulling her a few inches away from my body so that I could observe her better; she had spent the last few minutes pressed painfully against my chest, as if she was trying to burrow her way through to my very heart and find a hiding place within. 'Anastasia, my love, what has happened? I heard the gunfire. Who was shooting? Was it the Bolsheviks? The Tsar? Speak to me! Is anyone injured?'

She spoke not a word, but continued to stare at me as if I was not a man at all, but a figure from a nightmare that would dissolve into a thousand fragments at any moment. It was as if she did not recognize me, she who had spoken of love to me, promised a lifetime's devotion. I reached for her hands, and as I took them in my own it was all that I could do not to release them again in fright. They could not have been colder had she been destined for the grave. At that very moment, her composure left her and she began to shake violently, allowing a deep guttural sound of tortured breathing to

482

emerge from the back of her throat, the threat of a great scream to come. 'Anastasia,' I repeated, growing alarmed by her extraordinary behaviour. 'It is me. It is your Georgy. Tell me what has happened. Who was shooting? Where is your father? And your family? What has happened to them?' No response. *'Anastasia!'*

I began to experience the sensation of horror which succeeds the recognition of a slaughter. As a boy, I had been present while villagers in Kashin had suffered and died, their bodies wasted by starvation or disease. Since joining the Leib Guard, I had witnessed men being led to their deaths, some staunch, some terrified, but never had I observed as much contained shock as that which lay before me in the trembling body of my beloved. It was clear that she had witnessed something so terrible that her mind could not yet process the fact of it, but in my youth and innocence, I knew not how best to attend to her.

The sound of voices emerging from the house grew ever louder and I pulled us both deeper into the cover of the woodland. Although I was sure that we could not be seen where we lay, I grew concerned that Anastasia might suddenly return to her senses and expose us; I wished that I had a weapon of my own, should one be required.

Three Bolsheviks stepped out from the tall red doors at the front of the house, lighting cigarettes, speaking in low voices. I saw the glow of matches being struck over and over and wondered whether they were nervous too or whether the breeze was extinguishing the flames before they could take. I was too far away to hear their conversation, but after a few moments one of them, the tallest one,

483

let out a cry of anguish and I heard these words break the tranquillity of the night:

But if it is discovered that she has—

Nothing more. Eight simple words that I have pondered many times over the course of my life.

I narrowed my eyes, attempting to decipher the expressions of these men, whether they were cheerful, excited, nervous, penitent, traumatized, murderous, but it was too difficult. I glanced down at Anastasia, who was clutching me painfully tight; she looked up at the same moment, caught my eye, and a look of such terror crossed her face that I feared that whatever had taken place inside that cursed house had made her lose her reason. She opened her mouth, drawing in a deep breath, and, fearful that she would begin to scream and betray us both to the soldiers, I placed my hand across her mouth, as I had with her older sister two nights earlier, and held it there, every fibre of my being revolting against such an offence, until finally I felt her body slump against my own and her eyes look away, as if she had the lost the will to fight any longer.

'Forgive me, my darling,' I whispered into her ear. 'Forgive my brutality. But please don't be afraid. They are out there, but I will protect us both. I will take care of you. You must remain silent though, my love. If we are discovered, they will come for us. We must stay here until the soldiers return inside.'

The moon emerged from behind a cloud and for a moment I saw Anastasia's face bathed in a pale glow. She appeared almost serene now, calm and tranquil, the way I had always imagined in my fantasies that she would appear in the stillness of

484

the night. How many times had I dreamt of turning in my bed to find her there, sitting up to watch her as she slept, the only thing of beauty I had known in my nineteen years? How often had I awoken in a sweat, shamed, as her image dissolved from my dreams? But this serenity was in such conflict with our situation that it scared me. It was as if she had lost her mind. I feared that at any moment she might cry or scream or laugh or run through the woods, tearing at her clothes, if I was foolish enough to release her.

And so I held her tightly against me and, youthful as I was, indiscreet as I was, lustful as I was, I could not help but take pleasure in the sensation of her body pressed so close against my own. I thought, *I could have her now*, and loathed myself for my perversion. We were faced with a terrifying situation, where discovery could mean extinction, and my primary emotions were base and animal. I disgusted myself. But still, I did not let her go.

I watched through the trees, waiting for the soldiers to leave.

And still, I did not let her go.

*   *   *

The only thing I knew for certain was that we had to get away from there. What had been intended as a romantic tryst between two young lovers had been replaced by something else entirely, and if my alarm was less physically manifest than hers, it was no less real. I had anticipated Anastasia slipping into my arms filled with laughter, the same warm, giddy, affectionate creature whom I had fallen in love with in exalted surroundings, her radiance

485

only slightly diminished by the time spent in Yekaterinburg. Instead, a traumatized mute had been my reward, and the sound of gunshots was the music that rang in my ears. Something terrible had occurred within the Ipatiev house, that much was obvious, but somehow Anastasia had escaped it. If we were to be discovered, I believed we would not survive until the morning.

Although the night was dark and cold, my instinct was that we should make our way westward without delay and seek relief from the elements in a barn or coal-house, if such a place could be found. I bundled Anastasia to her feet—she seemed unwilling still to loosen her grip on me—and took her chin in my left hand, turning her face upwards so that our eyes would connect. I stared at her, attempting to draw her absolutely into my gaze and confidence, and only when I felt that she was alert and listening to me did I speak again.

'Anastasia,' I said quietly, my voice filled with purpose, 'I do not know what has taken place tonight and this is not the moment to share confidences. Whatever has happened cannot be undone. But you must tell me one thing. Just one thing, my love. Can you do that?' She continued to stare and gave no signal to me that she understood my words; I took it on faith that there was a part of her brain that remained sentient and responsive. 'You must tell me this,' I continued. 'I want to take us away from here, to leave this place entirely, right now, not to send you back to your family. Anastasia, is this the right thing to do? Am I right to take you away from here?'

Such a stillness existed between us at that moment that I did not dare to breathe. I was gripping her forearms between my hands, pressing so tightly against her skin that at any other moment she might have cried out in protest at the pain of it, but she did nothing now. I watched her face, desperate for any sign of an answer, and then—such relief!—an almost imperceptible nod of her head, a slight turning westward as if to indicate that yes, we should make our way in that direction. It allowed me to hope that the true Anastasia was present within this strange countenance somewhere, although the effort of making the tiny signal was too much for her and she slumped against my chest once again. My mind was resolved.

'We begin now,' I told her. 'Before the sun comes up. You must find the strength to walk with me.'

I have thought of that moment on many occasions throughout my life, and picture myself bending down to lift her from the ground and carry her not to safety, but in the direction of safety. This, perhaps, would have been the heroic gesture, the detail which would have made a fitting portrait or dramatic moment. But life is not poetry. Anastasia was a young girl of little weight, but how can I express the cruelty of the atmosphere, the impertinent *froideur* of the air, which bit at any exposed parts of our bodies in a manner reminiscent of the Empress's loathsome puppy. It was as if the blood had stopped moving beneath the skin and turned to ice. We had to walk, we had to keep moving, if only to ensure that our circulation was maintained.

I was wearing my greatcoat, and three layers of clothing beneath it, so removed this outer layer and wrapped it around Anastasia's shoulders, buttoning it at the front as we began to walk. I focussed completely on maintaining a rhythm as I pulled the two of us along. We did not speak to each other and I became hypnotized by the sound of my footsteps, all the time maintaining a consistent pace so that we might not lose our momentum.

Throughout this, I remained alert for the sound of the Bolsheviks behind us. Something had taken place inside the house that night, something terrible. I knew not what, but my mind reeled with possibilities. The worst was unthinkable, a crime against God himself. But if that which I dared not put into words had indeed taken place, then surely Anastasia and I were not the only two people running away from Yekaterinburg; there would be soldiers following us—following *her*—desperate to bring her back. And if they found us . . . I dared not think of it and quickened our pace.

To my surprise, Anastasia did not appear to be finding this march in any way difficult. Indeed, not only did she match my consistent strides, at times she outpaced me, as if she was, despite her silence, even more eager than I to put as much distance between herself and her former prison as possible. Her stamina was beyond human that night; I believe I could have suggested that we walk all the way to St Petersburg and she would have agreed and never sought rest.

Eventually, however, after two, maybe three hours, I knew that we had to stop. My body was protesting with every step. We had a great distance to travel and needed to rally our energy. The sun would be coming up soon and I did not want us to remain where we might be seen, although to my surprise there did not seem to be any sign at all that we were being followed. I spotted a small animal-hut about half a mile ahead, and determined that we would break our march there and sleep.

It smelled terrible inside, but it was empty, the walls were solid, and there was enough straw on the floor for us to rest in reasonable comfort.

'We will sleep here, my love,' I said. Anastasia nodded and lay down without protest, staring up at the roof, that same haunted, hollow look in her eyes. 'You do not need to tell me anything,' I added, ignoring the fact that she had spoken only one word, my name, since we had met that night and showed no sign of wanting to tell me what had taken place. 'Not yet. Just sleep, that is all. You need to sleep.'

Again the small nod, but on this occasion I felt her fingers close around mine a little more tightly, as if she wanted to acknowledge what I was saying. I lay beside her, wrapping my body around hers for warmth, and knew that sleep would overtake me in seconds. I tried to stay awake to watch over her, but looking at her eyes as they stared up at the roof of our hut hypnotized my spirit and my exhaustion quickly got the better of me.

*   *   *

It was three days before Anastasia spoke again.

The morning after we awoke we were fortunate enough to secure transport on a wagon heading in the direction of Izhevsk; the journey took an entire day, but the farmer who granted us carriage sought no more than a few kopecks for his kindness and offered us bread and water along the way, which we accepted gratefully, for neither of us had eaten since the previous afternoon. We slept fitfully in the rear of the vehicle, stretched out flat on the wooden slats, but every bump in the road jolted us back to consciousness with a start and I prayed that this torture would end soon. Every time Anastasia awoke, I noticed how it took her a moment to recollect where she was and what had brought her to this place. Her face would appear relaxed and untroubled for the briefest of seconds and then it would cloud over, a sudden eclipse of her brilliance, and her eyes would shut firmly once again, as if she was willing sleep—or worse—to take her. Our driver made no conversation and did not recognize the princess of the Imperial line who sat silently behind him, her back to his. I was grateful for his silence, as I did not think that I could bear to feign friendliness or sociability in the circumstances in which we found ourselves.

At Izhevsk, we stopped and ate at a small café before making our way to the train station, which was much busier than I had expected, a fact that pleased me, as it meant that we could blend into the crowd without difficulty. I was concerned that there would be soldiers waiting at the entry-ways, watching out for us, looking out for *her*, but nothing out of the usual appeared to be taking place. Anastasia kept her head bowed at all times, and covered her blonde hair with a dark hood, so that she looked like any other farmer's daughter who passed us by. I still had most of the roubles I had found the previous afternoon and made a reckless decision to spend almost twice as much as necessary in order to secure us a private compartment on board the train. I purchased two tickets to Minsk, a journey of over a thousand miles. I could think of nowhere further for us to go. From Minsk, I knew not where we might travel next.

There are curious moments of joy in life, unexpected pleasures, and one such instant occurred as we pulled away from the station. The guard blew his piercing whistle, a series of cries to urge any final passengers on board was heard, and then the steam began to rise as the railway buffers cranked into gear. A few moments later, the train was accelerating to a decent speed, heading westwards, and I looked across at Anastasia, whose face was a sudden picture of relief. I leaned over and took her hand in mine. She appeared surprised by the unexpected intimacy, as if she had forgotten that I had even boarded the train alongside her, but then she looked at me and smiled. I had not seen that smile in eighteen months, and I returned it gratefully. Her smile filled me with hope that she would soon return to her former self.

'Are you cold, my darling?' I asked, reaching up and taking a thin blanket from an overhead shelf. 'Why not place this across your legs? It will keep the chill away.'

She accepted the blanket gratefully and turned her head to look through the window at the stark countryside passing us by. The land. The crops. The *moujik*s. The revolutionaries. A moment later, she turned to look at me again and I held my breath in anticipation. Her lips parted. She swallowed carefully. She opened her mouth to speak. I saw her throat rise gently in her pale neck as the signal passed from brain to tongue to talk, but just as she was about to summon words for the first time, the compartment door opened violently and I turned my head in fright, relieved to see the conductor standing there.

'Your tickets, sir?' he asked, and before reaching for them I glanced at Anastasia, who had turned away from us both. She was looking out of the window again, clutching the neck of my greatcoat around her chin, and trembling. I reached across, unsure where to touch her.

'*Dusha*,' I whispered, before being interrupted.

'Your tickets, sir,' repeated the conductor, more insistently this time. I turned and glared at him, my face expressing such sudden fury that he took a half-step backwards and looked at me nervously. He opened his mouth to say something more but thought better of it, remaining silent as I slowly removed the tickets from my pocket and handed them across.

'You're travelling to Minsk?' he said a few moments later, as he examined them carefully.

'That's right.'

'You must change at Moscow,' he replied. 'There will be a separate train for the final leg of the journey.'

'I'm aware of that,' I said, wanting him to leave us alone. Perhaps I had not intimidated him quite as much as I thought, however, because rather than hand the tickets back to me and leave us in peace, he held on to them, hostages to his curiosity, and stared across at Anastasia.

'Is she quite well?' he asked me a moment later.

'She's fine.'

'She seems troubled.'

492

'She's fine,' I repeated without hesitation. 'My tickets are in order?'

'Madam?' he said, ignoring my question. 'Madam, you are travelling with this gentleman?' Anastasia said nothing, but continued to stare out of the window, refusing even to acknowledge the conductor's presence. 'Madam,' he continued in a harsher tone. 'Madam, I asked you a question.'

What felt like a very long few moments followed and then, as if no greater insult had ever been sent her way, Anastasia turned her head and stared coldly at him.

'Madam, can you confirm that you are travelling with this gentleman?'

'But of course she's travelling with me, you fool,' I snapped. 'Why else would we be seated together? Why else would I have both our tickets in my pocket?'

'Sir, the young lady seems troubled,' he replied. 'I wish to satisfy myself that she has not been brought here under duress.'

'Under duress?' I said, laughing in his face. 'Why, you must be mad! She is simply tired, that is all. We have been travelling for—'

Before I could finish my sentence, Anastasia had reached across to me and laid her hand against my arm. I looked at her in surprise and watched as she took it away again and, no longer trembling, stared at the conductor defiantly. I turned to look at him and could see that he was taken aback by two things: her sudden composure and her dignified beauty.

'I have not been kidnapped, if that is what you are implying,' she said, her voice croaking a little as she spoke in reaction to how long it had been

493

out of use.

'I apologize, madam,' he replied, looking a little embarrassed. 'I didn't mean to suggest that you had. You looked uncomfortable, that was all.'

'It's an uncomfortable train,' she said. 'I wonder that your People's Government does not invest some of its money in improvements. It has enough of it, does it not?'

I held my breath, unsure of the politics of such a remark. We had no idea who the conductor was, after all, who he answered to, where his allegiances lay. Anastasia, who was accustomed to answering to no man save her father, had clearly rediscovered her own inner strength through his insolence. Silence filled the compartment for a few moments—I was unsure whether the conductor would challenge us further and felt concerned that if he did, we would come off the worse for it—but finally, he handed the tickets back to me and looked away.

'There is a dining car at the end of the train if you are hungry,' he said gruffly. 'The next stop is Nizhniy Novgorod. Have a pleasant journey.'

I nodded in reply and he took a final look at the two of us—Anastasia was still staring at him, daring him to challenge her further—before turning away, closing the compartment door and leaving us alone together. I let an enormous sigh escape my body, feeling my chest collapse in tension before me, and then looked across at Anastasia, who was smiling weakly at me.

'You have found your voice,' I said.

She nodded a little. 'Georgy,' she whispered, her voice filled with sorrow.

I took her hand in mine.

494

'You must tell me,' I insisted, betraying no note of urgency in my tone, but rather kindness and sympathy. 'You must tell me what happened.'

'Yes,' she said. 'I will tell you. And only you. But first, you must tell me something.'

'Anything.'

'Do you love me?'

'But of course!'

'You will never leave me?'

'Only death could separate me from you, my darling.'

Her face fell at these words and I knew that I had chosen badly. I held her hands tightly in mine and urged her once again to tell me, to tell me all. To tell me everything that had happened at the Ipatiev house.

*   *   *

The guards did not treat us as if we were prisoners. In fact, they permitted us to wander the grounds at will, even to take long walks in the surrounding countryside on the understanding that we would return to the house afterwards. Of course, we obeyed them. There was nowhere for us to go, after all. We would not have been able to conceal ourselves in any town or village in Russia. They said that we were safe in Yekaterinburg, that they were protecting us, hiding our location from a country filled with people who hated us. They said that there were people who wanted us dead.

They were friendly, too, which always surprised me. They spoke to us as if they did not control our lives. They acted as if we were free to stay or go and never questioned any of us when we went outside, but the guns on their backs told a different story. I wondered whether the day would come when I would walk to that door and they would raise a hand to stop me.

Marie told me that you had come for me. I couldn't believe it at first. It was like a miracle. She swore that it was true, that she had seen you and spoken with you, and I was almost out of my mind with happiness, but Mother wouldn't let me leave the house, insisting that I stay and continue with my lessons. Of course, I couldn't tell her why I wanted to go. She would never have permitted me to leave again if I had. The idea that you were so close made me happy, though, especially when Marie said that you would come again that night. I could hardly wait, Georgy.

When it was dark I slipped downstairs. I could hear the guards talking together in one of the parlours on the ground floor. It seemed curious to me that they were gathered together like that, as one of them was nearly always stationed by the door. The grounds were empty, but I walked slowly. I was frightened that the sound of my shoes on the gravel would alert someone to my absence. It's strange to think of it, Georgy, but my concern was not the guards discovering where I was going, but Father or Mother learning who I was going towards.

I crouched down as I passed the window of the parlour and something made me hesitate for a moment. They sounded as if they were arguing. I tried to listen and one voice was raised above the others and they all stopped to listen to what it had to say. I thought nothing more of it and walked quickly towards the gates with only you on my mind. I longed to be in your arms. I even imagined, I dreamed that you would take me away from Yekaterinburg, that *you would reveal our love to my father and that he would embrace us both and call you his son, and that everything we had been, we would be again. Perhaps Marie was right. She said I was foolish to think that we could ever be together.*

By the time I reached the gate, I realized how cold I was. My heart told me to run on, to find you, that your arms would warm me soon enough, but my head said to go back to the house and bring a coat. There was one hanging in the hallway by the door— Tatiana's, I think, she would not miss it. I walked back and noticed that the room where the guards had been talking was empty now. I thought this strange and hesitated, wondering whether my desire for the coat would lead to my discovery. I expected that some of the soldiers would emerge from the door at any moment and stand outside as they smoked. But no one appeared. I didn't want them to, Georgy, and yet it disturbed me that they did not.

A moment later, I heard the heavy thud of boots on the stairs, many boots, and I ran quickly through the front door and around to the side of the house, crouching low beneath a window. A light went on above my head and a crowd of people entered the room. I could hear my father's voice asking what was happening and one of them replied that it was no longer safe in Yekaterinburg, that in order to protect our family it was imperative that we be transported somewhere else immediately.

'But where?' asked my mother. 'Can it not wait until the morning?'

'Please wait here,' he replied, and then all those heavy boots left the room once again and only my family remained within.

By now, I was torn between duty and love. If they

497

were to be transported to a different city, then surely I should be with them. But you, Georgy, you were waiting for me. You were so close. Perhaps I could see you once more and tell you where we were going, and then you would follow us and find a way to save me. I was trying to think what to do for the best when I heard a soldier enter the room again and ask a question I could not hear, and my father replied, 'I do not know. I have not seen her this evening.' I guessed that they were talking about me, that the soldiers were looking for me, but I stayed where I was and after a few moments the room went silent again.

Finally, I stood up. The window was high, so only that part of my face above my mouth would have been visible to anyone on the inside. I looked at the room that I had seen on so many occasions in the past. It had always been bare, but now there were two chairs by the wall. Father was sitting in one of them, with Alexei on his knee. My brother was half asleep and dozing in his arms. Mother was seated beside them, looking anxious, her fingers twirling the long row of pearls around her neck. Olga, Tatiana and Marie were standing behind them and I felt guilty that I was not there too. A moment later, perhaps sensing the intensity of my gaze, Marie glanced towards the window, saw me, and said my name.

'Anastasia.'

Father and Mother turned to look in my direction and my eyes met theirs for only a moment. Mother looked shocked, as if she could not believe that I was outside, but Father . . . he shot me a look of fierce intensity, his eyes strong and determined. He lifted his hand, Georgy. He held the palm out flat, telling me to stay exactly where I was. It felt like an order, a Tsar's command. I opened my mouth to try to say something, but before any words could come the door of the room was flung open and my family turned quickly to look at their captors.

The soldiers were standing together in a row and no one spoke for a moment. Then their leader removed a piece of paper from his pocket. He said that he was sorry but our family could not be saved, and before I could even comprehend the meaning of his words, he pulled a gun from his pocket and shot my father in the head. He shot the Tsar, Georgy. My mother blessed herself, my sisters screamed and turned to hug each other, but they had no time to speak or to panic, for every soldier drew a gun at that moment and slaughtered them. They shot them like animals. They killed them. And I watched. I watched as they fell. I watched as they bled and as they died.

And then I turned.

And I ran.

I remember nothing other than wanting to reach the trees, to leave the house behind, and I focussed on the copse, where I knew you would be waiting for me. And as I ran I tripped over something and fell. I fell and I landed in your arms.

I found you. You were waiting for me.

And the rest . . . the rest, Georgy, you know.

*   *   *

It was almost two days before we arrived, exhausted, in Minsk. We stood in the train station, staring at the timetable and the list of destinations, dreading having to spend more time in a railway carriage but knowing that we had no alternative. We could not stay in Russia. It would never be safe for us there.

'Where shall we go?' Anastasia asked me as we looked at the list of cities to which we could make connections. Rome, Madrid, Vienna, Geneva. Copenhagen, perhaps, where her grandfather was king.

'Anywhere you like, Anastasia,' I replied. 'Anywhere you feel safe.'

She pointed at one city and I nodded, liking the romance of it. 'To Paris, then,' I announced.

'Georgy,' she said, taking my arm urgently. 'There is just one thing.'

'Yes?'

'My name. You must not call me by it any more. We cannot risk detection. They won't be looking for you, no one knew of our relationship except Marie and she . . .' She hesitated, composed herself and continued. 'You cannot call me Anastasia from this day.'

'Of course,' I said, nodding my head in agreement. 'But what shall I call you, then? I cannot think of any better name than your own.'

She bowed her head for a moment and considered it. When she looked up, it was as if she had become a different person entirely, a young woman embarking on a new life for which she had no expectations.

'Call me Zoya,' she said quietly. 'It means *life*.'

1981

It's almost eleven o'clock at night when the phone rings. I'm seated in an armchair before our small gas fire, an unopened novel in my hands, my eyes closed, but not asleep. The telephone is close to me but I don't pick it up immediately, allowing myself a final moment of optimism before I must answer it and face the news. It rings six, seven, eight times. Finally I reach out a hand and lift the receiver.

'Hello,' I say.

'Mr Jachmenev?'

'Speaking.'

'Good evening, Mr Jachmenev,' says the voice on the other end, a woman's. 'I'm sorry to phone you so late.'

'It's all right, Dr Crawford,' I say, for I recognize her immediately; who else could it be, after all, at this time of night?

'I'm afraid it's not good news, Mr Jachmenev,' she tells me. 'Zoya doesn't have very long left.'

'You said there might be weeks yet,' I reply, for this is what she told me earlier in the day, shortly before I left the hospital to return home for the evening. 'You said that there was no cause for immediate concern.' I'm not angry with Dr Crawford, just confused. A doctor tells you something, you listen and you believe it. And you go home.

'I know,' she says, sounding a little contrite. 'And that is what I thought at the time. Unfortunately, your wife took a turn for the worse this evening.

Mr Jachmenev, it's entirely up to you, of course, but I think you should come in now.'

'I'll be there shortly,' I say, hanging up.

Fortunately I haven't yet changed for bed, so it takes me only a moment to retrieve my wallet, keys and overcoat and head for the door. A thought occurs to me and I hesitate, wondering whether it can wait, deciding that it can't; I return to the living room and the telephone, where I call my son-in-law, Ralph, to let him know what's happening.

'Michael's upstairs,' he tells me, and I'm glad to hear it, for I have no other way of contacting my grandson. 'We'll see you shortly.'

Outside on the street it takes a few minutes to locate a taxi, but finally one approaches, I raise my hand and he pulls in to the kerb next to me. I open the back door and before I can even close it again I have given him the name of the hospital and he's pulling out on to the road. I feel a quick breeze in my face and pull the door firmly shut.

The streets are less quiet at this time of night than I expect them to be. Groups of young men are emerging from the public houses, their arms around each other, fingers pointing in each other's faces in their determination to be heard. Further along, a couple are fighting and a young woman is trying to separate them by placing herself between the blows; I only see them for a moment as we pass, but their expressions of hatred are disturbing to observe.

The taxi takes a sharp left turn, then a right, and before I know it we are passing by the British Museum. I glance at the two lions standing on either side of the doors, and can see myself hesitating there for a moment before I step inside to meet Mr Trevors for the first time on the morning that he interviewed me, the same morning that Zoya began her position as a machinist at Newsom's sewing factory. It was so long ago and I was so young and life was difficult, and I would give everything I have to be back there once again and to understand how lucky I was. To have my youth and my wife, and our love and our lives before us.

I close my eyes and swallow. I will not cry. There will be time for tears tonight. But not yet.

'Here OK for you, sir?' says my driver, pulling up next to the visitors' entrance, and I tell him yes, this is fine, and hand him the first note that comes to hand; it's too much, I know it is, but I don't care. I step outside into the cold night air and hesitate before the hospital doors for only a moment, only walking forwards when I hear the taxi drive away.

Zoya is no longer in the oncology ward, I am told by a tired, pale young woman at reception. She has been moved to a private room on the third floor.

'Your accent,' I say. 'You're not English, are you?'

'No,' she says, looking up at me for only a moment and then returning to her paperwork. She's chosen not to tell me where she comes from, but I'm sure it's somewhere in Eastern Europe. Not Russia, I know that much. Yugoslavia, perhaps. Romania. One of those countries.

I step into the lift and press the button for '3'; even if the phone call had not been explicit enough, I know what it means to be moved into a private room at this stage in an illness. I'm glad the lift is empty. It allows me to think, to compose myself. But not for long, as I soon emerge on to a long, white corridor with a nurses' station at the end. As I walk slowly towards it I can hear two voices engaged in conversation, a young man and an older woman. He's talking about an interview he is soon to undertake, presumably for promotion at the hospital. He stops when he sees me standing before him and an irritated expression crosses his face at my interruption, even though I have yet to speak. I wonder whether he mistakes me for one of the elderly patients from the many wards which spread out like the arms of an octopus all along this corridor. Perhaps he thinks I'm lost, or cannot sleep, or have soiled myself in my bed. It's ridiculous, of course. I'm fully dressed. Just old.

'Mr Jachmenev,' says a voice from behind him, Dr Crawford's, as she reaches for a clipboard heavy with documentation. 'You made it here quickly.'

'Yes,' I say. 'Where is Zoya? Where is my wife?'

'She's just through here,' she replies softly, taking my arm. I shrug her off, perhaps more violently than necessary. I am not an invalid and I won't be treated like one. 'I'm sorry,' she says quietly, leading me past several closed doors behind which are . . . what? The dead and the dying and the grieving, three conditions I will know myself before very much more time has passed.

'What happened?' I ask. 'Tonight, I mean. After I left. How did she become worse?'

'It was unexpected,' she says. 'But not unusual, if I'm honest. I'm afraid the last stages of the disease can be unpredictable. A patient can be no better or worse for weeks, even months on end, and then one day she can suddenly become very ill. We

504

moved her out of the ward and into this room so you would have some privacy.'

'But she might . . .' I hesitate; I want neither to fool myself nor to be treated like a fool. Still, I need to know. 'She might improve yet, do you think? As quickly as she became worse, she could become better?'

Dr Crawford stops outside a closed door and offers me a half-smile as she touches my arm. 'I'm afraid not, Mr Jachmenev,' she says. 'I think you should just focus on spending whatever time you have left together. You'll see that Zoya is still attached to a heart monitor and a feeding tube, but other than that, there are no more machines. We feel it's more peaceful this way. It offers the patient more dignity.'

I smile now, I almost laugh. As if she or anyone else could possibly know how much dignity Zoya has. 'My wife was raised with dignity. She is the daughter of the last martyred Tsar of Russia, the great-granddaughter of Alexander II, the Tsar-Liberator who freed the serfs. The mother of Arina Georgievna Jachmenev. There is nothing you can do to diminish her.'

I want to say this, but of course I do not.

'I'll be at the nurses' station when you need me,' says Dr Crawford, opening the door. 'Please, come and get me any time you want.'

'Thank you,' I say and she steps away now and leaves me alone in the corridor before the door. I push it open.

I look inside.

I enter.

* * *

505

'Is it safe?' I asked her as we sat outside the café in Hamina, on the south-eastern Finnish coast, looking towards the islands of Vyborgskiy Zaliv in the distance, towards St Petersburg. Of course, Zoya had planned this all along. It was to be our last trip together. It was she who had chosen Finland, she who had suggested that we travel further east than we had originally planned, and she who had insisted upon our taking this last voyage together.

'It's safe, Georgy,' she told me, and I said that if it was what she wanted, then it was what we would do. We would go home. Not for long. A couple of days at most. Just to see it. Just to be there one last time.

We stayed in a hotel next to St Isaac's Cathedral, arriving in the late afternoon, and sat by the window staring out at the square, two tall mugs of coffee before us, finding difficulty in speaking to one another, so moved were we to be back.

'It's hard to believe, isn't it?' she asked, shaking her head as she watched the people walking quickly along the street outside, doing their best not to be run over by the cars driving quickly every which way. 'Did you ever think you'd be here again?'

'No,' I said. 'No, I never imagined it. Did you?'

'Oh, yes,' she said quickly. 'I always knew we'd come back. I knew it wouldn't be until now, until the end of my life—'

'Zoya . . .'

'Oh, I'm sorry, Georgy,' she said, smiling tenderly and reaching across to place her hand on top of my own. 'I'm not trying to be morbid. I should have said that I knew I would come back when I was an old woman, that's all. Don't worry, I have a couple of good years left in me yet.'

I nodded. I was still growing accustomed to Zoya's illness, to the idea of losing her. The truth was that she looked so well it was difficult to believe that there was anything wrong with her. She looked as beautiful as she had on that first evening when I had seen her standing with her sisters and Anna Vyrubova at the chestnut stand on the bank of the Neva.

'I wish we had brought Arina here,' she said, surprising me a little, for she did not often speak of our daughter. 'I think it would have been quite something to show her where she came from.'

'Or Michael,' I said.

She narrowed her eyes and looked less certain. 'Perhaps,' she said, considering it. 'But even now it might be dangerous for him.'

I nodded and followed her gaze outside. It was night-time, but darkness had not yet fallen. We had both forgotten, but remembered at the same moment.

'The White Nights,' we said in unison, bursting out laughing.

'I can't believe it,' I said. 'How could we have forgotten the time of year? I was beginning to wonder why it wasn't getting any darker.'

'Georgy, we should go out,' she said, filled with sudden enthusiasm. 'We should go out tonight, what do you think?'

'But it's late,' I said. 'It may be bright, but you need to rest. We can go out in the morning.'

'No, tonight,' she pleaded. 'We won't stay out for long. Oh please, Georgy! To walk along the banks

507

of the river on a night like this . . . we cannot come this far and not do it.'

I gave in, of course. There was nothing she could ask of me that I would not agree to. 'All right,' I said. 'But we must dress warmly. And we cannot stay long.'

*   *   *

We left the hotel within the hour and walked down towards the banks of the river. There were hundreds of people strolling along arm in arm, enjoying the late brightness, and it felt good to be at one with them. We stopped and looked at the statue of the Bronze Horseman in the Alexander Garden, watching as the tourists had their photos taken in front of it. We said little to each other as we walked, knowing where our feet were taking us, but not wanting to destroy the moment by speaking of it until we arrived.

Passing by the Admiralty, we turned right and were soon confronted with the General Staff quarters circling Palace Square. Before us was the Alexander Column and standing before it, as bright and powerful as I remembered it, the Winter Palace.

'I remember the night I arrived here,' I said quietly. 'I can recall passing the column as if it was only yesterday. The soldiers who brought me here dumped me by the side of the palace, and Count Charnetsky looked at me as if I was something he had discovered on the heel of his boot.'

'He was a grump,' said Zoya, smiling.

'Yes. And then I was brought inside to meet your father.' I shook my head and sighed deeply to prevent myself from becoming overwrought with memories. 'That's more than sixty years ago,' I said, shaking my head. 'It's impossible to believe.'

'Come,' she said, leading me forward towards the palace itself, and I followed her cautiously. She had grown silent, her mind no doubt filled with many more memories than I had myself of this place; she had grown up here, after all. Her childhood, and that of her siblings, had been spent inside these walls.

'The palace will be locked at this time of night,' I said. 'Tomorrow, perhaps, if you wanted to go inside—'

'No,' she said quickly. 'No, I don't want that. Just this. Look, Georgy, do you remember?'

We were standing in the small quadrangle between the front gates and the doors, the twelve colonnades surrounding us where the horseman had gone by too quickly, startling her, and she had fallen into my arms. The place where we had kissed for the first time.

'We hadn't even spoken to each other,' I said, laughing at the memory of it.

Zoya leaned forward and embraced me once again, standing before me in the place where we had stood all those years before. This time, when we separated, it was difficult to speak. I could feel myself growing overwhelmed with emotion and wondered whether this had been a bad idea, whether we should have come here at all. I looked back towards the square and reached into my pocket for my handkerchief, dabbing at the corners of my eyes, determined that I would not lose control of my emotions.

'Zoya,' I said, turning back to her, but she was no

longer beside me. I looked around anxiously and it took only a moment to locate her. She had slipped into the garden that stood between us and the palace door, and was sitting by the side of the fountain. I watched her, remembering when I had seen her at that fountain once before, in profile, and as I did so she turned her head and looked at me and smiled.

She might have been a girl again.

*   *   *

We walked slowly back towards the hotel along the bank of the Neva.

'Palace Bridge,' said Zoya, pointing towards the great structure that connected the city, from the Hermitage across to Vasilievsky Island. 'They finished it.'

I laughed out loud. 'Finally,' I said. 'All those years of a half-completed structure. First, they couldn't complete it in case the noise kept you awake at nights, and then—'

'The war,' said Zoya.

'Yes, the war.'

We stopped and looked at it, and felt a surge of pride in the fact of it. It was a good thing. It had been completed at last. Connections could now be made with those on the island. They were no longer alone.

'My apologies,' said a voice to our right and we turned to see an elderly man, dressed in a heavy greatcoat and scarf. 'Could I trouble you for a light?'

'I'm sorry,' I said, glancing at the unlit cigarette he held out towards me. 'I'm afraid I don't smoke.'

'Here,' said Zoya, reaching into her bag and removing a packet of matches; she didn't smoke either and it surprised me that she would have them, but then the contents of my wife's handbag have long been a mystery to me.

'Thank you,' said the man, taking the box. I glanced to his left and noticed his companion—his wife, I assumed—staring at Zoya. They were about the same age, but, like my wife, age had not diminished her beauty. Indeed, her elegant features were spoiled only by a scar that ran along her left cheek to a point below the cheekbone. The man, who was handsome with thick white hair, lit his cigarette, smiled and thanked us.

'Enjoy your evening,' he said and I nodded.

'Thank you,' I replied. 'And you.'

He turned to take his wife's hand and she was staring at Zoya with an expression of tranquillity upon her face. None of the four of us spoke for a moment and then, finally, the woman bowed her head.

'May I have your blessing?' she asked.

'My blessing?' asked Zoya, the words catching in her throat even as she said them.

'Please, Highness.'

'You have it,' she said. 'And for what little it is worth, I hope that it brings you peace.'

*　　*　　*

It's bright now, it's morning time, and the living room looks cold and unwelcoming as I open the door and let myself in. I stop for a moment, glance towards the table, the cooker, the armchairs, the bedroom, this small place where we have made our

511

lives together, and hesitate. I'm not sure if I can go any further.

'You don't have to come back here,' says Michael, also hesitating in the doorway behind me. 'It's probably a good idea if you come back with me and dad today, don't you think?'

'I will,' I say, shaking my head and stepping forward into the room. 'Later on. Tonight, perhaps. Not right now, if you don't mind. I think I'd like to be here. It's my home, after all. If I don't come in now, I never will.'

He nods and closes the door and we both step into the centre of the room, take our coats off and place them on one of the chairs.

'Tea?' he asks, already filling the kettle, and I smile and nod. He's so English.

He leans against the sink as he waits for the kettle to boil and I sit down in my own armchair and smile at him. He's wearing a T-shirt with a comic message printed across the front; I like that—it didn't even occur to him to dress in a more sober fashion.

'Thank you, by the way,' I tell him.

'For what?'

'For coming to the hospital last night. You and your father. I'm not sure that I could have got through the night without you.'

He shrugs and I wonder for a moment whether he is going to start crying again; three or four times over the course of the night he has broken down in tears. Once when I told him that his grandmother had passed away. Once when he came in to see her. Once when I took him in my arms.

'Of course I'd be there,' he says, his voice nervous and emotional. 'Where else would I have been?'

'Thank you anyway,' I say. 'You're a good boy.'

He nods and wipes his eyes, then puts teabags into two cups and fills them with boiling water, pressing them against the sides with a teaspoon rather than making a pot. If his grandmother was here, she'd roast him alive.

'You don't have to think about it right now,' he says, sitting opposite me and putting the cups down. 'But you know that you can come to ours, don't you? To live, I mean. Dad will be fine with it.'

'I know,' I say, smiling. 'And I'm grateful to you both. But I think not. I'm healthy still, don't you think? I can manage. You will visit me though, won't you?' I ask nervously, unsure why I am asking this since I already know the answer.

'Of course I will,' he says, his eyes opening wide. 'God. Every day, if I can.'

'Michael, if you come here every day, I won't open the door,' I tell him. 'Once a week will be fine. You have a life of your own to lead.'

'Twice a week, then,' he says.

'Fine,' I say, not looking to strike any deals.

'And you know my play is coming up, don't you? Two weeks from now. You'll be there for opening night, won't you?'

'I'll try,' I say, unsure whether I can really go without Zoya by my side. Without Anastasia. I can see the look of disappointment on his face and I smile and reassure him. 'I'll do my best, Michael,' I say. 'I promise.'

'Thanks.'

We sit and talk for a little while longer and then I tell him that he should go home now, that he must be tired, he's been up all night.

'I will if you're sure,' he says, standing up and stretching his arms in the air, yawning loudly. 'I mean, I could sleep here if you want.'

'No, no,' I say. 'It's time you went home. We both need some sleep. And I think I'd like a little time on my own anyway, if you don't mind.'

'OK,' he says, putting his coat on. 'I'll call around later tonight and see how you're getting on. There's . . .' He hesitates, but decides just to say it. 'You know, there's arrangements that have to be made.'

'I know,' I say, walking towards the door with him. 'But we can talk about them later. I'll see you tonight.'

'Later then, Pops,' he says, reaching forward and kissing my cheek, hugging me, and then pulling away before I can see the expression of grief on his face. I watch as he bounds up the steps towards the street, those long, muscular legs of his that can take him anywhere he wants to go. To be so young again. I watch and wonder at how he always manages to leave just as a bus is appearing, as if he refuses to waste even a moment of his life by waiting on a street corner. He jumps on the back of it and raises a hand to me, the uncrowned Tsar of all the Russias waving at his grandfather from the back of a London bus as it speeds off down the street while a conductor approaches him, demanding money for his fare.

It's enough to make me laugh. I close the door behind me and sit down again, considering this, and truly, I find it so funny that I laugh until I cry.

And when the tears come I think *aah* . . .

So this is what it means to be alone.